BODIES FROM THE LIBRARY 2

Forgotten stories of mystery and suspense
by the Queens of Crime
and other Masters of the Golden Age

Selected and introduced by

TONY MEDAWAR

COLLINS
CRIME
CLUB

COLLINS CRIME CLUB
An imprint of HarperCollins*Publishers*
1 London Bridge Street
London SE1 9GF
www.harpercollins.co.uk

This edition 2019

For copyright acknowledgements, see page 387.

A catalogue record for this book
is available from the British Library

ISBN 978-0-00-831875-8

Typeset in Minion Pro 11/15 pt by
Palimpsest Book Production Ltd, Falkirk, Stirlingshire

Printed and bound in Great Britain by
CPI Group (UK) Ltd, Croydon CR0 4YY

CONTENTS

Introduction vii

NO FACE 1
Christianna Brand 19

BEFORE AND AFTER 21
Peter Antony 36

HOTEL EVIDENCE 41
Helen Simpson 54

EXIT BEFORE MIDNIGHT 57
Q Patrick 135

ROOM TO LET 137
Margery Allingham 168

A JOKE'S A JOKE 171
Jonathan Latimer 177

THE MAN WHO KNEW 181
Agatha Christie 187

THE ALMOST PERFECT MURDER CASE 189
S. S. Van Dine 204

THE HOURS OF DARKNESS 209
Edmund Crispin 277

CHANCE IS A GREAT THING 283
E. C. R. Lorac 291

THE MENTAL BROADCAST 295
Clayton Rawson 300

WHITE CAP 303
Ethel Lina White 320

SIXPENNYWORTH 323
John Rhode 345

THE ADVENTURE OF THE DORSET SQUIRE 347
C. A. Alington 356

THE LOCKED ROOM 359
Dorothy L. Sayers 384

Acknowledgements 387

INTRODUCTION

'A great many crime short stories continue to be written with nothing but entertainment in mind.'

Julian Symons

As with the first volume of *Bodies from the Library* (HarperCollins, 2018), the aim of this volume is to bring into the light more lost or previously unknown short fiction by some of the best-known writers active during the Golden Age of crime and detective fiction, a period that can be loosely defined as starting in 1913 and ending in 1937. These dates mark the publication of two major titles: *Trent's Last Case*, in which the journalist E. C. Bentley provided an antidote to Sherlock Holmes; and *Busman's Honeymoon*, described as 'a love story with detective interruptions' by its author Dorothy L. Sayers.

For our purposes, there is also a loose definition of crime and detective fiction and in this volume, as well as stories that conform to S. S. Van Dine's requirement that 'there simply must be a corpse', there is a story that sets out merely to deceive the reader by only appearing to be criminous, one that blurs the distinction between fact and fiction and another that was published after the end of the Golden Age but playfully tweaks its tail . . .

Enjoy!

Tony Medawar
February 2019

NO FACE

Christianna Brand

They sat in their silent ring in the darkened room and their touching fingers trembled and jerked apart and touched again . . . He was trying frantically to get through to them. 'Listen to me! Listen! They were wrong, warn them, they'd got it all wrong!' But they did not hear him; over his voice the sweet piping treble was burbling on of the peace and sunshine over here on the Other Side, and all the flowers. No ear for his soundless screaming: 'It's all going to begin again . . .'

Ringing up the police—Miss Delphine Grey. 'Mr Joseph Hawke to speak to Superintendent Tomm.'

The weary voice. 'Yes, Mr Hawke?'

He was half hysterical, gibbering with excitement. 'You know, Superintendent, Joseph Hawke, famed clairvoyant. I sent you that article I published after the last time. The man is a lunatic—'

The murderer killed apparently at random, anyone, any time, any place. The swift incapacitating stab in the back, the body turned over and stabbed and stabbed and stabbed again. A plastic sheet would be throw down, which had protected the killer from the spurting blood; and for the rest, no sign left, ever, no clue for a police force stretched to its limit, on the edge of desperation. And every crank in the country ringing up, writing in, with their crack-pot theories. 'Well, so, Mr Hawke—'

'—helpless, a psychotic, I showed that in my articles. Some

childhood experience? Witnessed a killing? A stabbing? No face!—he told you that he had no face . . .' (The ghastly, gobbling, whispering 'phone calls to the police, taunting them, daring them, and yet perhaps with an inherent cry for help. 'You'll never catch me. How would you know me?' And the terrible choking cry, 'I have no face.') 'Now, a man who says he has no face, Superintendent, he's a psychopath, he looks in the mirror and he dares not see himself. A man who has no face—'

'—is a man who wears a stocking-mask. Now, Mr Hawke—'

'Yes, but one moment! This time I have something positive to tell you. I've seen him. In the crystal—scrying, we call it. A small man, five foot six or less, clerk type, regulation suit, knee-length mackintosh—'

'Strikingly different from half the male population of this town. Including for example, yourself. Now, I'm frantically busy—'

'But there's more—'

'—so goodbye and thank you.' He could not forbear from adding: 'Don't call us, we'll call you.'

He fell into one of his terrible rages, hunched like a monkey in the big séance room armchair, and for a moment lost consciousness, blacked out as of late he so often did, sometimes for hours at a time, coming to spent and exhausted, deeply troubled by forgotten dreams. But Delphine was with him now, gently dabbing with a damp cloth at the haggard, narrow white face. 'What does it matter, Mr Hawke? A dumb policeman!'

'I could have told them—the man has red hair. But they'll never believe in me, in my Gift—'

'*I* believe in you,' she said. 'I *know*.'

Coming up to her in the crowded store, a total stranger. 'Don't be afraid, I only want to help you.' But she *had* been afraid. Other shoppers had gathered protectively about her: was there not a mass murderer abroad? He introduced himself to them. 'Joseph Hawke—famed clairvoyant, you'll have heard of me. And

I've had this vision, you see, in the crystal, I know that she's in deep trouble.' She had cried out—how could he possibly have known?—gone with him and confided, ashen-faced, 'I've had a telephone call from him. From No Face, slopping and gobbling. It was terrifying. He said—he said, "You're next!"' But she was incredulous. 'How could you know?'

He knew because he had watched her an hour ago, praying in the church before the statue of St Jude, Refuge of the Despairing. He learned a good deal from watching in churches—the widow in her mourning dress at the foot of the crucifix, the woman before the altar of St Antony of Padua who would help you to find lost things.

Horn-rimmed spectacles, mac turned inside out, a nylon wig, perhaps—he was adept at disguises, simple or elaborate: follow the victim to some busy spot where your revelations will attract potential clients for future séances. His current assistant would follow up the clues in old newspapers, parish registers, graveyards, even; and they would be duly astounded at how much he could tell them of themselves.

Delphine, frightened, without family or friends, had fallen a natural prey and in time replaced the latest helper to have departed, faith eroded by so much of fraudulence; grateful and trusting, Delphine had accepted sensibly the need of any practitioner to pad out for the credulous, trivialities unworthy of the true psychic gift. Pretty, sweet and blessedly naïve Delphine!—he might have come to love her if he could ever have felt love for anyone, poor squinny little orphanage boy, looking only inward, unto himself; but he felt only that she was caring and kind. He had never known that either.

Now she suggested: 'Never mind the police. Tell the media.'

The media seized with joy, as ever, upon anything hinting of the occult. And here was Joseph Hawke, famed clairvoyant, describing a vision of a small man, white-collar type, and with red hair . . .

Two mornings later, the police issued a statement; the victim of last night's murder had clutched, as though torn out in the struggle, a curl of black nylon: and mixed in with the nylon, two short red hairs.

Mr Joseph Hawke was a famed clairvoyant indeed.

The public were ripe for exploitation. Terror stalked in their midst. The authorities seemed helpless. But now—a Saviour! Queues formed to attend his scrying séances. He saw what they wanted him to see—the chances, he said to Delphine, were high against any of them falling victim to No Face. And of course very often, it was a genuine vision.

'You never see *me* in the crystal?' she asked, wistfully.

'I'd have told you, wouldn't I?' He knew that she longed to stay with him in safety, but with this upsurge of fame he must be circumspect and she was nightly packed off to creep back to her lonely flat at the other end of town. 'Use different exits from here, keep him guessing. You'll be all right.' He was impatient to get on with the affairs of Joseph Hawke. His correspondence was growing enormously. 'If only we dared bring in some secretarial help!'

'There's so much stuff in the flat.' The wired-up séance room, the rolls of fine plastic for the ectoplasm during mediumistic trance; the disguises for the follow-ups, the painted gas balloons looking down from the ceiling with dear Father's fine features or mother's sweet smile—it was incredible what people would believe when, in grief and anxiety, they wanted to believe. He agreed: 'No, it's too dangerous. We'll have to make do with tricks, the slates and all that, and meanwhile I'll train you in the scrying.' He said sharply: 'Did you hear what I said? You seem very distrait today.'

'Yes, well . . . I've been trying to pluck up courage to tell you. The police have been questioning me. They asked how you could have known that the man has red hair. If I thought *you* had ever dyed your hair.'

'Oh, my God!' It had never occurred to him. 'They think I

know, because I'm No Face myself!' His voice grew shrill, hysteria rose up in him like a scream. 'They'd kill me—if such a rumour got around, the people would lynch me!' And he began casting about, his head moving this way and that as though he might literally see a way out. 'I'll have to somehow prove . . . What proof can I show them . . . ?' And the darkness grew, and the swimminess, the build-up to unconsciousness; and sharply into the darkness and swimminess, a bell pealed. 'Oh, Christ!' he cried out. 'They've come for me!'

'It's the people for the séance,' she said.

By the time she had led them in, awed and silent, he was sprawled back in the chair, his hands lying flaccid on the table-top, the crystal abandoned. 'He's already in trance. Very quietly—sit down, join your hands in a ring. His two neighbours—just put your hands on his hands.' In the ordinary way there would be noise, music, spirit movements all over the darkened room; if he wanted to be free, he simply jerked his hands, let his neighbours, groping in the dark, find each other's hands, leaving him outside the ring. But this time was going to be different. She stood quietly aside, looking, herself, a little frightened. And he began to speak.

Or through him, someone began to speak. The police had published recordings, every soul in the room clearly recognised that voice—the horrible, gasping, half-whispering voice with its slurring of consonants, slobbering out the words. A woman shrieked, hands jumped apart, scrambled to re-form the circle; but the voice gabbled on. 'Must have it! Must have it! Killed . . . The smell of their death . . . Must have it again . . .' And the terrible cry: 'They can't stop me—they can't find me: I have no face!' An incomprehensible muttering and then: 'But *you* know me! *You* described me! My name, tell them my name!' The mumbling died away, glottic as the plops in a bubbling saucepan; died into silence . . .

Broken at last by a different voice, the voice of the medium.

Strangely quiet after the hubble-bubble of that terrible voice. Spelling out—letters. An F. A pause and then an O; and then without interval, C-A-N-E. His name, he had said: and his name was F. O. Cane.

Into the stillness, Delphine said quietly: 'Rearrange the letters and it spells—No Face.'

He got rid of them all, rushed to the telephone. The wooden voice tinged with exasperation. '*Yes*, Mr Hawke?'

'His name,' he said triumphantly. 'I can tell you his name. And it is *not* my name.'

'Oh, that. I never very seriously thought it was.'

His mind shook. To have offered this precious secret on a plate, which all the time might have been saved for some world-shattering revelation when the time was ripe!—and to find that after all, he needed no such proof of his innocence. But he had blurted it out already. 'His name is F. O. Cane.'

A moment's silence, and then: 'You've been playing at anagrams, Mr Hawke, you and that pretty young lady of yours. F. O. Cane—No Face. But why not A. F. Cone? or C. O. Fane? Or F. Ocean, that would be rather a jolly name, F. Ocean. The Red Sea, perhaps, considering his fondness for blood?'

The narrow, hatchet face grew pinched with fury, he clung to the receiver with a juddering hand. 'All right! You'll be sorry! I'll tell you nothing more, let him kill and kill and kill, you'll get no more help from me!' And to reclaim something at least from disaster, he broadcast widely that during a mediumistic trance, the murderer himself had come through and revealed his name. It would be safest not yet to make this public but he would deposit it in a sealed envelope, and one day the world would know that he had been right.

And indeed that night, the voice called the police—they had arranged code words with him to save themselves from hoaxers—and his name was F. O. Cane.

Delphine was uncertain about it, uneasy. 'He'll know that you know—and that probably I do too. Tonight; he may know tonight, if they get it on the nine o'clock news.' She looked very pale and drawn. 'I feel a bit scared going home. I suppose, just for once—?'

But he was tired, exhausted. 'You'll be all right, he doesn't know yet, get back and lock yourself in, you'll be perfectly safe.' After all, what else was there to do about it? Give her shelter here? But he simply could not risk scandal now. 'I'm sorry, but I'm totally worn out by the séance. And then that fool of a policeman—' At the thought of it his voice began to rise, he felt sick with it, physically sick with the rage and the despair. 'Real—this time it was real. But they'll never believe . . .' And the darkness descending, and the blackness . . .

But at four o'clock in the morning, he was wide awake and dialling her number. 'Delphine—he's rung me up!'

'Oh, Mr Hawke—!'

'About you! He says he's going to . . . He says—tonight!'

She gave a sort of scream, broke into terrified sobbing. 'His voice came through again, Delphine. It was real, it was genuine, believe me! I came to and found myself by the telephone. Now, look—lock yourself in, bar the door, put something against it.'

'Oh, God,' she sobbed, 'I'm so frightened! He—he stabs them and stabs them. I can't stay here, I can't be alone—'

'Don't go, don't leave your flat, I'll call the police—'

'Please come,' she cried, imploring. 'Please come, please come!'

'Yes, but I can't remember—Delphine! Your address?' But her voice said, 'I'm going to . . . Passing out . . .' and there was the clatter of the dropped receiver. He called her name urgently, but there was no reply.

When he got through to the police station, it was from a call-box. A night-duty officer this time. Cagily. 'He rang you? Any code word?'

'Code? *I* don't know. I was in trance—'

'Oh, in trance, sir, were you?'

'Some word did keep coming through. Silver?—could it be—?' All caginess vanished. The voice snapped: 'Name and address?'

Her name, yes. 'But I can't remember—'

'Telephone?'

'You can try but she seems to have fainted. And it's a rented flat, the 'phone's not in her name.' And time passing, time passing. 'Anyway, you find it, I can't wait—I'll have to try and remember the way. He could be there at this minute.'

He allowed himself only the smallest delay but it was almost an hour before he appeared at her flat. The police were there, the Superintendent himself. He gasped out: 'Delphine?'

Superintendent Tomm in his level way. 'The young lady's not here.'

'Oh, God, he hasn't—?'

'He's been here. The window was forced, he'd got in over the roofs.'

'But Delphine?'

'She heard him at the window. Tore open the door and escaped. There's a call-box just outside the flats, she rang us from there. We've got her safe. But meanwhile, of course, he'd been here and gone.' He remarked coolly: '*You* took your time.'

'There's thick fog—'

'We noticed. Still—an hour! You started out from home?'

'Well, of course.'

'I ask, because you rang the station from a call-box.'

'She didn't replace her receiver. That disconnected my 'phone. I got lost, I've been driving round and round, hardly knowing what I was doing.'

'Yes, well . . . We'll keep the girl for the night, she's in a pretty bad way . . .'

She had pulled herself together by the time she came to him next morning, but she still looked terrible, pale as death and with dark arcs beneath her eyes. He was sitting collapsed in his chair and did not even look up at her. She knelt at his side. 'Don't be so upset! I'm all right now. I got away safe.'

He said dully: 'Before I started, I rang round the media. I told them there'd be another killing. Last night, I said. A girl. In her own home. It's been broadcast everywhere. And now I shall be proved wrong.'

She got to her feet, stood staring down at him. 'Oh, my God—Mr Hawke! You'd rather I *had* been killed. Killed, murdered, slaughtered—if it would keep them believing in your powers!'

'Oh, no!' he cried out. 'No, no!' And he fell on his knees, caught at her hand, holding it against his worn face, clammy and cold. 'Of course I wouldn't sacrifice one hair of your head, Delphine!' And yet . . . 'It means so much to me. I have the gift, you know that: it's so terrible to me that nobody will believe. Last night—the 'phone call: that was a genuine experience, I swear to you that it was. And now, if I'm proved wrong—'

She slid away her hand, stepped back, looking down at him. The horror seemed to fade away from her face, pity took its place. 'It's all right,' she said. 'You're safe. He did kill again last night.'

Now it was Superintendent Tomm's turn to call on Joseph Hawke. 'This time you weren't quite so bang on. A girl was killed, yes. In her home, yes. But a man was killed too, the boy friend, visiting. You didn't foresee that?'

'Well, but . . .' He said quickly: 'That would be fortuitous. He meant to kill a girl—well, he meant to kill Delphine. But the man appeared, he had to kill him too.'

'You're still offering this as a psychic revelation?' said the Superintendent, curiously.

'I was in trance. I have these—well, what *you* would call dreams, very troubled, I wake up exhausted as though—'

'As though you'd been walking in your sleep, perhaps?'

'In this case as though I'd had the telephone call. A psychic revelation: yes, just the right phrase. How else could I have known the code word?'

'You had a genuine 'phone call from No Face and he mentioned it?'

He fell back in despair. 'You'll never believe me, will you? No one will ever recognise my powers. Did he ring me, those earlier times, and describe himself to me? Did he ring and tell me that he has red hair? Did he ring and give me his name?'

'I don't know,' said Superintendent Tomm. '*You* tell *me*.'

He fought against the old inevitable rise of hysteria. 'Are you suggesting that I'm nothing but a fraud?'

'Well, as to that—people do talk, you know.'

'Oh, yes, I'm sure. Dismissed assistants. Who would listen to *them*?'

'*I* would. Because you see, we have three choices. If, as you insist, you've had no actual 'phone calls—and if, as *they* insist, you have no true psychic powers—then there's only one way that you would know as much as you do about this murderer.'

'You mean—? Oh, my God!' Fear rose up, choking him, darting questions scuttled about in his mind like rats. 'You think I'm him? You believe I'm the killer? You suspected it once before . . .'

'And you immediately came across with a 'proof' of your innocence. You gave us his name.'

'Well, there you are then!'

'But after all, that could have been yourself ringing up and confirming yourself.'

'How could I, if I didn't know the code word?'

'Ah, *but*, Mr Hawke,' said Superintendent Tomm, 'what does that make you, if you did?'

He sat for a long time saying nothing, and slowly the hysteria ebbed away, leaving his mind cold and clear. He said at last, slowly: 'If I tell you something, will you swear—?'

'I'll swear to nothing. But I won't unnecessarily give away your secrets.'

'Well, then. I see now that I have to convince you that I am not No Face; whatever conclusion *you* in the end might come to—if such a rumour got about—God help me! So I must tell you. I saw him. Not in the crystal—I saw him in a church. I noticed this man go into the confessional box. He was there a long time and when he came out he flung himself down on his knees and buried his face in his hands. And the priest came out of the box and went away quickly and he was as pale as death. I followed, I saw the priest kneeling out of sight of the rest, before a side-altar, with his hands clasped, looking up at the crucifix, tears pouring down his face. I knew then that he had heard something terrible, but he couldn't break the seal of the confessional, he was powerless to do anything about it. And there was a mass murderer abroad.

'I went back down the aisle. I touched the shoulder of the kneeling man and spoke some name. He shook me off, muttering, "No, no. Go away!" I gave him a sort of apologetic pat on the head and said, "Sorry, mate!—I thought you were someone I knew!" But in those two moments—we're trained in these tricks, Superintendent, that's how we get our information—I'd flicked the handkerchief out of his breast pocket and seen the name printed across the corner; and I'd gently shuffled back the nylon wig and got a glimpse of the red hair underneath. And that's all there was to it.' He gave a small, despairing shrug. 'So now you know. But at least it proves that to know what I knew about him, I didn't have to be the killer.' He shrugged again. 'I suppose if, after that, I swear to you that I do sometimes exercise the true psychic gift, you will simply think me a fool.'

'A fool?' said the Superintendent. 'No, no, on the contrary. I think you are a very clever man.' He fell to musing upon it. 'A very, very, very clever man,' he said.

Delphine appeared in the doorway. 'Oh—I'm sorry—'

'No, no, Miss Grey. It was really you I came to see. This may be just a little to your comfort. After you'd left this morning, we had one of his calls. Out of the usual horror emerged the fact that he was gloating over the two people murdered last night. In his childhood, he'd witnessed a double killing—a fight between his parents. With knives—so one up to you, Mr Hawke, you always suggested something of the kind!—and recently, I suppose, something triggered off the reaction. He has a craving, like a drug, for what he calls the smell of death.'

'Yes—he said that to Mr Hawke, during last night's séance.'

The Superintendent did not look at Mr Hawke. 'He didn't mention the word "surfeit"? No, the séance took place before the double killing. But he said it this morning, over and over. I'm hoping it just may mean that he's satisfied. All the same . . .' He suggested to Delphine: 'You've had a bad time—this is twice he's threatened you. You wouldn't consider getting out of town for a bit?'

'Oh, she can't do that,' said Joseph Hawke. 'I need her here.'

She remained but now she was given police protection indeed, with safe-conduct to and from her home, a man posted all night on duty at her block of flats, even prowling the corridors outside of Joseph Hawke's apartment. The work was ever-increasing, but they had been able to rent, from people fleeing from danger, a flat in the same building and there install a couple of secretaries. Three months passed by: No Face, appetite apparently appeased, struck no more. Gradually she seemed to forget her terrors, gave herself over to her study of the crystal ball. A success; she invented a little gimmick of her own, allowing the sitter to peer over her shoulder down into the wavery depths of the globe on its bed of black velvet then, once they were sufficiently mesmerised, slipping under the crystal a picture or photograph—by that time, almost anything more would do—and with a little guidance soon having them in amazed recognition of the dear old homestead complete with lost loved ones right down to dead doggie, Rover. But she herself proved somewhat too susceptible to the hypnotic effect—like gazing into deep, deep water, she would dreamily say, moving gently to a cloudy turbulence. An evening came when, after a particularly long, hard day's work, he found her apparently unconscious, sitting nursing the glittering ball in her hands. 'Delphine?'

No flicker of response. He was about to bring her round, gently, when she began to speak, to mutter in the high, bird-like voice she affected for her professional sessions. 'Something moving. In the crystal—moving.'

To be clever at interpreting nonsense was one thing; a genuine rivalry in scrying was quite another. 'What do you mean?' he said sharply. 'Moving?'

She seemed not to hear him. 'Shadowy . . . All swirling . . . A picture of, a picture of . . .' And she cried out suddenly: 'It's my flat! I can see the clock. The clock says midnight. It's midnight. It's tonight. There's a girl—' The high voice faltered. 'There's blood, there's blood!' and she gave a sharp scream and cried out 'No! No! NO!' and her hands dropped away from the crystal globe, she fell across the arm of the chair and lay there, still.

Oh, dear God—Delphine! His gentle and loyal Delphine, the only true friend that in all his life he had ever known—butchered to death by a maniac come alive again to his craving for blood! But it's all right, he thought; there's masses of time to warn the police, she can stay in the office flat, she needn't go back home . . .

On the other hand . . .

He sat for a long, long time, watching her. Almost certainly what she had seen in the crystal would be obliterated from her mind. Let her go, then; and *then* inform the police, let them set a trap and—maniac caught red-handed in a murder attempt, and all through his own amazing predictions.

And yet, again . . .

She had seen in the crystal the spilled blood of a deed accomplished. She had seen into the future. What use, after all, to interfere, to protect, to warn?—only to have the prediction of the crystal come true; to be seen to have failed. Should not one simply 'foresee' what inevitably must be?

But foreseeing, why not have warned in advance? I must leave it to the last moment, he thought, pretend to have just come out of trance, rushed to the telephone. Then immediately call the media and . . . The maniac caught, not in the attempt but actually in commission of the deed: a small man, red-headed, whose name would prove to be F. O. Cane. Just dare the very universe, after that, to question the psychic powers of the great Joseph Hawke!

If in his heart he recognised that here was an infamy beyond the imagination of any decent man—his mind over-rode the thought. Within him the passion to be accepted for what he knew himself indeed to be had grown like a weed, to suffocate all other caring. At five minutes to midnight, call the police, call his contacts; and meanwhile let her, in happy ignorance, go home.

She stirred at last, opened her eyes, looked mildly astonished. 'Oh, dear—did I pass out? This thing—I fall for it far too easily. Like staring down into a pool, into swirling water.'

He said: 'Did you see anything in the water?'

'Well—I seem vaguely to remember something—something rather horrid, like waking up from a nightmare one's forgotten. I didn't say anything?'

He dragged out the words. 'No, you didn't say anything.'

'Goodness, how late it is! I must get home. Would you like me to get you something to eat before I go?'

'No, no,' he said, almost violently. Even he could not accept kindness from her, could not share with her such a meal as this. The last supper, he thought: she and Judas.

The last supper. He knew, then, didn't he?—deep in his

consciousness he had known all along—that he was sending her out to die.

The waiting was terrible—terrible. He began to be afraid that the tension would bring on one of those ever more frequent black-outs, of not coming to in time to make his 'phone calls. And indeed he did lapse into some sort of uneasy dream, returning fully to awareness only a few minutes before midnight—ill, exhausted, as though instead of lolling there a prey to nightmares, he had been through some tremendous effort . . .

Coming to full awareness—to a sudden full realisation of what he had done.

Save her, he thought—I must have been mad, I must save her, must save her!

Telephone her flat, then? To the police? But it was almost twelve, wouldn't that make him too late to catch the television people? On the other hand . . . With his mind split three ways, he stumbled over to the telephone.

And the telephone was dead.

Panic hit him like a hurricane, whirled him into the familiar darkness, only one thought clear in his mind. Time's running out. I must ring the press, ring the television people, I must tell them about it before it becomes known, before there is any normal way for me to have found out.

But the telephone was dead. The office, he thought: the office flat! I can use the 'phone there. Not waiting for the lift, he fled down the single flight of stairs. The church clock boomed the hour as with a trembling hand he thrust the key into the lock. He flung open the door and tumbled into the flat.

And she was waiting for him there.

The uplifted arm, the plunge of the keen blade that seemed to flash down and into his heart, as though through a sheet of shining water. He gave one shrill rabbit-scream of pain; and she was down on her knees, bending over him, sniffing at the blood that spurted through the slit nylon, snuffling like a pig after truffles. 'The smell! The smell! More of it, I must have more!' But she dropped the raised hand.

'No, no, I mustn't!' She muttered and mumbled. 'Only one stab. Self-defence . . .' His head rolled helplessly as she forced on to it the dark nylon wig. Muttering . . . Echoes of the gruesome mutterings of the telephone voice. 'Can't call them till he dies. So die, can't you?—die!' She scrambled up, perched on the edge of a chair, leaning over him, her eyes fixed on his face. Her voice relaxed into something more nearly human. 'But you'll die—No Face, the maniac murderer with his nearly human thirst for the smell of death! Oh, you signed your death warrant, didn't you?—the day you published that first article. Mad am I? Well, helpless lunatic I may be, but I got you into my power from that hour on. Watched you, got on to your tricks in the churches . . . Didn't you ever think, poor deluded fool, that it was all a bit too slick and easy? Picking me up there—so naïve and trusting! And the confessional! I suppose that poor wretch still believes he heard the confession of a killer who would kill again. A trap for you—a trap! All laid on by the pitiful lunatic with his terrible childhood experiences. Terrible, it wasn't terrible, it was wonderful, I hated them, I hated them for doing it all in front of me, their child—fighting each other with knives, fighting to the death. I wanted the smell of it again, the smell of their death in my nostrils. And again and again. But I needed a fall guy—the police were getting close, even if they didn't yet know it. And who more suitable than you, who had spilt out your lies to the world. Mad, was I?—who was up to all your shifts and contrivances, playing you along, selling you to the police. Watching over me?—they were watching *you* with your precious scryings and seeings. The murderer's voice ringing you up!—who knew that?—they knew only that you told them he rang you up. Do you think they believed you? *I* believed you: after all it was I who rang you. And all the disguises here, right down to the sheets of sheer plastic: this is one of your own wigs, they'll find plenty of clues in that. They thought you might even not know it yourself, I described the blackouts, how you'd come to exhausted, strange dreams . . . I didn't mention the little doses in all those warm drinks I used to bring you, kind, caring Delphine! But of course, all that was after the double killing . . .'

His ears were closed now, deaf for ever. His eyes were sightless for ever, staring blindly up at the animal face that could turn in a moment so charming and sweet—snout out-thrust at the savoured memory of that spilling of blood after which she had written SURFEIT. But, dead or alive, she needed an audience now. She gloated on. 'Oh, the two of them—didn't I have you all on a merry-go-round that time? Ringing you in my No Face voice—waiting till you called me; begging you to come. Not replacing the receiver so that your own telephone was disconnected, you had to ring the police from a call-box. And you played right into my hands; for what other reason had I chosen a foggy night?—driving around "not knowing what you were doing", getting yourself lost. They thought you'd rung up from the call-box outside my flats, got in through the window and away again before they could arrive there. From then on—oh, you were for it, Mr Hawke! No clues, nothing to pin on you yet; but now they *knew*. They let me stay and spy on you in the flat, I was safe while mobs of people were coming in and out; but they watched you, night and day. It was wearisome, no more killings for those three hungry months, but I'd had a good deal from the double killing, I could last. Till the time came—I had to get more. Not that you've provided me with a lot, but once you've gone and the police relax, break up all this elaborate operation—then I can safely begin again. What a laugh!—took you in completely, didn't I?—with the scrying act! You—drinking it all in, the final warning that I would be killed tonight. Murdered, slaughtered, by the maniac psychopath—and you let me go home to it! But I didn't go home, you see: I just came here. I knew how your mind would work, I knew you'd never warn the police, you'd rather get your triumph with the media—and I'd quietly disconnected your telephone, you'd have to come down here to do it. And you came.' Calm now, calmed by the assuaging of the long unsatisfied craving, she leaned over and sniffed long and ecstatically at the thickened seeping of the blood around the wound; rose and, re-settling her features into those of a sick and terrified girl, went across, already weeping, to the telephone. 'Oh, Mr Tomm! Oh, it's so dreadful! He came at me with the knife . . .'

And so now, here he was, trying to get through to them, to the circle sitting there in the darkness with their touching hands. Screaming, silently screaming. 'Listen to me, listen! Tell them, warn them, implore them to believe in me! They've got it all wrong. Yes, I cheated sometimes, but I had the Gift, I had it, and here I am now to prove it to you, speaking to you . . . Tell them I wasn't the killer, tell them it's all going to begin again!'

But they would not hear him. Heard only the sweet, familiar piping. 'Very happy. Yes, he's happy now, he's met them all on the Other Side, his sins are forgiven him. All peace and joy on the Other Side, sunshine and flowers everywhere, just sunshine and flowers . . .'

Sunshine and flowers; and no one to believe in his warning—this very night, it's all going to begin again.

CHRISTIANNA BRAND

Mary Lewis, née Milne, was born in Malaya in 1907, the daughter of a tea planter. She wrote under the pen names Mary Brand, Mary Roland, Mary Ann Ashe, China Thompson, Annabel Jones and, the one as which she is best known, Christianna Brand, which joined her mother's first name to her grandmother's maiden name.

After several happy years at school at a convent in Berkshire, Brand was told she would have to leave by her father, who had been declared bankrupt. At the age of seventeen, she found herself 'literally penniless' and with no training whatsoever for earning her own livelihood. She moved to London where, known by her friends as 'Quif', she drifted from one job to another, eventually becoming a dance hostess (which, incidentally, was not a euphemism for something less respectable). This inspired her earliest published short story, a light romance entitled 'Dance Hostess' (1939) and it led to her meeting her husband, a surgeon called Roland Lewis. The couple married in 1936 and, when the Second World War broke out, Roland Lewis joined the Royal Army Medical Corps and was posted overseas.

On her own in London, Mary Lewis moved in and out of a variety of jobs, eventually taking on a role that was to change her life—she became a shop assistant. While she was not a great success in the job, the job led to a great success for her because she detested the manager of the shop so much that she decided to kill her . . .

in a novel. The hate-fuelled result, *Death in High Heels* (1941), is set not in a shop but in a high-class Mayfair couturier, drawing on another of her many early jobs. There is a poisoning and the detective is the brash young Inspector Charlesworth.

With the return of her husband to England, Mary Lewis settled down with the intention of writing for the rest of her life. Her second novel, *Heads You Lose* (1941), won the $1,000 Red Badge prize offered by publishers Dodd, Mead for the best mystery of the year, but it was her third book, *Green for Danger* (1944), that made her a household name, not least because of the film version, which was released in 1946 and starred Alastair Sim as her best known detective, Inspector Cockrill. That same year, she was elected to the Detection Club, and she continued to write books of various kinds under various names.

By the late 1950s, Mary Lewis was recognised as a leading name in the crime and detective genre. Sadly, and for private reasons, she decided to give up writing mystery novels. However, she could not abandon writing altogether and, as well as a few newspaper serials and some short stories for *Ellery Queen's Mystery Magazine*, she wrote a series of 'true life' novellas for *Woman* and several short books for children featuring Nurse Matilda, a character based on her own nanny.

And then, twenty years since his last case, Inspector Charlesworth returned, in *The Rose in Darkness* (1979), a strange, almost dream-like book in which a reclusive actress and her small group of friends are caught up in what appears to be murder. The return was very warmly welcomed by critics and readers alike but Mary Lewis had been suffering from a painful illness for some years and she died in March 1988.

At the time of her death, Mary Lewis was working on a new detective story featuring Inspector Cockrill and, while that was not finished, a collection of largely unpublished material is due in 2020 from an American publisher, Crippen and Landru.

'NO FACE' has not been published previously.

BEFORE AND AFTER

Peter Antony

It was nine o'clock on a warm summer's morning when Nurse Stephens discovered the body of her employer. Even in death Mrs Carmichael's face still held the irritability of one forced to lean on others who were all too often engaged elsewhere. For fifteen years she had been paralysed from the waist down. Now a tiny hole, drilled neatly through her right temple, had made the top half of her body as immobile as the lower half.

It was all most unfortunate, particularly for Nurse Stephens, who had a most unprofessional attitude to the sight of the little blood there was. She managed, however, to 'phone the doctor and the police.

Inspector Swallow was nominally in charge of the party who arrived at Delver Park at ten o'clock—assorted 'experts', finger-print men, a photographer and the doctor. After a telephone conversation with Inspector Rambler of Scotland Yard, Swallow had been advised by that gentleman to bring with him on the case Mr Verity, who happened to be staying in the locality, and whenever Mr Verity ventured on a case, no one could possibly deny that he, not the police officer, was in charge of it.

'You will certainly find him a little difficult to get on with,' Rambler had said to Swallow over the 'phone, 'but he is really a remarkable man. He always finds the truth. If he is in the area you can't afford to neglect his services. In any case, I don't suppose you will be able to. He has an infuriating habit of tendering them unasked.'

Inspector Swallow had not waited for that event, but had picked Mr Verity up in the police car on his way to Delver Park, and he now stood regarding the lifeless features of Mrs Carmichael with faint distaste.

Mr Verity was an immense man, tall and proportionately broad. His blue eyes shone brilliantly out of a pointed, bronzed face, which was completed by a well-tended, chestnut Vandyke. Despite the earliness of the hour, he was smoking a long, black Cuban cigar with the most curiously theatrical gestures.

'She does make a particularly unlovely corpse,' he said at length. 'And I thought that death was meant to have a softening effect on the features.'

Inspector Swallow interposed: 'If you've finished your inspection, could we have a few details, doctor?'

Doctor Hendrikson, neat, bird-like and laconic, straightened up.

'She was killed with something like a very thin knitting-needle. It was driven with a considerable amount of force through her temple here. A quick-closing wound with very little blood. Time of death 10.30 to 11 o'clock last night. That's about as accurate as I can get it.'

'Clear enough. Munby, get finger-printing, and you, Brandt, do your stuff.'

Brandt, a young recruit to the Force, took his camera and leant over Mrs Carmichael's tightening face. He giggled nervously.

'Watch the dickie bird,' he said with bravado.

Mr Verity scowled.

'The contagion of Mr Raymond Chandler!' he snorted.

'Let's go and see the family,' said Swallow.

Together the two detectives went downstairs to the library

where the dead woman's husband and the nurse were waiting for them.

Robert Carmichael was a tall, austere man still in his late thirties, with a fine forehead, darting brown eyes, a rather sharp nose and an unexpectedly weak mouth and chin. Nurse Stephens was good-looking in a coarse, full-blown sort of way. Neither appeared distraught though they were essaying a reasonable facsimile.

Swallow was good at this game, being at once urbane, sympathetic and slightly menacing.

'Now, let's start from tea-time yesterday.'

Nurse Stephens was ready and willing.

'Tea was at 4.30. Mrs Carmichael had her medicine at 4.45, and after that I wheeled her down to the garden. About five, Mr Carmichael took her photograph and went off to the village to develop it, whilst I sat with Mrs Carmichael for an hour or so before wheeling her off to bed. I remained on duty until seven o'clock, when relieved by the night nurse, Wimple.'

'And everything was all right before you left?'

'Certainly, Mrs Carmichael was asleep and everything in order.'

'And later on that evening?'

'At 7.30 we all went over to Colonel Longford's house for dinner and bridge. We arrived back here at about one in the morning,' Robert Carmichael put in.

'All?'

'Nurse Stephens, my brother-in-law Doctor Sanderson, Sandra my stepdaughter, and myself.'

Mr Verity grunted reflectively.

'There seems to be a pretty comprehensive interest in that curiously anti-social pastime, eh, Mr Carmichael?'

'I beg your pardon, sir?'

'I refer to bridge.'

'Yes, we all play.'

'Tell me, Mr Carmichael, did your wife have any mortal enemies that you knew of?'

'I'm afraid I can't help you there, Mr Verity. I am as much in the dark as you are.'

'Never mind, Mr Carmichael. I have a wonderful capacity for illumination.'

With a wave of the hand he dismissed them.

That evening after tea, Inspector Swallow and his elderly colleague saw Dr Sanderson, the dead woman's brother.

The old man started the ball rolling with typical charm.

'Well, sir. You've lost a sister and made £15,000. Some people would consider that you have made a profit on the day's activities. What do you think?'

Doctor Sanderson, balding, eagle-nosed and tubby, was indignant.

'Really, Mr Verity, I do resent that most earnestly. After all, I was very fond—'

'I know all about it. Your sister left it to you. I saw Riggs the lawyer before tea. And don't say you didn't know . . . Looks of incredulity are lost on me. I have seen too many of them to be deceived into thinking that you only expected a little something . . . an extra pipe of tobacco a week maybe, or that odd pint.'

'But it's true—'

Inspector Swallow interposed tactfully.

'Oh, come now, sir. It is our duty to check up on people, and we have discovered that you've been borrowing money on the strength of your expectations. Considerable sums, too.'

Doctor Sanderson paled.

'Oh, so you know about that. You certainly work fast.'

His face set defiantly; assumed pain gave way to spleen.

'All right, then, if you know so much about me, what about the others? Have you seen my sanctimonious brother-in-law? He's not the sort of man to be chained to a hopeless invalid all his life and do nothing about it.'

Mr Verity was yawning hugely.

'In the words of the vulgar, do you imply that we *cherchez la femme*?'

'And not so far either.'

'You refer, of course, to the angel of mercy. You could be right.'

'No "could be" about it. And there's Sandra. Money in trust. Love's young dream, and the missing parental consent. Why not have a look at all that before picking on me?'

'It's not a question of picking on anybody,' murmured Mr Verity sweetly. 'I just always like to take suspects in order of repulsion.'

Doctor Sanderson stormed out of the library in a fury.

Both detectives stayed to dinner. It was a homely little meal, marred perhaps for the hypersensitive by the arrival of the mortuary van. Mr Verity was in great form and talked incessantly about a portrait of an old man in polychromed clay executed by Guido Mazzoni in the late fifteenth century which he had just purchased for his collection of statuary at his Sussex home 'Persepolis'. The company, with the exception of Sandra, Carmichael's stepdaughter, bore his recondite conversation with fortitude. She, however, was noticeably distressed, and it was with some diffidence that the two men set out after dinner to find out exactly why.

'Believe it or not,' she began, when at last they were alone together in the library, 'I had a great affection for my mother.'

'That is not the voice of vulgar rumour,' said the old man.

'You can love a person and not always get on with them, Mr Verity.'

'So the Bible continually reminds us.'

Swallow scratched his head and said gently:

'Your mother had £20,000 in trust for you. I understand you were to receive this sum, or the income thereof, on your marriage, provided your mother gave her consent. Is that correct?'

'Perfectly. Have you ever heard anything so monstrous? It was my father's idea.'

She said this as if her father's death had been no great loss to her.

'And the position was that, having hunted down one Harry Logan as your intended mate, you could not persuade your mother that the alliance of Harry and £20,000 was a holy one.'

Mr Verity smiled benevolently at her over his black cigar, and patted his inflated stomach affectionately.

Sandra Collins was almost crying. Her top lip trembled mutinously.

'So—?'

'So, if I might say it without offence, my dear Miss Collins, murder for money is still a highly favoured motive, not only amongst those who write on matters of crime, but amongst those who investigate it.'

Wishing to avoid an hysterical scene, Inspector Swallow left the world of conjecture conjured up by his colleague, and returned to the world of fact.

'Tell me, Miss Collins,' he began suavely, 'what did you do last night?'

'I went out to dinner with the others. You can soon find out whether that's true or not.'

'I have already done so.'

Sandra was openly weeping now.

'I didn't kill her, Inspector,' she sobbed, '. . . my own mother . . . You can't say I did.'

'Which at the moment of speaking is perfectly true,' grunted Mr Verity, blowing a smoke-ring.

'Oh, you're impossible,' she cried, and with the tears pouring down her face hurried from the room.

'Mr Verity, I don't like this case,' Swallow said when they were alone. 'All of them had motives for killing her, yet none of them could have done it.'

Mr Verity beamed.

'Don't let it prey on you. 10.30 to 11 o'clock is the time to keep in mind. Surely we can punch a hole in one of their well-rehearsed narratives.'

'It seems impossible. They were all over at Colonel Longford's between 7.30 p.m. and 1 a.m. He lives twelve miles from here and there was absolutely no opportunity for one of them to take an unnoticed hour off, to drive back here, do the murder and drive back again. I checked up on it and no one left. Besides, the excellent Nurse Wimple was on duty in the passage outside Mrs Carmichael's room the whole night, so no one could have got in.'

Mr Verity looked glum.

'Oh lord! Not another locked room. My last locked-room case was a shattering business . . . all centring round some dreadful woman in a wardrobe. Besides, the excellent Wimple probably spent half the night dreaming she was in the arms of Tarzan.'

'I'm afraid she claims all-night consciousness. And, further, she had no motive to kill the old lady.'

'Of course she didn't do it. If she had, she would have taken good care to provide herself with an alibi.' The old detective yawned. 'Come, Inspector, adjourn with me to the local hostelry. A pint or two of good ale, a cigar and a little light discussion on the terra-cotta work of Antonio Pollaiulo will do wonders for our tired brains.'

The next morning Inspector Swallow, calling on Mr Verity, found him in a state of high excitement.

'Here, Inspector, look at this. Interesting, eh?'

He pointed with a well-manicured forefinger at the centre-page advertisement in the morning's copy of the *Daily Grind*. It showed two photographs of Mrs Carmichael 'Before and After Taking *Toneup*, the wonderful restorative for Invalids . . . "I felt absolutely washed out until I started taking *Toneup*," says Mrs Carmichael, a chronic invalid of Delver Park . . .'

'Yes, I know all about it.' Inspector Swallow said. 'It was Mrs Carmichael's idea. I asked her husband. He sent it off the same night she got killed. Just another manifestation of the invalid's craving to be noticed, I suppose.'

'I suppose so,' Verity replied, thoughtfully brushing his Vandyke with the back of a huge hand. 'But I wonder why she is looking so sour in the "After" photograph. It's most curious. In this kind of picture the patient is always equipped with a smirk of imbecilic glee. Here she looks like a professional mourner.'

Swallow studied the 'After' picture in perplexity.

'Maybe it's the cigarette smoke getting in her eyes.'

Mr Verity took out a small pocket magnifying-glass and scrutinized the picture again.

'You must excuse the Sherlock Holmes touch . . . Yes, that is another curious point. There is certainly plenty of cigarette smoke there. But where is the cigarette?'

'I think I can barely see it . . . there between her fingers.'

Inspector Swallow pointed to a dark smudge on the picture.

'That is very odd indeed. One might almost say it is the first real rift in the leaden clouds of deceit which have surrounded us since the start of our investigations.'

'Do you think she was dead then?'

'Certainly not. The doctor said she died between 10.30 and 11 o'clock, approximately six hours later. I never believe doctors on questions of health, but on questions of death I have always found them infallible. Besides, the maid up at Delver Park confirms she was alive at six o'clock. She helped carry her upstairs in the wheel-chair.'

Inspector Swallow ran a harassed hand through his thinning hair.

'I don't understand it at all, Mr Verity. A woman is murdered in a room where no one could have reached her without being seen, and at a time when everyone was miles away. What do we do now? What is the significance of this photograph, if any?'

'It certainly is significant. In fact, it tells us everything.'

Mr Verity lit a Cuban cigar and looked dreamily in front of him.

'You really must have patience, Inspector. As to what we are to do now, there is only one thing to do.'

'And that is?'

'We must pay a visit to the morgue . . . No, don't ask why. You will see when we get there.'

They had to stand five minutes in the antiseptic half-light of the mortuary before the attendants had sorted out Mrs Carmichael. Nervously Swallow pulled back the sheet and studied the body intently.

'Observe her right hand,' murmured Verity over his shoulder.

The Inspector whistled, and the noise had a horrible flat ring in that desolate room.

'She must have been a heavy smoker. The whole finger is stained with nicotine, and the flesh is badly scorched on the side there.'

Mr Verity's satanic face wore a smug look.

'Just so. Mrs Carmichael must have suffered a considerable amount of pain in allowing that cigarette to burn down to that point.'

'She must have been asleep when her husband took that "After" picture,' said Swallow.

'Fiddlesticks,' roared Verity. 'She was unconscious.'

'And just what is the point of shunting an unconscious woman around in a bath-chair, posing her for a personality picture, dumping her in bed and going off to a bridge party?' the Inspector enquired, suddenly startled by the old man's explosion.

'The point should be obvious to an intelligence considerably meaner than yours, my dear Inspector. Come, I want to make a telephone call.'

'To whom?'

'To the station, of course. I want them to arrest our two murderers, and take them into custody. Come, don't stand there as if you had been struck by lightning. I'm sure they must have a 'phone here; if not for the convenience of the inmates, at least for casual visitors.'

Whilst the Inspector saw that the body of Mrs Carmichael was safely returned, Mr Verity found the 'phone and got through to the police-station. His instructions were brief but effective.

Ten minutes later, after Mr Verity had meticulously examined some Corinthian-style pillaring which had caught his fancy on the exterior of the little town hall, the two detectives were speeding back to the police-station in the Inspector's car.

'After all, we don't want to keep our prisoners waiting,' Mr Verity explained as he urged his colleague to exceed the speed limit. Inspector Swallow, his mind in a baffled whirl, drove steadily.

Once at the station, Mr Verity jumped out of the car with all the deftness of a rhinoceros in labour, and charged inside.

'Well, where are they?' he enquired of a constable behind the desk.

'Waiting inside, sir.'

Next door sat Robert Carmichael and Nurse Stephens, white-faced and very angry.

'You'll pay for this, Verity,' Carmichael roared. 'False imprisonment. I'll get £10,000 damages.'

'The only damage you'll get is to your neck,' the old man replied benignly.

'You can't prove a thing. On your own evidence, the murder was done between 10.30 and 11 o'clock. Nurse Stephens and I were miles away at the time. I have half a dozen witnesses.'

'Saving your presence, Nurse Stephens, I wouldn't give a damn if you had the whole population of Central London as witnesses. You may have been miles away when your wife died, but that doesn't mean you didn't murder her. You ran the whole job up between you—a very natural alliance seeing that you planned to carry the partnership on to the legalised sex level when the obstacle was safely in her coffin.'

'This is absurd,' screamed Nurse Stephens. 'Supposing you prove it.'

'I can do that, too,' Mr Verity replied, taking a deep puff at his cigar and exhaling slowly. 'From the burn on Mrs Carmichael's finger, I was convinced that at the time you took that photograph your wife was unconscious. Therefore some drug was suggested and at the same time a wonderful opportunity for administering the stuff—Mrs Carmichael's medicine.

'What happened was this. Nurse Stephens slipped an overdose of some suitable narcotic, probably chloral hydrate, into the medicine, and though the victim lost consciousness within half an hour she did not die until close on 11 o'clock. What simpler than for your nurse to come along in the morning and drive a thin implement through her head, the idea being to make it look as if Mrs Carmichael had been murdered at 11 o'clock, the time of death, when she and her accomplice were twelve miles away playing bridge. A very thin weapon, even if it had been used when the victim was alive, would cause so very little blood that Doctor Hendrikson was unable to tell that the wound was inflicted after death. Again, a drug like chloral hydrate would not be suspected if there were other evidence to account for death, like a wound in the temple. Ingenious and all well within a qualified nurse's knowledge.

'It really was very foolish of you, Mr Carmichael, to give way to your macabre egotism and put a picture of your dying wife in the newspaper with a caption plugging her superb health. It wasn't really necessary to prove that she was alive at five o'clock. There was plenty of independent testimony on this point. On the other hand, it clearly showed me the way to your conviction . . . You can lock them up now, Sergeant.'

Protesting, they were led below. Inspector Swallow came up to the old man and held his hand out.

'Many congratulations, Mr Verity. I should never have guessed.'

'Nonsense, my dear fellow,' he replied, pumping the other's hand. 'No guesswork was required. You would have got there if you had thought about it long enough . . . Perhaps you will lunch with me so that we may talk of other and pleasanter things? I suggest you join me at "The Stag" at one o'clock. I must first pay a brief visit to your local museum. I have heard they possess a quite excellent bronze of Antonio Rizzo; a Venetian youth, I believe. See you at lunch.'

Inspector Swallow watched him go down the street, still gesticulating wildly, his small beard and the smoke from his cigar being blown about by the wind, and disappear round the corner into the High Street. With a shake of his head he returned inside to the comparative calm of the police-station.

PART II

Mr Verity had gone. Inspector Swallow mopped his brow as he climbed the steps of the police-station.

'Say, Inspector—'

'Why, Harry!' Swallow positively beamed at the local reporter. 'I want some information from you.'

'Me? I just came for the latest—'

'I know, I'll give you something later. Look, you're in the newspaper business. Supposing an advertising agency wanted to insert an advertisement in a national newspaper, how long before publication would they have to get the pictures and things ready?'

'The way clients change their minds and alter the ads, I'd say a month or so.'

'No, seriously. What's the shortest time?'

'Well, let's see. The national papers close for press for advertisements the evening of the second day previous to publication—earlier, some of them. Then the agency would need a day for their layout men to draw the ad out and so on, another for making the illustrations, especially if they're half-tones, another for casting the block. About four days. It *has* been done in less time, of course, in emergencies and with top-level pushing.'

'The photo of the old woman was posted at six,' Swallow was murmuring to himself, 'to reach London next morning. I say, Harry, could it be done in under a day?'

'Not on your life. Now, Inspector—'

But Swallow had hurried in.

Robert Carmichael and Nurse Stephens were still very angry and considerably on their dignity. Swallow beamed at them a little nervously.

'I'm terribly sorry about all this.'

'We want—'

'Oh, Carmichael,' said the Inspector hurriedly, 'that photo you took of Mrs Carmichael the afternoon of the tragedy, what was it for?'

'I tried to tell you. Mrs Carmichael is—was—being featured in a "Toneup" advertisement, "Before and After"—you know the sort of thing.'

'Yes, I've seen it.'

'Have you? Then you'll have noticed how terrible she looks in the "After" shot. The "Toneup" people wanted to use the advertisement again next month, and they asked for a more cheerful photograph. I was taking it, that's all.'

'Quite. Sergeant, have you got those interviews with the servants at Delver Park? Can't think why Verity ignored them so completely.'

'Yes, sir; it's all sorted out now. The person you suspected is inside here.'

'Confession?'

The sergeant nodded.

'Nurse Wimple, the night-nurse,' he said, 'confirms now that the maid came up about 10.30. Very tired she was and complained about running up and down stairs for invalids all day. "There now," said the maid, "I'm so tired I've been and forgotten your cocoa, Nurse. And the water's all on the boil." Nurse Wimple said she looked so done in that she offered to go down and get it herself. I quote: "I'll go down, dearie. You just stay here a minute."'

'Time enough,' Swallow commented.

'*See, where my slave, the ugly monster Death,*
Shaking and quivering, pale and wan for fear,
Stands aiming at me with his murdering dart.'

'Verity would appreciate that. Persepolis, indeed!' Inspector Swallow snorted.

'Yes, sir. And we've got the motive. Neurotic hatred of the invalid, built up over the years—'

Nurse Stephens nodded in sympathy: 'She could be hard. Look at her treatment of Sandra, Logan's a good man.'

'—and there was a good fat legacy. She knew—at least, it was common gossip according to the cook. But we didn't get anything on the burn.'

'On Mrs Carmichael's hand?'

'I know about that,' said Nurse Stephens. 'She used to sit in her room sometimes in her chair. She tried to poke the fire a day or so ago and nearly fell in it—caught her finger on a coal.'

The sergeant looked a little worried. 'I thought Verity said it showed in the photograph in the paper?'

'Verity's imagination,' Swallow smiled. 'The fingers had come out dark, the nicotine stains probably—you could never identify that burn smudge on a newspaper reproduction. Coincidence, though.' Inspector Swallow sighed. 'So it was just another simple tragedy, after all.'

Robert Carmichael had simmered down now. He smoothed back his thinning hair.

'There's just one thing, Inspector,' he said. 'Why did you let that Verity fool make such a nuisance of himself, upsetting everyone?'

Swallow paused a moment. 'I feel I owe you some sort of apology, but it's strictly in confidence. We had orders from the Yard to let him have his head—they're suspicious because he happens to be around when so many murders crop up. But he had nothing to do with this one.'

'Nothing at all. Ah!' said the sergeant as a constable brought in a tray of tea mugs.

PETER ANTONY

'Peter Antony' was an alias adopted by the Shaffer twins, Anthony and Peter, both of whom became rather more famous under their own names. The twins were born in Liverpool in 1926 and, after the family moved to London, they attended St Paul's School and then spent three years as Bevin boys in the Kent coalfields. At the age of 21, under the name 'Peter Antony', the brothers collaborated on what would be the first of three mysteries, *The Woman in the Wardrobe* (1951), *How Doth the Little Crocodile?* (1952) and *Withered Murder* (1955). The novels feature Mr Verity, a detective cast very much in the mould of the sleuths of the Golden Age of crime and detective fiction.

On his release from the mines, Anthony Shaffer went up to Cambridge where he read Law at Trinity. In the early 1950s, he worked as a barrister and in 1954 he married his first wife, Henrietta Glaskie. The marriage ended four years later and Glaskie named the actress Fenella Fielding and two other women in her divorce suit.

Considerably more at home with the written word than the spoken one, Anthony did not enjoy the life of a barrister and moved into reviewing books and copy-writing for advertising company Pearl & Dean. In 1963, he produced his first play *The Savage Parade*, which had its roots in the abduction and trial of the Nazi Adolf Eichmann. The play was criticised by some for taking an insufficiently serious approach to the Holocaust and by others because, in the words of one critic, it included 'so many cases of mistaken identity as to be laughable were the subject not so serious and the author so obviously well intentioned'. The young writer learned from the criticism but nonetheless carried some elements of his first play into his next, *Sleuth* (1970), in which he celebrated the work of John Dickson Carr and other Golden Age writers while accurately skewering the more unpleasant tropes of the genre. Described by one critic as a 'who-dun-what-to-whom', *Sleuth* was an enormous success, playing for some years in London's West End and in New York on Broadway.

While other stage thrillers would follow—including the over-elaborate *Murderer* (1975) and the unwisely titled *The Case of the Oily Levantine* (1977)—none would achieve the same success as *Sleuth*. He also wrote for the cinema, beginning with the charming *Mr Forbush and the Penguins* (1971) and the thriller *Frenzy* (1972) for Hitchcock before adapting his own play into Joseph L. Mankiewicz's memorable film of *Sleuth* (1972) with Michael Caine amd Laurence Olivier. His next screenplay—for the cult mystery *The Wicker Man* (1973)—would eventually bring him almost as much fame as *Sleuth*, and he had begun his first of three high-profile Agatha Christie film adaptations, *Death on the Nile* (1978), before returning to his own work with another twisted mystery, *Absolution* (1978), directed by Anthony Page. He also worked with the director Nicholas Meyer on *Sommersby* (1993), which relocated a sixteenth-century mystery of imposture to the American Civil War.

Towards the end of his life, Anthony Shaffer lived in Australia with his third wife, the actress Diane Cilento, and it was here that his final two plays were performed, *Widow's Weeds* (1977) and *The Thing in the Wheelchair* (1996), a 'melodrama' adapted from 'The Case of the Talking Eyes', a short story by Cornell Woolrich.

After his stint as a Bevin boy, Peter Shaffer also went up to Cambridge, on a scholarship, to read history. He graduated in 1950 and moved to America where he worked in the New York Public

Library and then in a bookshop. It was while living in New York that he wrote his first script, *The Salt Land* (1955), a television play about the formation of the state of Israel. On returning to London, he worked for the classical music publisher Boosey and Hawkes on catalogues and publicity, specialising in the symphonic section, and he also reviewed books for the magazine *Truth*. As well as writing the libretto for a comic opera, he wrote a television play *Balance of Terror* (1957), a spy thriller about the theft of plans for an intercontinental missile by an unspecified foreign power, and a radio 'parable' called *The Prodigal Father*. His first major theatrical success was *Five Finger Exercise* (1958), a play about a warring family. Though it seemed to some critics rather old-fashioned, others praised the play for the way it explored sensitive issues without the strident tone of other playwrights of the new wave. Either way, the play won him recognition as the Most Promising British Playwright of the Year in the *Evening Standard*'s prestigious theatre awards.

Peter Shaffer believed that theatre 'should lead people into mystery and magic. It should give them a sense of wonderment and, while entertaining, reveal a vision of life.' His many plays include *The Royal Hunt of the Sun* (1964), which explored Spain's genocide of the Incas, the 'farce in the dark' *Black Comedy* (1965), *Lettice and Lovage* (1987) and *Amadeus* (1979), which probed the death of Mozart and the possible involvement of the composer Salieri. For many, *Amadeus* is Peter Shaffer's finest play and it was filmed by Milos Forman in 1984, winning eight Oscars including one for Shaffer's screenplay. But there is also *Equus* (1973), an ingenious whydunnit in which a psychiatrist explores the motives and meaning behind a case of horse-mutilation. The play was a sensation on both sides of the Atlantic, although, as the playwright observed, 'In London, *Equus* caused a sensation because it displayed cruelty to horses; in New York because it allegedly displayed cruelty to psychiatrists.'

Anthony Shaffer died in London in 2001, the year in which his brother was knighted; Peter Shaffer died in 2016 while on a family visit to Ireland.

'Before and After', the only short story to feature Mr Verity, was published in *London Mystery Magazine* (Issue 16) in 1953, and 'Part II: Mr Verity's Investigation' appeared in the following issue, credited to 'J. M. Caffyn', the name of a surgeon in Bram Stoker's *Dracula*.

HOTEL EVIDENCE

Helen Simpson

Henry Brodribb was engaged in an argument with his wife; or, rather, he was pacing the room, wordless, trying to take in the sense of her final proposal. His wife, calmly stitching an undergarment, watching him, was aware of his throes, and allowed time to elapse before she continued:

'It's no good our going on living together when there's no reason for it and we don't suit each other.'

'Don't we?' interjected Mr Brodribb ironically.

'No,' said his wife, disregarding the irony, 'we don't. Now, Arthur and I do. We like the same sort of plays, and there's bridge, and he's ever so good-looking. But, as I said to him, I won't have anything underhand.'

'Nothing underhand,' Mr Brodribb repeated, 'only a pack of lies for me to tell in court. Only perjury and collusion. What about the King's Proctor?'

'People can't be expected to tell the truth,' said his wife comfortably, 'with the silly way the law is. I'm sure if there was any other reason they'd let you have, I'd have no objection to your divorcing me. But there's only infidelity for a woman. As I said, there's never been anything of that between me and Arthur. Besides, it wouldn't be good for him in his business.'

'And what about my business?' Mr Brodribb inquired, sarcastically.

'You'll be all right,' his wife replied, disregarding the sarcasm.

'Nobody'd ever dream of your doing anything wrong. It 'ud be a change for both of us.'

To this Mr Brodribb's imagination gave involuntary assent. He pictured home without Cissie, a life free from comment, in charge of a good cook-housekeeper. It was alluring. Also, he could move from the country into the town. But he sounded a protest, as was right.

'I never heard of such a thing. I won't listen to another word about it.'

And he sat down in the chair opposite hers and shook out his evening paper. Mrs Brodribb, biting off a length of yellow silk. resumed:

'Nobody thinks anything of it, nowadays. Look at these countesses, and Lady This and Lady That; always in and out of the divorce courts.'

Mr Brodribb beat the paper into more convenient folds and replied severely:

'We're not countesses.'

It was a shot fired in flight, at random, which could not give pause for an instant to the victorious advance of his wife. She had made up her mind.

Mr Brodribb realised this, and was appalled. Only once before had he known her to make up her mind. She had not argued with him then, but she had used other methods without scruple, and he had turned up at the church on the day she named. Having secured him by this display of resolution she had laid decision aside until now, when all the slow force of her will was once more arrayed to be rid of him. Cowering behind his paper, Mr Brodribb sank deeper into his chair and prepared to offer such resistance as pride demanded.

'I was afraid,' said Mrs Brodribb calmly, 'that it might be expensive. But it's not so very, Arthur says, if the case isn't defended. Arthur's been finding out about it. Of course, he'd share expenses. Arthur—'

'How dare you mention that fellow's name to me?' Mr Brodribb inquired. 'It's bare-faced. You don't seem to have any sense of what's right and proper.'

'I've told you,' Mrs Brodribb answered with dignity, 'there's nothing wrong at all between me and Arthur. And won't be.'

Mr Brodribb dashed down his paper, rose, and retired to the only refuge that owned him for master, the tool shed. Mrs Brodribb showed no emotion at his exit, did not lift her eyes from her sewing; but some minutes later she smiled.

This was the first of a series of encounters whereby, at the end of a fortnight, Mr Brodribb was finally brought to reason. Towards the result his wife's arguments contributed in some degree; but in the main she owed her victory to that unknown ally, Mr Brodribb's imagination, which displayed him to himself a free man. Only that wicked preliminary, the necessary infidelity, alarmed him. He made guarded inquiries, confirmed Arthur's estimate of the expense, and admitted one evening that he might think it over. His wife kissed him, and telephoned to Arthur to come round at once.

The meeting passed off without awkwardness, owing to Arthur's tactful praise of Mr Brodribb's generosity. Indeed, the evening ended with a kind of impromptu supper, during which healths were drunk in whisky and water. After all, as Mrs Brodribb pointed out, it was not as if they had any of them anything to be ashamed of. It was she who steered the men towards action, with:

'All very fine, but what do we do first? You can't sit with your hands folded and expect a judge to come to you.'

Mr Brodribb involuntarily consulted Arthur with his eyes.

'Restitution of conjugal rights,' said Arthur, responding. 'That's the first step.' Mr Brodribb cleared his throat.

'No question of that, old man. Restitution, I mean. She's never been deprived.'

'Well, you've got to deprive her,' said Arthur.

Mr Brodribb looked helplessly about the comfortable room; at the ferns he had tended all the winter long; at the black marble clock, shaped like a tomb, that the firm had given him on his marriage; finally, at his wife.

'You don't have to do it for long. You go to some nice boarding-house—there's a little place in north London I could give you the address of, a private hotel—well, you go off, and you write Cissie a letter, saying you're gone for good. Then off *she* goes to a solicitor and shows him the letter, and he sues you.'

'What for?'

'Restitution. You don't answer him. He sues you two or three times more—'

'Who's going to pay for all this?'

Arthur waved the question from him.

'And that's all, as far as that goes.' He coughed, and went on delicately: 'There's one or two other things. But you'd better get a solicitor to put you up to all the dodges.'

Mrs Brodribb, with healthy feminine contempt of delicacy, said:

'Yes, the infidelity; what about that? I don't know that I like the idea of Henry going off with goodness knows who.'

'I think you'll find,' Mr Brodribb ventured at last, 'that it's only a form.'

'That's it,' Arthur agreed, relieved; 'that's all. A form.'

Mrs Brodribb, with feminine bad taste, laughed.

'Fancy, Henry!' said she.

They separated, and Mr Brodribb, making his way to the spare bedroom, felt that he had taken that night another step towards freedom. Next morning, at breakfast, it was arranged that he should leave home on the following Monday.

'It's always nicer,' said Mrs Brodribb, 'to start the week clear.'

The intervening days went smoothly by. Mr Brodribb secured a room in the little place in north London at a reasonable figure. During the Friday lunch hour he was measured for a new suit.

At home Mrs Brodribb passed his underclothing in review, darned, packed, and began to look younger. With the near prospect of escape, home became tolerable to both. They were considerate and friendly.

On Sunday night, as he knelt by his suitcase, affixing the label, Mrs Brodribb entered the spare room. In her right hand was a brown paper parcel. She held it out timidly and said:

'Got any room in your case?'

'Plenty,' said Mr Brodribb. 'Hello, what's this?'

'Hot water bottle,' his wife answered. 'Extra strong, guaranteed. You know what your feet are, and I thought, perhaps now—'

Mr Brodribb unwrapped the parcel, revealing the gift, whose outer cover appeared to be made of tiger skin. His wife went on, justifying her display of sentiment:

'If it leaks any time in the next six months, Prosser's'll give you a new one. Only don't let them fill it with boiling, whatever you do. If you fill it with boiling, they won't guarantee.'

'Right,' said Mr Brodribb. 'I'll tell them. Thanks, Cis.'

He was touched, and uneasy. Still on his knees, he wrapped the bottle again in its paper and stowed it with care in a corner of the suitcase. When he lifted his head his wife was at the door.

'All aboard,' said Mr Brodribb, to lighten the tension. 'You be off.'

He made a threatening gesture, in play. His wife lingered.

'Is that place comfortable you're going to?' she asked.

'Seems all right,' said Mr Brodribb, 'there's a nice bit of garden at the back.'

'Oh,' said his wife. 'Well, good-night.'

'Good-night, Cis,' Mr Brodribb responded. 'I won't forget about that hot bottle.'

Nor did he. On Monday evening in the boarding-house bedroom, his belongings strewn about him ready to be absorbed into drawers and cupboards as yet uncharted, Mr Brodribb paused to hand on his wife's instructions to the housemaid, who, regarding the disorder with that sympathetic mockery which is the everyday attitude of woman to man, replied:

'I know all about that. You leave it to me. I was filling bottles before you were born.'

Mr Brodribb, who had guessed her age at about twenty-five, was flattered. He handed over the bottle, and felt in his pocket for a coin which should ensure her continued interest in him. He found two, and bestowed them. Instantly the housemaid informed him that her name was Ivy and that she never could bear to see a gentleman trying to do things for himself. On this Mr Brodribb thankfully abandoned the struggle with his belongings and went for a stroll with a cigar; retiring, he found order, and the temperature of the bottle judged to perfection.

In the kitchen Ivy sketched his portrait for the benefit of Queenie and the cook.

'That's a nice little feller in number four,' said Ivy. 'Good clothes, and not pernickety, I should say. No scent or brilliantine.'

'Married?' Gladys inquired.

'Ought to be,' Ivy responded. 'A bit shy, though. And no photographs. No, single, I should say. But a nice little feller. The sort you can soon learn their ways.'

This prophecy was fulfilled. In a week such ways as Mr Brodribb had were learned, and the routine of 'Melrose' began to fit him like his waistcoat. His life appeared to the other boarders to be entirely uneventful.

They could not know, nor could the servants know, the significance of certain letters in blue envelopes which arrived for him from time to time and were immediately destroyed. These letters, which denounced Mr Brodribb as a vagabond and wife-betrayer, called upon him to return without delay to his duty, and stated in clear type what steps, in the event of non-compliance, would be taken. Each letter troubled him, not by its black and white accusations of guilt but by its wordless reminder that these were, as yet, unfounded. He knew that the step must be taken. He knew that Cissie, and Arthur, and two impeccable forms of solicitors expected it of him, and he was resigned; but, also he was afraid. He procrastinated. Time went by.

It was a chance word from Ivy that in the end, strangely, gave him courage. She appeared one evening unusually early to turn down his bed, announcing that she had the evening off.

'Oh,' said Mr Brodribb, 'what'll you do? Pictures?'

'Pictures!' Ivy repeated with scorn. 'Why, last time a feller started trying to flip my suspender elastic. I had the attendant on to him, quick. No, it's dancing I'm mad over.'

And she described the joys of the Alexandra Palais de Danse, with its twin bands, its delectable sixpenny partners.

'You ought to go,' said Ivy, summing up.

'I might, some time,' Mr Brodribb replied. 'Good-night. Have a good time.'

'Watch me,' Ivy responded, and withdrew.

The next evening Mr Brodribb slipped out and took a taxi to the Palais de Danse. The exterior alarmed him; it was garish with light. But indoors, the large room into which he blundered was dim, save for a moving radiant circle in which two figures shifted to hushed music. This, he knew, must be an exhibition dance; it looked easy, artless; nevertheless Mr Brodribb's neighbours bent forward to observe with the rapt stillness of trees and mountain tops attentive to Orpheus' lute.

It was ended; the band, long spent, burst into a frenzy of syncopation, and Mr Brodribb, looking about him in the restored light, began to feel lonely. Couples formed the assembly, sitting, dancing, dallying: nowhere could he see a woman unattached. The couples were respectable, they danced with decorum, as a social rite, unsmiling, while above their heads the music raved and pranced, kicked high, and came slithering down on a wail from the saxophone.

At last a woman appeared in the doorway alone. She was fair, small, not so very young, not so very pretty. Her nice average face was masked with paint, and her dress was showy. Mr Brodribb wondered at her presence in that place, for he had no illusions as to her calling. Neither, it seemed, had the attendants, who watched her, questioned each other with glances, and then, nodding to each other, bore down. Calmly, civilly, they edged her towards the door. The group was almost out of sight when Mr Brodribb, stepping forward and craning to see the last of the episode, caught the woman's eye over an attendant's shoulder. Without hesitation she pushed the man aside and came towards him, widely smiling. Dimly he heard her greeting:

'Well, George, wherever have you been hiding? Keeping me standing about—'

'This lady with you, sir?' the attendant asked, doubtfully.

'Can't you see I am?' she interrupted, and took Mr Brodribb's arm, which he did not withhold. Reassured, the attendant moved away.

'Well,' said Mr Brodribb to his companion, 'since you're here and I'm here, suppose we have a dance?'

'I don't mind,' the lady replied, surveying her face by the swift circular motion of a mirror two inches square; and without further reference to his chivalry disposed herself for him to clasp. She had a snub nose, which he liked. Her hair's metallic refinement matched that of her voice. If her scent was pervasive, her feet kept their distance. Not a bad little woman at all, he decided. Silently they shuffled, while the music raved.

'Often come here?' Mr Brodribb asked.

'Not so often,' she replied, and was instantly in full conversational sail. 'They don't like a girl to come here without a gentleman. Of course I saw at once you were what I call a real gentleman, or I wouldn't have spoken.'

'Very glad you did,' said Mr Brodribb, 'I was wondering what to do for a partner.'

'Come on your own?' she asked.

He explained that he lived quite near.

'Lucky!' said she. 'It's a nice part.'

'And where do you live?' Mr Brodribb asked, with no ulterior motive; but her answering glance dismayed him, reminded him. Through the hurry of his own thoughts he heard her say:

'Not so far. Like to come along? I'll make you a cup of tea.'

Mr Brodribb rose.

'That's right,' said his partner, 'and there's a nice pot of salmon paste I haven't opened.'

During the drive she told him that her name was Edna, and asked for his. He gave it, with some reluctance; unnecessarily, since she disliked it and elected to call him George as before.

But the room into which she led the way surprised Mr Brodribb from his brooding. It was small and tidy.

Mr Brodribb watched her preparations for tea through a cloud of thought. Where, he asked himself, could he find a correspondent more suitable in every way? Impulse overcame him; and as she handed him the cup he made his suggestion.

Edna doubted, mocked, required assurance, read the ultimate letter from the solicitor, and was convinced.

'It would have to be some hotel,' said Mr Brodribb, 'so as to get the servants' evidence. I dare say you know of some place.'

'Well, I do,' she responded without enthusiasm, 'but they're not what I'd call very nice. What's this place like you're in?'

Mr Brodribb described 'Melrose' at some length. She pondered.

'Sounds the sort of place I'd like,' she said at last. 'I'm sick of these flash hotels. Everybody knows what you're there for. Now, what I'd liked be some nice quiet boarding-house, or somewhere like that, just for once in a way.'

Mr Brodribb, too, had been pondering. What, after all, was 'Melrose' to him? No final refuge, since he would have to leave as soon as the case came on. There was a vacant room next to his own.

'But it would have to be as my wife,' said he, thinking aloud.

'Well, rings are cheap,' she answered, unperturbed.

A week later Mr Brodribb introduced a small mouse-coloured woman to 'Melrose' as his wife; he let it be understood that they had been married some months ago, but that Mrs Brodribb had been nursing a sick mother in the country.

The good time ended by reason of financial pressure. Mr Brodribb, assessing his expenses for the half-year, which included two homes, a retaining fee for Edna, and a month of junketing for two, decided that the experiment could no longer continue. Edna approved.

Mr Brodribb gave notice to the proprietress that they would leave in a week's time, and sent a letter with the same information to the solicitors. At the prospect of losing them, upper 'Melrose' showed tepid surprise; nether 'Melrose' lamented, prophesying wrath to come, boarders in their stead who would be neither tidy, civil nor generous. For the guilty couple, grateful to the establishment which had sheltered their idyll, had no way save one of showing gratitude. On the night before their departure Ivy and Queenie were summoned. Each received garments from Edna, and from Mr Brodribb largesse. Queenie and Ivy, dismissed, descended to the kitchen almost in tears, declaring to the cook that never again would 'Melrose' see the like of the Brodribbs, and vowing eternal regard. Upstairs, Mr Brodribb, on his knees beside his suitcase, looked up to find Edna standing by him, a parcel in her hand.

'What's this?'

'It's just a little thing I got for you,' Edna replied, 'to look nice on your mantelpiece.'

He unwrapped the gift, revealing a brown plaster monkey six inches high, dressed in striped bathing drawers and playing the fiddle left-handed. The pedestal on which it stood was pierced with holes.

'For pipes,' Edna explained. 'Cute, isn't it? How ever they think of these things I don't know.'

Mr Brodribb, overcome, acknowledged her thought for him and the genius of the inventor.

'It hasn't been such a bad old time, has it?' he asked wistfully.

'I believe you,' Edna replied. 'As good as a trip to the sea. You tell your wife from me she doesn't know a gentleman when she sees one.'

They left next morning, some two hours before the arrival of a young man who made inquiries. This young man, having told his errand, and assured the proprietress, anxious for the good name of 'Melrose', that only servants' evidence would be required, sent for Ivy and Queenie, whom he interviewed in her presence. He questioned them, took notes, made clear their duty, and within twenty-five minutes departed. He was a brisk young man, who now and then sacrificed other things to promptness, and he did not on this occasion take time to observe the demeanour of the witnesses, which was, to say the least, reluctant. But three months later, when the case of Brodribb v. Brodribb and Another was called, he and his employers had cause to regret this economy of time.

For plaintiff's counsel, seeking to establish the facts of Mr Brodribb's desertion and adultery, met with a check when he called upon Ivy Blout to prove that Mr Brodribb had for weeks lived in an intimacy unsanctioned by law. Having ascertained her name, age and calling, he suavely inquired:

'You were housemaid at this address from October 5th last until December 10th?'

'Yes, sir,' Ivy replied.

'During that time was the defendant a paying guest in the house?'

'I don't know.'

Counsel halted, staring.

Ivy, contemplating Mr Brodribb, repeated without hesitation or haste:

'I don't know that gentleman.'

'You lived in the same house, in constant attendance on this man for weeks, and you say you don't recognise him?'

'No, sir.'

Counsel took another tack.

'You understand that you are on your oath?'

'Yes, sir.'

'Do you quite understand what is meant by perjury?'

'Telling lies.'

'Telling lies on oath, yes. A serious offence, punishable by imprisonment. Do you still insist, on your oath, that you don't know the defendant?'

'Yes, sir.'

'Why do you suppose you were brought here into court at all?'

Ivy, for the first time, permitted herself a smile.

'I really couldn't say.'

He fared no better at the hands of Queenie; words, questions and threats alike broke in spume against her unshaken gratitude. At last, on a note from his instructors, he sat down. There was a chill pause, into which the ironic comments of the judge fell softly as snowflakes. The case was dismissed.

On their way home, in the 'bus, Queenie said to Ivy:

'That was 'is wife, her in the blue hat. Think of it; sitting there with a face like that, and trying to get rid of that nice little feller.'

'Cheek!' Ivy agreed. 'She ought to be thankful for a husband like him. Whatever Mr Brodribb's done,' said Ivy, 'he's a real gentleman, and they don't get their dirty evidence out of Ivy Blout.'

In the restaurant off Fleet Street where they had met as arranged Mrs Brodribb lamented to Arthur:

'Now what? Do I have to take him back?'

'Not him,' said Arthur. 'We'll get more evidence, other witnesses. Prosecute these witnesses. Whatever can have happened I don't know, but it's not his fault, I'll bet. He's been having no end of a time on his own.'

'Yes; well, if that's how he's been going on,' said Mrs Brodribb with decision, 'he'd better come home. I'm not going to be made a laughing-stock again. Going over it all again, and the same thing happening, most likely. Like trying to get a number on the telephone.'

'That's your look-out,' Arthur answered, hurt, but jaunty. 'If you like to take him back slightly soiled, you're welcome.'

'Oh, Arthur,' said Mrs Brodribb, suddenly overcome, 'and we'd even chosen the bedroom suite.'

Lunching alone in a chop-house in the city, and waiting for his cheese, Mr Brodribb thought with affection of a brown plaster monkey in bathing drawers, playing the fiddle left-handed; then, suddenly recollecting, of a hot-water bottle, dressed in tiger skin, which, after only five months' use, had begun to leak at the seams, and which Prosser's, according to their guarantee, were obliged to replace without charge. He made a note on his cuff there and then.

HELEN SIMPSON

Helen de Guerry Simpson was born in 1897 in Sydney, Australia, where she was brought up on a sheep farm. At the age of seventeen, after her parents' divorce, Simpson was sent by her father to study in France, but with the outbreak of war she travelled to England to stay with her mother. In September 1915 she went up to Oxford to read French, but after two years she left the university and joined the Women's Royal Naval Service, working in the Admiralty as an interpreter and cipher clerk until the end of the war. A competent flautist and pianist, Simpson decided to return to Oxford, this time to read music as she now intended to become a composer. Although she composed a few songs and—in her own words—'fragments for piano', she soon realised that her future did not lie in music and finished without a degree.

While at Oxford Simpson became very interested in the theatre, and she founded the Oxford Women's Dramatic Society. This led to her first book, *Lightning Strikes* (1918), a collection of four playlets including one in which a vampire makes a compact with the devil. She also wrote longer pieces including the fantasy *Pan in Pimlico* (1923) and *A Man of His Time* (1923), a more substantial but episodic work about the renaissance polymath Benvenuto Cellini. As well as plays, Simpson wrote poetry, and a selection was collected in the well-received *Philosophies in Little* (1921), together with some verse translations from French, Italian and Spanish.

Simpson's first novel, *Acquittal*, was published in 1925, having been written in five weeks as the result of a bet after Simpson had described modern novels as being 'written in six weeks by half-wits or persons under the influence of drink'. The book concerns the aftermath of a murder trial, and it sold sufficiently well for Simpson to decide to take up writing full time, always using pen and paper rather than a typewriter which, for her, would shatter 'the peace and quietness necessary to the creative artist', and always working in a room without a distracting view. Her next book, *The Baseless Fabric* (1925), was a collection of strange and sometimes sinister short stories, while the awkwardly titled *Cups, Wands and Swords* (1927) took her back to Oxford.

Around this time, Simpson married Dennis Browne, a fellow Australian and a children's surgeon at the Hospital for Sick Children in London, now better known as Great Ormond Street. She also met the writer Clemence Dane. The two became firm friends, so much so that Simpson named her daughter after Dane, and they collaborated on three novel-length detective stories, two of which—*Enter Sir John* (1929) and *Re-Enter Sir John* (1932)—feature Sir John Saumarez, an actor-manager. They also co-wrote a stage play and the screenplay for *Mary* (1931), an atmospheric thriller directed by Alfred Hitchcock, whose film *Murder!* (1930) had been based on *Enter Sir John*. Simpson also wrote another crime novel, but without Dane. This was *Vantage Striker* (1931), described by one critic as 'the jolliest murder case we've had for a long, long while'. Her next novel, *Boomerang* (1932), drew on the history of her mother's family and won the prestigious James Tait Black Memorial Prize.

Among Helen Simpson's many hobbies was the study of witchcraft and demonology, which were the subject of the many rare books that formed the 'Library of the Devil' in her London home, where she also made her own wine. In 1932, she and her husband travelled to France and Hungary to research sightings of werewolves and vampires as well as to investigate the alleged involvement of satanists in the brutal murder of a typist in Strasbourg; Simpson would draw on this research for a radio talk, 'On Witchcraft Bound', which made headlines when it was first broadcast by the BBC in 1934 for its frank discussion of ritual murder. She also presented radio programmes for the BBC on homecraft and cookery, and she took part in several celebrity panel shows. Simpson also continued to write. Her other novels include *The Woman on the Beast* (1933), a long triptych fantasy set partly in 1999, as well as two historical novels: *Saraband for Dead Lovers* (1935), about the doomed romance between Sophie Dorothea of Celle and Count Philip Christoph von Königsmarck, and *Under Capricorn* (1937), about Australia's early settlers. As well as the libertarian organisation PEN, Simpson was a member of the Detection Club and she contributed to two of the Club's round-robin mysteries and to *The Anatomy of Murder* (1936), in which Dorothy L. Sayers and others explored notorious real-life crimes—in Simpson's case, the murder of Henry Kinder in 1865.

In 1937, Helen Simpson embarked on a lecture tour of Australia and made various broadcasts for charity. In 1939, she was chosen as a parliamentary candidate for the Liberal Party, but the General Election was postponed because of the Second World War. Her final novel, *Maid No More*, a strange story of slavery and Caribbean beliefs, was published in March 1940. At this time, Simpson and her husband were living in a flat above the hospital where her husband worked and, on 9 September 1940, the hospital was hit by a bomb during an air raid by the Luftwaffe; together with nursing staff and air raid wardens, they helped to extinguish the flames and move the sick children to safety. Just over a month later, the hospital where Simpson was recovering from a cancer operation was bombed and she died of shock. Her last literary assignment had been a series of articles giving a woman's perspective of the war in response to views expressed by an American columnist.

'Hotel Evidence' was first published in *Woman's Journal* in May 1934.

EXIT BEFORE MIDNIGHT

Q Patrick

It was a relief to escape from the office for a while, even though she did have to go back later. Here at the hairdresser's, Carol felt almost human again for the first time in days. Nothing was expected of her. She could just relax and leave all the worrying to Lucille.

The rush of work during the past week had been simply hectic. Carol had not realized how much temperament and typing were entailed in the winding-up of a company. She had thought that some bigger firm just came along, took one bite, a swallow and—gulp—it was all over! But the preparations for the merger of the little Leland and Rowley Process Company with a great monster like the Pan-American Dye Combine had been one headache after another. As harassed secretary to a harassed president, most of the headaches had devolved upon Carol Thorne.

But the company's headaches, at least, would soon be cured, she was thinking as Lucille's expert fingers ran soothingly over her fair hair. After all, a head couldn't ache when it had been cut off. And the shareholders of Leland and Rowley's were, at that very minute, meeting in Mr Rowley's office to go through the formalities necessary for profitable self-decapitation.

It was bad enough that, in their hurry to collect the proceeds they should have picked on New Year's Eve for their meeting.

It was bad enough that she would have to go back to a gloomy, deserted office building at a time when she should have been at home balancing the allure of backless black velvet against sleeves and simplicity for her very important dinner date with Peter Howe. But Carol didn't mind working overtime; nor was it a desire to pay herself back for the extra hours put in lately that had prompted her to slip out of the office before the shareholders arrived.

Her chief reason had been a reluctance to meet Miles Shenton. Also, although she had reconciled herself to the company's extermination, she just couldn't bear to be there when the blow actually fell. Leland & Rowley's had been her first job, and she was absurdly sentimental about it. And, unfortunately, her job would end at midnight with the firm's corporate existence. The prospect of unemployment was the best possible excuse for an expensive and quite unnecessary hair-do.

'Make it the best ever, Lucille,' she said. 'I want to face the New Year with all flags flying.'

'Is this the same date as the Christmas Eve manicure and shampoo, Miss Thorne?' Lucille stood back a moment to survey her very creditable handiwork; Carol's soft, naturally fair hair and the intriguing line of her forehead always put the artist in Lucille on her mettle. 'I mean the good looking young research chemist?'

Carol's dark amber eyes widened slightly and she was annoyed to see in the mirror that her cheeks had flushed. Who could have told Lucille about Miles? And did she—did anyone—know he had let her down on Christmas Eve? That was the worst of hairdressers. They sort of anaesthetised you, and you let things slip out before you realised. Or, if you didn't, the other girls in the office did it for you. Mabel Gregg, for example.

'You're out of date on my dates, Lucille,' she said crisply and glanced at her watch. It was after half-past five. 'Heavens, I've got to fly!'

She slipped from the chair, pulled the hood of her camel hair coat carefully over the soft curls and paid the bill.

'Good night, Miss Thorne. And Happy New Year.'

Happy New Year! Lucille's conventional phrase rang in Carol's ears as she joined the home-going thousands on Manhattan's snowy sidewalks. Would it be a happy new year as Mrs Peter Howe—the wife of Mr Rowley's nephew? Could it be a happy new year until she'd learned to forget Miles Shenton, to forget what a fool she'd been and what a fool he'd made of her?

And she'd never have had to see him again if Mr Rowley hadn't asked her to go back and tidy up the corpse of the poor old company after the shareholders had voted it to death. She knew that Miles and Peter would both be at the meeting—up there.

Instinctively, Carol had glanced up at the Moderna Building which loomed just ahead of her. The newest and emptiest of New York's skyscrapers was almost completely dark. Only the offices of Leland & Rowley's glimmered in bright miniature from the top of the tower.

She had entered and left the Moderna Building practically every day, but she had never noticed before how deserted and dreary it looked at night. Now, seen through the pall of snow and silhouetted against the starless December sky, the huge structure seemed somehow sinister. It was like a strangely-shaped dagger, she thought—a dagger stabbing the darkness. And the tower was a blade—a gigantic blade upon whose tip, lonely and isolated, were impaled the offices of a dying company.

She was indulging in these gloomy reflections as she hurried into the main building and shot upwards in the lift, past empty offices and dark passages. She was even more conscious of the sense of isolation when, at the thirtieth floor, she changed to the single lift which served the tower.

'You're going to wait for the shareholders, aren't you?' she reminded the lift man.

'All services except the lift in the main building close at six. New Year's Eve.' The man let her out at Leland & Rowley's whose offices took up the whole top floor. 'If the meeting's not through, it won't hurt them shareholders to walk down ten flights through the tower. They'll be feeling so rich anyway, they wouldn't mind doing the whole forty.'

Realizing that further argument would be fruitless, Carol made her way into the office.

Most of the lights had been turned out. In this sombre illumination, the familiar desks and chairs looked oddly different. Already they seemed to have ceased to be a part of Leland & Rowley's. They were just desks and chairs, waiting for the new occupants.

The strongest light came from the half-open door of Mr Rowley's office which was used as a conference room and where the meeting was still in progress. A pale shaft struck out, gleaming on Carol's desk and on her typewriter.

The typewriter looked different, too, thought Carol idly. Why? Of course. A sheet of paper had been slipped into it. She was certain she had left nothing unfinished when she sneaked out for her appointment with Lucille.

Curious, she moved towards her desk. From the president's office she could hear Mr Rowley's rather breathless voice telling the shareholders how the firm had been steadily losing ground since Mr Leland's death in June and what wonderful things the merger with Pan-American Dye was going to do to their shares.

She pulled the sheet from the machine, holding it up so that the oblique light shone on it.

MEMORANDUM to:

Mr Rowley, Mr Howe, Mr Shenton, Mr Whitfield, Miss Gregg, Mr Druten, Miss Leland.

But that was absurd. Memorandum to Marcia Leland! The daughter of the firm's founder and heiress of his twenty thousand shares! She didn't work for the company. And Mr Druten—he was the representative of Pan-American Dye. What was it all about? Who had typed it? When?

Carol read on. She felt the blood draining from her cheeks as she took in the amazing phrases of the actual message.

> This is to remind you that the merger with Pan-American Dye is not going through. Of course, you're planning to have it carried at the meeting by an overwhelming majority. *But it is not going through.*
>
> Remember—it doesn't become valid until midnight, anyhow. If enough of the largest shareholders died before then, fifty-one per cent of the stock would change hands, wouldn't it? The heirs of the deceased would undoubtedly demand a new vote. Think that over when you turn in your ballot slips.
>
> Because, if the merger is passed, I have decided to murder several of you—possibly all of you.
>
> You'll have plenty of time to consider whether you want to—EXIT BEFORE MIDNIGHT.

A threat of murder! This was a threat of murder!

Carol stared dazedly. Obviously it had been put in her typewriter for her to see while the meeting was still going on. Was it just a hoax? A practical joke fixed up by one of the girls? She didn't think so. There was something brutally purposeful about those terse sentences—an alarming ring of veracity to the threat.

'So you're staying to be in at the death, Miss Thorne?'

Carol spun round. Little Mr Whitfield, the company's lawyer, had slipped out of the president's office. His thin birdlike fingers were picking up the briefcase which he had left on her desk.

A lawyer! Just the person.

'Mr Whitfield . . . !'

Carol threw out a hand to detain him. But the little man had scurried back into the lighted room. She was alone again in the bleak half darkness with that crazy memorandum.

In at the death. How ironical Mr Whitfield's phrase had been! Carol made up her mind swiftly. She could not risk the responsibility of keeping this to herself. She would have to go in there, interrupt the shareholders meeting at once.

Mr Rowley had finished his speech. When Carol entered his office, the large room was portentously silent. Grouped round in chairs, the score or so of shareholders were bending over ballot slips, signing their names.

So it was too late to do anything about it anyway. The vote was actually being taken at this moment.

Carol hesitated by the door. She noticed Mr Rowley's gaze on her, inquiring, annoyed. Some of the other shareholders had glanced up, too. To whom should she take this mad memorandum? Not to her boss, Mr Rowley; the shock might bring on one of his heart attacks.

Peter, of course.

The young vice-president was sitting at the far end of the room next to Mr Druten from the Pan-American Dye Combine. There was something reassuring about Peter Howe's athletically square shoulders and forthright face. He typified all that was normal, regular. Crazy murder threats and sane, sensible Peter just didn't go together.

Carol hurried to his side and slipped the note into his hand. 'I found it in my typewriter. Just now.'

His smile faded as he read. His wide grey eyes became grave. 'Better stay in here, Carol.'

As he passed the memorandum to Mr Druten, Carol dropped into an empty chair at his side. Miss Gregg, the firm's plump, bespectacled treasurer, was bustling officiously round, collecting up the ballot slips. The merger was going to be carried, of course.

Carol knew it had always been a foregone conclusion. But after the meeting—what was going to happen then?

While the shareholders waited expectantly for the result of the vote, the names on the memorandum kept repeating themselves in Carol's mind. Miss Gregg was one of them, little Mr Whitfield, Mr Rowley and Peter. And Mr Druten from Pan-American—the stocky, dynamic man who sat alert and bushy-browed at Peter's side.

Then there was Miles. Although she deliberately did not look at him, Carol was acutely conscious of Miles Shenton, the erratic but brilliant young protégé of Nathaniel Leland who had inherited the old man's unfinished work and his position as head research chemist for the firm. He was sitting over by the curtainless window next to Marcia Leland.

There was a maddening half smile on his dark face with its excitingly high cheek bones and its narrowed insolent eyes. He had smiled like that when she had found him in the office late on Christmas Eve after he had broken their date earlier in the evening. He had smiled like that when he had made love to her and had then casually informed her that he had designs on the wealthy Marcia Leland as a 'permanent meal ticket'. He would smile like that, she knew, when he heard about this threat of murder. Miles Shenton never took anything seriously. Nothing, Carol added viciously, except his own bread and butter.

And his future bread and butter, Marcia Leland, was sitting impassively at his side. Slim, young, exquisitely dressed, like some fragile sea nymph, thought Carol, with her dark hair cut to her shoulders and those green, strangely observant eyes. No wonder Miles was trying to land her. With twenty thousand shares and that figure—and brains, too—she would make a satisfactory 'meal ticket' even for the most fastidious of breadliners.

Peter and Mr Druten were bent together over the note. She could hear them whispering earnestly. Were they going to say anything now? Or were they going to wait until the result of the vote had been announced?

Miss Gregg's brisk fingers had counted through the ballot slips. Her spectacles flashing, she stooped and said something to Mr Rowley. Rather shakily, the president rose, his thin fingers absently twisting the long steel paper knife which always lay on his desk.

Once this transaction with Pan-American Dye had gone through, Peter's unmarried uncle was retiring after a thirty year association with Leland and Rowley's. Carol knew he was taking it rather hard. This final farewell to the company must be an ordeal for her almost-ex-boss.

'Ladies and gentlemen—' there was quiet dignity in his tone—'the merger has been carried. Ninety per cent of your votes are in favour of it. The papers which Mr Druten and I will sign are dated January the first. The merger will therefore go into effect legally at midnight.'

Amidst a flutter of approval from the shareholders, Mr Druten crossed to Mr Rowley's side. The two men were signing their names. Carol glanced anxiously at Peter who still held the fantastic memorandum clasped in his hand.

'Peter,' she whispered, 'what are you going to do?'

'Ask the people concerned to stay behind afterwards. Don't want to make a fuss in front of everyone.'

'You—you don't think it's serious?'

She could tell from the expression in his eyes that he was worried, but he smiled lightly.

'Probably just a crank. You and I are going to exit before midnight anyhow. We're going to Longval's to knock the old year for a loop.'

Longval's with Peter on New Year's Eve—it sounded very gay and—unmurderous.

Mr Rowley's short tribute to the genius of the late Nathaniel Leland had drawn to a conclusion. He bent over his desk and speared with his paper knife the final sheet of the old year's calendar which lay there next to an unnecessary one for the new year. He held it out with a little dramatic flourish.

'December the thirty-first, ladies and gentlemen. The end of an old year, the end of a fine company and the end of my own business activities. As shareholders of the Pan-American Dye Combine, we can all wish ourselves a happy and a prosperous New Year.'

The meeting had started to adjourn as Peter rose but there was something about his tall, virile body and the set determined angle of his jaw that compelled immediate attention. Gloves remained half drawn on; coat sleeves hung poised in mid air.

'Miss Thorne,' he said quietly, 'has brought me a rather unusual communication. Perhaps the following people would care to stay behind for a few moments to consider it.'

As he read out the list of names, a ripple of polite curiosity stirred the gathering. Then those shareholders who had not been mentioned moved, chattering, to the door and out into the main office. Peter slipped away to speak to his uncle. Carol was left alone.

'So the beautiful secretary has done something dangerous to her hair.'

She glanced up sharply. Miles Shenton had lounged to her side, his faun-like eyes regarding her ironically through cigarette smoke. 'You shouldn't, you know. It's not fair to the male members of the staff.'

'The male members of the staff have just been voted out of existence.'

'But they're still male.' He moved a little closer. Carol hated herself for being so conscious of his nearness. 'I was wondering whether an ex-secretary felt like drowning her sorrows tonight with an unemployed chemist. How about a—?'

'Another broken date?' cut in Carol with dangerous sweetness.

'Blondes and elephants never forget.' He shrugged ruefully. 'Perhaps I might try explaining Christmas Eve.'

'Why bother? I quite understand how important your—er—business engagement with Miss Leland was.'

'That sounds very ominous. No armistice then? No New Year's Eve debauch?'

'Strange as it seems,' said Carol tersely, 'no.'

As she moved away the lift doors clanged shut behind the batch of departing shareholders. The sound echoed drearily through the room.

She glanced at her watch. Exactly six o'clock. So the tower lift had made its last trip for the night.

She found herself thinking of Leland and Rowley's offices as she had seen them from the street, perched high and lonely on the top of the Moderna Tower. Now that the lift had stopped working, there was nothing but the stairs in the fire tower to connect them with the active bustling life forty floors below.

Exit before midnight. She shivered.

Mr. Rowley's large office seemed austere and empty now that the majority of the shareholders had left. The people whose names had been typed on the memorandum were grouped curiously around the desk. As Carol joined them, Peter started to read out the message.

'*This is to remind you . . .*'

Carol watched the faces round her. Marcia Leland listened with absorbed impersonal interest; Miss Gregg's tight-lipped mouth dropped open with surprise; little Mr Whitfield, looking like an agitated but very legal robin, shot startled glances at Mr Rowley.

For a moment there was unbroken silence. Peter laid the memorandum down on the desk.

'I thought you all ought to hear it, he said. 'Presumably this was fixed up to try and frighten us into voting against the merger.'

His mouth moved wryly. 'Personally, I don't think these formidable threats will be put into action. But if anyone feels at all nervous—'

'Certainly I'm nervous,' snapped Miss Gregg, the woolly tassel on the front of her blouse quivering indignantly. 'We must consult the police at once. A threat of murder! Disgraceful!'

'But ingenious.' Miles had strolled over to join them. 'Killing off the major shareholders to get a new vote on the merger. If he wants fifty thousand shares to change hands before midnight, he'll have to be pretty wholesale.'

'We cannot afford to treat this lightly, Mr Shenton,' chirruped Mr Whitfield, the company's lawyer, his pince-nez trembling on the thin bridge of his nose. 'Even if we do not inform the police, we should each of us take adequate precautions until midnight.'

'I agree.' Mr Rowley's thin, ascetic face was even more drawn than usual, his voice was weary. 'We have no reason to suppose this is a hoax. Mergers always cause bad feeling. This was probably written by some employee who's losing his work. He may conceivably be desperate enough to attempt something—er—rash.' He turned to the bushy-browed representative of Pan-American. 'This is most unfortunate, Druten. I feel we owe you an apology.'

Marcia Leland alone seemed completely unaffected by the general consternation. Her soft green eyes turned to Carol.

'But where did you find this extraordinary note. Miss Thorne?'

'In my typewriter. I'd just slipped out about four-thirty. It was there when I came back.'

'So any of the employees or the shareholders could have put it there?'

Carol nodded. 'Yes, anyone at all.'

While she was speaking, Mr Whitfield had been moving the zipper of his briefcase jerkily to and fro. Now he gave a sudden little exclamation.

'Wait a minute!' he cried. 'I think I can explain.'

They all stared at him. Carol was astonished at the change in the lawyer's appearance. Behind the pince-nez his pale eyes were bright with a strange expression of alarm. His cheeks were ashen white.

'This threat *is* serious—terribly serious. Some of us are in real danger. We—' his voice was high, breathless. 'As Mr Rowley's lawyer, I have no right to make a statement. But I can see no alternative. This is a question of life or . . .'

But he never finished his sentence—for, suddenly, without the slightest warning, the lights in the president's office went out, plunging the room into swift, blinding darkness.

With the sudden descent of darkness, Carol felt a stab of alarm. What had Mr Whitfield been going to say? Why . . .? Around her the others were moving confusedly. There were voices calling out; arms brushing against her. But she could think only of this darkness. The lights, she knew, were controlled from the floor itself. They could not have turned them off from downstairs. It must have happened here. Could it—could it have been deliberate?

Instinctively she groped her way to the switch. When she reached it, someone else was already there. She heard a click and her fingers touched the rough material of a coat.

'The switch doesn't work.' It was Miles's casual voice, close to her ear. 'Fuse must have gone.'

'Most annoying.' Mr Rowley's voice rose above the clamour, weakly querulous. 'Where is Miss Thorne? Perhaps she—'

'Miss Thorne's here.' So Miles had sensed it was her next to him there in the darkness. 'I'm afraid even the efficient Miss Thorne can't do much. If the fuse's gone, all this side of the floor will be in darkness. And the main office, too.'

'Better move over to my office.' Peter's suggestion was calm and steady. 'It's on the other circuit.'

There was a general movement towards the door. Carol felt

Miles's warm fingers slipping down her arm and closing around her hand. He was drawing her forward.

'Christmas Eve with you in a dark office; now New Year's Eve,' he whispered. 'I seem to be lucky with Eves.'

Carol would have been glad to have anyone else near her; there was something unnerving about Miles. This enforced intimacy seemed part of the crazy evening—part of its intangible menace. She tried to pull her arm away, but he wouldn't release his hold, he was pressing it close against him, so close that it hurt.

At the rear of the uncertain little procession, they passed out into the main office which separated them from the group of private offices on the east side of the building. Miles had been right. All the lights here had gone, too. It was profoundly dark.

Peter hurried ahead. In a few moments a beam of light, filtering towards them over the tops of the desks, showed that he had snapped down the switch in his office.

Thank heaven there was nothing wrong with the fuses on that circuit!

In a minute they were all hovering anxiously round the desk in Peter's smaller office, blinking at the unaccustomed brightness.

'Well, Mr Whitfield—' Peter's voice was abrupt, jerky— 'you had something very important to tell us and . . . '

He broke off. Carol looked round quickly and saw what was wrong.

The lawyer was not in the room.

There was a murmur of startled comment. Mr Rowley glanced at the open door and then at Carol.

'Perhaps you would ask Mr Whitfield to come here, Mss Thorne,' he said curtly. 'I have no idea what he was going to say, but it's getting late and . . .'

She moved to the door, the president's voice trailing impatiently after her as she hurried out again into the main office—away from the beam of light.

It was somehow uncanny being in the darkness alone. As quickly as possible, she retraced her steps to Mr Rowley's office and paused at the door.

'Mr Whitfield.'

There was no sound. She crossed the threshold. Was this dark cavernous room really the old familiar office where she had scribbled so many miles of shorthand notes?'

'Mr Whitfield!' she called again.

She was a little frightened now. There was no use trying to kid herself. Mr Whitfield must be here. He couldn't have slipped away. *Some of us are in very real danger*. She tried to keep back the crazy thoughts that were invading her brain. They were absurd, ludicrous. And yet, there it was, that phrase from the memorandum, writing itself across the darkness in front of her.

'*. . . exit before midnight . . .*'

'Mr Whitfield!'

Step by step, she moved forward. She stumbled against a chair—another. And then her foot touched something lying on the carpet. Instantly she froze. The darkness around her seemed to stir.

She forced herself to bend, to touch that thing with her finger. It was hard, shiny—the leather of a shoe. Her hand moved, groping through the darkness. It touched something else, something soft—limp.

Carol knew what it was—knew with absolute certainty. Her fingers had touched a human hand.

At first she just stood there, numbed by the shock. She could only think: I have touched a dead man.

And then she heard her own voice. She hardly recognized it, it sounded so small and lost. She was calling:

'Quick—Mr Rowley. Come quick.'

She could hear footsteps, faint and then nearer—hurrying. In a few seconds there were voices, rustlings, movements all round her in the darkness. A hand gripped her arm, and Peter's voice, low, urgent, was asking:

'Carol, what is it? What's the matter?'

She felt overwhelmingly grateful for Peter. He was so real, so alive after—after that dead thing. Thank God, she wasn't going to faint.

'It's—it's someone,' she faltered. 'Lying there in front of me. I felt his hand. I—I think he's . . .'

The others were all pressing round now, stifling her by their nearness. Someone struck a match. It was Miles. Carol could see his dark, high-cheekboned face—the only illuminated thing in that room. Then another match was struck and another. The little troop of flames lighted up the carpet in front of her.

Mechanically her gaze moved downward. She could see them now—the shoe and the hand. Somehow they weren't so ghastly now she could see them. But it was all ghastly enough.

Mr Whitfield was lying there, slumped beneath the desk—looking pathetically small and unobtrusive, with his fingers still clutched around his briefcase. The matchlight gleamed on his pince-nez, casting strange little rays across his face. The matchlight caught something else, too. Still adorned by the crumpled sheet from the calendar, the shining steel handle of Mr Rowley's paper knife protruded from the lawyer's waistcoat, just above the heart.

Matches flashed and lingered like slow-motion fireflies. Carol caught stray images of people round her—Mr Rowley's haggard face, blank and horrified; Mr Druten's black hair and his eyes, wide and bright beneath the thick brows.

Peter had dropped to his knees and was bending over the body. Carol waited for him to speak, but she knew before he said it what it would be.

'Dead.'

'Murdered! And—and he was one of the largest shareholders.'

Miss Gregg's tone was oddly strangled. 'So he actually means what he said—the man who wrote the letter.'

A fresh sputter of matches. And then Peter's voice again, suddenly different.

'Look!'

Rapidly his fingers were smoothing out the sheet from the calendar which, still impaled on the knife, was half thrust into the wound. With the others, Carol peered down in the uncertain matchlight. She saw at once what he meant.

The date which the president had speared during the meeting had been December 31. Now, glaring up at them in bold black print was:

JANUARY
1

At the furthermost edge of the arc of light, Carol could just see the loose-leaf calendar for the new year on the desk. It showed January 2.

'You see—' Peter's voice rose again, steady but very grim—'he put it there, the murderer. Number One. He meant us to know that Mr Whitfield was the first—that there will be others . . .'

Gradually Carol's mind began to take in the full implications of this appalling thing. The person who had typed out that note must somehow have fused the lights on this circuit and crept into the room in the consequent confusion. He was carrying out his incredible threat. If enough of the large shareholders were murdered before midnight when the merger became valid, there would have to be a second vote. Mr Whitfield had carried ten thousand of the hundred thousand shares outstanding. He had been the first to go.

But who could be doing this? Who could have this insane hatred of the merger? Why the macabre complication of the calendar slip, speared on the knife?

The last match had flickered out now and no one seemed to

think to light another. There was a long, helpless silence. Then Carol heard the familiar clatter of the telephone receiver and Mr Rowley's distracted voice at the desk, shouting:

'Hallo, hallo, give me the police station at once. Hallo—'

'You won't get any reply, Mr Rowley,' Carol said. 'The operator left the switchboard at five.'

'Operator?' echoed the president. 'Oh, yes, of course. Well—'

'I'll try and work the switchboard,' offered Carol.

'Yes, yes. Thanks, Miss Thorne.'

'You're not going alone, Carol,' cut in Peter's voice. 'I'm coming with you. None of us must touch anything,' he ordered. 'We've got to leave everything exactly as we found it for the police. There may be fingerprints.'

All this seemed part of the nightmare—to hear voices and to see nothing. Somehow Carol found Peter and they were groping their way out into the main office.

His arm was round her, strong, protective.

'Oh, Peter, isn't it ghastly? What—what are we going to do?'

'Call the police,' he said grimly. 'And get away from this darn place as quickly as possible.'

The switchboard lay in a corner of the main office, close to the lift shaft. They found their way to it with nothing to guide them but the faint light emanating from Peter's distant office.

Carol sat down at the board, struggling to remember what little she knew about it. She put on the earphones and started to push in plug after plug.

'Hallo—hallo . . .'

One plug after another. She worked with growing anxiety. But it was no use. The instrument seemed absolutely dead.

The others had left Mr Rowley's office now. They were all crowding round her in the darkness as though none of them could bear to have the group divided.

'I'm sorry, Mr Rowley,' she said at length. 'I'm afraid I can't work it.'

There was a spurt of light. Carol saw Miles Shenton with a cigarette lighter cupped in his hand. He was bending forward, peering behind the switchboard. He gave a low whistle.

'I'm not surprised Miss Thorne can't work it. The wires are cut—all of them.'

'Cut!' echoed Miss Gregg weakly. 'You mean deliberately?'

'Deliberately and most competently. I doubt if even a regular electrician could fix them before midnight.'

Once again a strained silence descended on the darkness. Finally, Mr Rowley's voice rose, hoarse, uncertain.

'Then we must use the lift. Go down to the ground floor, Peter, and tell the night watchman—'

'I've been ringing the buzzer, sir. Nothing happens.'

'It's no use anyway,' said Carol faintly. 'The tower lift stopped running at six. The man wouldn't stay. There's no one to work it.'

'But—but what can we do?'

'The fire stairs,' said Carol. 'We'll have to walk down to the main building and take the regular lift there.'

Her words galvanized the others into action. They all started to hurry back through the main office, stumbling over chairs and desks. Carol felt herself pushed along with the rest of them.

They reached the door to the stairs. Someone struck a match. Miss Gregg gripped the handle and pushed. Nothing happened. She pushed again and then gave a little sob.

'It's locked.'

'But it can't be,' said Marcia Leland's cool voice. 'A fire escape door can't be locked. It's against the law.'

More matches. Peter tried. Then Miles. They all pushed together feverishly. But it did not give. Peter dropped to his knees, peering under the door in the flickering matchlight. He looked up, his face strained, almost gaunt.

'It must be wedged,' he said 'Wedged from outside. We'll never open it.'

For the first time Carol felt real panic invading her. This was all part of the plan then—telephone cut, door jammed. They were to be shut up there in the darkness until the murderer had achieved his mad purpose.

'But the fire alarm.' It was an unfamiliar voice—Mr Druten's. 'There must be a fire alarm.'

Carol answered, 'It's outside the door—on the fire tower. We can't get to it.'

The others were standing absolutely still now in the darkness. She could sense they were like herself—stunned by the ruthless deliberation, the cold-blooded planning that underlay it all.

'Cut off!' It was Mr Rowley's voice, shrilling to a crescendo. 'It can't be true.'

But Carol knew that it was. Locked in, forty floors up with a dead body, in an office that was less than half-lighted. Cut off in the very heart of New York! They were as isolated as if they had been on a desert island.

She stood there, her arms limp at her sides. Once again she had conjured up the image of the Moderna Tower as she had seen it from the street.

A gigantic dagger thrusting up into the cold December sky. And the offices of the Leland & Rowley Process Company impaled, helpless and lonely, on its tip.

No one spoke or stirred in that dark pall of silence. It was as if they were afraid that the slightest move might plunge them into some unknown danger.

It was Peter who finally said, 'There's no use standing around here. Better get back to my office.'

The others followed through the shadowy obscurity of the main room. Their footsteps echoed, dull and queerly muffled, like sounds half heard in a dream.

To Carol it was an immense relief to get back into the brightly lighted room. The mail-basket on the desk, the sales charts on the wall, the shiny swivel chair—they were so essentially a part of normal business routine, so essentially part of Peter.

And it was to Peter, instinctively, that the others looked for the next move. Mr Rowley had sunk into a chair, his eyes fixed unseeingly on the floor. He, obviously, had been crushed by the successive shocks of the past half-hour.

Peter stood by the high, curtainless window, his face very grave, his chin thrust forward grimly.

'Well,' he said, 'we're up against it all right. But we've got to keep our heads.'

'But there must be some way out,' exclaimed Mr Druten.

The representative of Pan-American Dye had sat down behind the desk—a short, stocky figure with his thick black hair and shrewd eyes. This must seem craziest of all to him, thought Carol. What a reception he was getting from Leland and Rowley's!

His gaze was moving incredulously around the room.

'A modern office—cut off. lt's impossible. Surely we could do something—drop a message out of the window.'

'On to the roof of the main building ten floors below,' said Miles ironically. 'It stretches all round. You couldn't get anything down to the street from here.'

'Then we must shout for help,' exclaimed Miss Gregg brokenly.

'Forty floors up? New Year's Eve? Try and do it, Miss Gregg.' Miles dropped on the couch next to Marcia Leland. 'No, my friends, we're the proverbial rodents in a proverbially improbable trap.'

Mr Rowley looked up with a harsh, bitter laugh. 'So we've just got to wait here and let ourselves be killed off one by one before midnight—like poor Whitfield!'

'But there must be a night watchman!' persisted Mr Druten.

'There is,' said Peter. 'He's due to get up here about midnight.'

'If he's sober,' added Miles. 'He has a marked tendency towards celebrating holidays. I very much doubt whether he'll attain to the top floor for a long time.'

'So we *will* be here.' Miss Gregg's voice rose to a stifled little sob. 'We will be here until midnight.'

In the sudden shock of finding themselves shut in, they had not thought of that—had not thought how long it would be before they could hope for release. Carol's heart sank. Shut in all night—without food, without any sense of safety. What couldn't happen? What . . .?

And then she remembered something—something which happily brought with it an overpowering sense of relief.

'The cleaning service!' she exclaimed. 'It works at night. They'll be here soon.'

'Good for Miss Thorne.' Miles grinned. 'Saved by the scrub-women. I never thought of them.'

'When do they get here. Carol?' Peter was looking at her, the anxious line of his mouth relaxing.

'I don't know. But I think somewhere about nine.'

Marcia Leland glanced at her watch. 'It's nearly seven now. Only two more hours.'

Only two more hours! Somehow those words made all the difference between sanity and insanity.

'Well, it's obvious what we've got to do.' Peter's voice was steady, authoritative. 'Stay together in this lighted room and not leave it under any circumstances. No—er—danger can come to us here.'

'But this—this maniac who killed poor Mr Whitfield!' The treasurer was twisting her plump fingers together convulsively. 'He said in that note he's going to try to kill us all to stop the merger. How do we know he's not still here in the office? Somewhere—somewhere out there in the darkness?'

'Exactly, Miss Gregg.' Peter's glance moved to Miles. 'Shenton and I had better make sure of that at once. We'll turn on all the lights that work on this side of the office and search the place thoroughly.'

'Quite a tricky proposition—searching for a murderer in the dark,' murmured Miles. 'Does anyone have anything practical? I'm sure you were a Boy Scout, Howe. Don't you carry a revolver or a flashlight or something equally prepared? '

Marcia Leland had been sitting apart as if absorbed in her own thoughts. Now she pushed the dark hair back from her shoulders and said surprisingly:

'You could use paper spills. I'll make some for you.'

She rose, moving to the desk. Swiftly she twisted pieces of paper into tapers. She gave some to Peter, some to Miles.

'That ought to be better than nothing.'

'The superwoman!' Miles's smile was coolly admiring as he glanced at her grave face. 'I always had a feeling you'd be an asset in time of stress, Marcia.'

He and Peter set matches to the spills. Cupping them in their hands, they slipped out of the room—out into the darkness of the main office.

With their departure, the rest of the group started to talk feverishly, to plan, to speculate. Who could be doing this? Was it an employee of the firm or some unknown maniac? How could he have killed Mr Whitfield and escaped?

Carol was only half conscious of the agitated voices round her. She had moved to the door and was peering out, following with her eyes the little flickering lights that marked the two men's progress away through the office. She heard them exchange an occasional remark, heard their footsteps growing fainter. Then there was no sound—no light.

She was horribly afraid for them. What if they did find this—this person lurking somewhere in the darkness? He had already murdered one man. He would be desperate, probably armed. What could they do against him without weapons—anything?

She thought of poor little Mr Whitfield, lying there in Mr

Rowley's room, pathetic, untended, with the paper knife thrust in his heart. Why—why wasn't there just as much danger for Peter and Miles?

Peter and Miles! How absurdly trivial her own problems seemed now. How absurd that just an hour ago her date with Peter had seemed so terribly important. She had been worrying whether or not she could bring herself to tell him the truth; that she liked him more than anyone she knew; that she respected him; that there was nothing to stop her growing to love him, if only it hadn't all happened so suddenly, if only she could shake off those maddening memories of Miles.

And how absurd that even now she felt that tingling excitement when she thought of Miles; that burning anger when she remembered Christmas Eve, the broken date, his kisses and his cynical remarks about Marcia as a 'meal ticket'. The romantic dilemma of an ex-secretary! What did it matter now?

'. . . I knew we should have called in the police the minute Miss Thorne brought us that terrible note.' Miss Gregg's emphatic voice broke into her thoughts. 'None of this would have happened if we had called the police.'

'But we never had a chance.' Marcia Leland's answering tone was cool, imperturbable. 'Don't you see, Miss Gregg? Everything was worked out beforehand. Probably the telephone was already cut and the door jammed before the note was put in Miss Thorne's typewriter. This person knew exactly what he wanted and saw to it that he got it.'

Carol glanced curiously from one woman to the other. It was strange, she thought, how shock and danger brought out characteristics one would never have guessed. Miss Gregg had been the firm's treasurer ever since anyone could remember. For years she had bullied the girls, harassed the executives and kept her ledgers with machine-like accuracy. Mabel Gregg, Carol would have thought, could have stood up against anything.

But now the treasurer was obviously on the verge of a collapse.

She looked old and helpless and her normally brisk fingers were ineffectually twisting and untwisting the wool tassel on her breast.

And it was Marcia Leland who had risen to the occasion. Marcia Leland, the young, fragile girl just out of college, the woman whom the merger was to make a millionairess and for whom life must always have been padded by the luxurious upholstery of wealth. Carol had been jealous of Marcia, antagonistic because of Miles. She admitted that to herself. But she could not help admiring her now. Marcia was so very much old Nathaniel's daughter.

But then, of course, she had already faced death that year. Carol remembered how, at the time of his final attack six months before, Nathaniel Leland had been alone with his daughter in Florida, working in a makeshift laboratory against doctor's orders. The old man had guessed he was marked by death and had been desperately eager to complete his new chemical processes which were going to revolutionize the industry and restore the prosperity of Leland & Rowley's. But death had cheated him. He had died, leaving behind him only a few worthless note-books. And this slight girl had taken care of him herself and nursed him to the very end. Peter and Mr Rowley who had flown down to Florida when the news of Leland's death came through, had returned full of admiration for Marcia's courage and control.

Footsteps outside in the main office deflected Carol's attention. She turned and saw the vague light of tapers, quivering in the darkness. Miles and Peter were coming back.

Within a few seconds, the two men were crossing the threshold. Instantly the tension shifted its centre.

'Well?' asked Miss Gregg sharply.

Peter moved to Carol's side, giving her a brief, fleeting smile.

'We couldn't find a spare fuse or a flashlight, but we turned on all the lights on this circuit. And we've searched everywhere. Absolutely everywhere. There's no one there.'

'But that's impossible!' exclaimed Mr Druten. 'How could this man have got out?'

'Simple.' Miles dropped down again on the couch next to Marcia, his eyes resting for one moment on Carol. 'He must have got the wedges all ready and kept them outside on the fire tower. After the murder, he just had to slip out of the door and jam it behind him.'

'But I can't believe that.' Marcia Leland leaned forward. 'We know from the note that this person is trying to kill off the major shareholders before midnight. If—if he really means that, he'd never leave us all locked up here and go away.'

'He would,' explained Miles slowly, 'if he intended to come back.'

'Come back!' echoed Miss Gregg.

'Why, of course. He's bound to enter before midnight again.' Miles's smile was slightly mocking. 'Several times, in fact. After all, Mr Whitfield only owned ten thousand shares. Our friend has to kill off at least thirty-one per cent more if he wants a new vote on the merger. The evening has just begun.'

Carol drew in her breath sharply. Of course, Miles had to be flippant about it, if what he said was true. If the threat were really to be carried out, Mr Whitfield's death was a mere prologue.

'Then if the murderer's not here at the moment,' she said quickly, 'we've got to think out some way of stopping him getting back.'

'The efficient secretary speaks!' Miles gave her a mocking bow. 'In spite of Howe's scornful comments, I have already contrived a burglar alarm. An ingenious device of my own invention. Three chairs piled against the door with a glass water carafe perched on top. If anyone opens that door—we'll hear soon enough. A resounding crash of glass means—enter the murderer.'

'Provided your theory's correct, Shenton.'

Carol started at the sound of Peter's voice. She glanced at him quickly. The lines round his mouth had deepened, there was a strained, worried look in his grey eyes.

'Does anyone really believe Shenton's theory?' he asked.

'You mean that the murderer will come back?' asked Marcia.

'No.' Peter moistened his lips, a little nervous trick Carol knew so well. 'I mean, do you believe the murderer ever left the office?'

'But you searched,' cried Miss Gregg. 'You looked everywhere. You didn't find anyone.'

'We didn't. But does what Shenton says make sense? Could anybody have fused the lights in some other room and then crept into uncle's office and committed the murder? How would he have known where the paper knife was—or the calendar? And how could he tell in the darkness that it was Mr Whitfield he was attacking?'

For the first time Mr Rowley seemed to hear what was going on. He started, staring blankly at his nephew.

'Peter, what are you driving at?'

'I hate to say this, uncle. But we've got to face it. It's very unlikely that any outsider murdered Mr Whitfield.'

Miss Gregg gasped.

'Outsider?' queried Mr Druten harshly.

Peter looked down at his strong, capable hands. 'If I'd been clever enough to have staged all this, I would certainly have been clever enough to have added my own name on that memorandum. It would have been easy to jam the door, go down the fire stairs and come up again in the lift.'

Carol leaned impulsively forward. 'Oh, Peter, you can't think—'

'Yes.' He shrugged almost apologetically. 'I'm afraid it's far more likely that the murderer of Mr Whitfield is one of us—*one of the seven people in this room*.'

'One of us!'

The words echoed dully from Mr Rowley. Then there was utter silence.

Carol could hear the quick beat of her own heart. Of course, what Peter said made perfect sense—only too perfect. For the murderer to shut himself in with them here, to pretend he was as much a victim as they! It would be the logical thing to do, and it fitted in so well with the other incredibly efficient actions of this incredible person.

She glanced dazedly round the room. Those pale, familiar faces! Could one of them really be the face of a murderer? Against her will, suspicions began to stir in her mind. Mabel Gregg—she was losing her job through the merger—the job she had held for almost thirty years. Neither she nor Miles was being taken on by the Pan-American Dye Combine. And Mr Rowley—this transaction was forcing him into a retirement which was only half voluntary. It was just possible that one of them was more desperate than they had guessed.

And the others? Peter was getting a big job with Pan-American. The merger meant everything to him. So it did to Marcia Leland whose great holding of shares would be trebled in value at midnight. And Mr Druten—the representative of the firm that was taking over. Surely none of those three could have a motive for fearing this merger by which they seemed to profit?

Carol shrugged wearily. Here she was potentially accusing all the others of murder. And some of them were probably doing exactly the same about her. After all, she was being thrown out of work, too, and she didn't even benefit by the exchange of shares. Carol Thorne was the most likely suspect of all!

'There's something else,' Peter was saying quietly, 'that makes me pretty certain the murderer *is* one of us. We've been forgetting that Mr Whitfield was trying to tell us something when—'

'You mean he had it all worked out?' cut in Miles swiftly. 'He suddenly realized it was one of us and was going to let on?'

Peter nodded. 'That would explain why the murderer fused

the lights at that particular moment—to stop him. Only one of us in the room could have done that.'

There was a long, uneasy pause. Carol could tell that the others were more than half convinced of the fantastic truth that a murderer was in their midst.

Mr Druten shot a swift glance at the president. 'There's something none of us has brought up, Rowley. Just before the lights went out, Mr Whitfield mentioned your name. He acted as if you knew what he was going to say.'

'Yes,' added Miles curiously. 'He said something about having no right to make a statement because he was your lawyer. What did he mean?'

They had all focused their attention on the president. He stirred uneasily in his chair, a faint flush diffusing his cheeks.

'I haven't the slightest idea,' he said weakly. 'Not the slightest idea.'

Suddenly Carol remembered how Mr Whitfield had been in conference with Mr Rowley all that afternoon. During the past few days, too, the lawyer had been coming in regularly. And while he was there the door of the office had invariably been shut—a sure sign that they were discussing something too confidential even for the ears of a private secretary.

Impulsively she turned to her employer.

'It wasn't anything to do with those conferences you've been having with Mr Whitfield lately?'

Mr Rowley started. There was an almost angry gleam in his eyes.

'Really, Miss Thorne, my private business with poor Whitfield has nothing whatsoever to do with this. We were discussing a purely personal matter—purely personal.'

Another awkward moment of silence followed. Carol could see the veins on Mr Rowley's temples, standing out blue and taut against the pallor of the skin.

It was Marcia Leland who spoke first.

'I've just remembered something.' Her voice was brisk. 'I never would have thought of it if Mr Howe hadn't brought up the matter of the fused lights.'

'The lights?'

'I was listening to Mr Whitfield at the time. I think we all were. That's why I only heard it more or less subconsciously.' There was a touch of pink in the white coral of her cheeks. 'But just when the lights went out, I heard a very faint spluttering sound.'

Peter took a quick step forward. 'The fuse going?'

'Yes. Don't you see? That means it was blown from the room where we all were. That would prove it was done by one of us.'

Miss Gregg stared at her over her spectacles. 'Provided you really did hear the sound.'

'Oh, she heard it all right,' put in Miles, smiling sideways at Marcia. 'Trust Miss Leland on the technical details. Electricity is her own backyard. Honours graduate in physics, Vassar. Nothing can be more efficient.'

'And so,' Marcia was continuing, 'if we can find out which outlet was fused, we might be able to remember which of us was standing near it at the time.'

Carol remembered now that Nathaniel's daughter had given up a brilliant career as a physicist to look after her father. Find the fused outlet—remember who had stood next to it—discover Mr Whitfield's murderer. It was as simple as that and it had taken the calm, flower-like Marcia Leland to arrive at it.

'An excellent idea, Miss Leland.' Mr Druten from Pan-American was gazing at the girl admiringly as though at last a suggestion had been made of which he approved. 'One of us better go right away and look at those outlets.'

'I'll do it,' volunteered Miles.

'No, Miles.' Marcia Leland rose, a slim but oddly authoritative figure. 'I don't think any *one* of us should go. After all, if there's a murderer here in this room, we're all equally under suspicion. We don't want to give anyone a chance to destroy evidence.'

'You're a very logical person, Miss Leland.' Peter gave a wry smile. 'What do you suggest? '

'That we all go together.'

'Very sensible,' approved Mr Druten.

'I think it's terrible,' cut in Miss Gregg. 'Going back to that room? With poor Mr Whitfield lying there? I—I couldn't do it. I'll stay right here.'

'You'd better not hang round alone, Miss Gregg.' There was a faun-like twist to Miles's mouth. 'You never know what might happen.'

The treasurer started, flashed an uneasy glance through the open door into the darkness of the main office, and then rose hesitantly. The others were rising, too. This opportunity to do something definite seemed to have restored a more normal atmosphere.

'We'll have to use spills again.'

Marcia Leland moved to the desk, Carol joined her, and together they folded sheets of paper.

They had started towards the door when Peter exclaimed, 'Wait a minute.' His hands were fumbling through his pockets. 'Darn it, I've used all my matches. Has somebody else plenty?'

'Afraid I haven't.' Miles shrugged. 'My last match went in search of the mythical murderer. I've got my lighter, though.'

There was an uneasy ripple of comment. Mr Druten brought out a book with two matches in it. Marcia and Miss Gregg did not smoke. Mr Rowley and Carol had about six between them.

Peter looked rather worried. Miles said:

'We'll have to go easy; that's all.' He solemnly handed his lighter and the matches to Carol. 'I think we can trust the efficient secretary with the illumination. Use the lighter, Miss Thorne, and save the matches for emergencies. The emergencies being a crack-up of the lighter. It's very unpredictable.'

Carol put the matches in her bag and kept the lighter in her hand.

Instinctively keeping close together, the little group moved out into the main office.

Now that all the bulbs in the east block of private offices were burning, it was not so dark as it had been. An eerie radiance illuminated the nearer desks and chairs. But it was no easier to see. In fact, by contrast, the gloom beyond seemed thicker and even more impenetrable.

In taut silence, they moved out of the restricted area of half-light into a shadowy obscurity. With uncertain fingers Carol lighted a spill, sending a cone of flame wavering up. Its weak rays struck on the dislocated switchboard, then on the black shaft of the lift as they left the lighted offices further behind.

It was a rather weird sensation. There seemed no light in the world but this little taper. They were all pressed round it like moths. Surely, thought Carol, this is the strangest crime investigation there has ever been. Seven people shut in a dark office forty floors above the streets returning to the scene of the crime in search of a clue that might prove one of them a murderer!

They were passing the fire escape door now. Carol caught a glimpse of the chairs tilted grotesquely against it and the heavy glass carafe gleaming dully on top. The burglar alarm! They wouldn't be needing that now, she reflected grimly.

When they reached the door of Mr Rowley's office, they paused for one indecisive moment by Carol's desk. The spill was burning low. Carol lighted another. Then Miss Gregg gave a little sob.

'I can't,' she whimpered. 'I can't go in there. Not with poor Mr Whitfield—lying murdered.'

'You'll be all right. Don't worry, Miss Gregg.'

Peter's voice was soft, reassuring. He slipped an arm round the treasurer's plump waist. It was that incongruous, rather pathetic picture that held Carol's attention as they all stepped over the threshold into the room.

Carol held the taper up so that its rays shone as far as possible into the office. In the fitful light, there was something horrible about this dark, deserted room. The murder that had been committed here less than an hour ago seemed to have charged all the familiar objects with some subtle, sinister unreality. Only one thing seemed real—vividly real—the huddled body of the little lawyer, lying beneath the desk with one arm flung helplessly out and the other still gripping the black briefcase.

'Miss Thorne, perhaps you know where the outlets are.' Marcia Leland's voice was brusque as she moved into the centre of the room.

'Yes. There's one by the window.'

Carol joined her. The others followed, Miss Gregg still pressed nervously against Peter's side.

While Carol held the taper low, Marcia stooped to inspect the plug in the wainscot. She looked up, her green eyes gleaming like a cat's.

'No. We can't tell anything from that.'

It was amazing, thought Carol, this calm scientific efficiency in the presence of death.

'Some sort of insulated gadget must have been used,' Marcia was saying. 'I don't think the murderer would have been foolish enough to keep it. I imagined we'd find it left by the outlet. is there another plug?'

'Yes, there's—there's one in the wall right by my desk.' Mr Rowley's voice was rather hoarse. 'I had a desk lamp for a time and—'

'And we were all round there when the lights went out,' cut in Miles. 'That's probably the one he fused.'

Carol held the burning end of her taper to a fresh one. With Marcia and Miles hurrying ahead, they moved through the darkness, grouping round the desk.

'There!' Mr Rowley was pointing to a plug in the wall a few inches from the desk and on the same level as its surface. 'I had it put in specially.'

'A very convenient place,' mused Marcia. 'Anyone could have pushed something in there without having to bend and attract attention.'

'And here it is.' Miles's voice rang out excitedly. 'Clue number one.'

They all spun round. From beneath a sheaf of papers on the desk he had produced a small, two-pronged kitchen fork with a wooden handle.

'Of course!' Marcia took it and slipped it into the outlet. It fitted perfectly. 'The ideal thing for fusing a plug. Easy to use and easy to hide afterwards. The murderer must have brought it in with him.'

'But who . . . ?'

Pale faces gleamed faintly in the taper light. Eyes moved uncertainly to eyes.

'Yes, who?' echoed Marcia. 'Which of us was standing there to the left of the desk?'

Carol was wracking her memory, trying to recreate in her mind that tense tableau which had formed there just before the lights had gone out. If only someone could remember, this whole ghastly thing might be solved. But everything was blurred. And yet—wait a moment. Hadn't Miss Gregg been standing just there while Mr Whitfield began his extraordinary speech?

'I thought it was you, Miss Leland.' It was the voice of the treasurer that cut into Carol's thoughts. 'Weren't you standing there?'

'I,' said Miles softly, 'thought it was Howe.'

Mr Druten's eyes were intent on the president. 'Didn't you move over there, Rowley, just after you'd been speaking?'

'No, indeed. No.' Mr Rowley's voice was crisp. 'I was on the other side of Mr Whitfield—to the right.'

'Well, one thing's definite,' Peter's voice broke in dryly. 'We're not going to get anywhere from this angle. In thirty seconds we've accused three different people. To be perfectly frank, I haven't the slightest idea where anyone was at the time.'

'I'm afraid I agree,' said Marcia. 'When something startling happens, like the lights going out, you don't remember what went before. My idea wasn't very successful.'

'Then what—what shall we do?' Miss Gregg asked weakly.

There was a long moment of inaction. They could do absolutely nothing, of course, thought Carol. They had found out where the lights had been fused, and how. But that was all.

'We might as well go back to Mr Howe's office,' she suggested. 'After all, the cleaning women ought to be here soon. There's not much longer to wait.'

She turned. As she did so, the light from the spill struck fanwise across the surface of the desk. She gave a gasp.

'Look!' she exclaimed 'Look!'

'What is it?'

'Where . . .?'

The others swung round, reacting instantly to the alarm in her voice.

Carol was pointing at the loose-leaf calendar for the new year. Just a moment before she had been feeling calm, efficient. Now, once again, there were swift stirrings of panic.

When last they had been in this room the calendar had shown January 2. Now the light of the taper revealed:

JANUARY
4

'You see?' she asked faintly.

Miles gave a low whistle. 'The second and third—someone's taken them.'

'And it must have been one of us.' Mr Druten's voice was sharp with incredulity. 'One of us must have taken them while we've been here at the desk.' Beneath the thick brows his eyes were bright with alarm. 'That definitely proves that the murderer is here—here in the room.'

In the uneasy silence, Marcia Leland moved forward. Her dark head bent over the vaguely illuminated calendar. She looked up, her lips very pale.

'It also means,' she said, 'that the danger isn't over yet. Number Two and Number Three. Apparently the murderer has decided to kill two more of us.'

Carol gave a little shiver. It had been so horribly cold-blooded, taking those calendar slips while they were all there. The murderer, whoever he was, must be utterly sure of himself. It was almost as though he took pleasure in letting them know what he intended to do next. Marcia was right. The danger was certainly not over yet.

'Come on. Let's get back to my office,' said Peter brusquely. 'You lead the way with the light, Carol.'

She was only too glad to obey him, only too glad to leave this room, where Mr Whitfield lay dead and where the atmosphere of murder seemed to hang thickest.

Shielding the taper with her hand, she moved quickly to the door and out into the darkness of the main office.

Ahead, she could just make out the faint glow from the lights in the private offices.

She hurried towards it—vaguely conscious of the others behind her, of their voices, low and rapid, and the hard click of their footsteps as they followed her light.

Her vague, unreasoning fear was growing.

'One of them,' her mind kept repeating dully to itself, 'one of those six people is a murderer.'

She passed the chairs piled bizarrely against the fire stairs door. She passed the steel gates of the lift. She was almost half-way to the safety of light when she heard something that made her stop dead—something that made the hair at the back of her neck crawl. Her thoughts started to reel crazily. It wasn't possible; it couldn't be true . . .

And yet she knew that it was.

From the darkness behind her had come an ominous rattle. Almost immediately it was followed by a crash that resounded like thunder around the invisible walls—the heavy crash of chairs falling and the splintering crash of broken glass!

The trap they had set on the door had been sprung!

The echoes, dying away, gave place to utter silence. Carol had never been so acutely conscious of the absence of sound. Somewhere there in the darkness, the others must be standing, paralysed into immobility.

But there was not the slightest whisper, the slightest rustle to hint at their presence.

The trap had been sprung. That could mean only one thing. They had been wrong. The murderer had not been one of them.

He had been waiting out on the fire stairs and now he had slipped in through the door. At that very moment he was somewhere there in the darkness around her—somewhere . . .

In those fleeting seconds, Carol had forgotten the taper. She gave a little cry. It had burned low, searing the skin of her finger.

Before she realized what she was doing, she had dropped it. In horror she watched the flame flicker a moment on the floor and then wink out.

Some remote part of her brain was conscious of the others. They had burst into hectic life. She could hear them stumbling against desks and chairs, calling out to each other, shouting for lights.

Lights! She was still gripping Miles's lighter. Mechanically her fingers started to struggle with it. She struck and struck again. A grudging spark flashed and then died. It wouldn't work.

And then one voice rose above the vague babble around

her, loud and authoritative. It was Peter and he was shouting loudly:

'Get back to the lighted office—all of you. Get back.'

The lighted office! Safety! Once Carol's mind grasped that idea, she could think of nothing else. She forgot she had control of the lighter, all the matches. With a little sob, she turned and ran as fast as she could towards the faint radiance ahead.

When she reached Peter's room she sank into a chair. Her hands were trembling and she could not stop them. She had never thought she could possibly feel like this—starkly, physically terror stricken.

There were hurrying footsteps outside. Someone else dashed into the room. It was Peter.

'Quick, Carol. The spills and the lighter. Quick.'

Shakily she gave them to him and he was away again before she could speak.

The others were entering now. Mr Rowley, a frail, ghost-like figure; Mr Druten; Miss Gregg, her greying hair falling loose and dishevelled over her forehead.

None of them spoke. They just stood by the open door, gazing out, straining their ears for sounds out there in the darkness.

Carol crossed to join them. At last Miles and Peter appeared. Their faces were very grim.

'We were fooled,' said Miles curtly. 'No one came in through that door. We've looked at it. The trap was knocked over from inside.'

' By one of us?' exclaimed Mr Druten.

'Yes.' Peter's eyes were moving rapidly round the room. 'It was a false alarm. The murderer must have done it to . . .' He broke off with a cry. 'Where's Miss Leland?'

'Marcia!'

Throwing a swift glance around the group, Miles dashed out into the darkness. Peter followed instantly, lighting a taper as he went.

'Marcia, Marcia . . .' Miles's voice trailed back to them.

Carol's gaze flickered helplessly from one face to another. She had been too numbed by her own panic to notice that Marcia Leland had not come back.

'She's been murdered!' screamed Miss Gregg suddenly. 'I know it. In the darkness, she—'

Her fingers plucked at each other. Her shoulders started to quiver spasmodically. Her voice rose to a high hysterical laugh.

'For heaven's sake, stop it, woman,' barked Mr Druten. He spun round, gripping her arms. 'Stop that infernal noise.'

Carol would never forget those moments. Miss Gregg's convulsive sobs; her own growing fear for Marcia; and Miles's echoing voice in the darkness outside.

From the door she had been able to follow Peter's progress by the lighted taper in his hand. It threw an uncanny radiance around his tall silhouette as he passed through the main office, holding the spill first to the right, then to the left—searching.

Suddenly he stopped, somewhere near the lift shaft. For a second he stood absolutely still. Then he stooped and shouted anxiously:

'Quick, Miles!'

Carol drew in her breath. From where she stood she could just discern the outlines of what Peter had found, what lay there, stretched on the floor.

The light of the downward pointing taper had revealed the prostrate figure of a woman.

The spill burned out almost immediately, and darkness swallowed up what Carol had seen. Behind her in the lighted office, Miss Gregg had stopped sobbing now. Carol could hear her voice whispering softly:

'I was right then. He did kill her—did kill her.'

Kill her! Carol's thoughts flashed jerkily through her mind.

How horribly clever to spring the trap on the door; to throw them into a panic; and then to choose his next victim. But Marcia Leland—the lovely, self-possessed Marcia.

As Carol peered urgently forward, she saw figures approaching through the gloom of the main office. Peter first—then Miles. In his arms Miles was carrying a vague, slim form.

The others shifted back as Peter hurried in.

'Miss Leland,' exclaimed Mr Druten. 'Is—is she . . . ?'

'No.' Peter crossed to the couch and piled the cushions up at one end. 'Looks as though someone had tried to strangle her. But she's still breathing, thank God!'

Miles had come now. He carried the unconscious girl to the couch and very gently set her down.

Carol moved forward. Her gaze lowered to the girl's throat. There, livid against the skin, were long inflamed marks and a single scratch, gleaming with tiny drops of blood.

'She was unconscious when I found her,' Peter said grimly. 'Something must have interrupted the murderer.'

Mr Rowley was fluttering helplessly around. 'But one of us attacking Miss Leland! It's impossible! I can't believe it.'

'On the contrary, she's the ideal victim. Twenty thousand shares.' Miles's voice was sardonic. He had brought water and was bending over Marcia, trying to force some between her teeth. 'Poor kid. I'm afraid I'm developing an intense dislike for someone in this room. I can appreciate ingenuity up to a point. But I draw the line at strangling young women and . . .'

He broke off with a little grunt of surprise. Carol saw his fingers slip down the front of Marcia's dress and bring out a crumpled piece of paper.

'What is it?' asked Mr Druten sharply.

'I could make a shrewd guess.'

Miles rose from the couch, smoothing out the sheet. The upward slant of his eyes was dangerously accentuated.

'A very methodical murderer.'

Even before he held it out, Carol realised what the paper would be. Those calendar slips! She had forgotten them.

The crinkled scrap of paper showed:

JANUARY
2

'Murder with all the trimmings,' commented Miles. 'Too bad he slipped up on this one.'

The others were crowding around, gazing in mute astonishment and horror at the crumpled leaf from the calendar.

Peter glanced down at Marcia. He exclaimed suddenly:

'She's coming to.'

The dark head against the cushions was stirring. The long lashes quivered slightly; then Marcia's eyes half opened, staring blankly up at Peter's anxious face.

'What happened?' Miss Gregg had sprung forward. 'Tell us what happened, Miss Leland.'

'Give her time.' Peter's voice was curt. He had taken Marcia's hand and was holding it gently in his. 'You're all right, Miss Leland. Back in my office.'

With an effort, the girl pushed herself up against the cushions. Her gaze shifted slowly from one face to another as though she were striving to remember exactly where she was. She swallowed painfully, then her lips parted in a rueful smile.

'I'm sorry. It was foolish of me to faint.'

'Foolish!' echoed Miles. 'My dear, you were half strangled.'

'Those bruises on your throat,' cut in Peter. 'Can't we do something for them?'

'Oh, they're all right.' Marcia's fingers moved slowly over the dull red weals on the delicate skin of her neck. 'It was my fault, anyway. I had the idea of going back to look at those outlets. If we'd stayed here in the light nothing could have happened.'

Her green eyes suddenly clouded. 'But the trap on the door was sprung by someone. What—?'

'Just a blind,' explained Peter. 'The door hadn't been opened.'

'I see.' Marcia's impassive gaze slowly scrutinised each of them in turn. 'So it was one of you six that tried to kill me.'

'But you must be able to remember what happened,' exclaimed Mr Rowley agitatedly. 'Surely you know who it was that—'

'I remember what happened. Perfectly.' Marcia pushed the dark hair back from her forehead. 'But it won't help.'

'You haven't any idea who attacked you?'

'None at all. You see, when—when the water carafe crashed, I ran towards it. I don't know why. I suppose I had some crazy notion of trying to catch the murderer.'

'Just like you.' Miles's mouth moved in a smile. 'The gallant Marcia.'

'I hadn't any idea where the rest of you were. I heard someone—Mr Howe, I think it was, telling us all to go back to the lighted office. That made me more sensible. I turned and started to grope my way back in this direction.'

'Yes?' put in Miss Gregg.

'Then I felt a hand on my arm. It was quite a gentle grip. I felt myself being drawn along.' Marcia shrugged. 'I wasn't frightened. I thought it was probably Miles or someone taking me under their wing. The hand dropped from my arm. It moved over my dress. Before I had time to realise what was happening, both hands were closing round my throat.'

She gave a little shiver.

'I tried to cry out, but I couldn't. I remember stumbling backwards, feeling myself choking. That's all.'

'But it must have been a man,' urged Miss Gregg. 'You must have known it was a man.'

Marcia glanced at the treasurer quickly. 'No, Miss Gregg, as I said, the grip was very gentle at first. It—it was never particularly violent. It might just as well have been a woman.'

There had been something essentially unemotional in the girl's story. Even now, thought Carol, Marcia Leland had perfect control of herself. She had been the victim of a murderous attack. Any other girl would have been terrified. But Nathaniel Leland's daughter seemed to look upon it merely as a technical problem on which to concentrate the trained mind of a physicist.

She was glancing at her watch.

'Twenty-five minutes to nine,' she said. 'If Miss Thorne's right, the cleaning women will be here in about half an hour. What are we going to do?'

No one replied for a moment. The small office was very quiet as though the fast falling snow were muffling sound even here in the room.

Miles dropped like a tired man on the couch; Mr Rowley, Miss Gregg and Mr Druten found chairs. Peter crossed to the window, a tall, strong silhouette against the vague curtain of snow outside.

There was a new kind of tension in the atmosphere. The fear of immediate danger had worn off and once again speculations and suspicions were breeding in everyone's mind. Carol knew what they were all thinking.

'One of the seven people in this room is a murderer. Can it be you—or you—or you?'

'Half an hour,' said Peter suddenly. 'I think it's about time we started to consider the really important question—which of us is doing all this? It's not exactly pleasant. But presumably the police will be in charge soon. Everything's going to be a lot simpler if—if we can get some points cleared up before they come.

'Precisely.' To Carol's surprise, it was Miss Gregg who spoke. The treasurer seemed miraculously to have re-acquired her normal brisk manner. 'I think that's a very sensible idea.'

'I suppose we all agree,' continued Peter quietly, 'that this terrible business only concerns shareholders and employees of Leland and Rowley's. Whoever arranged this trap must have known everything about the office. I can't understand why Mr

Druten was included on that memorandum. But as the representative of Pan-American Dye, he obviously has nothing to do with these—these crimes. I suggest we give him absolute authority and let him cross-examine us all. We've got to have someone in charge.'

'Excellent.' Miles brought lighter and cigarette together. 'Of course, a lurid imagination could conjure up a case against Mr Druten. Pan-American may have got cold feet about the merger and sent him over to murder us all.' He grinned. 'I notice he came early for the meeting. He had plenty of time to cut the telephone and jam the door. Still, I'll second Howe's recommendation.'

In a vague murmur, the others agreed.

Mr Druten was gazing rather angrily at Miles. Apparently he was not used to being treated flippantly. Carol looked at his dark, square-featured face.

Obviously, however, he was not a person to be taken lightly. The shrewd eyes beneath the thick brows, the determined mouth, the aggressive nose—they belonged very definitely to a major executive in an enormous combine like Pan-American Dye.

His alert fingers were twisting a long yellow pencil.

'I agree with Mr Howe,' he said. 'We should do our utmost to clear the dreadful matter up amongst ourselves. And I think it should be fairly easy.'

'Easy!' echoed Mr Rowley.

Mr Druten nodded. 'Things have been happening so quickly we haven't had time to think. But we know from the memorandum that the murderer has some very strong reason for wanting to stop the merger. Clearly we have to look for the criminal among those of you who stand to lose rather than gain by our absorption of your company.'

Mr Druten had the situation formidably under control now. His voice was sharp, unemotional.

'Even without the note, the motive would have been

obvious. Mr Whitfield had ten thousand shares; Miss Leland has twenty thousand. If the murderer had been successful in killing her, thirty per cent of the stock would already have changed hands. His scheme is not so far-fetched as it appeared at first.'

'In fact, it looks horribly like being successful,' put in Miles.

Mr Druten held up a large hand against interruption. 'If the murderer has so strong a feeling against the merger, it is reasonable to suppose that he voted against it. Before we go on, I should like to see the ballot slips.'

'Not a bad idea,' cut in Peter.

'They're in my office,' offered Miss Gregg. 'I took them in with some other papers after the meeting and . . .'

She broke off at a strangled little exclamation from Mr Rowley. The president had hardly spoken since their return to the lighted office. Now he had half risen, his cheeks the colour of cigarette ash.

'Ballot slip!' he breathed hoarsely. 'Calendar slip. That third calendar slip! We've forgotten it. Means another of us will . . .'

His hand moved jerkily to his heart. With a gasp he sank back into his chair, doubling forward with an expression of acute suffering on his haggard face.

'Mr Rowley!'

Carol knew her ex-employer had a weak heart. She had seen an anginal attack like this only a week before, after Mr Druten had come to the office to discuss the final arrangements for the merger. She hurried towards him.

But Peter was already at his side.

'Pocket!' Mr Rowley was whispering. 'Right-hand coat pocket.'

Peter's fingers slipped into his uncle's pocket. He produced a small ampoule and crushed it swiftly beneath Mr Rowley's nostrils.

While the others hovered nervously around, Carol noticed to

her astonishment that Peter was concealing something in his left hand—a small piece of paper.

He saw her looking at it and shot her a quick warning glance. Then he thrust his hand into his trousers pocket. It came out empty.

None of the others had seen. Carol was sure of that. But what had Peter been hiding? Why?

Mr Rowley's breathing was becoming more normal now. The agonized lines around his mouth gradually relaxed, and he forced a pallid smile.

'Just the heart,' he muttered. 'Been acting up lately. The shock.'

No one spoke for a long moment. Peter was staring down anxiously at his uncle. At length his eyes moved to Mr Druten.

'I'll get you those ballot slips,' he said.

He crossed to the door and paused, glancing over his shoulder at Carol.

'Perhaps you'll come with me, Miss Thorne. It's only next door.'

Carol thought once again of that slip of paper in his pocket. She knew he had something he wanted to tell her—alone.

'Yes,' she said. 'Yes, of course.'

Miss Gregg's office was next to Peter's. Neither he nor Carol spoke as they hurried to it. Peter closed the door behind them. His grey eyes looked down at her seriously.

'You saw it, didn't you, Carol?'

'You mean the piece of paper?'

He nodded. 'I expect you guessed what it was.'

He thrust a hand into his trouser pocket and produced the crushed ball of paper. He smoothed it out and gave it to her.

Staring up in that heavy, horribly familiar type was:

JANUARY 3

'I found it in uncle's pocket when I got out the ampoule,' Peter was explaining. 'I was afraid to let him see it just after he'd had that attack.'

'Number three.' Carol stared at it. 'Peter, how awful. But how did it get there?' '

'I suppose the murderer might have planted it on him. His voice was hesitant. 'But I don't see why, unless—'

'Peter,' cut in Carol suddenly. 'You don't think Mr Rowley was the one who took those slips; that he's—he's been doing all this?'

She could tell from his expression that the idea had at least entered his mind.

'I can't believe it, Carol. But I'm terribly worried about uncle. He hasn't been well for some time. The idea of the old firm having to be broken up's been preying on his mind.' He crushed the slip back into his pocket. 'Listen, Carol, you're his secretary. You're as close to him as anyone. You know how reserved he is; never talks about himself or what he's feeling. Has he done anything at all strange lately? Anything that makes you think he might . . . ?'

He broke off. Carol knew how beastly this must be for Peter—to have to suspect the bachelor uncle who had always been like a father to him. But, as her mind moved back over the hectic events of the past weeks, she felt a slow suspicion stirring in her. Her employer—a murderer! It seemed incredible. But then, whatever the solution, it would seem incredible. One of them was guilty. Why not Mr Rowley?

'Peter, I hate to say this,' she began impulsively. 'But he—he has been rather odd lately. And then, just after Mr Druten came here to the office the day before Christmas, he had a heart attack like the one he had tonight.'

'Mr Druten!' exclaimed Peter blankly.

'Yes. Mr Rowley made me promise not to say anything about it. Just after Mr Druten left the buzzer went and I—I found your uncle doubled forward over the desk. He managed to tell me about the ampoule and he was all right again in a few minutes. But I had a feeling he'd heard something that worried him—that had given him a shock.'

Peter's eyes were anxious. 'That was the day Mr Druten came round to discuss the final arrangements for the merger, wasn't it?'

'And it was the next day that Mr Rowley started to have those long conferences with Mr Whitfield.'

'You don't know what they were talking about?'

'No. They kept the door shut. I was told not to disturb them for any reason. But this afternoon they sent for me to witness a signature and . . .' Carol paused. 'Oh, Peter, I never thought about it at the time, but I've just remembered. When I went in there this afternoon, Mr Whitfield had borrowed my typewriter. He was sitting there—typing.'

'Typing!'

They stood perfectly still, staring at each other. Carol knew what he was thinking; she could think of nothing else herself. That memorandum. *Exit before midnight*. Had—had Mr Rowley and Mr Whitfield somehow compiled it together? Had that been what Mr Whitfield had been about to confess when the lights went out?

'What are we going to do, Peter?' she asked quietly.

'Whatever we think, it's only a theory. We've got no proof.' Peter's voice was taut as though he were trying to convince himself rather than her. 'Carol, we can't tell the others. It's not fair to uncle now he's so ill. The police will be here soon. If—if they find out anything, well, they find it out, but—'

'All right,' murmured Carol.

What if they were conspirators? It seemed only to draw them

closer together. Maybe some good had come out of this nightmare evening, she thought. It had taught her to appreciate Peter—sane, loyal Peter.

'New Year's Eve!' She looked up at him with a little grimace. 'Just a few hours ago I was having my hair done and planning to dazzle you with my new black velvet at Longval's!'

He did not reply for a moment. The light gleamed down on his short cropped hair, on his firm mouth and the little cleft in his square chin. Then his arms went around her and drew her towards him. His lips met hers, warm, passionate.

'Carol, darling,' he whispered. 'I know it's a crazy time to say it, but I've—I've got to tell you how crazy I am about you.'

He broke off, gazing down at her, his grey eyes anxious, uncertain like a boy's.

'Carol, darling, will you marry me? I know I'm not a particularly glamorous person. You're so clever, so—so beautiful, I expect you just think of me as a dull, inadequate kind of a mossback. But—oh, Carol, I love you so much.'

She let herself relax in his arms. It was comforting to feel him close to her. Life with Peter would be so safe, so secure. There was something strong, stable, even in his kisses. Peter, her tower of strength.

'Pardon a most untimely entrance.' Carol spun round at the sound of the quiet voice. There, his hands in his trousers pockets, his dark, mocking eyes fixed on them, was Miles Shenton.

'I had no idea this remarkable evening was breeding romance.' He drew a hand from his pocket and examined his nails. 'I'm sure the ex-employees of Leland and Rowley's will take great pleasure in organizing a wedding shower for the almost-ex-Miss Thorne.'

Carol felt sudden anger. She hated him for coming in; hated him for staring at her with those insolently amused eyes for being so—so disgustingly handsome.

Peter still had his fingers in hers. He was glowering at Miles.

'What did you come here for, Shenton?'

'For the same reason as you, Howe. I was hoping for a private talk with Miss Thorne. I wanted her to refresh my memory on a certain detail of our *tête-à-tête* here on Christmas Eve.'

Carol felt the blood flooding her cheeks. How exactly like Miles to bring up Christmas Eve! She swung round to Peter.

'Mr Shenton was kind enough to ask me out to dinner on Christmas Eve,' she explained acidly. 'Unfortunately, he discovered at the last moment that he had a very important business engagement. He rang up and broke the date.'

'Oh, I wasn't referring to that,' Miles grinned. 'I meant our little encounter here afterwards.' He glanced at Peter. 'Fate decreed we were not to be parted, Howe. I happened to drop into the office about half-past ten that night. And, lo and behold, who should appear but Miss Thorne herself. We had a very pleasant session together.'

Pleasant session! Carol remembered vividly every moment of that pleasant session. When Miles had phoned to say he would be unable to meet her, she had gone back to the office after a solitary dinner to retrieve some Christmas packages she had left behind. She had found him here, alone and in tails for his 'business engagement'. He had kissed her, made love to her. For some mad reason she had let him. And then he had suddenly broken away, saying, '*Well, Marcia Leland's waiting for me downstairs. A practically unemployed chemist can't afford to keep his potential meal ticket waiting.*'

Pleasant session!

The two men were gazing at each other steadily. She could sense an ever-growing current of antagonism passing between them.

'Your office is down at the laboratories,' said Peter quietly. 'What were you doing here at half-past ten on Christmas Eve?'

'Robbing the safe.' Miles's smile was less humorous than usual. 'As a matter of fact, I was on a very innocent mission.

That afternoon your uncle rang me up at the laboratories. It was the first time, incidentally, that I'd heard about the merger. He wanted me to send him all the unpatented processes and the notebooks old Leland kindly but quite unprofitably bequeathed me in his will. I sent them up.'

He took out a cigarette. 'As Miss Thorne told you, I had a business engagement. Marcia and I happened to be passing and I wanted my notebooks back. So I came up here and collected them. But we seem to be wandering from the point I intended to bring up with Miss Thorne.'

'There's no need to bring up any other points now,' cut in Carol curtly. 'We'd better be getting back to the others.'

'Miss Thorne is probably right—as usual.' Miles held his lighter to the cigarette. 'We are forgetting that a murder has been committed tonight. As I remember, you two were sent here to collect up the ballot slips.'

His eyes moved to the desk.

'You seem to have become sidetracked from your original purpose.'

He crossed and picked up the ballot slips.

'*Oh, careless love*,' he murmured.

The atmosphere was still very tense when they rejoined the others. Carol's mind was struggling with the complexities of her thoughts. First there had been the suspicions of Mr Rowley. And now, Miles—had he really given them the true explanation of what he had been doing in the office on Christmas Eve?

Miles took the ballot slips up to Mr Druten. The executive from Pan-American Dye glanced through them, his eyes widening.

'Well,' he said briskly, 'I was hoping to narrow the murderer down to those of you who voted against the merger. I'm afraid I was rather ingenuous. The murderer has voted in favour of it presumably to avert suspicion. Every one of you present in this room voted aye.'

Surprised murmurs stirred the group. All voted for it! Miss Gregg, who was losing a twenty-seven-year-old job; Miles, who also was to be put out of work; Mr Rowley . . .

'But even so,' continued Mr Druten's level voice, 'I think we may reasonably eliminate those of you whose interests are obviously bound up with the carrying of the merger.'

He glanced at Peter. 'By the terms of the agreement worked out by Mr Rowley and myself, Mr Howe is to have a very remunerative position with Pan-American. I fail to see how he could have the slightest motive for committing these crimes.'

An emphatic gesture of the hand eliminated Peter. While the group waited in silence, Mr Druten's gaze shifted to Marcia.

'And Miss Leland, too. Even if she had not been brutally attacked, she owns twenty thousand shares and the merger will greatly enhance their value.'

Marcia inclined her head. 'As a matter of fact, I'm very anxious for the merger to go through. I need the extra capital badly. You see, I'm planning to endow an institute for non-commercial research in—in memory of my father.'

'I can confirm that,' put in Miles. 'The proposed Leland Institute is Marcia's sole passion. Cross her off the list.'

Mr Druten's thick brows lowered as he glanced at Carol.

'Miss Thorne, I understand, is losing her job through the merger. Is that so?'

'It's absurd to suspect Miss Thorne,' broke in Peter. 'Besides, she has an alibi. When the trap on the door was sprung, she was at the other end of the office. You could tell that by the lighted taper.'

Carol smiled at him gratefully. Dear Peter, how thoughtful of him to have produced an alibi.

Mr Druten seemed convinced. 'That is true,' he said. 'We may eliminate Miss Thorne.'

The atmosphere in that small room was growing increasingly electric as the circle of suspicion narrowed its circumference.

Suddenly Miss Gregg leaned forward in her chair, the eyes behind her spectacles strangely bright.

'There's no need to suspect me,' she said calmly. 'I know what some of you are thinking. Poor old Miss Gregg who's been with the firm twenty-seven years and who's given her life to it—maybe she couldn't stand the idea of having to start all over again; maybe she's just an old spinster driven crazy by the idea of the merger—driven crazy enough to commit murder.'

She snorted. 'Well, you're wrong. I'd never murder anyone to prevent that merger going through; but I might murder someone who tried to stop it.' She drew herself up. 'The merger means more to me than anything in the world. It's going to treble the value of my shares; give me a big enough income so's I won't have to work. And I'm through with work. I want to have a good time—I want to travel before I'm too old to enjoy it.'

She crossed her hands in her lap and looked around her defiantly.

'You can cross me off, too.'

Absolute silence greeted this uninvited outburst. Miles smiled wryly and murmured:

'That's the spirit. Good for you, Miss Gregg.'

Mr Rowley had been listening with rather tense interest. Now he lifted a hand.

Carol thought of the calendar slip they had found in his pocket; thought of those strange conferences with Mr Whitfield. She shot a swift glance at Peter.

'As Miss Gregg has explained her point of view,' began the president quietly, 'I might as well explain mine. Some of you, I know, realize that my heart wasn't in the merger. Perhaps I was sentimental, but, with my old friend Nathaniel Leland, I started this firm—it meant everything to me. In the back of my mind I hoped that we would be able to struggle along without losing our corporate existence.' He smiled faintly. 'But that was only a sentiment. As a large shareholder I have as much to gain as anyone by the merger. Besides, like Miss Thorne, I have an alibi.'

He threw out his hands in a small gesture of finality.

'Only my nephew, Peter Howe, knows this, knows why I could have no motive for interfering with something which no longer concerns me. Last week my doctors gave me just three months to live. Ladies and gentlemen, my alibi is—death.'

There was a calm dignity on his drawn face. Once again Carol glanced at Peter, who was gazing down at the floor. So this was why he had pleaded with her not to mention to the others their half-formulated suspicions of his uncle. He had known Mr Rowley was a dying man.

There ran through the group a spontaneous ripple of shocked and sympathetic comment. They lapsed into silence until the sharp click of a lighter drew all attention to Miles. He was leaning back against the cushions of the couch, a faint trail of smoke issuing from his nostrils.

'I seem to be the only suspect left,' he said. 'I might as well save you all the trouble and give you the case against myself. It's not such a bad one at that. The merger is removing my job. I happen to be in fairly desperate need of money. Mr Leland, who was so generous to his other dependants, failed to be generous to his protégé. He left me no shares in his will, only a few and regrettably sketchy notes of the experiments he was working with at the time of his death. Presumably, he trusted me to turn them over to the company if any of them showed commercial possibilities—but they were too incomplete to show anything. In other words, I am the only one who has any kind of logical motive for committing murder to stop the merger going through.'

He grinned. 'As defence, I merely state the fact that I did not murder Mr Whitfield. I certainly did not attack Marcia to whom I am very devoted. And my motive is not quite as strong as it appears since Marcia has offered me a job with the proposed Leland Institute.'

'That's true,' broke in Marcia swiftly. 'As soon as I heard of the merger, I called Miles up and persuaded him to join me. Although he's too modest to mention it, I want him as head research chemist. And I know he's as excited about the Leland Institute as I am. It's ridiculous to pretend he could have any motive.'

Carol felt an overpowering sense of relief. Of course, Miles didn't mean anything to her. Why should he? But . . .

'So'—it was Miles's voice that broke in calmly—' we have gone around the mulberry bush and we're back again exactly where we started. We've proved that none of us has the slightest motive for inaugurating this mass exit before midnight.'

'But,' blustered Mr Druten, 'there must be some mistake. We—we know that one of us has been doing this. We—'

'Why don't we give up being detectives for the time being?' asked Miles. 'Besides, I have a rather uneasy suspicion which I feel I must share with you all.'

His eyes moved gravely to Carol. 'I was hoping to talk this over with Miss Thorne before making a public announcement, but she did not seem particularly interested. Miss Thorne and I happened to meet here in the office on Christmas Eve. The time was about ten-thirty and, I may be wrong, but I don't remember noticing any signs that the cleaning women had been here.'

So that was what Miles had been trying to say when he had joined her and Peter in Miss Gregg's office. Carol stared at him, her eyes gradually widening.

'You're right,' she breathed. 'The charwomen hadn't been.'

Miles nodded. 'From which I can draw only one conclusion. Christmas Eve was the day before a holiday. So is tonight. Charwomen don't put in an appearance on the eve of holidays. They don't come tonight. They won't come till tomorrow night.'

'Of course,' said Carol weakly. 'The lift man told me all services stopped at six on New Year's Eve.'

Miss Gregg gave a little horrified gasp. 'So—so we won't be let out. We *will* be here until midnight.'

'Undoubtedly, Miss Gregg,' said Miles.

There were a few moments of complete inaction. Instinctively they had all buoyed themselves up with the inner certainty that release must come soon. Now all hope seemed suddenly swept away. They were to be shut in indefinitely with only the problematic arrival of the night watchman to look forward to—shut in with a murderer who would grow increasingly sure of himself, increasingly determined as the hours moved on towards midnight.

'But we've got to find some way of getting out.' Miss Gregg voiced the thoughts of them all. 'We can't let ourselves be trapped here—let him do what he wants with us.'

'Yes.' Mr Rowley was gripping the arms of his chair. 'Here in the heart of New York, we can't be cut off. There must be something we can do.'

'There is a chance—just a chance.' Miles's cool voice broke in. 'We know the lift, the telephone, the stairs are out. But we can always revert to this most primitive method of attracting attention. Fire.'

'Fire?' echoed Mr Druten. 'But how?'

'By making people in the street think the Moderna Tower is on fire. By having smoke pouring out of all the windows.'

Miles's face was very serious. 'I've been thinking this out for some time, and I've got a fairly workable plan. There are some samples of one of our specially processed dyes here in the office which smokes like hell when you set fire to it. Each of us gets a metal scrap basket stuffed with paper. Each of us takes a window. I've got some lighter fluid in my desk. We can make little individual bonfires. It'd be a smoky unpleasant job—but we could put up quite a convincing impression of fire. Some New Year's Eve reveller might turn in an alarm.'

This idea seemed to rouse the others to a kind of desperate eagerness.

'Yes. We could put the scrap baskets on the sills.' It was Mr

Rowley speaking, quickly, excitedly. 'There are seven rooms and just seven of us. Excellent. An excellent scheme.'

'But the darkness!' cut in Miss Gregg. 'It means going out again—out there in the darkness.'

'Leave that to the most stalwart of us, Miss Gregg.' Miles rose. 'You ladies can share the lighted offices.'

The next ten minutes were hectic. Here was a practical suggestion for escape at last. Miles hurried off to find the samples of dye while Mr Druten, Peter and even Mr Rowley trooped out into the darkness of the office, gathering up scrap baskets and paper.

Eventually they all reassembled in Peter's room. Miles announced that he had collected four boxes of matches from the stenographers' desks. Seven metal scrap baskets were set down on the floor. Each was stuffed with paper, Miles sprinkled some of the powdery dye on them and then added to each a frugal share from the small bottle of lighter fluid.

Peter was moving around arranging quietly who would take which rooms. His face was very grave.

'We'll have to be careful,' he said. 'If we did actually set fire to the place, there wouldn't be much of a chance of getting out.

'Exactly,' added Miles. 'No one must leave his post. There's an extra supply of paper by each window. So keep stoking as long as you can. And don't forget in your—enthusiasm, that one of us is still a murderer.'

Everything was ready now. Miles's words echoed eerily in Carol's mind, as, gripping her scrap basket, she moved with the others to the door.

Marcia Leland had been left behind to look after the window in Peter's room, while Miss Gregg was to take charge of her own lighted office. The rest of them started in silence through the semi-darkness.

Carol had been allotted the central window in the main office.

She felt a little twinge of fear as the four men slipped away from her into the deeper obscurity, leaving her alone in that large, silent room.

She moved towards the vaguely looming expanse of window. A faint shaft of illumination took the edge off the darkness. It made a grotesque twilight, casting across the carpet distorted shadows of the familiar desks and chairs. Carol's hand brushed against a vase of chrysanthemums which one of the girls had brought in that morning. She smelt their cool, bitter-sweet perfume. Only a few hours ago Miss Beale had been sitting there, sniffing and telling the other girls how she had caught a cold at a dance on Christmas Day. All that seemed part of another world.

Carol gripped the sash and pushed the wide window up. A little gust of chill air rushed in, bringing with it a swirl of snowflakes. It was still snowing. She had not thought of that.

The snow was icy against her hands as she banked it up on the sides of the sill to make room for her scrap basket. Ahead and below, the vast panorama of Manhattan stretched out, garishly bright, tantalizingly alive. Over the edge of the broad roof beneath her, she could see the dark ribbon of a street with cars, taxis and tiny black spots that were men and women. So near—so inaccessible.

From around her in the office, she could hear the occasional creak of boards, the harsh grating of other windows being thrown open. Leaning over the sill, she saw a cloud of blackish smoke bellying out of Peter's office. Marcia Leland had already started to work.

Carol put her scrap basket down on the sill. She fumbled for a match in her box. Then, suddenly, she stiffened.

From the darkness behind her had come the soft sound of footsteps.

One of us is still a murderer. Miles's sentence jangled wildly in her brain.

They were closer now—the footsteps. So close that she could hear soft breathing, feel the presence there behind her. For a second she could not move. Then she spun round blindly.

'Who's . . . ?'

Her voice faded. An arm had slipped purposefully around her waist. She felt breath warm on her cheek and then lips pressing against hers.

As soon as he had touched her, she had known it was Miles. It was a strange, intoxicating sensation—part anger, part relief, part excitement. She tried feebly to break away from that long, aggressively male kiss. But she was still weak, confused.

Gradually his arms relaxed around her. He drew back. And with the moment of his moving away, she felt anger rising to swamp all other emotions.

'Miles!'

'I had to kiss you to stop you screaming.' The vague light from the Manhattan sky struck in through the window, softly accentuating his bright eyes and the ironical curve of his lips. 'We've had enough shocks tonight without having to submit to an unnecessary shriek.'

'You choose somewhat unconventional methods,' said Carol scathingly. 'What are you doing here, anyway? You said none of us was to leave our window.'

'Just part of my policy. I thought it would be a good opportunity to have a talk with you alone.'

'And what is there to talk about?'

'Your private life.' Miles moved towards her again, twisting his warm fingers around hers. 'Carol, you're not going to marry Howe, are you?'

'I shouldn't have thought it mattered to you what I did. There'll always be lots of other girls to make dates with—or break them!'

'Listen, Carol, you're being a fool and you know it.' His arm had slipped around her again. His face, very close to hers, was dark, earnest. 'Christmas Eve was all a mistake. I'd have explained it days ago if I'd ever realized what you were thinking. I went out with Marcia because she rang me up to offer me this job with her Leland Institute. It was a business engagement. Heaven knows, there's nothing more emotional between Marcia and me than the mutual respect of two scientists and a brotherly-sisterly friendship—never has been.' He gave a little laugh. 'Maybe you misunderstood my remark about a meal ticket. Whatever you did, you're not going to marry Peter Howe. I'm not going to let you.'

His lips were moving softly over her hair. She tried to cling on to the slipping reins of her anger; tried to fight against a dangerous feeling of elation.

'If you've got any sense, Carol, you know I'm crazy about you. I—well, when I heard about the merger I knew that my job was on the skids. I didn't exactly feel like asking you to be the wife of an unemployed chemist until I was sure of something else. But I'm going to have a job now with Marcia— a good one.'

He gripped her arms and gazed down at her.

'You don't want to marry a stuffed shirt like Howe. You'd be bored in a week and you know it. Of course, I'm not much of a catch. I don't have an executive position with Pan-American, and I don't inherit the Rowley fortune like Howe, but—you'd have a better time with me, Carol. You'd have fun. You're going to give up fooling around with what you don't really want—and marry me.'

Still Carol could not speak. He kissed her again almost fiercely. Then he gave a short laugh.

'Two proposals in an evening. You *are* in demand.'

Abruptly he turned away.

'I say, you haven't lit your bonfire yet. What sort of a fireman are you?'

While she stood there, breathless, he struck a match and bent over the scrap basket, brushing off the snowflakes. He set the flame to the paper and immediately a trail of smoke curled up.

'Which just goes to show that you can't get on without me.' He touched her arm. 'Make up your mind, dim-wit, and don't mess up your young and beautiful life.'

She heard his footsteps growing fainter as he disappeared into the shadows.

She was alone again.

For a moment she stood still, her lips numbed by the harshness of his kisses, thinking dazedly of what he had said. He had explained Christmas Eve; his explanation was perfectly reasonable. Probably she had made a fool of herself. But—but could she believe him? Did she want to? Only a few minutes ago she had decided, knowing that life with Peter would be safe, sane. And now Miles had come along and complicated things again.

She wouldn't think about it now. She forced herself to concentrate on the moment. The paper in her scrap basket had been too closely packed, and the snow had dampened it. The flames which Miles had started were dwindling. She cupped her hand to shield them from the breeze. And as she did so, she noticed her own name on one of the crushed sheets.

She looked more closely. It was her signature.

Carol Thorne.

And then, above it:

Samuel P. Whit . . .

The flames shivered and died out.

Stooped as she was over the sill, she could see the smoke streaming from Marcia's basket. On the other side of her was Mr Rowley's office. Smoke was issuing from that window, too, and she caught a glimpse of the president's pale, lined face bent intently over his scrap basket.

Suddenly it all seemed so pitifully inadequate—these frail strands of smoke trailing out of office windows forty floors above the street. To the people below the windows themselves could have seemed no larger than postage stamps. What chance was there that anyone would notice these slight signals of distress?

The crazy exhilaration which Miles's presence had brought with it drained away. Uneasy fears began to return.

As she stood there, leaning out of the window, the snowflakes fell, crystal cold, against her face; the chill night air tugged at her hair. She could still see the smoke eddying slowly from the president's room and the dull glow of burning paper.

And then, suddenly, the smoke curled crazily. She saw Mr Rowley's scrap basket lurch forward, topple and crash from the sill, falling like a miniature comet down the dark side of the tower.

While she watched, her nerves tense, an arm was flung wildly out through the window next to her. Another arm. Then the vague figure of a man was poised there over the sill.

She screamed, but her voice seemed to dissolve without sound into the night air. The figure had jerked forward. She caught one blinding glimpse of Mr Rowley's pale, distorted profile. His legs and arms were flailing helplessly. Then he too was hurtling downwards, downwards.

Dazedly, her eyes followed the precipitous descent of that figure. From behind her, the scent of chrysanthemums was suddenly overpowering, stifling.

A piece of burning paper had slipped loose from the fallen scrap basket. It was still twisting its slow way downward. She saw it reach the roof of the main building ten floors below, saw the flames glow there a second before they winked out.

And, in that brief moment, they had cast a faint radiance across the body of Mr Rowley, stretched dark and hunched there across the white, unbroken snow.

Carol never quite knew what happened next. Somehow, she found the others, told them of the dreadful thing she had seen. She remembered Peter's face, pale with shock and anger; she remembered thinking: *perhaps this would never have happened if we'd warned Mr Rowley of the calendar slip in his pocket.*

Vaguely she was aware of Peter and Miles dashing to the window. Then they were all back again—a shaken, silent little group—in Peter's office.

No one seemed to have spirit enough left to talk—or to think. Miles's attempt to attract attention by smoke had been an obvious failure; everything had been a failure. They had played once more into the murderer's hand. Mr Rowley was dead. Half-heartedly they tried to find out which of them could have crept into the president's office and killed him but, as before, there were no results. Each person had been watching his scrap basket too intently to notice any movement in the darkness behind them. And the murderer must have slipped up to Mr Rowley and jerked him out of the window before he had time to cry out. Once again this person had achieved the seemingly impossible.

There was nothing to do now but to wait—to wait in the safety of light for midnight. and to hope that the watchman would keep to his regular round that night.

After the first few minutes of horrified comment and speculation, they all lapsed into silence. It seemed hours before any of them spoke. And then only gradually did they make any attempt to re-open the subject. It was Miles who first spoke of it, a ghost of his usual smile moving his lips.

'And just before it happened,' he said, grimly, 'we'd proved with superb logic that none of us could be guilty.'

Marcia Leland looked up. 'We'd only proved that none of us had a motive for wanting to stop the merger, Miles.'

'That seems very much the same thing to me.'

'But it isn't.' Marcia's voice was slow, deliberate. 'We all benefit by the merger, and yet we know one of us has been committing these crimes. There's only one solution. We must have been working on the wrong motive.'

'The wrong motive!'

Her words shook the others into sudden attention.

'But that memorandum!' exclaimed Mr Druten. 'It said exactly what the motive was.'

'Why should we believe what the memorandum said?' Marcia smiled slightly. 'The murderer's been clever enough in every other way. Why couldn't he have deliberately given the wrong motive to put us off the scent?'

'But what other motive could there be?' asked Carol, perplexed.

'I don't know, but I have an idea.' Marcia's tranquil eyes were gazing straight ahead. 'I've been sitting here, thinking. Mr Whitfield and Mr Rowley had those private conferences together; Mr Whitfield tried to tell us something—and Mr Whitfield and Mr Rowley are the two who have been murdered.'

'Isn't it possible the merger and the rest of us were brought into this as an elaborate blind? That the murderer really wanted to kill only Mr Whitfield and Mr Rowley for some other—absolutely different reason?'

'But you, Miss Leland,' cut in Miss Gregg sharply. 'You're forgetting you were attacked, too.'

'But I wasn't killed.' Marcia's fingers moved absently over the clasp of her handbag. 'And, after all, if he'd really wanted to, the murderer could easily have killed me. He had plenty of time in the confusion after he'd sprung the trap on the door.'

'So—so you think you might have been attacked to throw us off the scent?' asked Peter incredulously.

'I do. If the murderer had wanted to make us believe he was trying to kill off the major shareholders, I was the obvious person to pretend to attack.'

Miles gave a low whistle. 'Maybe you have got something, Marcia. Mr Whitfield, Mr Rowley, and those conferences!' He turned to Carol. 'Do you have any idea what they were talking about?'

Carol shook her head. Quickly she outlined what she had already told Peter, how she had seen Mr Whitfield typing a document when she had been called in that afternoon to witness a signature.

'Typing a document!' broke in Miles. 'If there's anything in Marcia's theory, those papers would probably have something to do with it. Mr Whitfield didn't go back to his office before the stockholders' meeting, did he?'

'Why—no.'

'Then the documents are probably all in his briefcase.' Miles rose. 'Hold everything. I'll get it.'

He dashed out of the room, only to return a few seconds later. He was gripping the lawyer's briefcase in his hand. He shrugged.

'False alarm,' he said resignedly. 'The darn thing's empty.'

'Empty?' echoed Carol. 'But—but I know there must have been some important papers in it. Mr Whitfield had left it on my desk and he came out of the stockholders' meeting especially to get it.'

'He did?'

Quick, confused glances were exchanged. A deep furrow ploughed Mr Druten's forehead.

Peter rose and started to pace up and down the room. Suddenly Marcia Leland broke in:

'Then we are on the right track. Don't you see? Mr Whitfield and Mr Rowley must have been killed because of those papers. And the murderer's stolen them.'

'Stolen them? But—'

'Of course,' exclaimed Miles. 'That's how Mr Whitfield must have worked things out. He was moving the zipper of his brief-case to and fro when we were all discussing the memorandum. He must suddenly have seen the papers had gone and put two and two together.'

'But what could the papers have been?' exclaimed Miss Gregg.

'Exactly. What?' Miles threw out his hands. 'We've made elab-orate strides forward. But where's it going to get us?'

'Wait a moment,' broke in Carol. 'Mr Rowley had a heart

attack last week just after you'd been to see him, Mr Druten. I thought at the time that something you'd said had given him a shock. What did you talk about?'

For the first time, Mr Druten looked rather flustered.

'I—er—I merely came around to discuss a certain aspect of the merger.'

'What aspect?' demanded Peter.

'As a matter of fact, it concerned certain unpatented processes which had been turned over to our company with your patents, trade marks and other official documents. Our head chemist was very excited about them. He asked me to make sure from Mr Rowley that they were to become the property of the Pan-American Dye Combine by the terms of the merger. Mr Rowley assured me that they were.'

'Unpatented processes?' Miles's face was blank. 'But, Mr Druten, as head chemist of Leland & Rowley's, I know we didn't have any unpatented processes that were worth a damn.'

Mr Druten looked even more agitated. 'I do not understand. Of course, I am no chemist myself. But I was assured that certain processes for the artificial manufacture of aniline derivatives of indigo which Mr Leland left at the time of his death were extremely valuable.'

'But—but the notes for those processes were left to me personally,' persisted Miles. 'And I know they were worthless. Mr Leland hadn't finished them; he'd only left a few embryonic ideas. They were far too sketchy. Even a wizard couldn't have got anything out of them.'

'We must be talking at cross purposes,' spluttered Mr Druten. 'Our head chemist had seen the processes himself. He told me they had been worked out down to the last detail.'

There was a long, astonished silence. Then Marcia Leland rose, her delicate cheeks flushed.

'I always thought so,' she exclaimed. 'Just before he died in Florida, father was working desperately to get his results down on paper. Aniline derivatives are out of my field and above my head anyway. But I know father. He'd never have given in until he'd finished his job.' She turned to Miles. 'Don't you see what happened? Father *did* complete his experiments. We always thought it was strange he'd left you nothing in his will. He'd actually left you the records of his most important and revolutionary work.'

'And—'

'And you only received the few useless notebooks because someone stole the others.'

'You mean someone employed by Pan-American Dye?' asked the bewildered Miss Gregg.

'Of course not,' cut in Mr Druten crisply. 'But I'm beginning to agree with Miss Leland. If those processes really belonged to Mr Shenton personally, the thief must have had shares in Leland and Rowley's. He knew the firm was slipping; he knew Pan-American would never consent to a favourable merger without the inducement of those particular processes. He not only cheated Mr Shenton. He also cheated Pan-American. He persuaded us into this merger under false pretences.'

'That makes sense,' added Peter slowly. 'Uncle must have realised something was wrong after Mr Druten had brought up the subject of the unpatented processes on Christmas Eve.'

'And that's why he called me and asked to see the notebooks I had down at the lab,' added Miles. 'When he saw I still had them, he'd have known the ones Mr Druten talked about must be something different. It would have been easy to work out what had happened. He discussed it with Mr Whitfield.'

'And that was why they were murdered,' broke in Miss Gregg, her face creased with dawning understanding. 'Because they were the only ones who knew there'd been a fraud.'

Since Marcia's initial suggestion, developments had followed one another so quickly that they were all left rather breathless. Peter was the first to speak again.

'But, if Mr Whitfield and uncle knew there had been a theft, why didn't uncle realize what was back of all this? Why didn't he tell us we were on the wrong track as soon as Mr Whitfield was murdered?'

'Probably because the murderer had gone to a great deal of trouble to fool him,' explained Marcia. 'Perhaps that was the real reason why I was attacked, why the murderer used that theatrical device of the calendar slips. It was partly to confuse all of us, but mostly to throw Mr Rowley off the scent—to make him think there really *was* a madman among us who wanted the merger stopped at all costs.'

Miles lit a cigarette with fingers that shook. 'But where are we getting? We've suddenly decided that I've been cheated out of a legacy I never knew I had. We've fitted everything into a perfectly logical pattern. But so far as I can see, anyone could have stolen those processes when Mr Rowley brought them back from Florida. And anyone who knew old Leland could have guessed they were valuable without necessarily understanding them scientifically.' He shrugged. 'If only we'd been able to get those papers from Whitfield's briefcase.'

Until then Carol had been sitting in silence, trying to straighten out this sudden, unexpected turn of events. She looked up quickly.

'There's just a chance,' she said. 'Mr Whitfield may have made carbon copies. If so, they'll be in Mr Rowley's private safe. The murderer couldn't have taken them too, because I'm the only person who knows the combination.'

The atmosphere was tense, electric now. The fear and shock of the past hours had given way before a fast-growing excitement.

All the evening this little group of people had been the hunted. Now they were beginning to feel themselves the hunters.

'The safe! An excellent idea, Miss Thorne,' said Mr Druten.

Peter rose. 'Come on, Carol. Mr Druten and I will go with you.'

Carol followed the two men to the door and together they hurried through the main office back to Mr Rowley's room. Carol's fingers were trembling as she spun the handle of the safe. If there were any documents inside, she knew they would be the ones they were searching for. All of Mr Rowley's private papers had been removed the day before. The door swung open. Peter's flickering match gleamed on a single sheet of paper.

'Looks as though you're right, Carol.'

Mr Druten took the paper out, and the three of them hurried back to the others. The room was very quiet as the representative of Pan-American moved to the desk and sat down, bending over the document. He looked up.

'This,' he said slowly, 'is the carbon copy of a new will drafted by Mr Rowley this afternoon. It leaves his whole estate, both real and personal, to Miles Shenton.'

The others gazed at each other in bewildered silence. Then Miles asked softly:

'To me? Why on earth should Mr Rowley have left his money to me?'

'Don't you see?' exclaimed Marcia. 'This proves those processes *were* stolen. They were unpatented; once the chemists at Pan-American had seen them, they could not be protected. Mr Rowley would have realized they'd no longer be of any value to you or Leland & Rowley's. He also knew he was a dying man. He left his money to you to make up to you for what you'd been cheated out of.'

'But,' broke in Miss Gregg, 'I still don't see who—which of us murdered Mr Whitfield and Mr Rowley.'

'The person,' cut in Miles quietly, 'who stole Mr Leland's notebooks and passed them over to Pan-American so that the merger would increase the value of his shares.'

Slowly, deliberately, he lit a cigarette.

'I wonder which of you thought up that bright plan.' He glanced at the treasurer. 'It would have taken a keen financial mind like Miss Gregg's.' His eyes moved to Marcia. 'Or an earnest young physicist who wanted money for pure, non-commercial research. Or'—his amused gaze rested on Peter—'a far-sighted executive like Howe. One might even build up a case against Miss Thorne as the prospective wife of one of the people financially involved in the merger—and another strong case against Mr Druten.'

He gestured with his cigarette. 'But that doesn't get us anywhere in particular, does it? It only proves that, as the injured party, I am rather emphatically eliminated.'

They were all staring at him now. Carol noticed to her surprise that there was a dangerous, unfamiliar gleam in Peter's grey eyes.

'A very clever theory, Shenton,' he said quietly, 'involving everyone but yourself. I think I can offer you a better one.'

He turned to the representative of Pan-American. 'I wouldn't bring this up, Druten, if I didn't feel it absolutely necessary, there is another motive for my uncle's murder—a very strong motive.'

'What d'you mean?'

'Just that he could easily have been killed by someone who had a financial interest in wishing him dead.'

Peter's steady gaze had returned to Miles who was lounging back on the couch, the cigarette tilted to his lips.

'I presume,' said Miles, 'that's a crack against me as his last-minute legatee. You suggest—'

'I merely suggest,' broke in Peter, 'that there is only one person who could reasonably be supposed to have stolen those processes and used them to arrange a favourable merger with Pan-American—a person who had most of his money tied up in Leland & Rowley's shares, and for whom the merger would have made the difference between twenty thousand near-worthless stock and twenty thousand of the very valuable stock of Pan-American Dye.'

'But who is it?' asked Miss Gregg.

Peter glanced at her gravely. 'My uncle,' he said.

'Mr Rowley?'

'I hate even to have to think it, but don't you see how that would explain everything?' Peter's voice was deadly calm. 'Uncle could have taken the processes when we went down to Florida at the time of Mr Leland's death. Suppose Shenton found out about it, suppose he made an agreement with uncle not to expose him provided uncle changed his will in his favour. A form of blackmail.'

'Superb,' said Miles harshly. 'And spoken from the heart of a disinherited heir. To follow your train of thought, I arranged this party and murdered Mr Rowley to speed up the arrival of my new inheritance. Rather unnecessary of me, wasn't it—seeing that Mr Rowley had been given only three months to live by his doctors?'

'For all you know, you might have had to wait for years.'

Peter rose and moved forward so that he stood in front of the other man, his strong shoulders squared.

'Haven't you rather tripped yourself up, Shenton? You seem to forget that everyone in this room heard uncle say that no one except myself knew he was a dying man.'

In the silence that followed, Carol stared at the two men who still stood there, facing each other like combatants gauging each other's strength and weakness. She was struggling desperately with the confused thoughts that swirled in her brain. Now, suddenly, the solution came to her. What a fool she had been! She had really had the clue all the time.

Feeling rather dizzy, she rose.

'Wait a moment, Peter. You've got to let me say something.'

Both Peter and Miles swung towards her. She was vaguely conscious of the others grouped around her, their faces lined with surprise.

But now that she realized at last what had happened, she was angry—far too angry to think of anything or anyone else.

She moistened her lips.

'It—it sounds crazy to bring my own private life into this, but I see now that it's all linked up with what's been going on. Tonight'—her voice sounded very remote—'two men asked me to marry them. I'm afraid I was conceited enough to think both of them had been overwhelmed by my brains or my beauty or both. But I was wrong. One of them, I believe, was quite sincere. At least, I—I hope so. But the other—the other man asked me to marry him simply for the unflattering reason that he's afraid of me.'

'Carol—' began Peter, but she not seem to hear him.

'One of those men,' she went on, 'did arrange this trap, he did write that mad memorandum to throw us off the scent because he wanted to kill Mr Rowley and Mr Whitfield—the two people who knew about the stolen processes. But there was something else he had to do, someone else who had to be reckoned with. Mr Rowley's private secretary.'

Her fingers gripped tightly to the back of her chair. 'Even if he did manage to kill Mr Whitfield and Mr Rowley the private secretary was still a problem. How could he be sure she hadn't overheard something damning during those conferences last week? How could he be sure she wouldn't gradually put two and two together until she realized that they made four?'

She laughed rather bitterly. 'Being a gallant gentleman, he didn't actually murder her. He thought out a far more gallant way of keeping the snooping secretary's mouth shut. He made love to her, presumably on the theory that her dumb head would be so turned that she wouldn't know whether she was coming or going—let alone give any thought as to whether the wonder man might be a double murderer.'

'He was so gallant that I think he was even prepared to marry her to keep her mouth shut. And it would have served him right if he had.'

Her eyes flashed sparks of amber as she gazed from Peter to Miles.

'The funny part of it is, he needn't have bothered to try and fool me. I didn't know anything about the stolen processes or the new will; I was utterly harmless. But I'm not so harmless now. And I'm going to be perfectly shameless, too. I'm going to trot out something that all girls have to trot out at some stage of their careers—feminine intuition. Both these men kissed me tonight, and my feminine intuition's just getting around to realising which of them kissed me because he meant it.'

She broke off, looking rather wildly at the tense faces in front of her. 'And I've got something more tangible than kisses and intuition to offer. We know the murderer, my prospective husband, stole those documents from Mr Whitfield's briefcase. Well, he thinks he's destroyed them. He was very smart, he stuffed them in with the rest of the paper in my scrap basket, and took it for granted I'd burn them. But, as I was told this evening, I'm a very poor stoker. I let my fire go out and I happened to notice my signature there—on a document. That was the paper I was called into Mr Rowley's office this afternoon to sign.'

Once again her gaze turned to Peter and Miles. There was a crooked smile on her lips.

'I rather think,' she said, 'that we'll find what we want in that scrap basket. And I'm going to get it.'

Impulsively she turned and ran out into the darkened main office. She could hear exclamations, shouts from the others. Vaguely she was aware of hurrying footsteps, following her. But she was blind to all thoughts of her own danger now, carried away by a burning indignation against the man who had made a fool of her.

She felt a crazy sense of exhilaration that she herself was going to produce the proof of his guilt which lay in that solitary scrap basket perched on the sill of the main office window.

She hurried on, stumbling against desks and chairs. At last she reached the window. Swiftly she snatched up the scrap basket and slammed down the sash.

As she did so, she felt herself gripped from behind. She spun round, started to struggle, beating with her fists at the face of her invisible assailant.

The scrap basket had fallen from her hand and was rolling away. But in her sudden panic, she had forgotten everything about it. She was conscious only of the steel strength of the arms around her, the relentless force that was pushing her backwards—back against the closed window.

She tried to scream, but a stifling hand was pressed over her mouth. There was a mocking tinkle of broken glass, a gust of snowy air rushed in through the broken pane.

Although she fought desperately to keep her balance, she felt her feet losing hold of the ground. She was being lifted. Oh, God, any second now, she, too, would be hurtling downwards, falling as she had seen Mr Rowley fall only a short time ago.

And then, suddenly, miraculously, the vice-like grip loosened. She felt herself being jerked forward away from the window.

As she staggered against a desk for support, she realized that another shadow had loomed out of the darkness just in time to save her. Ahead of her, there in the obscurity, two men were fighting—fighting savagely. She could see them in vague silhouette, hear the crash of falling chairs, the sharp voices of the others.

Everything began to blur. She heard the dull impact of a blow, a little cry, and a heavy thud as one of the men stumbled backwards to the floor.

That was the last thing she knew before she lost consciousness.

When she came to, Carol was lying on the couch in the lighted office. Her temples were throbbing; the bright electric bulb in the ceiling seemed to be burning through her eyes.

She turned her head slowly. A man was bending over her.

'Nothing serious, darling,' he was saying softly. 'Only a cute little cut here and there, where your gentleman friend tried to throw you out of the window. The scratch on your nose makes you look like a kid who's been dipping in the jam jar.'

'But what . . .?'

'It's all over now.' The mockery in Miles Shenton's eyes had changed to tenderness. He sat down on the edge of the couch, his fingers slipping over hers. 'Quite a close shave, Carol. He knew you'd figured out the solution and he knew the game would be up if we found the papers in that scrap basket.

'I think he was just about desperate enough to have thrown you out of the window. But luckily my unpredictable left hook had one of its good days. I spent a very enjoyable few minutes, and both you and the scrap basket are safe.'

'But where—where is he?'

'Out very cold at the moment.'

Painfully Carol pushed herself up against the cushions. She looked around her. Marcia Leland and Miss Gregg were standing together by the desk, gazing solemnly down while Mr Druten trussed with pieces of stout cord the unconscious figure of Peter Howe.

'You were one hundred per cent right,' Miles was saying. 'We've got all the evidence the police'll need from the papers in the scrap basket. One was the signed copy of Mr Rowley's new will, rather charred but quite legal. The other was a personal note to me explaining exactly what kind of a skunk Howe was.'

Carol was still staring down in fascinated horror at the man who had asked her to marry him, the man who had just done his best to kill her.

'So—so it was Peter himself who stole those processes when he and Mr Rowley went down to Florida.'

'Exactly. And it was Howe who showed them to the chemist at Pan-American and made sure the merger would involve a fat job for himself.

'Mr Rowley knew nothing about it until Mr Druten came

round in all innocence the day before Christmas to talk about the unpatented processes. He realized then what had happened. But Pan-American had already seen the processes and the damage was done.

'I imagine he'd have exposed Howe, even though he was his white-headed nephew, if he hadn't known he was a dying man. That gave him the opportunity to make amends to me without having to drag the family name in the mud. This afternoon he made that new will cutting Peter out in my favour—the will you and Mr Whitfield witnessed.'

Carol still felt a little dizzy. She let her head lie back against the comforting warmth of Miles's shoulder.

'It's easy to see why Howe arranged this elaborate exit-before-midnight party,' Miles was saying. 'He found out about the new will and realised Mr Whitfield wouldn't be going back to his own office before the shareholders' meeting. If he could destroy the new will and murder his uncle and the lawyer before anyone else knew about the will, the old one in his favour would still be valid. He'd also have killed off the only two people who knew he was a thief.'

'And the shareholders' meeting gave him the ideal opportunity.'

'Of course. We all knew he had everything to gain by the merger. With any luck, no one would have guessed his real motive. That's why he wrote that memorandum, trapped all of us here and threw us off the scent by attacking Marcia, using those calendar slips and building up that imaginary bogeyman who was determined to stop the merger.

'At first he probably hoped the police would think it was all done by some crazy maniac who kept coming in and out of the fire-tower door. But my burglar alarm spoiled that and he had to change his tactics. Which he did admirably.

'As soon as he saw he had to, he was the first to switch round and point out the murderer was one of us. He even made use of the burglar alarm when he wanted to attack Marcia. And he took care to lead the investigation so that his fingerprints on the knife wouldn't be suspicious.'

'It was incredibly clever,' said Carol slowly. 'And Marcia must have been right. Mr Rowley might have guessed just the way Mr Whitfield did. But Peter took such pains to act honestly, he bluffed his uncle just the way he bluffed the rest of us.'

'Pretty brilliant bluff, too. No one would ever have dreamed a solid, respectable citizen like Howe could have thought up all those fantastic ideas. And I really believe he'd have got away with it if Marcia hadn't been so much on the scent, if there hadn't been a carbon copy of the will locked up in the safe, where he couldn't get at it and if you'd been a better stoker.'

'If my feminine intuition had been in better shape,' murmured Carol ruefully, 'he wouldn't have got away with as much as he did. I should have realized he was putting that calendar slip into his uncle's pocket instead of taking it out. I should have guessed when he kissed me that he was less interested in Carol Thorne than in finding out just how much the private secretary knew.

'If you hadn't broken in on us, I expect he'd have lured me into opening the safe for him.'

Her scratched nose crinkled up delightfully. 'The whole thing only seeped through my thick skull when he accused his uncle of stealing the processes and tried to get too smart turning that will into a case against you.'

Miles leaned over and kissed her hair.

'Darling, I'll never forget how gorgeous you looked when you went into that denunciation. A blonde fury with a stunning new haircut. But I wasn't listening to a word you said—not after you'd hinted that one of your two men wasn't exactly repulsive to you. Carol, did you really mean that?'

She glanced up at him, her eyes smiling. 'Dimwit,' she said.

'I seem to be quitting the old year in style.' Miles's lips moved ironically. 'Despite battle and murder, I rake off an unexpected inheritance and the heroine of the hour.'

'Not the heroine of the hour, darling. Just the queen of the dimwits.' Carol glanced down again at the bound and still unconscious figure of Peter Howe. 'To think I was dumb enough to imagine he loved me.'

'And to think you were dumb enough to imagine I didn't,' whispered Miles. 'But then blondes are always dumb.'

The others were moving over to their side now. Mr Druten gazed down at her, his face grave and worried.

'I'm glad to see you are all right again, Miss Thorne. This is terrible—terrible. But there is no question about Howe's guilt. I am sure, too, that he hoodwinked our chemist at Pan-American. I know he would never have been party to a fraud.' The bushy-browed eyes turned to Miles. 'Well, Mr Shenton, we always have a vacancy at Pan-American for a man of your calibre. Perhaps—'

'No, he won't, Mr Druten,' broke in Marcia's soft voice. 'Mr Shenton has promised to work with me and you're not going to lure him away.' There was a twinkle in her clear green eyes as she turned to Carol. 'I warn you, Miss Thorne, I'm going to get all the work out of him I can—and as much of his money as possible for the Leland Institute.'

Miles gave a mock groan. 'So I'm going to be a meal ticket for two unscrupulous women.'

It was Mabel Gregg's voice that brought them back to the realities of the moment. Her plump face was still bewildered—horrified.

'Mr Howe—a murderer,' she breathed. 'It's incredible . . . disgraceful. But—but what are we going to do about it, anyway? We may have tied him up, but we're still trapped here. How do we get out?'

Marcia glanced at her watch. 'Almost midnight. Any second now the merger will go through—and the New Year begins.'

As she spoke, there was a faint sound—a sound coming from somewhere outside in the darkness of the main office.

They all listened intently.

'It's somebody singing,' exclaimed Miss Gregg weakly.

They could hear it louder now—a male voice raised in emphatic if alcoholic melody.

'"Sweet Adeline"!' cried Miles. 'The night watchman—God bless him!'

They all dashed out into the main office, ran to the door of the fire stairs and started to bang wildly. Yes, there was no mistaking it now. The singing grew nearer and nearer.

Within a few seconds they would be free.

And then, as they stood there, another sound joined in the chorus of 'Sweet Adeline'. From forty floors below in the streets of New York, came a distant throbbing, the blaring of myriad car horns and toy trumpets, welcoming in the New Year.

Somewhere a clock started to strike. It boomed out the opening chime of midnight.

With one hand Miles was beating on the door. The other arm was around Carol's waist.

Very gently, his lips met hers.

'Happy New Year, darling,' he whispered. 'After all this, we deserve it.'

Q PATRICK

'Q Patrick' was a pseudonym used by two British-born writers Richard Webb and Hugh Wheeler for more than 20 mystery novels, a 'theoretical reconstruction' of the infamous 1892 Borden murders and many short stories. The two also wrote together as 'Jonathan Stagge' and 'Patrick Quentin', under which pen name Wheeler published eight more books after the collaboration ended.

Rickie Webb was born in 1901 in Burnham-on-Sea, Somerset, and he came to America where he worked for a pharmaceutical company in Philadelphia. Before his collaboration with Wheeler, Webb wrote two novels with Martha Mott Kelley using the pen name 'Q Patrick', derived from combining her nickname 'Patsy' with his own, adding the 'Q' for a touch of mystery. In 1933, Webb's writing partnership with Kelley came to an end when she married and moved to London, and he wrote the third 'Q Patrick' novel on his own. Two more novels followed, co-authored with Mary Louise White, a Quaker journalist who would go on to serve 12 years as Literary Editor of *Harper's Bazaar*.

Hugh Wheeler was born in 1912 in Hampstead, London, and in later years he would claim that he had started writing fiction when only eight years old. He was 19 when he first visited the United States and, after graduating from University College, London, he emigrated there in 1934. He would live in America for the rest of his life, becoming naturalised in 1942. Away from crime fiction, for which he won Edgar awards in 1961 and 1973, Wheeler was an acclaimed librettist. His best known work is perhaps his revision of the book for the 1974 production of Leonard Bernstein's *Candide* for which he won an Antoinette Perry Award for Excellence in Broadway Theatre, but there are also his Tony-winning books for *A Little Night Music* (1972) and *Sweeney Todd: The Demon Barber of Fleet Street* (1979), both developed in collaboration with Stephen Sondheim. Wheeler also had some success in the theatre, in particular with his first play *Big Fish, Little Fish* (1961), whose original production secured a Tony for its director, Sir John Gielgud. Wheeler also wrote a single novel under his own name, *The Crippled Muse* (1951).

In interviews after Webb's death, Wheeler claimed that the collaboration had initially come about because their families had been close friends in Britain. Whatever its origins the two became more than close friends. In 1940, they took over the rent of a place in Tyringham, Massachusetts and they later bought an eighteenth-century farmhouse, reputed to have once been a tavern, on the thickly wooded Chestnut Hill Road in nearby Monterey. When working on a story, Wheeler and Webb would develop the plot together, but while Wheeler usually claimed that the two had shared the actual task of writing, it largely fell to him as the more proficient typist of the two. Webb's heath deteriorated and their partnership came to an end in the early 1950s when he returned to England, where he died in 1966. In 1987, Wheeler was hospitalised with pneumonia and he died of multiple organ failure in Pittsfield, Massachusetts, leaving unfinished the book for a stage adaptation of the film *Meet Me in St Louis.*

'Exit before Midnight' was first published in *The American Magazine* in October 1937.

ROOM TO LET

Margery Allingham

ANNOUNCER: Tonight we are taking you over to the annual dinner of the November Club. It is not generally known that members of this exclusive gathering are all world-famous detectives who, regardless of nationality, meet each year in a different capital city to discuss new crimes and recall old ones. Last year their dinner was held in Buenos Aires. Next year it is hoped the gathering will take place in Oslo, but tonight it is London's turn. This year's President, Mr R. G. Peterson of New Orleans, is in the chair. Over to the November Club.

(*Fade in to after-dinner noises, polite clapping, some laughter, murmur of voices, etc., etc.*)

J.J. JONES: (*A fat old voice, packed with satisfaction. Very loud*) I thought I spoke *excellently*, didn't you, Le Blanc? Kept my end right up, what?

(*General laughter*)

INSPECTOR LE BLANC: (*A French accent, soft*) Silence, *mon ami.*

J.J.: Can't hear you if you mumble.

LE BLANC: *Mon vieux*, your microphone she is still alive.

(*Laughter*)

J.J.: Oh . . . Take this disgusting thing away, somebody!

(*Mike moved: voice changes*)

That better, huh? Unfortunate, perhaps. Not that I mind.

Nothing to hide. Well? Distinguished myself again, don't you think?

(*Faint tapping in the background*)

LE BLANC: My friend, I esteem you. I am even fond of you. You are also my guest. But here in this room are forty-five men at the very top of our profession, men who have been chosen . . .

J.J.: (*Angrily*) I know that.

(*Tapping louder*)

LE BLANC: Be silent, J.J. Let me finish. In such company it was not *comme il faut* to describe yourself as the only detective alive never to have a failure. The only—what was it?—Master Mind. No, that was inexcusable.

(*The tapping is fierce*)

J.J.: Poppycock! When you're as old as I am—I'm over eighty, if I don't look it—you'll know that truth will out. Modesty apart! . . .

CHAIRMAN: (*A pleasant American voice getting in at last*) (*Aside*) Inspector Le Blanc, could you hold our *enfant terrible* down while I get on with the programme? (*To the company*) Gentlemen, as you know, we usually spend this night discussing the crimes of the year, but this evening we have a very special guest . . .

J.J.: Eh? I didn't catch that. A little more of that port. Very good.

CHAIRMAN: (*Amid laughter*) Perhaps I should have said two very special guests. But apart from that Old Master, I had almost said that legend, J.J. Jones, from whom we have already heard at—ah—some length, we have among us tonight a man whom many of us have wanted to meet for a very long time. Newly retired from a great career in the Rhodesian force, here at last is Curly Minter in the flesh.

(*Applause*)

Our Vice-President, Assistant Commissioner Stanislaus Oates, and I have spent the best part of the day persuading him to give us here tonight the true facts of what I believe to be the most extraordinary crime of the present century. As we all know, once a murder has been thoroughly investigated, even though the criminal remains at large, the mystery has gone out of it, at least in the minds of the men in charge of the case.

(*Hear, hear*)

But there is one recorded crime which remains perennially interesting because it had no explanation. To all intents and purposes it was a miracle. I refer to the Marlborough Road murder here in this city, the case of the shot without a gun.

(*Applause*)

Minter is the only man alive who can give us the full details of that strange November story, and much against his will—for he is a modest, retiring kind of guy—he is going to tell it now. Curly, on your feet!

(*Applause. Enthusiastic noises*)

J.J.: (*Loudly*) Dam' silly! Quite absurd!

LE BLANC: *Incroyable*! Really! This is too much!

MINTER: (*An intelligent voice with a hint of country accent*) My dear J.J., if only you weren't wrong you'd be so right. Old Chief Inspector Pyne, who was in charge of the case—one of the grandest men of the day (*Murmurs of assent*) felt much the same about it. It was absurd and it was exasperating, but there was no answer then or now.

J.J.: (*Rumbling like God*) My boy, I like your face and I think you're honest, but there are no miracles in crime. Move over here so that I can hear you and give me the full facts. Then I'll give you the solution.

(*General laughter*)

LE BLANC: *Messieurs*, I feel I must apologise. My friend is old and . . .

J.J.: Getting up, Le Blanc? Good. Let him have your chair—mind my glass. Now, Captain Minter, keep your account very clear and when I see your miracle I'll expose it. Never had a failure. You'll get the living truth from me.

MINTER: I wonder. Very well, J.J.

(*Noise of shifting chairs*)

Now, sir. As I remember, it was a bright gusty morning in September nineteen hundred and four. I was twenty-two, a constable not long up from the village where I was born. My old sergeant and I were walking along the peaceful suburban road, afterwards so notorious. We were discussing a particularly horrible fire which had destroyed a small nursing home in the neighbourhood the night before. Police and firemen had done everything possible, but that morning there were five charred and unrecognisable bodies in the mortuary, and the best part of a dozen injured men in the hospital. I had not been employed in the actual rescue work, but old Sergeant Harris had behaved like a hero . . .

(*Fade in to a street scene. Heavy footsteps on the pavement. The sergeant is coughing like a sea-lion*)

SERGEANT: (*Elderly Cockney*) Wet through! Wet through to me skin, and that ain't *good* mackintosh. I said to the bloke with the 'ose, 'What d'you think I am, pillar of fire or Jonah's perishing whale?'

MINTER: (*A yokel guffaw*)

SERGEANT: That will do, young Minter. I 'ad a waistline narrower than yours when I was your age. (*Burst of coughing*) Lumme! I *'ave* caught it! Looks like this is the last thing old Jackie-boy will do for me. (*Lowering his voice*) 'E ain't in the 'orspital, so I suppose 'e's one of the other poor blighters, unless—(*More intense*) 'Ere, Minter: did you 'ear that doctor feller say somethink about a patient being unaccounted for?

MINTER: (*Younger; country accent stronger*) Can't say I did, Sergeant.

SERGEANT: Per'aps I'm wrong. I'm light-'eaded this morning.

Caught a 'eavy cold. But I wouldn't like to think old Jackie-boy was out again, not in my neighbour'ood.

MINTER: Who's that, sir?

SERGEANT: Eh? Never mind. That wasn't no ordinary nursing 'ome, you know. That was a private, what you might call a secret, loony bin, that's what The Towers was. I knew an old man 'oo worked there till 'e died a couple o' months ago, and it was through 'im I got to 'ear about old Jackie. Don't you go repeating this, my lad. This is confidential, this is.

MINTER: I understand, sir. Would you be talking about one of the patients?

SERGEANT: Yes. Jackie was a private patient up to two months ago. Very quiet, 'e was. Never 'd a visitor. Paid 's own way out of a registered envelope which come for 'im every Tuesday. But there was two little things about 'im which made me think. Are you listening, young Minter?

MINTER: Yes, sir.

SERGEANT: Ever heard anyone go like this? (*He sucks his breath through his closed back teeth, making a curious hissing sound*)

MINTER: Can't say I have, can't say I haven't.

SERGEANT: This was a regular trademark. You couldn't miss it. That was one thing. The other was 'e came to the 'Ome very sudden and secret, brought by two frightened gents in a carriage, and the date 'e came was November the ninth, eighteen eighty-eight . . . Mean anything to you, young 'un?

MINTER: November the ninth, eighteen eighty-eight . . . No that don't, unless . . . why, sir! You don't mean Jack the R—?

SERGEANT: Shut up! I'm not saying nothing. I shouldn't wonder but what I've got one of these fancy temperatures or I shouldn't be gassing. But I was stationed in Whitechapel at the time of the Ripper murders and I've never forgot it.

MINTER: (*Shocked*) We 'eard of him down in the country. You never caught him, did you?

SERGEANT: We never even see 'im. Week after week we 'ad murder after murder, each more 'orrible than the last, and then suddenly, after November the ninth, he was gorn.

MINTER: But surely you suspected someone, Sergeant?

SERGEANT: No. Some said 'e was a doctor, some said 'e was a lunatic, but no one ever saw 'im or 'eard 'im except one man—'e came driving into a pub yard practically on top of the man in the dark and 'e thought 'e 'eard a big snake 'issing just before 'is 'orse shied. No one took much notice of it, thinking it was fanciful, you see. But (*He sucks his teeth again*) I wondered.

MINTER: But, sir, oughtn't you to report it? If you know—

SERGEANT: No. I know nothing. If you're going to have a career in the Force, young Minter, that's somethink you'll 'ave to learn. Imagination don't necessarily mean promotion. All I'm saying is that there's one poor chap in the mortuary—and I 'ope 'e *is* in the mortuary—'oo I'm not so sorry for as I am for the others. You'd better forget what I've bin saying. 'Ere, ain't that your young lady cleaning the step over there? You like 'em what they call 'mature', don't you?

MINTER: (*Seriously*) Alice ain't my young woman! Why, sir, she's fifteen years older than what I am. We come from the same village, that's all.

SERGEANT: Ah. Per'aps she'd got a little sister back at 'ome.

MINTER: (*Amazed*) How did you know, sir?

SERGEANT: (*In a burst of coughing*) Call it second sight. So long, boy.

(*Sound of scrubbing*)

MINTER: 'Morning, Alice.

ALICE: (*Middle-aged country voice*) Oh. How you startled me, Curly. I can't stop. I haven't heard from home, if that's what you're after.

MINTER: It weren't. You look as if you've been crying.

ALICE: Well, I ain't. Been peeling onions, if you want to know.

MINTER: (*Gently persistent*) I wondered if your poor lady was ill. I see the young lady pushing her in her little chair yesterday. They didn't neither of them look too bright.

ALICE: Mrs Musgrave's perfectly well, and so is Miss Molly, and so am I. The washing's done and we're going to have duck for dinner. Anything else you'd like to know? (*Sharply*) Have you been by the house before, this morning?

MINTER: No. Why?

ALICE: Nothing. Nothing at all.

(*Clatter of pails*)

Well, I'm sorry to be short, Curly. See you another time, dear, and if Con writes I'll be sure to let you know.

MINTER: I was at a fire last night, Alice.

ALICE: If you were at a pantomime, dear, I couldn't wait. Goodbye.

(*A rattle and a clatter as she goes up the alley to the back door, which opens and shuts*)

Miss Molly?

MOLLY: In here. In the kitchen. Who was that?

ALICE: Only my little bobby from home. He hadn't noticed anything. Perhaps it's going to be all right. The To Let card wasn't in the window for more than half an hour.

MOLLY: I don't see that it matters. People have let rooms before.

ALICE: Not in this street, they haven't. I thought I'd have died when the Missis told me. A doctor's house letting rooms! Whatever next?

MOLLY: It's not a doctor's house any more. Daddy's dead and we've got to face it. Have you *seen* this man Mother's let the room to?

ALICE: Well, I opened the door to him. The Missis may be able to get about in her little chair, but I don't let her answer the bell, I hope!

MOLLY: Is he—all right?

ALICE: Oh, a nice quiet gentleman. In his fifties, I should say. Very timid and old fashioned, but quite the thing. A doctor, Miss.

MOLLY: A doctor?

ALICE: So he said. 'Doctor Charles', he told me, and said he was sorry he hadn't a card. Listen! That's the Missis now.

(*A brief silence in which the distinctive sound of a light hand-propelled chair is audible. An inner door opens*)

MOLLY: I'll wheel you through here, darling.

MRS MUSGRAVE: (*A deep attractive voice, very feminine*) Oh, please don't. I'm managing beautifully. I adore my little chair. Look, I can almost turn a pirouette.

ALICE: Mind the clothes-horse, Ma'am. Whatever next!

MRS MUSGRAVE: Sorry, Alice. I'm elated. Well, my dears, wasn't I right? Within twenty-five minutes of the card going in the dining-room window we get just the person we need. Do you know, I don't believe the people next door even saw it. I do hope not. People are so snobbish. Oh, Molly, cheer up. Things are going to be all right. We shan't even have to think of leaving this dear old house.

MOLLY: What's he like, Mother? Do you like him?

MRS MUSGRAVE: I think I do, dear. He's a qualified doctor. He's very kind. He asked about my accident. But I don't think we shall see much of him. He wants his meals in his room, and that would suit us if Alice can manage it.

MOLLY: But what's he like?

MRS MUSGRAVE: Well, you'll see him, dear. He's elderly, I suppose. Very big and powerful looking, with enormously long hands. His voice is educated and—er—well, not really unpleasant. I should think he had a strong personality.

ALICE: That's what I thought. When I let him in I thought, you're quiet but you're masterful, I thought. What about the luggage, Ma'am?

MRS MUSGRAVE: Oh. Yes, I forgot. Poor man, he's just come

from Leipzig and his trunks have been delayed. He's very worried about them because he doesn't seem to have a thing. I said you'd run out and get him what he wants, Alice.

ALICE: Of course I will, Ma'am. I'll go and see him now. Your oven's smelling, Miss Molly.

(*Sound of door as Alice goes out*)

MOLLY: Oh!

(*Noise of oven door*)

It's all right. I've caught it in time, thank goodness. Mother, if he's just come from Leipzig, why does he want to settle here of all places?

MRS MUSGRAVE: Darling, that really is his own business, isn't it? All we need to know is that he's perfectly respectable, and there's no question about that. If we can make him comfortable he'll stay, and that's all that matters. Are you going to wear your blue to the Atkinson's this afternoon?

MOLLY: I wonder if I ought to? It's the only really good frock I possess and—

MRS MUSGRAVE: (*Excited and happy*) Wear it, darling. It makes you look so awfully pretty. Look, I know I ought not to say this, and I can't promise, but I do believe things are going to be very much easier for us all from now on. Doctor Charles insisted on paying me such a lot of money in advance . . .

(*Last words fade: brief passage of time*)

MOLLY: (*Singing*) Little Dolly Daydream, Pride of Idaho, So now you know . . . (*Talking*) Oh, how I wish it wasn't *criminal* to colour one's lips. Now, gloves? handkerchief stay-lace quite safe? petticoat not showing? first hatpin, second hatpin . . . so. Splendid. Now then, Mr Atkinson, *prenez garde*!

(*Sound of her light high-heeled shoes on the lino. Door opens and shuts. She sings as she goes downstairs*)

Little Dolly Daydream, Pride of . . . (*Breaking off*) Oh. How do you do? I didn't see you there. It's dark by those curtains.

DR CHARLES: (*Just the sort of voice you'd think, but not over-*

done) Miss Musgrave? I am Doctor Charles. I am going to live here. Do you think you will like that?

MOLLY: I hope so. I mean of course I hope you will like it too. Is your room comfortable?

DR CHARLES: (*Dubiously*) It seems very light. I shall like it much better when it gets darker. In the winter. In November.

MOLLY: Will you?

DR CHARLES: Yes. Your mother has asked me to give you this. She didn't tell me what it was.

MOLLY: Oh, it's only the book-box to post. We share a library subscription with Mother's old aunt in the country. It's an absurd arrangement but the old lady likes it. She feels we keep in touch.

DR CHARLES: (*Sharply*) I understood you had no relatives.

MOLLY: Well, there is only Aunt Nell, I'm afraid. She's very old and a long way away.

DR CHARLES: I see. You're coming straight back, are you?

MOLLY: No, I'm going out to tea.

DR CHARLES: Nobody told me that,

MOLLY: Well, I don't suppose they would, would they? It's not very exciting.

DR CHARLES: You won't be late?

MOLLY: I don't think so. If I am someone will bring me home.

DR CHARLES: (*Softly*) That won't do. (*He draws his breath through his back teeth, making a most unpleasant hissing sound*)

MOLLY: I beg your pardon?

DR CHARLES: I said come back soon. Your mother is very helpless, you know.

MOLLY: Oh, but she's not! She's wonderfully strong although she's so little, all except for—for—

DR CHARLES: The paralysis in her limbs. Yes. Goodbye. I will shut the door.

MOLLY: (*Puzzled but not alarmed*) Oh, thank you. Goodbye, Dr Charles.

(*Fade in to a tea-party; chatter, laughter, tea-cups, piano in the background*)

ATKINSON: (*A hearty middle-aged business man*) Oh, terrible. A shocking thing. We saw the flames from here, you know. Began in the basement and the whole place became afire. Not a hope for any poor devil locked in his room.

MR PORTER: (*Same type, but younger*) Did you hear that extraordinary rumour that one of the patients had escaped?

ATKINSON: Nothing in it. I was talking to the Coroner. There was a scare and one of the assistant medicos said something stupid to the police, but the superintendent of the Home is very vehement that nothing of the sort could have happened.

PORTER: How did *he* know? The records were burnt and both the porter and the night-attendant were killed.

ATKINSON: Really? Well, in that case the superintendent's word is as good as anybody's. After all, they were his patients. I don't suppose he wanted to lose one.

PORTER: I can imagine a circumstance in which he might.

ATKINSON: Can you? I can't. Oh hallo, young man, who's this? Why, it's Molly. My dear you're so grown-up and so beautiful I didn't know you'.

MOLLY: Mr Atkinson, can I ask you something terribly important?

MIKE: Father, tell her she's being absurd. She wants you to give her a job in the office!

ATKINSON: God bless my soul! What post would you like, Molly? Managing Director?

PORTER: She'd improve the decorative scheme of your boardroom, old boy.

MOLLY: No, don't, please. Don't tease. Couldn't you, Mr Atkinson? Other girls go into offices nowadays.

ATKINSON: The things other girls do nowadays make my hair stand on end, young lady. We'll have you in Parliament next and then heaven knows what will happen.

PORTER: If Miss Molly is serious I think I might . . .

ATKINSON: (*Hastily*) No, no, we'll keep her in the family, eh, Mike? You run along, my dears. We'll go into this sometime, Molly. Your mother would have to be consulted, you know. Good heavens, I can see my old head clerk's face if you walked in on us one Monday morning! Go and play—er—croquet. Take her with you, Mike.

MOLLY: (*As they move*) He might have been more enthusiastic, but he didn't turn me down.

MIKE: It was Mr Porky Porter he was turning down. I loathe that man. Molly, just how bad are things at home?

MOLLY: They're perfectly all right, thank you.

MIKE: Listen, Molly, come out into the garden. I want to talk to you.

MOLLY: I've nothing to tell you. I just want a job, that's all. I've been thinking of it for ages. It's nothing to do with anything that's just happened.

MIKE: What has just happened?

MOLLY: Nothing. Really, nothing at all.

MIKE: Molly, I'm doing awfully well in Dad's office but I don't make much money yet, and—

MOLLY: Mike, don't, please. Hush.

MIKE: But I must talk to you. You see, I'm not in a position to ask anyone to marry me, and yet . . .

MOLLY: (*Softly*) Nobody axed you, sir, she said. (*Loudly*) I think I'd like one of those little pink cakes.

MIKE: I know nobody did . . . Oh, I'm so sorry, Mrs Phillips. Did I jolt your cup? . . . Excuse me . . . excuse me . . . Molly, do come into the garden a moment. Come and see those . . . those . . . oh, those pink and blue things.

MOLLY: (*Laughing*) Astors. Do you know, I think I'd better.

MIKE: (*Urgently*) Do you like them?

MOLLY: Yes. Yes, I do.

MIKE: How much? Could it be . . . awfully?

MOLLY: Yes, Mike. It might be . . . frightfully . . . I think.

(*Party fades. Mrs Musgrave's chair is heard moving up and down in some agitation*)

ALICE: (*Softly*) Give me a hand with the quilt, Miss, please. Keep still, Ma'am, do. You're doing yourself no good and fidgeting me.

MRS MUSGRAVE: (*Same low voice*) You're right, Alice. I'm sorry. Is the bed ready? Let me see if I can pull myself in. I believe I could.

ALICE: That you won't, Ma'am.

MOLLY: No, don't be silly, darling. Put one arm round me and the other round Alice. There. Comfy?

MRS MUSGRAVE: Wonderful. I don't know what I'd do without . . . Listen!

ALICE: (*After a pause*) No, it's all right. I can hear that latch of his a mile away, let alone just down here.

MOLLY: (*Laughing uneasily*) I don't know why we're all whispering. We've got rather like it these last few weeks, haven't we? Oh, Mother, why did we ever let him in the house?

MRS MUSGRAVE: I did make a mistake, darling. I know I did, but it's going to be all right. Wait just a little and we'll get him to go.

MOLLY: I wish I knew how. You've tried, haven't you?

MRS MUSGRAVE: I . . .

MOLLY: Haven't you?

MRS MUSGRAVE: I tried to indicate it, but . . .

MOLLY: Oh, what's the use? We may as well admit we're all afraid of him.

MRS MUSGRAVE: Molly, that's pure hysteria. I'm certainly not afraid, but lt *is* awkward, because he took the room for three months on trial, and like an idiot I let him pay for it. He won't go before his time without a silly scene, and as he hasn't done anything to which we can reasonably object . . .

MOLLY: Oh, hasn't he? Creeping about at all hours—interfering—hating anyone to go out—cross-questioning us when we come in—answering *our* front doorbell—snatching letters—turning down the lights—turning down the gas! The whole house feels as if—as if it had suddenly got overrun with rats!

MRS MUSGRAVE: Darling!

MOLLY: Who put his foot down when at last I persuaded Mr Atkinson to give me a trial in his office?

MRS MUSGRAVE: My dear, *I* was against that.

MOLLY: You weren't really. *He* settled it. It was he who said (*Mimicking*) 'Mrs Musgrave—hiss!—needs her daughter—hiss—by her side.' Yet you and Alice could have managed and I could have earned enough to do without him or anybody. He knows that.

MRS MUSGRAVE: I'll get rid of him, I will. I'll speak to—oh, listen, wasn't that something then? No, no, I don't think so. Just something in the road.

ALICE: (*Calmly*) If you ask me, he's waiting, Doctor Charles is.

MOLLY: Waiting? What for? Do you mean he expects a visitor, or a letter?

ALICE: No. It's your visitors and your letters he's interested in. As long as he gets his registered envelope on a Tuesday he's quite satisfied. He's waiting for November.

MRS MUSGRAVE: (*Eagerly*) Oh, Alice, I've thought that. Perhaps he means to go back abroad then. His trunks never came, did they? Perhaps they were never sent. Perhaps there was a quarrel at home and . . .

ALICE: Maybe. But I think he's waiting for the dark.

MRS MUSGRAVE/MOLLY: (*Together*) The dark?

(*Silence, followed by a rattle and a thud in the distance*)

MOLLY: (*Catching her breath*) Oh! . . . How silly, it's only the late post. I'll go.

MRS MUSGRAVE: (*In sudden panic*) No, Molly, don't!

MOLLY: Why? Mother!

(*A tap on the door, followed by the sound of its opening*) Quick, Alice.

DR CHARLES: (*From the doorway. He is very sure of himself now and the hiss appears more frequently from now on*) I have a letter here. It is addressed to Miss Molly, but I think I should hand it to Mrs Musgrave.

ALICE: The Missis is in bed, sir.

DR CHARLES: I don't think you'll regard this as an intrusion, Mrs Musgrave. After all, I am used to finding my patients in bed. Will you read this, please?

MRS MUSGRAVE: (*With forced naturalness*) It's for you, Molly. How kind of you to bring it in, Doctor Charles, but we did hear the postman.

DR CHARLES: I was in the hall when it came. It looked like a little grey tongue sticking out at me through the door. I didn't like it. There are too many lights in this room.

MRS MUSGRAVE: Oh, but I like it bright. It used to be our drawing-room before—

DR CHARLES: Your husband died and left you poor and a cripple.

ALICE: Well!

MRS MUSGRAVE: (*Trying to control the situation*) Exactly, Doctor Charles. And now I like it very much. Goodnight.

MOLLY: (*Who has not been listening and is now reading aloud*) '. . . called at your house and was told by an extraordinary person with a lisp that I was not and never would be welcome . . . convinced some absurd mistake, but puzzled. My love, my dear Molly. Mike Atkinson.' Doctor Charles! Did you send a visitor away from here yesterday afternoon?

DR CHARLES: I did. I send everybody away. I sent two spying old women packing today. I won't have people coming here.

MOLLY: But this is the limit! This is outrageous! Mother, Doctor Charles should be made to understand that this is *our* house.

DR CHARLES: Your mother is a very ill woman, much more ill than you realise. You are a very pretty girl, a very beautiful girl, but you are a fool. Too much of a fool altogether.

MRS MUSGRAVE: Doctor Charles, I am in my bed and I—I feel at a great disadvantage. Won't you leave us now? I should like to speak to you in the morning.

ALICE: Come along, sir. Come along to your room. You like it up there, sir, it's not so bright.

DR CHARLES: Eh? No, no, that's right. That's right, Alice. You're not beautiful. You're not a pretty woman.

ALICE: No, sir. I was never thought to be. Come along.

DR CHARLES: Very well. But it must be understood, no one must come to the house.

(*The door opens and closes*)

MOLLY: He must go, Mother, he must go at once. We must get rid of him.

MRS MUSGRAVE: (*Afraid*) Yes. Yes. I didn't realise that he was—well, quite as he is. Yes, he must go at once. We must get him out of the house. If we can—

(*Fade. The following disjointed scraps of conversation are connected by music suggesting urgency and apprehension*)

OLD WORKMAN: That's it. That's about the last of the leaves.

FIRST WOMAN: (*Cosily*) The evenings are closing in.

A MAN: (*Regretfully*) The evenings are closing in.

MRS MUSGRAVE: (*Fearfully*) The evenings are closing in.

(*Music*)

SECOND WOMAN: All the curtains are drawn at poor Doctor Musgrave's house. Has anything happened, do you know?

THIRD WOMAN: I caught a glimpse of the girl running out to the pillarbox on their corner. She wasn't in black.

SECOND WOMAN: Nobody calls there now. Have you noticed?

THIRD WOMAN: Oh, how the evenings are closing in! It's nearly dark at tea-time.

(*Music*)

MRS MUSGRAVE: Doctor Charles, my daughter and I feel we've made a foolish mistake. We've never . . . let a room before, and perhaps we ought not to have tried. Please understand.

(*Music*)

(*Firmly*) I've changed my mind, Doctor Charles. Will you look for other accommodation, please?

(*Music—continuing throughout the following*)

Doctor Charles, you force me to speak very plainly. I must ask you to leave.

MOLLY: We don't want to share our home. You must go, Doctor Charles.

ALICE: If I were you I should leave 'ere, sir. There's darker houses than this.

DR CHARLES: Not yet. Not yet. My plans may force me to make a change in November, but I'm not ready yet.

MRS MUSGRAVE: Be careful. Humour him. It's only till November.

MOLLY: It's only until November.

ALICE: He's waiting for November.

(*Music ceases*)

MOLLY: I can't ask anyone to the house, not yet. I don't want to explain, Mike. Do you mind?

MIKE: Of course, I don't. But it is rather awkward. Mother wants to call, naturally, and—

MOLLY: I want her to, oh, I want her to! But later. Later, Mike. After November.

MIKE: Well, can *you* come to see *us*?

MOLLY: I'll try, but it's not easy. Understand, Mike.

MIKE: I'm trying to, but you're making it terribly difficult.

(*Music*)

DR CHARLES: (*With suppressed rage*) You were talking to someone at the gate. Who was it? *Who* was it?

ALICE: Only a young policeman friend of mine, sir. I've known him since he was a baby.

DR CHARLES: What were you talking about, eh? What were you talking about?

ALICE: Mainly about his old sergeant, sir. He's dead. Caught a chill at a fire.

DR CHARLES: A fire? What fire?

ALICE: He didn't say, sir. Oh, sir! That great wardrobe put across your other window? How did you get it there?

DR CHARLES: I put it there. I am very strong, Alice, very strong indeed. It would surprise you. Never speak to anyone at the gate. Understand?

ALICE: Yes, sir.

(*Music*)

FIRST WOMAN: I assure you I was turned away on the step. No callers until after November! The maid looked positively terrified.

A MAN: Pure imagination. (*Coughs*) My dear, a hot toddy. My winter cough is starting again. The days are getting very short; Fogs next, I suppose. Oh, damn the people up the street, and attend to me!

(*Music*)

MRS MUSGRAVE: (*Whispering*) Wait until November. Only until November.

MOLLY: (*A breath*) November.

(*Chorus of Cockney kids, coming nearer*)

CHILDREN: Guy, guy, guy, stick 'im up on high, 'ang 'im on a lamp-post and there let 'im die! Guy, guy, guy! Spare a copper, Mister. Spare a copper, Lady. Spare a copper for the guy. Copper for the guy, copper for the guy!

ALICE: (*Softly*) He's taken to wandering out at night. Lock your door.

MRS MUSGRAVE: (*Softly*) Lock your door.

MOLLY: (*Softly*) Lock your door.

CHILDREN: (*Very close*) Guy, guy, guy, stick 'im up on 'igh, 'ang 'im on a lamp-post and there let 'im die! Guy, guy, guy!

MOLLY: (*Hurriedly*) There you are. Quick, take it. Run away.

KID: You don't 'arf look white, lady. Thank you, Lady, thank you.

MOLLY: Hush! Run.

(*A skelter of boots as she closes the window, turning back into the room*)

I don't think I'll go. I'll stay with you.

MRS MUSGRAVE: No, slip out, quietly. He's safe upstairs. Be careful coming back.

MOLLY: I don't like to leave you alone, just to go to a firework party.

MRS MUSGRAVE: I want you to. The Atkinsons are nice people. We may need nice people. Oh, Molly, don't you see we may have to do something terrible, like going to the—the police, if we can't get rid of him any other way. I have dreaded having to do that. People do talk so.

MOLLY: I think I'll stay. You're so helpless, darling, in that chair.

MRS MUSGRAVE: No, I'm all right. Alice will be in the kitchen. I shall stay here at my desk and finish my letters. Hurry, it's nearly eight. Have a *lovely* time.

MOLLY: (*Suddenly*) Mother, didn't Daddy have a—revolver?

MRS MUSGRAVE: (*Catching her breath*) He had, but he—he— must have got rid of it before he died.

MOLLY: Have you looked?

MRS MUSGRAVE: Yes.

MOLLY: Oh, mother darling, let me stay.

MRS MUSGRAVE: No! We're being absurd. We're becoming terrified, hysterical old women, crouching in this awful shrouded house. Hurry, dearest. You'll be late. Give my love to Mike.

MOLLY: Mike? Oh, all right. Goodbye, Mother.

MRS MUSGRAVE: Goodbye, darling. Be very quiet coming in.

(*Door closes. Silence. Children in the distance—Guy, guy, guy, etc. Silence. Door opens softly*)

(*Checking a scream*) Oh! Oh, it's you, Doctor Charles. I didn't hear you knock.

DR CHARLES: I didn't knock. I should have done so, I realise that. I wanted to talk to you. I'm going to sit down. We're alone in the house. Did you know?

MRS MUSGRAVE: Alone?

DR CHARLES: Yes, your daughter's gone out. I thought she would have told you. I've sent Alice down to the chemist's. I wanted a new razor. She may be quite a time.

MRS MUSGRAVE: I see.

DR CHARLES: Do you? I wonder. I haven't been able to consider you before because I've been so busy.

MRS MUSGRAVE: (*Faintly*) Busy?

DR CHARLES: Yes, with my plans. My plans take a lot of time because they have to be made with extraordinary care. Otherwise they wouldn't be so successful. It's vital that they should be successful. Mrs Musgrave?

MRS MUSGRAVE: Yes?

DR CHARLES: Do you know, I'm going to talk to you. I'm going to tell you. Long ago, when I made my plans before, they were all spoiled for me because I had no one to tell. Do you understand?

MRS MUSGRAVE: I—I don't think I do.

DR CHARLES: No. How could you? But you will. I'll tell you. My plans are all finished. Today is the fifth, you see, and in four days' time it will be the ninth. I shall begin where I left off. Then everyone will recognise me. That's logical, isn't it?

MRS MUSGRAVE: Do you mean that in four days you will be leaving here?

DR CHARLES: Oh, yes, I should hardly stay. No, I shan't stay here, but you will, you know; you and Molly and Alice. You'll stay here for ever.

MRS MUSGRAVE: Doctor Charles, what do you mean? What do you mean?

DR CHARLES: I'll show you. First I'll take your letters. Another book for that old aunt, I see. How kind you are, and how quiet. Then I'll show you my maps; the old one and the new one. I like maps. They're so useful if one's moving about in a hurry, or—in the dark. You'll find them fascinating.

MRS MUSGRAVE: (*With courage*) Yes, show me the maps. Go and fetch the maps.

DR CHARLES: You really want to see them?

MRS MUSGRAVE: Yes, yes, I do. Fetch them.

DR CHARLES: I will.

(*He goes out; the door closes*)

MRS MUSGRAVE: (*Laughing*) Lock the door. Quickly! Across the room. Oh, quickly!

(*Sound of wheeled chair*)

Round the table, over the rug. Ah . . .

(*Sound of a key in the lock*)

Oh, my God! Not yet. He's not coming yet. I can't hear him. Listen . . . Listen . . . Listen . . .

(*Sound of a shot*)

Oh!

(*Scream, giving place to a burst of music which continues for a minute, Mrs Musgrave shouting above it*)

(*Shouting*) Help! Please! Somebody come! Help! Help! Please! Help!

(*Banging on street door*)

A MAN: (*Muffled voice*) Can I help you? I can't get in. Open the door.

MRS MUSGRAVE: I can't reach. I'm on the floor . . . in the passage. Fetch the police.

THE MAN: The police? Did you say the police? All right. Wait a moment.

ALICE: (*From behind: she has entered the other way*) Why, Ma'am, what is it? What's happened? Oh, dear. On the floor in the cold passage. Your little chair on its side. Oh, Ma'am! Wait till I help you up.

MRS MUSGRAVE: Alice, I—I heard a shot.

ALICE: No, Ma'am. Lift up your arm. You 'eard a firework. They're going off all the time in the fog. Come up, now. Dear, oh dear, your letters all over the floor!

MRS MUSGRAVE: No. I tell you it was a shot. There was a shot upstairs, in—in *his* room. I came out of the sitting-room so quickly that I struck my wheels against the stair and the chair overturned. Someone's gone for the police.

ALICE: Then they'll fetch Curly. I've just walked up the road with him. We heard plenty of bangs, but I couldn't say I heard a shot.

MRS MUSGRAVE: Go up! Go up and see!

ALICE: But you're in a dreadful state, Ma'am. Your poor hands and dress that dirty.

MRS MUSGRAVE: Never mind me. I'm not hurt. Go and see.

ALICE: I will. I wonder he hasn't come out, with all this noise.

(*Steps on the stairs. Banging. Silence. More banging*)

(*From the top of the stairs*) He won't answer. Wait. I'll fetch somebody.

(*She comes down*)

MRS MUSGRAVE: Listen! There's someone there now.

(*There is a knock. Alice opens the door*)

ALICE: Ah, it's you, Curly. Missis thinks she heard a shot upstairs. The gentleman's door's locked and he won't answer.

MINTER: Evening, Ma'am. A shot, Alice? More likely one o' they fireworks. I'll go up, shall I?

ALICE: Yes, you do. Don't walk on the letters, boy. I'll take 'em and pop 'em in the box.

THE MAN: (*Returning*) I'll do that, shall I? I heard somebody call for the police and I happened on this officer not a dozen yards from the house.

MRS MUSGRAVE: Oh, that was kind of you! Yes, if you would take the letters. The plllarbox is just outside.

MINTER: (*From the top of the stairs*) Open up, sir!

(*Knocks*)

Open up, if you please! Open up!

(*Silence*)

(*Minter comes down heavily*)

He don't reply, Ma'am, and the door's locked, but the lights are on in there. If you've no objection I'll go and get a ladder and take a look through the window.

MRS MUSGRAVE: Yes, yes. That's the thing to do. Through the window. We've got a ladder, haven't we, Alice? I heard a shot. Oh, I know I heard a shot!

ALICE: There, Ma'am, there! Why, you're white as a sheet, and *that* dirty from the old passage. Let me push you in the bedroom and I'll put something round you and get you clean. The fall's upset you. The ladder's out at the back, Curly. You can't miss the shed.

MINTER: I'll find it.

MRS MUSGRAVE: Go with him, Alice. Something terrible has happened. I'm afraid . . . oh, I'm afraid!

(*Scene shifts to outside*)

ALICE: I'm 'olding the ladder. My word, this fog chokes you. Can you see anything, Curly?

MINTER: (*Above*) Not yet, I can't.

ALICE: There's a crack in the curtains. I can see the glow. Can you see in now?

MINTER: My lord! (*With excitement*) I'm a-going to break this 'ere window with my truncheon.

(*Splintering of glass*)

Hold hard on the ladder, Alice. I'm a-going in.

(*Fade back to the November Club, murmurs, etc. Minter's voice ages*)

Well, gentlemen, everybody in the world now knows what I found that night. The man who called himself Doctor

Charles—we never found another name for him—was lying on his face on the floor. He had been shot clean between the eyes. The door was locked on the inside and the key was on the mat. There was also a bolt on the door which was thrust firmly home. On a table near the body were two roughly drawn maps, without lettering, and I remember getting a thick ear from my superior when I suggested that one of them traced exactly the itinerary of the Ripper murders of eighty-eight. But the most extraordinary thing was that there was no revolver either in the room or anywhere in the house. There was a thorough police search—and I need not tell you what that means. To all intents and purposes the man died in a box sealed from the inside, and the gun he was shot with might well have been a phantom. There was never a trace of it found anywhere. The only possible weapons in the room were a very fine set of surgical instruments. Yet he was shot and the bullet was extracted from his head.

CHAIRMAN: Well, well! Fingerprints?

MINTER: That was early days. We weren't so scientific then. Some sort of smudge was found on the key but it proved nothing. The bolt was clean.

GUEST: (*Strong Czech accent*) But there were suspects at the time, yes?

MINTER: Well, there was the boy, Mike Atkinson, and the girl Molly. They admitted they had wandered away from their firework party, and their story was that they strolled about in the fog, talking. They were questioned but it seemed fairly obvious that neither of them could have entered or left a room whose only door was locked and bolted on the inside and whose only available window was twenty feet above ground and fastened. Alice had an alibi; she was with me.

SECOND GUEST: (*Pedantlc English voice*) Yes, a most extraordinary case. I remember it well. As I recall, the revolver was never found and the man was never identified.

MINTER: Never, Professor. The whole district was searched without result. And as for Doctor Charles, his only links with the outside world were his Tuesday registered letters and they ceased to arrive. The case had been widely reported in the press, you see. He left no papers other than the two maps. Nothing to show if he was the Ripper of eighty-eight or if he wasn't. I know what I thought at the time, though, and I know what I believe now.

CHAIRMAN: It's a swell mystery, Minter. Thank you. A swell mystery.

(*Murmurs of approbation. Some clapping*)

LE BLANC: (*With malice*) J.J., my friend, you are strangely silent.

J.J.: (*Grunting ferociously*) A fine wine, this. Very full, very round. The case? Oh, elementary. Perfectly obvious what happened.

(*Sensation*)

LE BLANC: Mon Dieu, mon ami, you are ungenerous. You are also absurd.

CHAIRMAN: Snap out of it, J.J. This is where you add a little zero to that famous list of yours.

J.J.: Not at all. I may say Minter has told his story very clearly, but there is a vital section he has left out. It is an important omission because—ah—it contains the solution to the mystery.

CHAIRMAN: Omission?

J.J.: Exactly. What happened between the time that Mrs Musgrave told Charles that she would like to see his maps, and the time she heard the shot?

MINTER: How do you mean, J.J.?

J.J.: I invite you to think back. Mrs Musgrave and Charles were in her sitting-room. She had been writing letters.

(*Fade back to Mrs Musgrave and Doctor Charles*)

DR CHARLES: I should hardly stay. No, I shan't stay here. But you will, you know; you and Molly and Alice. You'll stay here for ever.

MRS MUSGRAVE: Doctor Charles, what do you mean? What do you mean?

DR CHARLES: I'll show you. First I'll take your letters and put them in the hall, so.

(*Goes out, to return at once, his voice receding and then returning*)

And now I'll show you my maps. You won't understand them at first but I'll explain them. Shall we go?

MRS MUSGRAVE: I can't come up, Doctor Charles. I'm in my chair. You go and fetch them.

DR CHARLES: So that you can lock the door? Oh, no, that won't do. I'll take you up.

MRS MUSGRAVE: No, don't come near me. No!

DR CHARLES: I can carry you, chair and all. It's very light, you're very small, and I'm very strong. Hasn't Alice told you how strong I am?

MRS MUSGRAVE: Put me down. Oh, please, please! Put me down.

DR CHARLES: Don't make a noise. Don't make a noise. That might bring the neighbours and you'll have to explain. You wouldn't like that, would you? And besides, you're not the screaming sort, are you, Mrs Musgrave? When you're afraid you freeze, don't you, and that's so much more interesting.

MRS MUSGRAVE: (*With tremendous courage*) I'm not afraid of you, Doctor Charles. Not in the least. Not in the least.

DR CHARLES: I advise you to sit very still.

(*His voice, highly intelligent and with new authority, sounds softly through the other noises as Doctor Charles carries Mrs Musgrave up the stairs to his room. We hear him breathing heavily as he sets the chair down, the sound of its wheels, and the opening and closing of the door*)

J.J.: Isn't it evident that she was upstairs when the shot was fired? What was her story? She heard a shot and hurried out of the sitting-room so quickly that she struck the stairs and overturned? How could she have been coming at such speed if she had first to unlock the door? We can only guess at the ensuing conversation, but is that so very difficult?

DR CHARLES: (*His voice coming up as though he has already been talking for some moments*) And here, do you see here? It's a by-way off Spitalfields called Bucks Court. I've put a cross there. And here is the Commercial Road. Another cross there. Further on, further on through the dark, through the fog, we come to Mitre Court. A little cross there. Faster, faster, faster now, to Miller's Court. Miller's Court, on the ninth of November . . . don't these names mean anything to you, Mrs Musgrave? (*Pleadingly*) Don't you remember them? Didn't you hear of them? Surely you did. You were over twenty then. It's not so very very long ago. Don't you remember Miller's Court, November the ninth, eighteen eighty-eight?

MRS MUSGRAVE: (*Facing the truth with horror*) Miller's Court, eighteen eighty-eight! But that was Jack the . . . Oh! (*Suppressed scream*) No . . . no . . . no!

DR CHARLES: Be quiet. Don't you understand? I chose to tell you because you were so quiet.

MRS MUSGRAVE: Go away, go away! (*Screams aloud*)

DR CHARLES: Now you've spoilt it all. Now I shall have to start too soon. Fool! Now—What have you got there? *What have you got there?*

MRS MUSGRAVE: Go back. Go back, or I'll pull this trigger. I mean it, I mean it. Go back.

DR CHARLES: (*Advancing*) Put that revolver down. Put it down.

MRS MUSGRAVE: (*Whispering*) Go back. Go back.

DR CHARLES: (*Closer*) Put it down. Put it down. Put . . .

(*A shot, a sigh and a crash*)

MRS MUSGRAVE: (*Whispering*) What have I done? What have I done? Oh, dear God, what have I done? (*Pause*) *How shall I explain?*

J.J.: (*In the background*) It would not have been easy for her, would it? Of course she'd had her husband's gun concealed in her chair ever since Molly went out. She lied to the girl because she did not want to frighten her, but she knew where the gun was. Probably in the very desk at which she was writing. Men don't dispose of their revolvers before they die. Why should they? They tell some responsible person where they are—their wives, for instance. She was a brave woman, Mrs Musgrave, but too afraid of the neighbours' tongues. (*Slowly*) Poor terrified woman!

MRS MUSGRAVE: (*Breathing hard*) Lock him in! Lock him in! The key. I've got to get the key under the door . . . I can reach the ground, just . . . I can edge the chair close . . . close . . . close . . . now!—Ah—Now the stairs . . . The stairs . . . One flight down . . .

(*Sound of chair*)

I can pull myself out . . . I am strong . . . I told them I was strong . . . I can pull myself out by the banisters on to the floor. Now, my belt. I've thought of this. I've thought what I'd do if there was a fire and I was helpless in my chair. My belt round the axle. Now, push the chair over the edge . . . now down . . . slowly down . . . and me crawling . . . crawling . . . crawling head-first after it. When I was at school I could come downstairs head-first. I could . . . I can . . . I've got to. Chair first . . . dragging me . . . bumping . . . bumping . . . down . . . down . . .

J.J.: (*Quietly in the background while the dreadful sounds continue*) But when she reached the ground the chair overturned and the revolver fell out of the cushions on to the parquet. She couldn't get back, d'you see, and had to invent the tale of hitting the stairs.

MRS MUSGRAVE: (*Whispering, breathless with effort*) The revolver . . . they mustn't find Dad's revolver. Where can I hide it? Where can I hide it? I can't walk. I can't stand. Where can I hide it? . . . The library box! Nell's book box, with the letters on the chest. I can pull myself over to it, if I can only grip the lid. Yes . . . Yes . . . Yes . . . Now. Take out the book and hide it under the chest. Put in the revolver and close up the flap. Alice will post it. Nell will keep quiet. Nell, alone in the country reading the papers, Nell will understand. Now . . . The police! (*Shouting, as before*) Help! Help! Please! Somebody come! Help! Please! Help!

(*Fade back to the November Club. Murmurs of interest and approval. Some dissent*)

CHAIRMAN: Bravo, J.J.! That's dandy. I'll certainly hand it to you. You've got a grand imagination.

VOICES: Remarkable.

I concur.

Bravo!

Extraordinaire.

Ingenious, very.

Wunderbar!

Queer, damned queer.

CHAIRMAN: Curly is looking at you, J.J., as if he's seen some sort of apparition.

MINTER: (*Unsteadily*) Several, several. You've brought it all back like an old song, J.J. It was a grey damp evening, like tonight. Same amount of fog. The girl got her boy, by the way. There was opposition from his family, but he stuck to her, and they're very happy, somewhere up north . . . There's two or three kids, I believe. Mrs Musgrave died not so long ago, and Alice is down in her old home in the country. You're very shrewd, J.J.

CHAIRMAN: Maestro, it's just too bad that you're wrong.

J.J: Wrong? Eh? How's that? Speak up, speak up.

CHAIRMAN: Just one little omission. It's your own word, J.J. The door to the room was not only locked; it was bolted.

(*Murmur of assent*)

I've made a study of that case and I've read many theories. In all of them that bolt provided the one unanswerable snag. The door was firmly bolted on the inside and there were no pin-holes, no bits of string, no fancy-work around it. *It could not have been fastened from the outside.* No, J.J., a commendable effort. I enjoyed it, but it won't wash. That little zero must go up. The first zero on the list!

J.J.: Humph! Excellent port, Mr Secretary. Just fill my glass, will you, Minter? Well told, my boy. Good luck to you.

(*Laughter, chatter, fading into a street scene. Children*)

CHILDREN: Guy, guy, guy, stick 'im in the eye, 'ang 'im on a lamp-post and there let 'im die . . . Sixpence for the guy, Mister. Sixpence for the guy!

LE BLANC: Sixpence! *Tiens!* The times deteriorate. Very well, very well, hold out your 'ands, so. *Va t'en! Va t'en!*

(*Children scatter, run off shouting*)

So you are defeated at last, eh, J.J.? Beaten by a little bolt. It is sad, but then, *mon vieux*, one must be philosophical. Nemesis, they say—

J.J.: (*Furiously*) Philosophical, my boot! I told you it was elementary. It's obvious to a blind donkey who shot the bolt.

LE BLANC: (*Surprised*) How? You know?

J.J.: Le Blanc, use your thick head. Who was the only person who could have bolted that door? Who was the one person who, throughout the whole story, must have followed that wretched family's danger and misery at every step? Who must have heard every detail of the history as it occurred? Who knew the identity of 'Dr Charles' and yet could do nothing to prove it? Who must have seen the whole situation in a single blinding flash the moment his eyes rested on that locked door with the pitiful key probably thrust but half under it? Who alone could have shot the bolt home to make the family safe and the story a miracle?

LE BLANC: But who? You don't mean?—Who?

J.J.: The man who broke the window and found the body. The

man who told the story in such convincing detail tonight. Our guest of honour. That soft-hearted, quick-witted young constable, Curly Minter.

LE BLANC: *Mon dieu*, it is possible! It is conceivable! It is *true*, J.J.!

J.J.: 'Course it's true. Saw it at once.

LE BLANC: But you said nothing. Tonight when you might have triumphed you were silent. You were magnanimous, J.J. You were merciful. That is not like you. Why?

J.J.: (*Briskly*) Two reasons. First the feller asked me not to—all that stuff about the young people. Cry from the heart, that was. She shot in self-defence, d'you see.

LE BLANC: And the other reason?

J.J.: The port. (*With reverence*) Crofts' o-four. The year of the murder, d'you see? Couldn't spoil that. Beautiful stuff. Recognised it at once. No, Le Blanc, I may not be a gentleman, but hell's bells! I hope I'm an artist!

MARGERY ALLINGHAM

Margery Allingham (1904–1966), one of the so-called 'Big Four', remains one of the best known and most popular writers of crime fiction. She was born in Ealing, West London, and, as both her parents were writers and her grandfather an editor, it was not surprising that even as a child she should enjoy writing, producing at the age of seven a journal for her family entitled *The Wag-Tale*, which included serial stories, poetry, a recipe and even an advertisement—for 'sinite of potassium' . . .

Allingham's earliest short story, 'The Rescue of the Rainclouds', was published in April 1917 in *Mother and Home*, the sister magazine of *Women's Weekly*, which was run by her aunt. The author was thirteen years old. By the time she was seventeen, she had written countless poems as well as several monologues and plays, including a three-act drama *Dido and Aeneas*, which was performed at King George's Hall in central London. And the precocious young teenager also completed *Blackkerchief Dick* (1923), a story of pirates in Stuart times, which her father claimed his daughter had been inspired to write by a series of séances.

In 1927, Allingham married Philip Youngman Carter. At around the same time, she resumed her writing career with *The White Cottage Mystery* (1928). This novella was first published as a newspaper serial and, as an innovation in deceit, the solution stands up against other classics of the genre such as Christie's *The Murder of*

Roger Ackroyd. Given the enormous popularity of crime fiction at the time, it was not surprising that the young writer would next try her hand at a full-length mystery and, in emulation of Dorothy L. Sayers and others, create a 'great detective'. That first book was *The Crime at Black Dudley* (1929) and Allingham's sleuth was the dilettante Albert Campion who may or may not have been a viscount or a baron . . . or even a King-in-waiting.

Campion would go on to appear in 17 novels, numerous short stories, and another novella, *The Case of the Late Pig* (1937). At her death Allingham left an unfinished 18th novel, which her husband completed; he would go on to write two more Campion novels and to start a third, which was completed on his death by Mike Ripley, who has also produced four other Campion novels so far. If Campion is Wimseyesque, his manservant certainly has nothing in common with Wimsey's Bunter; the 'large and lugubrious' Magersfontein Lugg is a most original creation, 'graceful as a circus elephant'.

As well as the Campion stories, Allingham wrote many other short stories and novellas, as well as a romantic thriller *The Darings of the Red Rose* (1930), originally published anonymously, and the non-series mystery *Black Plumes* (1940). There is also the trio of thrillers that were originally published as magazine serials under her own name but, when published in book form, were credited to Maxwell March, whom Allingham described as 'a first class hack—he makes the cash' and went on to note that 'Margery Allingham thinks of her reputation'. That reputation rests not only on her ability, like Dickens, to create truly memorable characters and to capture the atmosphere of a place, but also on her considerable strengths as a writer and her clever and playful approach to the construction of a mystery.

However, Allingham's best book may be her least well-known. Written at the request of an American friend, *The Oaken Heart* (1941) is set in the Essex village of Auburn which, even when the book was published, was readily identified as a lightly disguised version of Tolleshunt D'Arcy, the village where Allingham made her home after leaving London with her husband. Her only published book-length work of non-fiction, the book was acclaimed by contemporary critics as an outstanding portrait of how the inhabitants of a typical English village reacted to events, from the slow burning summer before the Munich Conference through to the arrival of evacuees and the coming of the Luftwaffe.

After the Second World War, Allingham would play her part in healing D'Arcy and she would go on to write more novels, including the book that many consider to be her best, the Campion thriller *Tiger in the Smoke* (1952) and the final novel to be published in her lifetime, *The Mind Readers* (1965), which sadly reads more like a children's thriller than a mystery.

'Room to Let' was first broadcast on the BBC Light Programme on 11 November 1947, produced by Martyn C. Webster. It was previously published in the journal of the Margery Allingham Society and in strictly limited editions, on the same day, by the American publisher Crippen & Landru, and the small British publisher The Pyewacket Press.

A Joke's a Joke

Jonathan Latimer

I remember it started the night Barnes played the joke on Tony Paletta. Barnes laughed that hearty laugh of his and hung up the telephone and said, 'Will Tony be surprised when he gets down to the morgue and finds it isn't his wife!' He hit his thigh with the soft palm of his hand.

'That's not funny,' Stewart said. 'It's a damn dirty trick. Try a joke on me and I'll beat your brains out.'

Barnes just laughed. I never could make out if he was afraid of Stewart. He hadn't played a joke on him up to this night I am telling you about, but I think it was only because he had been waiting for the right joke. It seemed as though Barnes had been set down on the earth expressly to play jokes.

It was a year and a half ago he came to work on the copy desk—sometime in November. I didn't have much to do with him until he was put on the dogwatch in May. Until then I saw him only a short time each day and his hands were the one thing I noticed about him. They were very soft and white, like the well-cared-for hands of an old woman.

George used to tell me about his jokes. George didn't like him very well because of the joke he played on Emma Doyle. She did obits and interviews for the paper and her eyes watered when she looked at anybody and there was always a wisp of mud-coloured hair across her cheek. Barnes played the joke on her in January, on the day after she had interviewed Kent Porter, the motion picture star, at the Palace Hotel. She had come back to the office, George said, full of cocktails and very excited over the intimate conversation she had had with Porter. He was the kind of man she hadn't believed existed outside novels, she told George, pushing back the wisp of hair that was like a smudge of soot across her cheek. She was so excited she couldn't work her typewriter and when Cowles, one of the rewrite men, offered to do her story and asked her what she wanted to write, all she could say was: 'He's simply divine! He's wonderful!'

The next afternoon there was a phone call for Emma. It was Barnes imitating Kent Porter's voice. He asked Emma if she would like to go to Hollywood with him. He said she resembled his mother and was the only girl he'd seen with whom he felt safe and would she go?

'As your secretary?' Emma asked over the telephone.

'As my wife,' said Barnes in Porter's voice.

Emma's face got pale and her eyes filled with tears and she ran into old Bronson's office and quit her job and took a cab over to the Palace Hotel, George said. Only Kent Porter had left for Hollywood on the morning train.

Barnes thought this was a great joke even though Emma was too ashamed to come back to work and had to go live with her folks in Vermont when she couldn't get another job.

He did pull some good jokes. You are bound to hit upon a funny gag if you keep trying long enough. He certainly tried. He had all the small-boy tricks: electric shock machines, imitation ink wells that looked as though they had been overturned and had spilled ink over everything, exploding cigars, a water-shooting stickpin device that buzzed when you shook hands with him—I don't remember how many other things. And the faces he'd make! Suddenly he'd stare under the copy desk with bulging eyes, pretending there was a snake or something on the floor. Or he'd pretend he was dying of a heart attack. Once he put soap in his mouth and pretended he was mad. It got so nobody would pay any attention to him.

Nobody except Stewart. It was Barnes's laughter that annoyed Stewart—and his slapping his thigh with that soft old woman's hand. 'Shut up!' Stewart would yell when we three were together on dogwatch. 'Shut up or I'll beat your brains out.' Barnes would just go on laughing.

Most of the time we three got along well enough. We'd talk after the First Final had been put to bed. Barnes would talk about the jokes he had played and about his wife. I don't know which he thought about most. I never saw his wife, but George met her with Barnes at Jacques' Cabaret over on Whiteacre Street one Saturday night. He said she was beautiful. He said she sat at a table with Barnes all evening, tall and slender and dark. Barnes talked and laughed that hearty laugh of his; his eyes fixed on her face like an adoring hound dog, but she didn't look at him. Her dark, oval face was impassive, uninterested, almost sullen. She had jet black eyes, but when she looked at you there were golden specks in them, George said. He wondered how Barnes had managed to marry her until he heard she came from a little town. Barnes had probably seemed like the best she could do.

Stewart, when he wasn't sore at Barnes, would talk about women. He was a handsome man, and a lady-killer. He had a new girl every month or so. When most of us got involved with a woman we floundered around like a fish in a rowboat. But Stewart would make a clean break. They'd call him on the telephone just once. I don't know what he'd say to them, but they'd never call again. They'd simply disappear from his world.

That was the kind of thing they'd talk about until the night Barnes played the joke on Tony, sending him down to the morgue to identify his wife. Of course, his wife wasn't there. She'd run away from Tony three years before and hadn't been heard of since. It was just Barnes's idea of a joke. It certainly upset Tony. But what I am telling you about started that same night with a woman calling Stewart. I remember Stewart looking puzzled while he talked. I heard one sentence he said: 'But I assure you I am nice when you know me.'

When he finished he came up to the city desk.

'More girl trouble?' I asked.

'I don't know,' he said. 'That dame called me just to say she doesn't like me.'

For a week the woman called Stewart every night to tell him how much she disliked him. He was intrigued and tried to make a date with her. Each time the conversation was longer. Then, about the tenth day, she let him take her out to supper. He came to work that night very excited, saying she was the best-looking girl he'd ever seen. But she hadn't promised him another date; had only agreed that he might possibly take her out to supper again.

'I don't understand what she wants,' Stewart said. 'I certainly never saw her before.'

Barnes burst out laughing.

'What's so funny?' Stewart asked.

Barnes just laughed.

After a couple more weeks I could see Stewart was hard hit. With all his other girls he had set the pace, dictated how often and where they'd meet. But this one was different. She dictated. He'd been able to take her out to supper twice more, but that was all. She wouldn't tell him her name or where she lived, or when they could have another date.

'I've never seen a girl like her,' he said.

Barnes shouted with laughter and slapped his thigh with his soft hand and later that night, while Stewart was out for coffee, he told me about her.

His wife was the woman on the phone. It was all a joke on Stewart. The idea was to get him really mad about her and then have him out for dinner. 'Imagine his surprise,' said Barnes. 'Finding his dream girl married to me.'

The idea was to carry it on for two more weeks. 'I'll give him one more date with her,' he said. 'That's all.'

The next day he let the rest of the office in on the secret. Everybody thought it was a good joke on Stewart, figuring it was time he took a beating from a woman. And from then on Barnes chuckled all the time. He was certainly pleased with his joke. I think he felt the night Stewart came to dinner and was introduced to Mrs Barnes would more than even the nasty remarks he had taken from him.

In fact the score was being evened right along. One night Barnes was talking about some cornbread his wife had cooked.

'Who wants to be married to a hag who can cook?' Stewart said. 'You can always hire a cook.'

'Mary Lou's pretty,' Barnes said. 'I'll bet you she's just as pretty as the girl who's always calling you up.'

'Don't be dumb,' Stewart said. 'No girl with looks would marry a slob like you.'

Barnes laughed and slapped his thigh.

One night shortly after Barnes had let the others in on the joke, George dropped in to see me on his way home from a party. It was Stewart's night off, and George said he'd seen him and Barnes's wife dancing at the 21 Club.

'She can act,' he said. 'You'd think she was nuts about Stewart. They danced cheek to cheek and most of the time she had her eyes closed.'

Later I asked Barnes when he was going to hold the dinner for Stewart.

'After he's had the date with her,' Barnes said.

'I thought you told me last week you were only going to let Stewart have one more date,' I said.

'I did,' Barnes said. 'I haven't let him have it yet.'

I didn't say anything, but I was just as well pleased, when the time came for the pay-off, that I had to work and couldn't accept Barnes's invitation to the dinner. Knowing, or maybe suspecting what I did, I would have been uncomfortable. George went, though, and I heard all about it.

'They either act well or you're wrong,' George said.

Stewart turned fire red when Barnes introduced him to Mary Lou and made an obvious effort to hide his surprise.

'Why . . . why, how do you do!' he said to her.

Barnes's laughter filled the room and Stewart turned to him, at first astonished and then angry. 'I get it,' he shouted. 'Another of your funny jokes.'

He took his hat and started to leave, but Barnes begged him to stay. Suddenly he laughed. 'That was a good one,' he said. 'Imagine my falling in love with Barnes's wife.' He looked at Barnes. 'I never thought she'd be beautiful.' He looked at Mary Lou. 'Or so good an actress.' There was just the right shade of bitterness in his voice.

After that the dinner went along fine, George said, except for Barnes's hearty laughter breaking out at intervals and making the plates rattle. Mary Lou was very quiet and kept her eyes on the table, not looking at Barnes or Stewart. She had beautiful eyelashes, George said.

Of course, Stewart took an awful kidding from the boys in the office. That is, up to the time he ran away with Mary Lou.

JONATHAN LATIMER

The son of a lawyer, Jonathan Latimer was born in Chicago in 1906. He was named, like his father, after Major Jonathan Latimer, an ancestor who had served with George Washington in the American War of Independence.

In the late 1920s, after graduating from Knox College in Galesburg, and travelling in Europe, Jack Latimer became a crime reporter and re-write man for the *Chicago Herald Examiner* and, later, the *Chicago Tribune.* Latimer enjoyed journalism and in 1934 he came to the attention of Harold Ickes, Roosevelt's Secretary of the Interior and director of the Public Works Administration. Impressed by a 'needle job' that the young journalist had done on him for the *Tribune*, Ickes offered Latimer a job at double his newspaper salary and it was this, as well as perhaps his father's friendship with the politician, that led him to change careers and move to Washington. At the PWA, Latimer worked as part of a team engaged to ghost-write for Ickes a book on the PWA's role and achievements. That Latimer's duties were light is clear from the dedication to his first novel, thanking the PWA 'which made this project possible', and the experience of working alongside 'Honest Harold' Ickes would be reflected ten years later in Latimer's screenplay for the Faustian thriller 'Alias Nick Beal', released in 1949.

In Latimer's first novel, *Murder in the Madhouse* (1935), a private detective has himself admitted to a sanitarium to investigate queer goings on which lead, of course, to murder. The mystery would be the first of a series of five books featuring the 'glib-tongued, hard-eyed' and hard-drinking gumshoe Bill Crane and his sidekick Doc Williams. The Crane mysteries combine a 'tough' crime story with wisecracks, and three were filmed with the American actor Preston Foster in the leading role.

Jack Latimer found mystery-writing easy: 'Some people get the solution first and write backwards', he told one interviewer, 'but that's the coward's way out. I just get a good, bloody situation—a couple of corpses reeking of whiskey and a stray redhead—and then I solve the crime myself.'

During the late 1930s, alongside the Crane mysteries, Latimer got the closest he ever came to a classical detective story, writing *The Search for My Great Uncle's Head* (1937) under the pen name of Peter Coffin. This was followed by the atypical Congo-set adventure *Dark Memory* (1940), which harked back to Latimer's first published story about slave-running in Africa, for which he had earned $250. In 1941 a non-series 'hard-boiled' mystery, *Solomon's Vineyard*, was published, but the novel was considered so violent that it was edited and the unexpurgated text was not published in America until some 40 years later.

Around this time, Jack Latimer and his wife moved to La Jolla, California, where he played tennis daily and began writing for the cinema, mainly for Paramount and RKO, working from 8 o'clock to noon each day in a room overlooking the sea. Taking from 10 to 12 weeks to deliver a screenplay, he wrote for Frank Capra, among other directors. Some of Latimer's most notable scripts are *The Big Clock* (1948), based on Kenneth Fearing's classic novel, and *Night Has a Thousand Eyes* (1948), adapted from the novel by Cornell Woolrich, originally published under the pseudonym George Hopley. Another is the survival thriller *Back from Eternity* (1956), filmed with Anita Ekberg, and the William Holden vehicle *Submarine Command*, (1951), which was informed by Latimer's experience of working with the US Navy during the Second World War.

In the late 1950s, Latimer wrote two more mysteries, which would turn out to be his final novels: *Sinners and Shrouds* appeared in 1955, 14 years after *Solomon's Vineyard*, and the last, *Black is the Fashion for Dying* (published in Britain as *The Mink-Lined Coffin*) was published in 1959.

As a writer, Latimer's philosophy was simple: 'Analyse what will sell and write that.' In the 1930s, after his sinecure in Washington, he was satisfied that mysteries were the easiest way to earn what he called 'eating money'. By the 1940s, it was clear that writing for the cinema would be even more profitable, and by the late 1950s he recognised that the future was in television. Between 1960 and 1965, he wrote dozens of scripts for the immensely popular series *Perry Mason*, starring Raymond Burr. The high fees, and more importantly the lucrative residuals he earned from the widely syndicated repeats of *Perry Mason*, made Jack Latimer rich. By 1968, in his early 60s, he had simply lost his incentive to work: he was, he felt, 'no longer a hungry writer'. Apart from a single episode for the television series *Columbo*, first broadcast in 1972, he never wrote again.

In 1983, Jonathan Latimer died of lung cancer at his California home. 'A Joke's a Joke' is his only known short story and was first published in *This Week* on 1 May 1938.

THE MAN WHO KNEW

Agatha Christie

Something was wrong . . .

Derek Lawson, halting on the threshold of his flat, peering into the darkness, knew it instinctively. In France, amongst the perils of No Man's Land, he had learned to trust this strange sense that warned him of danger. There was danger now—close to him . . .

Rallying, he told himself the thing was impossible. Withdrawing his latchkey from the door, he switched on the electric light. The hall of the flat, prosaic and commonplace, confronted him. Nothing. What should there be? And still, he knew, insistently and undeniably, that something was wrong . . .

Methodically and systematically, he searched the flat. It was just possible that some intruder was concealed there. Yet all the time he knew that the matter was graver than a mere attempted burglary. The menace was to *him*, not to his property. At last he desisted, convinced that he was alone in the flat.

'Nerves,' he said aloud. 'That's what it is. Nerves!'

By sheer force of will, he strove to drive the obsession of imminent peril from him. And then his eyes fell on the theatre programme that he still held, carelessly clasped in his hand. On the margin of it were three words, scrawled in pencil.

'Don't go home.'

For a moment, he was lost in astonishment—as though the

writing partook of the supernatural. Then he pulled himself together. His instinct had been right—there *was* something. Again he searched the small service flat, but this time his eyes, alert and observant, sought carefully some detail, some faint deviation from the normal, which should give him the clue to the affair. And at last he found it. One of the bureau drawers was not shut to, something hanging out prevented it closing, and he remembered, with perfect clearness, closing the drawer himself earlier in the evening. There had been nothing hanging out then.

His lips setting in a determined line, he pulled the drawer open. Underneath the ties and handkerchiefs, he felt the outline of something hard—something that had not been there previously. With amazement on his countenance, he drew out—a revolver!

He examined it attentively, but beyond the fact that it was of somewhat unusual calibre, and that a shot had lately been fired from it, it told him nothing.

He sat down on the bed, the revolver in his hand. Once again he studied the pencilled words on the programme. Who had been at the theatre party? Cyril Dalton, Noel Western and his wife, Agnes Haverfield and young Frensham. Which of them had written that message? Which of them *knew*—knew what? His speculations were brought up with a jerk. He was as far as ever from understanding the meaning of that revolver in his drawer. Was it, perhaps, some practical joke? But instantly his inner self negatived that, and the conviction that he was in danger, in grave immediate peril, heightened. A voice within him seemed to be crying out, insistently and urgently: 'Unless you understand, you are lost.'

And then, in the street below, he heard a newsboy calling. Acting on impulse, he slipped the revolver into his pocket, and, banging the door of the flat behind him, hurriedly descended the stairs. Outside the block of buildings, he came face to face with the newsvendor.

''Orrible murder of a well known physician. 'Orrible murder of a—paper,' sir?'

He shoved a coin into the boy's hand, and seized the flimsy sheet. In staring headlines he found what he wanted.

HARLEY STREET SPECIALIST MURDERED.
SIR JAMES LAWSON FOUND SHOT THROUGH
THE HEART.

His uncle: Shot!

He read on. The bullet had been fired from a revolver, but the weapon had not been found, thus disposing of the idea of suicide.

The weapon—*it was in his pocket now*: why he knew this with such certainty, he could not have said. But it was so. He accepted it without doubt, and in a blinding flash the terrible peril of his position became clear to him.

He was his uncle's heir—he was in grave financial difficulties. And only that morning he had quarrelled with the old man. It had been a loud bitter quarrel, doubtless overheard by the servants. He had said more than he meant, of course—used threats—it would all tell against him! And as a culminating proof of his guilt, they would have found the revolver in his drawer . . .

Who had placed it there?

It all hung on that. There might still be time. He thought desperately, his brain, keen and quick, selecting and rejecting the various arguments. And at last he saw . . .

A taxi deposited him at the door of the house he sought.

'Mr Western still up?'

'Yes, sir. He's in the study.'

'Ah!' Derek arrested the old butler's progress. 'You needn't announce me. I know the way.'

Walking almost noiselessly upon the thick pile of the carpet, he opened the door at the end of the hall and entered the room.

Noel Western was sitting by the table, his back to the door. A fair, florid man; good looking, yet with a something in his eyes that baffled and eluded. Not till Derek's hand touched his shoulder, was he aware of the other's presence. He leaped in his chair.

'My God, you!' He forced a laugh. 'What a start you gave me, old chap. What is it? Did you leave something behind here?'

'No.' Derek advanced a step. 'I came to return you—*this*!'

Taking the revolver from his pocket he threw it on the table. If he had had any doubts, they vanished now before the look on the other's face.

'What-what is it?' stammered Western.

'The revolver with which you shot James Lawson.'

'That's a lie.' The denial came feebly.

'It's the truth. You took my latchkey out of my overcoat pocket this evening. You remember that your wife and I went in the first taxi to the theatre. You followed in another, arriving rather late. You were late because you had been to my rooms to place the revolver in my drawer.'

Derek spoke with absolute certainty and conviction. An almost supernatural fear showed upon Noel Western's face.

'How—how did you know?' he muttered, as it were in spite of himself.

'*I* warned him.'

Both men started and turned. Stella Western, tall and beautiful, stood in the doorway which connected with an adjoining room. Her fairness gleamed white against the sombre green of the window curtains.

'I warned him,' she repeated, her eyes full on her husband. 'Tonight, when Mr Lawson mentioned casually something about returning home, I saw your face. I was just beside you, although you did not notice me, and I heard you mutter between your teeth "There'll be a surprise for you when you do get home!" And the look on your face was—devilish. I was afraid. I had no chance of saying anything to Mr Lawson, but I wrote a few words on the programme and passed it to him. I didn't know what you meant, or what you had planned—but I was afraid.'

'Afraid, were you?' cried Western. 'Afraid for *him*! You still may be! That's why I did it! That's why he'll hang—yes, hang—hang—hang! Because you love him!' His voice had risen almost to a scream, as he thrust his head forward with blazing eyes. 'Yes—I knew! You loved him! That's why you wanted me to see that meddling old fool, Lawson, who called himself a mental specialist. You wanted to make out I was mad. You wanted me put away—shut up—so that you could go to your lover!'

'By God, Western,' said Derek, taking a step forward with blazing eyes. He dared not look at Stella. But behind his anger and indignation, a wild exultation possessed him. She loved him! Only too well he knew that he loved her. From the first moment he had set eyes on her, his doom was sealed. But she was another man's wife—and that man his friend. He had fought down his love valiantly, and never, for one moment, had he suspected there was any feeling on her side. If he had known that—he struggled to be calm. He must defend her from these raving accusations.

'It was a conspiracy—a great conspiracy.' The high unnatural voice took no heed of Derek. 'Old Lawson was in it. He questioned me—he trapped me—found out all about my mother having died in an asylum (Ha ha! Stella, you never knew that, did you?). Then he spoke about a sanatorium—a rest cure—all lies! Lies—so that you could get rid of me and go to your lover here.'

'Western, you lie! I've never spoken a word to your wife that the whole world couldn't hear.'

Noel Western laughed, and the laugh frightened them both, for in it was all the low cunning of a maniac.

'You say so, do you? *You* say so!' Carried away by fury, his voice rose higher and higher, drowning the protests of the other, drowning the sound of the opening door. 'But I've been too clever for you! Old Lawson's dead. I shot him. Lord! what fun it was—knowing who'd hang for it! You see, I'd heard of your quarrel, and I knew you were in pretty deep financial water. The whole thing would look ugly. I saw it all clearly before me. Lawson dead, you hung, and Stella—pretty Stella—all to myself! Ha ha!'

For the first time, the woman flinched. She put up her hands to her face with a shivering sob.

'You say you saw it all clearly before you,' said Derek. There was a new note in his voice, a note of solemnity. 'Did you never think that there was something *behind* you?'

Quelled in spite of himself, Noel Western stared fearfully at the man before him.

'What—what do you mean?'

'Justice.' The word cut the air with the sharpness of steel.

A mocking smile came to Western's lips.

'The justice of God, eh?' he laughed.

'And the justice of men. *Look behind you!*'

Western spun round to face a group of three standing in the doorway, whilst the old butler repeated the sentence that his master's words had drowned before.

'Two gentlemen from Scotland Yard to see Mr Lawson, sir.'

An awful change came over Noel Western's face. He flung up his arms and fell. Derek bent over him, then straightened himself.

'The justice of God is more merciful than that of men,' he said. 'You do not wish to detain me, gentlemen? No? Then I will go.' For a moment his eyes met Stella's, and he added softly: 'But I shall come back . . .'

AGATHA CHRISTIE

Agatha Christie (1890–1976) was born and raised in Torquay, Devon. After completing a rather sentimental 'first novel', *Snow upon the Desert*, Christie—thankfully—turned her hand to crime. For *The Mysterious Affair at Styles*, inspired by a local group of Belgian refugees, she created Hercule Poirot, one of the best loved and most enduring sleuths of the Golden Age. Although the book had been rejected by at least two publishers before being accepted by Bodley Head, it was an immediate sensation and more books followed, as well as short stories. These included three Poirot series for *The Sketch*, which were very similar in style to the Sherlock Holmes adventures of Sir Arthur Conan Doyle.

For over five decades, demonstrating the truth of her own description of herself as 'a perfect sausage machine', Christie produced novel after novel, play after play and short story after short story. While some, inevitably, are less good than others, the quality of her output, especially in the 1930s and '40s, is simply incredible with undisputed classics of the genre including *The Murder of Roger Ackroyd* (1926), *Murder on the Orient Express* (1934), *The ABC Murders* (1936), *Hercule Poirot's Christmas* (1938), *And Then There Were None* (1939), *Five Little Pigs* (1942) and *Death Comes as the End* (1945). Although her reluctance to give interviews resulted in her remaining an enigma throughout her life, her technique and work have been the subject of several extremely entertaining books since her death, including *A Talent to Deceive* (1980) by Robert Barnard, *Agatha Christie's Secret Notebooks* (2009) by John Curran and *Curtain Up: Agatha Christie's Life in Theatre* (2015) by Julius Green.

In 2019, more than 40 years since her death, all of Christie's books remain in print around the world, her work is a staple of the Christmas television schedules and stars clamour to be in films of her best known mysteries such as Sir Kenneth Branagh's *Death on the Nile* (2020), while *The Mousetrap* (1952) continues its record-breaking West End run and an immersive courtroom staging of her story *Witness for the Prosecution* (1925) is well into its second year. Other writers have their day but Agatha Christie seems set to go on and on forever.

The Man Who Knew comes from an updated typescript written some time between 1918 and 1923. It was first published in *Agatha Christie's Murder in the Making* (2011) by John Curran.

THE ALMOST PERFECT MURDER CASE

S. S. Van Dine

Philo Vance lay back in his chair and smiled sardonically.

'You're much too trustin' for this wicked world, Markham,' he said. 'There are any number of perfect crimes. Only, because they *are* perfect the world doesn't hear of them. It's the failures that come to our attention. And it's not always the murderer's fault that he is caught. Fortuitous circumstances often counteract the best laid plans. Very sad . . .'

Vance and John F.X. Markham—New York's district attorney—and I were seated in the lounge-room of the old Stuyvesant Club. We had fallen into the habit, after the solution of the Bishop murder case, of coming together on Sunday nights; and Vance, who at the time was deeply interested in criminology, often discussed famous cases with us.

He had already related on previous Sunday nights the Germaine Berton case, the Pruscha case, the Jaroszynsky case and the Ebergényi case—all of which I have set down in these columns—and tonight, apropos of Markham's comments on 'the perfect crime', he told us of the Wilhelm Beckert murder which took place in Chile in 1909—an almost incredible record of a carefully plotted crime, the detection of which hinged on a mere misunderstood connotation of a simple Spanish word.

'I like to see genius succeed, don't y'know,' Vance remarked lazily, lighting one of his adored Régie cigarettes; 'whether it be in art or commerce or crime. And somehow, I'll always feel that the murderer in the Beckert case was, as the doughty Sergeant Heath would say, given the needle by an unkind fate.'

Early in 1909 (*Vance began, settling himself luxuriously in his chair*), the town of Santiago de Chile was the scene of a crime which, for various reasons, holds unusual interest, both psychological and criminological.

Imprimis, the crime was committed on the premises of the Imperial German Legation. Not only did it give rise to many absurd and fascinatin' complications, legal and otherwise, involving the exchange of letters, notes and memoranda, such as only the ponderous punditic minds of diplomats could have conceived, but the circumstances in themselves were such that, under ordinary conditions, the criminal would probably never have been apprehended.

Its chief interest, however, lies in the astonishing foresight and uncanny powers of minute scheming developed by the perpetrator—qualities which stamp him as one of the world's most distinguished murderers, despite the paltry motivation of the act.

Moreover, only an almost infinitesimal oversight prevented the success of his plot. It was almost a perfect crime. *Eheu!* . . .

The German Legation in Santiago was situated on the ground floor of a two-storey building in the Via Nataniel near the Avenida de las Delicias. The premises consisted of two rooms—a front office and a rear room used for the storage of the diplomatic archives. The staff was composed of the minister, Baron von Boodmann, the secretary, Baron von Welseck, and a clerk named Wilhelm Beckert.

In addition, there was a messenger, porter and general

factotum, Exequiel Tapia, who was an ex-sergeant of the Chilean army.

The duties of this little staff were not arduous: they consisted mainly, I imagine, of friendly luncheons and dinners with various government officials.

In 1907 this *dolce-far-niente* life was temporarily disturbed by an incident which, though rather unimportant in itself, was to have the most astonishin' consequences.

In the little village of Caleu the native peasants had attacked a party of German settlers, who indignantly appealed to the Legation for redress. The matter was investigated with that charmin' leisure so characteristic of diplomatic affairs; but nothing much came of it.

The next year, however, members of the German Legation began to receive sinister letters signed 'Various Chileans'—*varios chilenos*. In these letters the minister was accused of having unjustly prosecuted innocent peasants who had acted in ignorance rather than malice. The letters warned Baron von Boodmann against continuing the suit, and threatened the lives of the members of his staff. Black Hand letters, in fact.

A little later—September of the same year, to be exact—a similar letter was sent to the minister himself, who straightway turned it over to the Chilean police authorities. These noble upholders of the law, anxious to avoid any unpleasantness with the representatives of a foreign government, made a valiant though futile effort to find the author of the sanguinary epistles.

Neither the minister nor Baron von Welseck paid much attention to these threats. But Beckert, who was rather a timid, good-natured soul, was torn asunder. His anxiety mounted by leaps and bounds: repeatedly he expressed his conviction that he was a doomed man. His state of nerves, to judge from the records, was rather pitiful. He was thoroughly convinced that the *varios chilenos* were thirsting for his blood and would some day swoop down on him and end his earthly career.

Beckert was then in his thirty-ninth year. He was a Bavarian by birth, the son of a well-to-do merchant. In 1889 he had emigrated to the new world and entered a Jesuit monastery in Santiago. Two years later, however, he decided that what we euphemistically call marital bliss was more to his liking than a career of pious meditation, and leaving the order, he turned Protestant. In 1899 he married the daughter of a Chilean merchant—a lady named Natalie López—and entered the diplomatic service of his native country as clerk of the Legation.

A few months after the receipt of the threatening letters Beckert dashed excitedly into the office of Baron von Boodmann and reported that three suspicious-looking Chileans had, on the preceding night, chased him for several hours through Santiago's deserted streets. The minister thereupon insisted that this timorous and terrified clerk carry a revolver—much to that gentleman's distress; for Beckert had an instinctive horror of all death-dealing devices.

At this time Beckert developed an almost morbid anxiety for his wife, and at the end of October, 1908, he entrusted to a friend a letter addressed to the German Minister, with instructions that it be delivered after his death, which he believed imminent. In it he thanked his chief profusely for the many considerations shown him, and asked that an enclosed communication be forwarded to Señor Manuel Montt, who was then the President of the Chilean Republic.

In this communication to President Montt, Beckert requested that his murder be not avenged, giving as his reason the fact that, above everything else, he was desirous of avoiding any animosity between his native and his adopted country. He stated that he was convinced that the *varios chilenos* had acted from a mistaken sense of patriotism. His one concern was for his wife, and he asked that she be provided for.

In all, the letter was a rather pathetic outpouring of a man who, as he worded it, considered himself a *reo en capilla*—to wit: a man under sentence of death.

(*Vance sighed lugubriously and crushed out his cigarette.*)

On Friday, February 5th, 1909, about eleven forty-five a.m., the minister and the secretary appeared at the Legation, where they found Beckert at work as usual. The legationary messenger, Exequiel Tapia, had, at half past ten, gone to the residence of Baron von Boodmann and had departed therefrom a quarter of an hour later, ostensibly to return to the Legation. The minister was therefore surprised not to find Tapia at the office. Beckert, in fact, said he had not seen Tapia that morning.

At a quarter of one Baron von Boodmann and Baron von Welseck departed from the Legation, leaving Beckert behind.

Half an hour later, several neighbours saw smoke issuing from the windows of the Legation, and instantly turned in a fire alarm. But the apparatus arrived too late—the roof had already collapsed and the entire building was tottering. The minister himself was informed of the fire about three p.m., and when he arrived it was impossible to save anything. The building had been destroyed.

Baron von Boodmann was naturally anxious about Beckert, especially as the chap was known to have suffered from fainting spells. He feared the worst, and at nine o'clock that night his fears became a certainty when, in the ruins of the rear office, under a stack of office files, a body was discovered totally carbonized. Near the body were found Beckert's silver cigarette case, a nickel watch with fragments of a chain, and a pince-nez.

In view of the threatening letters which had been received, of Beckert's morbid fears, and of the fact that Tapia still remained *perdu*, Baron von Boodmann requested a judicial investigation and demanded that a post-mortem be performed by the Chilean police surgeon.

On the fingers of the charred body were found Beckert's diamond and sapphire ring and his wedding ring bearing the initials 'N.L.' (Natalie López) and the wedding date: 13.3.99. In the ruins of the building a number of telltale articles were unearthed: fragments of clothing, a bloodstained handkerchief, a dagger which had been used as a paper cutter, a blackjack and a blow-lamp.

The result of the post-mortem was far from satisfactory. The official surgeon declared that the state of the body made it impossible to ascertain the cause of death. There was apparently little mystery about the fire, for it was Beckert's habit to burn all office memoranda each day after answering the Legation's correspondence; it seemed obvious that the fire had started in this manner and that Beckert had been stunned by a falling filing cabinet, as the top of his head was badly battered.

On February seventh, Baron von Boodmann received another letter from the *varios chilenos*, which had been posted in Santiago on the morning of the tragedy. In this letter the murder of Beckert and the burning of the Legation were mentioned and held up as a warning against further prosecution of the peasants in Caleu.

As it was known that a few days before the fire Beckert had received a similar communication, the minister felt that further investigation was called for.

Moreover, Tapia had not yet put in an appearance. He was known to have left his home at ten on the morning of the tragedy, and had stated that he had to leave the city that afternoon on official business—a statement which turned out to be untrue. After his visit to the residence of Baron von Boodmann at ten-thirty a.m., he had disappeared.

The minister, in order to quiet persistent rumours that Beckert had been assassinated, requested two German members of the faculty of the university to repeat the post-mortem.

Their report was a model of Teutonic thoroughness and brought to light several important bits of evidence. A piece of the left tibia, about three inches long, was missing: it appeared to have been burned off, probably with a blow-lamp. Also the bone of the left elbow was missing. The skin and the flesh of the skull had been completely destroyed, and the crowns of all incisors and canines in the upper jaw were missing, as well as the crowns of the left incisors and the left canine in the lower jaw. All the other teeth were in perfect condition, with the exception of a small caries in the upper right wisdom tooth.

There was an oval wound about one inch long in the chest. and it was now plain that the dead man had been the victim of foul play. Since the examination was only of a semi-official character, the minister requested that a new and official investigation be undertaken by a mixed body of physicians.

The Chilean authorities, however, anxious to avoid even a suspicion of partisanship in so delicate a matter entrusted the examination to Doctor Westenhoffer and Doctor Aichel, and merely appointed as an assistant the Chilean physician, Doctor Carlos Oyarzún.

The result of the post-mortem was this: the aorta had been severed, and the heart had been penetrated. In the thorax a metal splinter, evidently from a dagger or knife, was found. The injury to the skull had preceded the stabbing. There was a strong probability that the dead man had been struck over the head with a blunt instrument and subsequently stabbed to death. The lower part of the body had lain under some damp office files and had therefore escaped complete destruction; and there remained fragments of a green and white striped shirt bearing the initials 'G.B.'—to wit: Guillermo, or Wilhelm, Beckert.

Mrs Beckert unhesitatingly identified the shirt as her husband's. She was questioned in regard to her husband's teeth, and stated that they had been in perfect condition with the exception of some gold inlays in the upper incisors.

The following day, February ninth, a medical-legal-diplomatic meeting was held to discuss the findings. The Chilean police surgeon, who performed the first autopsy, spent a most uncomfortable half-hour, and finally admitted that he himself had not carried out the autopsy, but had turned over the uncongenial task to a servant at the morgue.

The testimony of Mrs Beckert referring to her husband's clothes and teeth was read, and it agreed in every particular with the findings of the second autopsy. Beckert had, years before, suffered from a fracture of the left tibia and was known to have had a conspicuous scar on his left elbow. It was obvious that these parts of the murdered body had been destroyed in order to make the identification impossible.

The conclusion of the conference, therefore, was that the charred body was that of Beckert, and that he had been stabbed and his body destroyed by fire in order to hide all traces of the crime.

Well, well. It was a most unpleasant situation for the Chilean authorities. Not only had the victim been a member of a foreign government, but the police surgeon had been lax in his examination.

At once there was a feverish activity on the part of the various Chilean government departments. Every possible effort was made to lay hands on the missing messenger, Tapia, whose guilt now appeared conclusive.

But there was one cynical gentleman who was unimpressed. He was the Examining Magistrate, Manuel Bianchi. He passionately resented the slur cast upon the Chilean judicial procedure, and proceeded to con all the reports with a suspicious and eagle eye. After hours of intensive study he discovered one item which seemed to hold out some hope of turning the tables on the *gringos*. And to this doubting magistrate must be given the credit for solving this most amazin' crime.

On the afternoon of February ninth, half an hour before the funeral was to take place, he sent Doctor Germán Valenzuela, the director of the Santiago School of Dentistry, to make a final examination of the teeth of the deceased. The German Minister magnanimously permitted the coffin to be reopened. But nothing was found that disagreed in any particular with the post-mortem findings and the casket was then resealed.

It was a most touching funeral, Markham. At five o'clock in the afternoon the cortège set out for the cemetery. President Montt sent his personal adjutant to attend the obsequies. The coffin was lowered into the grave by eminent Chileans, who had acted as pallbearers by way of showing their sorrow and esteem. Baron von Boodmann emitted various winged words of eloquent eulogy. And to confer upon the occasion an aesthetic atmosphere, the German Liederbund gave musical voice to several mournful dirges.

The same day the Chilean Cabinet called a special meeting, and after the reading of Beckert's letter addressed to President Montt, those assembled in solemn conclave voted unanimously to petition Congress for a grant of twenty thousand pesos for the bereaved widow.

It was most impressive and quite correct. But there was one sceptical gentleman who took the episode with tongue in cheek—to wit: the cynical Magistrate Bianchi. Shrewd fella! While the Liederbund were speeding their departed *Landsmann* into the Beyond with vocal harmony, this Bianchi and his friend, Doctor Valenzuela, were discussing a most startling discovery!

When the erstwhile Natalie López had been questioned regarding her husband's teeth, the two German professors had employed a Spanish-speaking German as interpreter; and this Teuton linguist had made use of the word *dientes* for teeth—a word which, in common Chilean usage, connotes only the incisors, or the teeth that are visible when one laughs. Molars, in Chilean usage, are called *muelas*; and the human teeth in their totality are referred to as *dentadura*.

Now, Mrs Beckert had truthfully answered that her husband's *dientes*—namely his visible incisors—had been perfect, and since she had not been asked about his *muelas*, she had volunteered no information on the subject . . .

Forgive me this little linguistic interlude, Markham old dear. The whole case hangs on it; and it simply goes to show that even 'the perfect crime' is, after all, a matter of chance.

The Chilean members of the commission had apparently overlooked this little difference between *dientes* and *dentadura*; but the perspicacious Bianchi had thought it worth a bit of scrutiny.

Doctor Valenzuela, at Bianchi's suggestion, now asked Mrs Beckert to describe her husband's *dentadura*; and she gave him the satisfyin' information that several of his molars had been missing. Whereupon Bianchi went to Doctor Juan Denis Lay, the dentist who had attended Beckert, and, with the help of the latter's records, ascertained beyond any doubt that five of Beckert's molars had been extracted only a few months previous.

(*Vance grinned a bit sadly.*)

Because of a philological nuance (*he sighed*), a lovely crime went to pot. It's most discouragin'. Since the charred body in the burned Legation possessed a complete set of molars, it now became obvious that the corpse was not that of Beckert. Furthermore, it became increasingly evident that the victim was none other than Tapia; for Madame Tapia informed Bianchi that all of her husband's molars had been intact with the exception of small caries in the upper right wisdom tooth!

In addition, Bianchi recalled, with chauvinistic delight, that Beckert and Tapia had been of similar physical build.

On February tenth, the day after the funeral, the morning papers of Chile published these disclosures. Baron von Boodmann promptly admitted to the Department of Justice that the body of the deceased could no longer be regarded as that of Beckert, and was, in all probability, none other than Exequiel Tapia.

It was now recalled that on February sixth a johnny named Otto—I forget his last name—had come to the police with the information that he had seen and spoken to Beckert between midnight and one a.m.—ten hours after the fire. But as Otto had an unsavoury reputation and was known to have been on bad terms with Beckert, he was not believed and was told to run along and mind his own business.

The German Minister and Baron von Welseck now remembered that, when they visited the Legation offices on the morning of February fifth, the floor had been newly washed, and that Beckert was not wearing his custom'ry pince-nez. The deduction appears inevitable that at that time the unlucky Tapia had already passed to his Maker and that his mortal remains lay hidden behind the office files—a supposition which agreed with the result of the post-mortem. It had been ascertained that death could not have been later than eleven-thirty a.m.

There was no longer any question that the charred body was that of Tapia; and the unescapable corollary was that Beckert had been the murderer, for the latter's belongings found by the body could have been placed there only by Beckert himself.

The German government immediately waived all diplomatic immunity for Beckert, and thus turned the case over to the jurisdiction of the Chilean authorities, who at once launched forth on the man-hunt with great gusto.

The body, which had been buried amid the inspirin' vocal strains of the German Liederbund, was now disinterred, and a third autopsy performed. A microscopic examination of the skin and hair proved that the dead man was of swarthy complexion and had dark hair, whereas Beckert was conspicuously blond.

Immediately following the fire a general alarm had been sent out for Tapia; and on February tenth, simultaneously with the discovery of the true identity of the corpse, a report arrived from the Chief of Police of Chillan, a little town on the Southern Railroad about two hundred miles south of Santiago.

The report stated that a traveller had appeared before the Chillan police with the information that on February seventh he had met a man on the train who, though representing himself as wealthy, had travelled second-class.

The chief of police had regarded this information as suspicious and had sent an inspector to Victoria, the train's destination. The inspector found and talked to a man bearing a passport made out in the name of Ciro Lava Motte, which had been issued by the State Department the preceding January for a voyage to the Argentine. But as the passport seemed to be in order, the inspector had returned to Chillan.

However, on the arrival of the news about Tapia the chief of police, thinking that the mysterious Señor Motte might be the missing messenger, telegraphed to Santiago for Tapia's description.

In Santiago the police immediately checked up on Señor Motte and discovered that in January Beckert had applied to the Foreign Office for a passport for his brother-in-law, giving as that mythical gentleman's name Ciro Lava Motte.

But even this was not sufficient evidence for the Santiago police. They were most careful and thorough. Within a few hours they had discovered that on the day in January when Beckert had applied for the passport he had also bought a blackjack at a local hardware store, had ordered three false boards and a brunet wig, and had bought a travelling suit, leather puttees, a trunk, and a rifle with a leather case—all of which he had inscribed with the initials 'C.L.M.' Beckert had also bought a revolver and cartridges and twenty yards of lamp wick.

While the police were thus engaged in checking up on the preparations of Beckert's perfect crime, the German Minister was endeavouring to find a motive for the murder. It didn't take long, for in going over the missing man's accounts it was discovered that for more than a year Beckert had been forging drafts and discounting them at the bank. It was estimated that he had diverted to his own pocket nearly 50,000 marks ($12,000).

But even this mass of corroboratory evidence did not entirely satisfy the Santiago police. They were treading on delicate ground—the honour of their fair nation was at stake—and so they turned their suspicious eyes upon Beckert's private life. They discovered that he had not been the virtuous family man and model husband that everyone had thought him. He was, indeed, a gay dog, and had spent many leisure hours in the company of charming but fragile *señoritas*.

To one of these light-o'-loves he had written several letters in a disguised hand, signed 'Tito Bera'. He had later confessed to his *dulcinea* the authorship of these amat'ry epistles. The lady produced the letters, and the chirography proved to be the same as that of the author of the letters signed by the *varios chilenos*.

In fact, all these threatening letters had been part of the preparation of Beckert's astoundin' plot. With them he had prepared everyone for his approaching murder. So well had he planted the whole idea that after the crime the identity of the body was hardly questioned.

There was now enough evidence even for the squeamish Santiago police, and a telegraph order for Beckert's arrest was sent to all stations along the Southern Railroad. Beckert had by this time quitted Chillan and was proceeding toward the

Argentine border. But on February thirteenth, barely six miles from the frontier, the *carabinieri* overtook their quarry; and on February sixteenth the author of the almost perfect crime was safely lodged in the bastile at Santiago.

The preparation for Beckert's trial took over six months—the Chilean authorities wished to have an absolutely clear case to present to the court. Also, the legal aspects of the case had to be gone into with great care, for the question of extraterritorial immunity was raised by the defence.

The trial, however, took place on September 2nd, 1909, and ended with Beckert's conviction on all counts. He was not only sentenced to death but given thirty-eight years' penal servitude and fined sixteen hundred pesos—a sweet bit of legal inconsistency, but quite characteristic of legal procedure, don't y'know.

Beckert naturally appealed. Even in Chile such processes are part of the noble game of jurisprudence. But the Supreme Court denied the appeal; and after several stays of execution—so reminiscent of our own legal procedure—the unfortunate gentleman faced a firing squad on the fifth of July, 1910.

Vance lighted another Régie.

'Y'know Markham, my sympathies are all with Beckert. He did a noble and thorough piece of work. He spent almost two years concocting a perfect crime. Really, he should have succeeded . . . No, I fear that I shall never go in for murder. The fickle goddess of chance . . . The perfect crime! Yes, yes. The cards were stacked against the unfortunate Wilhelm. Most distressin', eh what?'

'Yes, very distressin',' mocked Markham. Then: 'There have been curious parallels of the Beckert case in America. There was the H. H. Holmes case, for instance, and the Udderzook case—both attempted insurance swindles.'

'Oh, quite,' Vance returned indolently. 'Criminals are not original. Circumstances, don't y' know. There are parallels in most crimes, human nature bein' what it is. Especially is this true of *crimes passionnels*. They're based on the caressin' theory that one woman differs from another. Silly notion, what?

'Regard our own Snyder-Gray case. Lovers eliminatin' a husband. Very sad. And yet, lovers have been eliminatin' husbands since time immemorial. I shall never be a husband, Markham. Much too dangerous.'

S. S. VAN DINE

'S. S. Van Dine' was the pseudonym of Willard Huntington Wright (1887–1939), art critic, philosopher and champion breeder of Scottie dogs. Wright was born in 1888 in Charlottesville, Virginia, the son of relatively wealthy parents. He was fiercely intelligent and in 1906 he went to Harvard. However, he came down a year later, claiming that 'they had nothing more to teach me'. His first story had been published in 1906 and, after studying art for a year in Paris, he returned to America where in 1907 he married Katharine Belle Boynton, with whom he would have a daughter, and also became literary editor of the *Los Angeles Times*. Three years later he was among the journalists who escaped when the newspapers' offices were destroyed with dynamite, killing 21 staff.

As well as conducting interviews and delivering a regular column on 'New Books and Book News', Wright wrote for the *Times* on all sorts of literary subjects, the most significant of which was undoubtedly a piece lauding a book by H. L. Mencken: it was subsequently through Mencken's influence—and an incendiary essay on Los Angeles—that in 1913 Wright became editor of the prestigious *Smart Set* magazine at the age of only 25. A precocious talent, he was also in demand as a public speaker on literary matters and, more contentiously, on subjects such as the advantages of stupidity in dramatic censorship and England's continuing 'intellectual colonisation' of America as well as women's suffrage, which Wright vehemently opposed. He also reviewed books and theatre for *Town Topics* and other journals like the *North American Review* while remaining editor of the *Smart Set* until he was sacked in 1914.

1914 also saw the publication of *Europe after 8:15*, in which he wrote about Vienna and London while other cities were considered by his co-authors, H. L. Mencken and George Jean Nathan, then the *Smart Set*'s theatre critic; the three had collaborated before for the *Smart Set* under the pen name 'Owen Hatteras'. Other books followed, including *Modern Painting: Its Tendency and Meaning* (1915) and *What Nietsche Taught* (1915), as well as an unpleasantly misogynistic novel *The Man of Promise* (1916) and a series of short crime stories under the pseudonym 'Albert Otis', named for General Harrison Otis, former editor of the *Los Angeles Times*. Another book *Misinforming a Nation* (1917) criticised America's entry into the First World War, prompting some of his former colleagues to shun him, and towards the end of the decade this and various other issues led him to take up drugs.

While Wright worked as literary editor of the *New York Evening Mail* and wrote for magazines such as *Harper's Bazaar* and *International Studio*, his health declined. In 1923, after the publication of his book *The Future of Painting*, he suffered a complete breakdown and the story goes that his psychiatrist—or was it his doctor?—allowed him nothing more stimulating than detective stories which the patient read avidly for the next two years—or was it three?—before deciding that he could do better.

For what would become an immensely successful series of books, Wright adopted a pen name because he felt that 'detective stories come under the head of froth and frivolity' and so might damage his reputation as a serious critic. And so 'S. S. Van Dine' was born. When *The Benson Murder Case* (1926) was published—on the 13th of October, as all of the Van Dine novels would be—the publishers stated that Van Dine was a Harvard graduate, which Wright most certainly was not, and that Van Dine was also 'not only an expert in criminal psychology and in the various Continental and American methods of crime detection but a thorough student of the literature of crime both historical and fictional . . . for many years . . . collecting material and adapting it to detective form for his new series', which at least was partly true.

An untiring self-publicist, Wright made public appearances as Van Dine and also used the name for numerous newspaper and magazine articles in which the fictional Philo Vance analysed notorious non-fictional crimes such as the infamous Hall-Mills murders of 1922. In parallel, under his own name, Wright edited *The Great Detective Stories* (1927), an excellent anthology whose publication fuelled speculation that the famous critic and the reclusive author were one and the same, which was revealed in 1928 by Harry Hansen of the *New York World* not long after Wright, as Van Dine, had prescribed a set of rules for detective stories in *The American* magazine.

In 1929, with the popularity of the Philo Vance stories fuelled by William Powell's portrayal in the films *The Canary Murder Case* (1929) and *The Greene Murder Case* (1929), Wright took self-promotion to a new level when, as Van Dine, he agreed to serve as Police Commissioner of Bradley Beach, New Jersey. Expecting a sinecure, he was shocked when, not long after his appointment, a local man was murdered and he found he was expected to lead the investigation. With newspapers challenging S. S. Van Dine to solve what they termed 'The Pajama Murder Case', Willard Huntington Wright stepped down.

In 1930, not long after the divorce from his first wife, Wright married again, this time to the painter Eleanor Rulapaugh. As Van Dine, while continuing to write the Philo Vance novels, Wright also produced scenarios for twelve 'two-reel detective stories', which were developed into scripts by Burnet Hershey. The films feature the bullying Inspector Carr and Dr Amos Crabtree, a psychology professor; and the scripts of some were published in cartoon form with Philo Vance as the sleuth.

Almost one hundred years after the publication of the first of Philo Vance's twelve murder cases, the detective's affectations have dated badly and even as early as 1931 the character was ridiculed—Ogden Nash spoke for many when he joked that 'Philo Vance needs a kick in the pance'. Undoubtedly, the quality of the books diminishes, albeit erratically, and the last two—*The Gracie Allen Murder Case* (1938) and *The Winter Murder Case* (1939)—are little more than padded scenarios for films starring, respectively, the comedienne Gracie Allen and the ice skating champion Sonja Henje.

Nonetheless, the novels of S. S. Van Dine—at least the early titles—remain classic puzzles of Golden Age detection and Willard Huntington Wright one of the most important figures in the history of the American detective story.

Wright's health continued to decline through the 1930s and he died of a heart attack in New York in April 1939.

One of a series, 'The Almost Perfect Murder Case' was published in *Cosmopolitan* in July 1929.

THE HOURS OF DARKNESS

Edmund Crispin

1

At ten thirty-five p.m. on Christmas Eve, Noel Carter said to Janice Mond:

'This is perfectly senseless, Janice. What does it matter if we *are* discovered?'

'If you're going to play a game at all, Noel,' said Janice sententiously, 'you must play it properly.'

'I didn't ask to play the damned game. Anyway, it's obviously unfair to be hiding outside the house—quite apart from the fact that we shall both be laid low with pneumonia in a few hours. Good heavens, Janice, it's freezing. I don't know how you can stand it. You've got practically nothing on.'

'You ought to be very pleased,' Janice replied coolly. 'After all, Noel, the sole purpose of playing hide-and-seek is to allow people to make love in decent privacy for a few minutes. Nothing will make me believe that Duncan is actually *looking* for anyone.'

'I wish he'd find us,' said Noel unchivalrously. 'I wish he'd find us and take us back to the fire. I should like some whisky. I wish you were a salamander.'

Janice sighed, but made no remark. Noel got up and went to the door of the little summer-house, from which he surveyed the black bulk of Rydalls looming against a star-lit but moonless sky, and the thin sheet of snow, marked only with their own footprints, which stretched bleakly in every direction. A small but chilling wind was moving among the bare branches of the trees in the park, and the only sound was the distant howling of a dog. It rose and fell on the night air with a monotonous persistency which became, after a few minutes, extremely trying.

'Dogs only make that noise,' Noel observed, 'when there are vampires leaving their graves.'

'Come and make love to me, Noel,' said Janice from the gloom at the back of the summer-house.

'Darling, I should love to,' said Noel carefully, 'if it weren't for the fact that my animal heat—which, I may say, is always rather precarious—has now quite deserted me . . . How much longer do we have to stay in this detestable hovel?'

Janice felt in her handbag and produced a tiny gold cigarette-lighter. Its wavering flame lit up her ash-blonde hair and her pretty, petulant, childish features. She could not, thought Noel, be more than twenty. She looked at her wrist-watch, a tiny, jewelled rectangle on her slender wrist.

'Ten minutes,' she announced. 'Then they'll ring the gong, and we can go back, and you can have your damned whisky.' She paused, and then said:

'You don't approve of me, do you, Noel?'

'I think you're very attractive indeed,' he answered—with truth, since the lighter was gleaming on her slim and gently rounded body in its white slipper satin gown, and her bare arms were smooth and soft to look at.

'Then why don't you make love to me?'

'Because'—the remark sounded a trifle priggish—'I just don't make love to every pretty girl I happen to meet.'

'Why not?' she asked disconcertingly.

'I have principles,' Noel replied mendaciously. As a matter of fact he had none.

'You mean you're terrified of getting involved.'

'Very well.' Noel was annoyed at so much perceptivity. 'I'm terrified of getting involved. Also, I'm cold.'

'You needn't worry,' said Janice, with all the scorn of her youth. 'I shan't run after you . . . Damn, this thing's getting hot—'

The lighter fell with a clatter on to the uneven wooden floor of the summer-house. They were in darkness again. Noel dutifully groped about for it.

'I suppose the fact is,' Janice resumed in implausibly casual tones, 'that you're interested in Patricia.'

'Here's your lighter.'

'Thanks. Of course I don't blame you. Patricia's a very attractive girl, though I must say, I wish she wouldn't use that particular shade of lipstick.'

'Puss, puss.'

'Oh, don't be childish, Noel . . . I wonder who it was attacked her the other night?'

They heard a car coming up the drive, its tyres crackling in the frozen snow. The dog gave one last, devastating howl, and then was mercifully silent. When the ignition of the car was turned off, it was possible to hear the high, metallic singing of the telephone wires in the road beyond the low flint wall which bounded the little estate. A freezing gust of wind blew through the summer-house door; Noel shivered.

'A servant, I suppose,' he replied. 'Apparently it was just an ordinary attempt at petty thieving. If Patricia hadn't rushed in and tried to apply ju-jitsu, she wouldn't have got hurt at all.'

'Anyway, I've taken to locking my door at night.'

'Wise girl,' Noel commented ironically. 'But I shouldn't worry. A repetition's not very likely. Besides, nothing valuable was taken.'

'The diary.'

'I don't believe Patricia ever had a diary . . . Oh, what a comfortable way to spend Christmas Eve this is.'

'Will you please put your arms round me, Noel. I'm cold . . .

Lord, that can't be the gong, can it?' Janice sounded distinctly peevish. 'It's five minutes early.'

However, it was undoubtedly the gong. 'I'll tell you why it's early,' said Noel. 'They're making a last attempt to snatch us back from the jaws of the grave.'

'Race you to the front door.'

'You can't race in an evening dress. You'll fall.'

'I'll hold my skirt up. Come on.'

'How you would have enjoyed living in Sparta,' Noel remarked.

But Janice, with a finely feminine contempt for the laws of sport, had already left the summer-house and was running across the white expanse of lawn. A little slip of moon was rising above the trees of the park. Its light was just sufficient to give precision to the outline of Rydalls and to evoke a watery, answering gleam from the bonnet of the car which stood, some hundreds of yards distant, below the steps of the terrace.

Sighing deeply, Noel exerted himself to follow.

He ran clumsily, for his feet were so cold that he could hardly feel them, but he succeeded, nonetheless, in catching Janice up just as she rounded the corner of the house by the billiard-room. Lights flashed out from many of the windows; evidently the game was well and truly over. Giggling noisily, they panted up the terrace steps. These were dangerous, for the snow had hardened into a slippery, irregular surface; and Noel, cursing vehemently, nearly fell down on his face as he climbed them. They came in view of the windows of the long gallery.

'Look, Noel,' Janice gasped, catching him suddenly by the arm. 'Isn't—isn't that sweet?'

Secure in the conviction that Janice had only stopped the race because she knew she was going to lose it, Noel looked.

The long gallery was dimly illuminated by a lamp at the far end, where a door led into a vestibule giving on to the main hall; but in an alcove beyond the window at which they were standing a man and a woman were embracing beneath a branch of mistletoe. The man had his back to them, and since a dinner jacket, in a dinner-jacketed party, provides a very respectable form of anonymity, they were quite unable to make out who he was.

'But the girl's Louise,' Janice whispered.

'Louise?'

'Louise Munro. I know by the jade bracelet she's wearing.' A note of indignation came into Janice's voice. 'I must say, she's being very languid about it all.'

'Well, don't stand and stare at them. It's a perversion.'

'A perversion?'

'Called mixoscopy. Come in and get warm.' They walked on to the front door.

'Kiss me, Noel,' said Janice.

'If you'll promise to come inside immediately afterwards.'

'Of course I promise.'

Noel found it a disturbingly pleasant kiss. Janice knew this, and he knew that she knew. The whole thing, he reflected, was distinctly a defeat for him.

'Now you must keep your promise,' he said.

'Of course, Noel,' Janice replied demurely.

2

The drawing-room, when they reached it, was crowded; virtually the whole party had returned there at the conclusion of the game, and Noel and Janice seemed to be the last to arrive. Their host, Duncan MacAdam, approached them. He was a man of about forty, tall, slim, and immaculately dressed, with prematurely greying hair, the attractive accent of an educated Scot, and a mobile, expressive, rather plump face. He appeared to have money in his own right, and he had bought Rydalls seven years previously. He lived as comfortably as governmental extortions permitted, and spent the greater part of his time in giving house parties. In fact they ran almost non-stop at Rydalls, for MacAdam's circle of acquaintance was large. Yet he seemed to have no intimate friends, and no woman—though many had tried—had, as yet, succeeded in marrying him.

'You've been outside,' he said accusingly. 'That constitutes cheating.'

'I told you,' said Noel to Janice.

'Anyway, Duncan,' Janice returned, 'I don't believe *you* attempted to find anyone.'

MacAdam grinned. 'I found Murchison,' he said, 'who was rather inadequately concealed at the sideboard, and betraying his presence by swilling noises. After that, I admit, I didn't get much further.'

'Why the sudden recall?'

MacAdam grinned again. 'Sorry if it disturbed you. A new guest arrived *in medias res*. Poor fellow, he was a bit distressed at finding the whole house in darkness. I think it must have reminded him of *The Travelling Grave*—you remember?'

'Who is it?' Noel asked. 'Anyone I know?'

'Peter Hadow.'

'The man who writes detective novels?'

'Yes. Come and meet him.'

'Can we meet him somewhere in front of the fire?'

'Of course. You must be frozen. Come along.'

They pushed through the chattering groups of guests towards a huge edifice of flaming logs. The room was brilliantly lighted by two electric chandeliers and a profusion of standard lamps. It was in the Queen Anne part of the house, tall, long, panelled in pine, and richly ornamented on the overmantel, the cornice and the pediment above the door; but the furniture was modern throughout. 'I possess no aesthetic sense,' MacAdam was accustomed to say, 'but my bodily perceptions are very acute . . . Properly sprung chairs I must have.'

Peter Hadow was talking to Patricia Davenant and Richard

Neame. For a specialist in the macabre he looked remarkably jumpy. He was a man of about thirty-five, precise to the point of pedantry in his speech, with an untidy mop of dark hair, a long, thin, enquiring nose, and small, weak blue eyes. He held a glass in one hand, and with the other tapped his pince-nez, in a fidgety manner, against a waistcoat button.

The courtesies were observed; conventional enquiries as to health conventionally disposed of; an antiphonal commentary on the weather and the state of the roads duly accomplished. MacAdam departed to fetch drinks for Noel and Janice.

'Patricia dear,' said Janice, 'what *have* you been doing to your dress?'

'I must go and deal with it,' Patricia Davenant answered. She was a tall and lovely girl, with a splendid head of red hair and a curiously ingenuous manner.

'No further trouble, I hope?' asked Noel.

Patricia smiled and shook her head. 'Just an accident. My shoulder strap broke.'

She was holding the dress hunched up under her left arm. 'I'd better change.'

'Patricia dear, you look charmingly like a Maenad,' said MacAdam, returning with the drinks. 'But as the male element of this party is remarkable rather for modesty than for brains, you're embarrassing everyone. Would you like to be lent a safety pin?'

Richard Neame frowned perceptibly.

Patricia giggled. 'No, thanks. I'll get out of the wretched frock altogether. Excuse me.' She left the room and went upstairs.

'You won't'—Peter Hadow turned to MacAdam—'you won't of course inform the young lady of my reason for wishing to meet her? Or say anything about the book?'

'Certainly not,' MacAdam agreed; there was a twinkle in his eye. 'The young lady,' he explained to the others, 'is Louise. She was tied up with the Forrest case just before the war—or rather

her brother was. Peter based one of his novels on it, and wants to talk to her.'

'You know the book?' Peter Hadow enquired.

'Oh, yes,' said Noel and Janice simultaneously. 'Oh, certainly.'

'Splendid.' Hadow appeared pleased. 'Of course, it isn't published yet,' he added gently. 'There were certain difficulties about libel.'

'It was a murder case, wasn't it?' said Richard Neame. He was a rather colourless man of about thirty-five who was engaged to marry Patricia Davenant. 'Will she want to talk about it?'

'That,' said MacAdam, 'is the problem. Don't for heaven's sake upset the girl, Peter.'

'If she doesn't offer to talk about it,' Hadow assured him, 'I'll drop the whole thing . . . Can you point her out to me, by the bye?'

MacAdam craned his neck to look round the room. 'She doesn't appear to be in here.'

'She was in the long gallery when we came in,' said Janice, 'and I suppose may be there still. There was a man with her,' Janice added rather primly.

'This house seems to be a temple to Aphrodite Pandemos,' MacAdam observed. 'Well, I've no doubt she'll turn up sooner or later . . . Weren't we going to play charades?'

'I'm very good at charades,' Hadow announced unexpectedly, 'so you must put me in charge of one of the sides. But I think I'd better get my car under cover first.'

'Oh, I've told someone to deal with that,' said MacAdam. 'Have another drink, and then I'll show you your room, and then we can make a start. I don't suppose anyone has the least desire to play charades, but I refuse to allow dancing to begin until midnight.'

A quarter of an hour later he was issuing instructions to the party at large—with the exception, that is, of four people who had pleaded age and lack of histrionic ability and had slunk off into the library to play bridge. The party responded with cries of not unmixed enthusiasm.

'And by the way,' said MacAdam, 'it scarcely seems to me that we're all here. Isn't Patricia back yet?'

'Give her a chance,' said Richard Neame. 'You know how long women take over these things.'

'And where is Louise?' MacAdam's plump face grew comical with dismayed enquiry. 'Has anyone seen Louise?'

No one, apparently, had seen Louise since before the game of hide-and-seek.

'But you might check up on the men,' Noel suggested *sotto voce*. He was rather surprised when, in the event, all of them were accounted for.

'We'd better look in the long gallery,' said Janice. 'I hope she isn't ill, or anything.'

A voluntary search-party left the drawing-room. It consisted of Noel, Janice, MacAdam, Peter Hadow, Richard Neame and a middle-aged man named Simon Moore, who was correctly assumed by everyone to be trying to marry Louise Munro for her money. They crossed the hall, with its broad, green-carpeted staircase, passed through the vestibule and entered the long gallery.

It was the least used room in the house, but its size and its polished floor made it eminently suitable for dancing. Consequently there was little furniture in it at this time, apart from a tiny improvised bar, a large radiogram, and rows of chairs against the walls. The standard lamp by the door was still on, but blue velvet curtains had been drawn across the windows. Their footsteps echoed a little as they walked up to the far end.

MacAdam was ahead of the others. They saw him stop abruptly as he reached the alcove, and heard him utter a stifled exclamation. Louise Munro had always been considered an attractive woman, but strangulation and a blood-soaked body are not calculated to enhance anyone's charms.

3

Some fifteen miles away, in the North Oxford home of the university Professor of English Language and Literature, a children's party was in progress.

Its host was seated, glowering, at one end of the drawing-room. He was attempting, simultaneously, to construct a crane out of Meccano, drink a glass of whisky, and keep off a small and solemn-looking girl whose pleasure it seemed to be to buffet him disinterestedly about the ears. His clean-shaven face was ruddy with effort, and his brown hair stood up in spikes from the crown of his head. A few feet away from him, an aged colleague named Wilkes was engaged in improvising a rather lurid and improbable fairy story.

'Heh,' he was saying. 'So the wicked queen left the mirror and ran through the corridors of the great castle, and came to the huge deserted kitchen. And in the floor of the kitchen there was a heavy trap-door bound with rusty iron hinges. So the wicked queen lifted the trap-door and climbed down the damp and slimy steps into the dark dungeons. Heh.'

'Sounds corny to me,' said a rather unpleasant boy.

'What was it like in the dungeons?' asked a saccharine little girl with a blue bow in her hair.

'It was ruddy awful,' said Wilkes ill-advisedly.

'Ruddy awful,' screamed the children in chorus. 'It was ruddy awful.'

In the hall outside, the telephone could be heard ringing. Mrs Fen, a pleasant, plain, bespectacled woman, came in and approached her eccentric husband.

'Gervase,' she said, 'you're wanted.'

'Thank God for that,' said Fen, wiping his brow. The crane by now somewhat resembled a skyscraper in course of demolition by high explosive. 'Look here, it's late. Oughtn't all these children to go home?'

'We'll send them away,' said his wife soothingly, 'when Dr Wilkes has finished his story.'

'Ah,' said Fen. He rose to his feet. An aeroplane driven by elastic sailed across the room and caught him a glancing blow on the left temple. A freckled child of indeterminate sex had got hold of his whisky. Leaving his wife to deal with the situation, he beat a hasty retreat.

'Well?' he said into the telephone. 'Fen here.'

'This is Dick Freeman,' said the Chief Constable of Oxford from his house on Boar's Hill.

'Oh, is it,' Fen replied affably. 'And a Merry Christmas to you.'

'You're not sober,' said Sir Richard Freeman with some certainty.

'Well, don't you believe in celebrating Christmas, you puritanical old dullard?'

'No.'

'Every time you say that,' said Fen reproachfully, 'a fairy dies somewhere . . . What do you want?'

'There's been a murder.'

'A scientist, one hopes.'

'No, a girl. I thought it might interest you to go along.'

'Where is it?'

But for the moment this information was not forthcoming. Heralded by a sound like a cork coming out of a bottle, a feminine voice of positively obscene gaiety enquired whether they had finished.

'No, I haven't,' said Sir Richard Freeman. 'I've hardly begun.'

'A merry Christmas to you.'

'Don't you cut me off,' said Sir Richard with sudden suspicion. 'I'm the Chief Constable. You can't cut *me* off. I'm the—'

There was a dull crackling, like thorns beneath a pot, and then silence. Fen joggled the receiver-rest experimentally two or three times, and then replaced the instrument. From the drawing-room, Wilkes could be heard banging about with the fire-irons in attempt to simulate rattling chains. The freckled child who had seized Fen's whisky was hurried by Mrs Fen through the hall into the cloakroom to be sick. In a few moments the telephone rang again.

'The house is called Rydalls,' said Sir Richard. 'At Sanford Angelorum. And if the blasted exchange cuts me off again I'll have them all by the ears.'

'Or lay them all by the heels, of course,' Fen suggested. 'Sanford Angelorum's a long way away.'

'You've got a car, haven't you?'

'Yes,' said Fen, brightening. 'So I have. Are you going to be there?'

'No. I'm off to bed.'

'Who's in charge?'

'A local man—by name Wyndham. I'll let him know you're coming.'

'That's the way,' said Fen approvingly. 'Sleep tight.'

He rang off, and went into the drawing-room to announce his departure. It was accepted with indifference. A pugnacious little girl took a swipe at his leg, missed, and toppled over. Her wails pursued him out of the house.

He drove to Rydalls in his small red sports car, which was named Lily Christine III, and sang loudly to keep out the cold. His voice mingled hideously with the voices of peregrinating bands of carol singers, woke sleeping dogs, and bedevilled the dreams of rustics.

4

There were already two police-cars standing in the drive when he arrived at Rydalls. He was welcomed by Wyndham, an obese, gentle, worried-looking Inspector of police, and taken into MacAdam's study, which was being used as an office. It was a small room compared with the others in the house, snug, well-to-do, and little suggestive, despite its broad, flat-topped desk, of any kind of work. Despite MacAdam's pretensions to Philistinism, the pictures on the walls showed a certain taste.

'It's a mess, sir,' said Wyndham without further preliminary. He had an unexpectedly high, piping voice. 'And a cruel mess at that.'

'Who was the girl?'

'A Mrs Louise Munro. Youngish, it seems—somewhere in the late twenties, I should say, though no one seems to have any clear idea about her age. Her husband died in a flying accident during the war, when they hadn't been married more than six months. A much older man, I understand, and very well-off . . . Would you like to see the body? It's still on the spot, though we shall have to move it soon.'

'Right. You lead the way.'

They left the study and crossed the hall to the door of the vestibule which led into the long gallery, and which was guarded by a constable. The drawing-room door was ajar, and from it could be heard a subdued hum of conversation.

'Such a hell of a lot of them,' Wyndham commented gloomily. 'If I know anything about it, we shall be here half the night.'

The constable saluted. They entered the long gallery. A man who had been bending over Louise Munro's body came to meet them. He was young and neatly dressed, with a long, earnest face and a Roman nose.

'Well, doctor?' said Wyndham.

'Thank God I don't see *that* sort of thing very often,' said the doctor. 'The cause of death was strangulation, I fancy—though that won't be certain until I get a look at the internal organs. She may simply have died of loss of blood.'

'H'm,' said Wyndham dubiously. 'Well, I don't suppose it matters very much.'

'The slashing must have been done when she was still alive,' the doctor went on. 'Otherwise she'd hardly have bled so much.'

'H'm,' said Wyndham again. He turned to Fen. 'Look at that,

sir. I suppose the killer thought she was dead when he started his butchering.'

The body of Louise Munro lay on its back. She had been a tall, dark-haired, slender girl; and a dispassionate consideration of her face, even in death, might have seen there signs of weakness and indecision. The features were distorted to a hideous mask; the eyes were bulging; the flesh was cyanosed and swollen; and there were traces of bloodstained froth at the nose and mouth.

Wyndham bent and turned the body over. The black evening gown had left her back naked to the waist, and the soft white skin was now scarred with a dozen long, deep cuts, on which the blood was clotted and black. Indeed, there seemed to be blood everywhere on the body and on the floor round it.

'Yes,' said Fen, almost to himself, 'someone disliked that young woman very much . . . This is one of those occasions when the thought of judicial hanging gives me a positive pleasure. Is there anything else I ought to see?'

'The gloves,' Wyndham replied, 'and the knife. They're over here.' He crossed to the mantelpiece and Fen followed him. 'Both smothered in blood, as you'd expect. They were on the floor by the body. It seems that the knife comes from the kitchen. There are no prints on it. And no name in the gloves, which seem to be quite ordinary.'

Fen nodded. He had cast no more than a cursory glance at the exhibits. 'She was throttled?' he enquired.

'I think so. What's your opinion, doctor?'

'Almost certainly,' said the doctor. 'The bruising's distinctive.'

'Well, sir,' said Wyndham, 'if there's nothing else, I think we might have her taken away. Has the ambulance arrived, doctor?'

'It's just come, I think,' said the doctor, who was peering between the curtains. 'But there's a beastly little red sports car in the way of it.'

'Beastly?' said Fen indignantly. 'There's nothing beastly about Lily Christine. Still, I suppose I'd better go and move her.'

When he returned to the house, Wyndham was talking to a police sergeant in the hall.

'First of all, find out who has alibis for that game of hide-and-seek and who hasn't,' he was saying. 'And then when you've brought me the list you'd better go and search the girl's bedroom . . . Oh, and send'—he pulled out a notebook and consulted it—'Noel Carter and Janice Mond to me in the study.'

As they returned there: 'Hide-and-seek?' said Fen interrogatively.

'It happened during a game,' Wyndham explained, 'which of course means a general lack of alibi . . . The girl wasn't dead when they found her, you know.'

'Not dead?' Fen was startled. 'Oh, my dear paws. Was she conscious?'

'Yes, and said a few words. Nothing very revealing, though.' They had reached the study, and Wyndham lowered his considerable bulk with obvious relief into a chair. 'I'll get this fellow Carter to run over it for you.'

'Who's he?'

'Just one of the guests—a young man. He has an unassuming air and a good deal of basic conceit. Also he's rather more fussy and old-maidish than suits his years, but I think he's all right, and he appears to have a definite alibi.'

'And the girl—Janice somebody?'

'She was with him all through the game. They were canoodling in a summer-house.'

'Good God.' Fen was shocked. 'In this weather?'

'I know. Still, there are the Esquimaux, of course. I often wonder how they manage.'

'Igloos are very warm, I believe,' said Fen, interested.

'Yes.' Wyndham abandoned this topic with evident reluctance.

'Anyway, she's a forward little minx. *And* got her hooks in him. The more I see of women looking for husbands,' he added thoughtfully, 'the more I'm convinced of the total unscrupulousness of the sex.'

There was a knock at the door, and Noel and Janice came in. Fen noted with interest that the girl was considerably more at ease than the man, though both were a little pale. Wyndham motioned them to sit down.

'I'm sorry we have to trouble you again,' he said. 'But Professor Fen is interested in this business, and I think it would be a good thing if he heard your part of it in your own words.'

Noel shrugged. 'That's perfectly all right by me. You know, we've tried and tried, but neither of us has the least idea who that man was we saw. It can't have been someone from outside, I suppose?'

Wyndham shook his head grimly. 'We've checked on wheel marks and footprints in the snow, Mr Carter. The only wheel marks are those of Mr Hadow's car, the only footprints are yours and Miss Mond's, to and from the summer-house.'

'So that's that,' said Janice, absently twisting a sapphire ring on her finger. 'Our old friend, the Closed Circle.' Unexpectedly, she shivered. 'Thank God Noel and I are out of it. You don't suspect us of collusion, do you, Inspector?'

'I don't suspect anyone of anything at the moment, Miss Mond,' Wyndham answered evasively. 'Now, Mr Carter: you and Miss Mond were recalled from the summer-house by a prearranged signal—the ringing of the gong. That was at 10.40, wasn't it?'

'Yes. It was five minutes earlier than we expected. Hadow arrived, and Duncan—that's MacAdam—brought the game to a premature stop.'

'And you heard Mr Hadow drive up to the door?'

'Yes.'

'This isn't the detective novelist, is it?' Fen interrupted.

'Apparently, sir, yes.'

'Admirable,' Fen murmured. 'I've always wanted to meet him. *The King of the Groves* is almost as frightening a book as *The Burning Court*, and I can't say better than that . . . Sorry. Go on.'

Wyndham said: 'Then you must have arrived outside the windows of the long gallery at about 10.41?'

'I suppose so.' Noel frowned, without apparent reason. 'And were confronted with the spectacle of the murderer kissing the murderee under the mistletoe . . .'

'Noel,' said Janice with sudden urgency, 'I've only just thought . . . She must have been . . . That is, he must have started by then . . . I remember saying she looked very languid. Oh, God,' Janice concluded in a small voice.

'I don't see,' Noel protested, 'why it shouldn't have happened after we went away . . . Were we the last to get back to the drawing-room? It would seem to depend on that.'

'I'll check on it, sir,' said the Inspector. 'It may narrow down the times a little. Or again it may not. That kiss you saw could have been a perfectly innocent affair, with the girl alive and well. There's no reason, on the evidence, why the murder shouldn't have been committed *afterwards*.'

'But who by? We were all in the draw—Oh, hell. No, we weren't, though.'

Wyndham looked at him sharply, and tapped his pencil on the arm of his chair. 'Can you remember who was *not* in the drawing-room, Mr Carter—between the end of the hide-and-seek game and the discovery of the body?'

'Yes. I think I can, that is. Patricia—that's Patricia Davenant—had broken a shoulder strap, and went up to her room to change. Then four of the older people got up a bridge game in the library—old Murchison and his wife, and Mr and Mrs Joyce. I imagine, though, that they must have been together all the time. And Duncan went to show Peter Hadow his room.

But damn it all, it would have been abnormally risky at that time. And what would Louise have been doing, alone in the long gallery?'

'Waiting for someone, perhaps,' Janice suggested. 'And I suppose the assumption is that if the kiss we saw was a genuine innocuous affair, the man concerned is afraid to come forward after what's happened.'

Wyndham nodded. 'That's it, more or less. But I agree that the other notion's more plausible—namely, that the murderer heard you coming in the middle of his—activities, and snatched the girl up and kissed her—kissed her: my God, what a nerve—to put you off the scent. There's only one door to the long gallery, isn't there?—the one that leads through the vestibule into the hall? Well, then, if he'd just left her, and made for that, he would have been approaching the light and there would have been every chance of your recognising him . . .'

'*Hey!*' Fen howled. There was an astonished silence. 'You seem to forget,' he went on waspishly, 'that I know nothing whatever about all this. You daze me, with your alternative hypotheses. Let me get the set-up clear. When you looked into the long gallery, the lights were on?'

'A light was on,' said Noel. 'A small standard lamp at the end by the door. The *other* end, of course, where the couple was standing, was almost dark.'

'And all the curtains were open?'

'Yes.'

Fen muttered something unintelligible, and lit a cigarette. Then he went on: 'Doesn't it strike you as extraordinary that a murderer should go about his business in a lighted room—even a dimly-lighted room—with the curtains wide; and the rest of the party pottering about anywhere and everywhere in and out of the house?'

'I don't think he can have expected anyone to be *outside*,' said Noel.

'And then, you see, the lights were all turned off for the game,' said Janice.

'At the main,' said Noel.

'And then when they were all turned on again—'

'Five minutes earlier than anyone expected.'

'—it must have taken him completely by surprise.'

'And he can't have missed hearing us coming.'

'The lights went on just as we rounded the corner of the house.'

'So you see—'

'Yes, just a minute, please,' said Fen, eyeing them somewhat askance. 'I think I've managed to grasp all that. Can't you say anything definite about the man?'

Noel sneezed, and gazed reproachfully at Janice, who refused to look at him. Through the folds of his handkerchief he mumbled:

'Well, he was wearing a dinner jacket; but so was every other male in the party.'

'His waistline certainly wasn't more than average,' Janice added, 'which cuts out one or two people. I don't know about the height. Average, I should say.'

'Yes,' said Noel. 'And his head was in shadow, so he might have been dark or fair.'

Fen asked: 'Could it have been a woman dressed as a man?'

They stared at him. 'I suppose so,' said Janice. 'But then there would have been no time to change back again. All the women in the party were present and correct when we got back to the drawing-room—as far as I know, anyway.'

Fen turned to Wyndham. 'What about the servants?'

'They're out of it,' said Wyndham definitely. 'They went off duty at ten o'clock, and held a Christmas Eve celebration in their own sitting-room. They were all together during the whole of the relevant time. Thank God one can narrow down the field that far.'

'Ah,' said Fen gnomically. He resumed his questions. 'When

you left the window of the long gallery, you presumably didn't go straight back into the drawing-room? If you had, you would have arrived before, or simultaneously with, the person who was with Mrs Munro.'

'No, we didn't go straight back,' said Noel.

'Noel insisted on kissing me outside the front door,' Janice explained with maidenly prevarication.

'Well, I'm damned,' said Noel, and sneezed again.

'Very proper,' Fen commented, beaming at them like some sentimental old aunt. 'And you saw no one in the hall when at last you did get inside?'

'No one.'

'What makes you so sure that the girl you saw in the long gallery *was* Louise Munro?

'Now I come to think of it, said Noel blankly, 'I'm not at all sure. In fact, it was Janice who said—'

'She was wearing Louise's jade bracelet, anyway,' Janice interrupted. 'It caught the light. So obviously, I assumed it was Louise.'

The clock on the mantelpiece struck half-past midnight, in tiny, fluid chimes.

'All right,' said Fen with a sigh. 'Now, about finding the unfortunate girl. What time would that be?'

'About five past eleven, I believe,' Noel replied. He lit a cigarette and sucked at it dispiritedly. 'Five of us went across to the long gallery. We were in that deplorably jocose condition which always seems to be induced by playing children's games.'

'Who were the five?'

'Janice, myself, Duncan, Richard Neame and Simon Moore.'

'Who are Richard Neame and Simon Moore?'

'Richard's a master at some derelict boys' school or other. Very stodgy and earnest about Education. Also, he's quite insanely in love with that little b-i-t-c-h Patricia Davenant, and engaged to marry her. Simon Moore's middle-aged, very hail-fellow-well-met, and a professional week-ender. He wanted to marry Louise, but only for her money, I fancy.'

'It's a funny thing,' said Fen reminiscently. 'I always intended to marry some rich woman or other. But I never came across one,' he concluded with pathos. 'Well, well . . . Anyway, you were all together when you found Louise Munro.'

'Yes.' Noel absently stubbed out his cigarette, which he had hardly started to smoke, and lit another one. 'Janice let out a shriek like a startled gull—'

'Oh, don't be an idiot, Noel,' said Janice with exaggerated weariness.

'—and Duncan lifted Louise's head; she was lying on her back. He said: 'She's still alive', and then she opened her eyes and looked at us, and Duncan asked her who—who was responsible. I don't think I shall ever forget the sounds she made when she tried to speak, and what she finally said.' Noel paused, soberly.

'Well?'

'She said: "Patricia . . . in danger . . . help her." And then she stopped, and Richard looked round like a startled rabbit, and scuttled off with Simon Moore to Patricia's bedroom. MacAdam said: "Tell us who did this," and Louise muttered—poor girl, she must have been in horrible pain: "Mustn't be destroyed . . . I'll tell you . . . who . . ."

'And then she died.'

Noel put out the second cigarette. For a moment there was a silence. Fen broke it by asking:

'And what about this other girl—Patricia?'

'She was all right, but—' Noel turned to Wyndham. 'You know more about this part than I do.'

Wyndham stirred uneasily in his chair. 'Yes,' he said. 'It seems that Miss Davenant is in the habit of taking a tonic every night.' He paused, and added heavily: 'We found a large quantity of strychnine in it.'

5

Sergeant Stokes came in, and deposited a sheet of paper in front of the inspector. He was a ruddy, amiable young man.

'It's easier than we thought,' he announced. 'Only three men and one woman unaccounted for during the whole of the game. It would appear'—the Sergeant grinned unprofessionally—'that people hid, for the most part, in couples. Mr MacAdam and an old gentleman named Mr Murchison have partial alibis. They met about five minutes after the game started, and drank whisky by candle-light until Mr Hadow arrived. No one admits to having gone into the long gallery: they say it was too near and obvious a hiding-place.'

Wyndham uttered a faint grunt. 'The body's been taken away?'

'Yes.'

'In that case you can transfer Scott from the door of the long gallery to me here. I shall want to interview some of these people. You'd better go now and search Mrs Munro's room.'

The Sergeant vaguely parodied a salute, and departed. Wyndham read aloud from the paper on his knees.

'Patricia Davenant. Richard Neame. Simon Moore. Edgar Nathan. It seems they've none of them got alibis. Who's Edgar Nathan?'

'A ghastly man,' Noel explained obliquely. 'High church. Arty. Blue in the jowl.'

'And wearing a dinner jacket?' Fen put in.

'No. Clerical black . . . Oh, I see what you mean. Yes, from behind, and in a dim light, it would look like a dinner jacket.'

The constable who had been guarding the door of the long gallery came in.

'Sit down, Scott,' said Wyndham. 'I'll have something for you to do in a moment . . . Mr Carter, I suppose there's no doubt that Mrs Munro was all right immediately before the game of hide-and-seek?'

'No doubt whatever. I saw her myself.'

'Then there are two possibilities: either she was killed during the game, or she was killed in the interval between the end of the game and the time when she was found. Now: those without alibis for one or both of those periods are Patricia Davenant, Richard Neame, Simon Moore, Edgar Nathan, Duncan MacAdam and Peter Hadow. I include the last two on the assumption that MacAdam didn't stay with Hadow once he'd shown him up to his room. The bridge party I should think we could rule out. Is it *impossible* that either Neame, Moore or Nathan could have been the man you saw in the long gallery with Mrs Munro?'

'No,' said Noel immediately. 'It might have been any of them.'

'Was Mrs Munro the sort of person to allow virtually anyone to kiss her? I ask on the assumption that she was killed *after* the episode you witnessed.'

Janice had the grace to look uncomfortable. 'Yes, she was,' she said. 'Louise was quite promiscuous. I'm sorry if that sounds catty, but it happens to be true.'

Wyndham sighed. 'Thank you very much. Is there anything else you want to ask, Professor Fen?'

Fen, who had been fidgeting with a music box and had succeeded in inducing it to perform *The Bluebells of Scotland*, said:

'Yes, I've got two questions. First, are you sure Louise Munro wasn't raving when she said those few words after you found her?'

Noel hesitated, thinking back. 'No, I'm certain she wasn't,' he answered at last. 'I think she had something clear and definite and sane to say to us. Anyway, she was right about Patricia.'

'I quite agree,' said Janice with decision.

'And second,' said Fen, attempting to stop *The Bluebells of Scotland* and failing, 'how long did you two stay kissing outside the front door?'

'Not more than two minutes,' Janice replied primly. 'I wouldn't allow it.'

Noel made an incoherent noise, and sneezed a third time.

'Well, I must drive you away,' said Wyndham. 'But I'd better have one or two details for my report before you go. Age, Mr Carter?'

'Twenty-seven.'

'Occupation?'

'Assyriology.'

'Scarcely very funny, is that, Mr Carter?'

'Independent means, then. But my hobby's Assyriology.' ('Cripes,' said Janice.)

'Age, Miss Mond?'

'Twenty.'

'Occupation?'

'Bright Young Person.' Janice grinned. 'Schoolgirl emeritus. Prospectively, Mrs Noel Carter.'

'Like hell!' said Noel, startled. They went out, arguing.

'Well, there we are,' said Wyndham with some satisfaction. 'That clears things up a little.'

With a savage rending of clockwork, *The Bluebells of Scotland* came to an end. Fen hastily replaced the instrument on its table. 'Tell me about the strychnine,' he said.

'It's only an assumption as yet. But what ought to be an ordinary, watery tonic now tastes very bitter and unpleasant. Of course I shall have it analysed.'

'Strychnine.' Fen was thoughtful. 'Rather a silly poison to use: it can be detected so easily . . . How did you come to find out about it?'

'It was that fellow Neame. He's daft about the girl Patricia. As far as I can make out, he spent about half-an-hour searching her room for spring-guns and what not, forbade her leave his sight, and eventually thought of poisons and tasted this tonic. I could scarcely get a look at Mrs Munro for the fuss he was making about it when I arrived.'

Fen snorted. 'Well, *he* didn't try to poison her, that's certain. What do you propose doing now?'

'See these people without alibis, I should think. How about having MacAdam first?'

'Yes,' said Fen; and added hopefully: 'Since this house belongs to him, he might give us some whisky.'

6

This, in fact, was what MacAdam did; and Fen, restored to his normal good humour, punctuated the interview which followed with an unearthly rendering of *I saw three kings go sailing by*. 'I know there's something obscurely wrong about the words,' he admitted when remonstrated with. 'But the tune has always seemed to me a very nice one.'

Macadam was undoubtedly worried; the lines of his plump, mobile face were as if graven into it. He held an unlighted cigar between his fingers, and his greying hair was slightly dishevelled. The duties of hospitality performed, he sat down as though exhausted, and said:

'Well?'

'A few gaps to fill in, Mr MacAdam,' said Wyndham cheerfully. 'I won't keep you longer than I can help.'

MacAdam gestured vaguely. 'That's all right. I should have been up most of the night, anyway. So would the others. Fire away.'

'In this game of hide-and-seek, you were—what's the technical term?'

'"He". I didn't do much looking, though.'

'Apparently not. Did the people concerned expect you to do any looking?'

'I shouldn't think so. The fact is, Inspector, that there are quite a number of young people in the party, and they'd got to the stage when they were looking amorously at one another and wondering how in God's name they could find an excuse to get away and spoon in a dark corner. So I gave them the excuse. I'm sure no one regarded the hiding-and-seeking very seriously.'

'The game began when?'

'At ten twenty-five. I set a strict time-limit of twenty minutes—though in the event it was only fifteen.'

'You yourself turned off the lights?'

'Yes, from the main switch in the hall. I'd warned the servants about it, and provided them with candles. I'd also provided myself with a candle, I may say, as I didn't propose to sit about in darkness the whole time.'

'Where were you all when the game started?'

'Outside in the hall. When I said "Go" and turned the lights off, there were the inevitable whispers and giggles and shrieks and people bumping into one another.

'Then in a minute or two they all made off, *tant bien que mal*, and I could hear old Murchison cursing like a trooper as he tried to find the whisky on the drawing-room sideboard. I lit my candle and chatted to him until Peter Hadow arrived. Poor fellow, he must have had a nasty turn when I opened the door for him; he probably thought that it was his last hour, and that they'd come for him with a coffin and tapers. Anyway, I set Murchison to belabour the gong, and then turned on the lights.'

'And people came back more or less at once?'

'Yes. I think that as the gong was early they must have thought there'd been some kind of accident.'

'You didn't see anyone emerge from the vestibule which leads into the long gallery?'

'No. I went straight back into the drawing-room, as a matter of fact.'

'Can you remember in what order people returned?'

'Absolutely impossible, I'm afraid. I believe Simon Moore was *among* the first—I remember getting him a drink. And certainly Noel Carter and Janice Mond were last, because just before they arrived I'd been checking up to make sure everybody was there.

But beyond that, I really can't say; obviously one wasn't paying much attention.'

'Thank you. And what then?'

'I introduced Janice and Noel to Peter Hadow. Patricia Davenant disappeared upstairs to fix her dress. And I took Peter to his room.'

'Did you stay with him?'

'No. I told him to come down when he was ready, and left him to it.'

'You returned to the drawing-room immediately, then?'

'No again. I'd got somewhat grubby during the course of the evening, so I went to my own room for a wash.'

'That took you how long?'

'Oh . . . say ten minutes. Perhaps a little more.'

Wyndham paused for a moment to consider. Then said: 'As regards that knife that was used: I suppose unobserved access to the kitchen would be easy enough, wouldn't it?'

'After dinner was over and cleared away, yes. The servants have been having some sort of party in their own sitting-room.'

'I see.' Wyndham began drawing mermaids on a blank page of his notebook. Fen hummed furtively. MacAdam lay back limply in his chair; the cigar which he held was still unlighted.

'How long have you known Mrs Munro?' Wyndham asked.

'About four years, on and off. I met her at a first night in town, just before she was married. We continued to run across one another, but this is the first time she's been down here. As a matter of fact, I really only invited her because Peter Hadow wanted a chance to meet her.

'Why was that, sir?'

'It seems she was somehow connected with the Forrest murder case, just before the war.

'*What?*' Fen sat up with such suddenness that he nearly knocked over the glass of whisky which was balanced precariously on the arm of his chair. He rescued it in time, however, and clasped it tenderly between his hands. 'What was her maiden name?'

'Benest, I think.'

'Oh, my fur and whiskers,' Fen exclaimed. He generally had recourse to the White Rabbit in moments of high excitement. 'Sorry. Go on.'

MacAdam looked curiously at him. '*I* can't go on, I'm afraid. I don't take any interest in these things, and I only know the case by name. Peter's the man to ask. He's got it all at his finger-tips.'

Wyndham blew his nose. It was evident that his recollection of the trial in question was of the vaguest, and equally evident that he was not going to admit this in front of MacAdam. A premonitory rumbling in his throat suggested that some kind of evasive manoeuvre was in prospect, but whatever it was, Fen forestalled it.

'Can I make use of your constable for a moment?' he asked; and on Wyndham's assenting, hastily scribbled some names on a piece of paper, went to the door, opened it, and fetched in Scott, who was hovering about in the hall and was manifestly glad to be given something to do.

Fen handed him the paper and said: 'Will you go into the drawing-room, please, and ask the guests collectively if any of them either knew *or had heard of* any of the people on this list before August, 1939? You'd better read out the names one by one, and make a note of whatever response there may be in each case.' He turned to Wyndham. 'Is that all right as far as you're concerned, Inspector?'

Wyndham nodded. 'But what are the names?' he enquired when Scott had gone.

'Simply your list of suspects,' said Fen, grinning. 'Sorry to interrupt you.'

'I haven't much more to ask,' Wyndham admitted. 'Mrs Munro was well-off, wasn't she, Mr MacAdam?'

'I believe so.'

'Do you happen to know who was her heir?'

'I don't at all.'

'Well, I do,' Fen interposed complacently. 'Or at all events, I have a shrewd idea. But more of that when we've heard what Hadow has to say. I've got a question, too. There must have been some kind of attack on Patricia Davenant previous to this evening's business, mustn't there?'

Wyndham glanced at him sharply. 'Had you been told about that?'

'No,' Fen countered with some indignation. 'I deduced it. What's the good of a detective if he doesn't deduce anything? But what exactly happened?'

MacAdam shrugged. 'Well, we've only her account of it. She came down two evenings ago looking a bit bruised and dishevelled, and said someone—she didn't know who, or whether it was a man or a woman—had been robbing her room, and had stolen her private diary. It seems that she went into her room to fetch something, and was tripped up and tumbled on to the floor before she had time to as much as put the light on. Apparently some kind of brief wrestling match ensued, but Patricia banged her head against the chest of drawers, and the other person was out of the room and away before she had a chance to recover.'

'Where were the other guests at this time?'

'They were unpacking in their rooms. That's really the trouble. There was only Murchison and his wife and myself downstairs.'

'So it could have been any of them?'

'I suppose so.'

'What did you do about it?'

'What could I do about it?' MacAdam spread his hands in a gesture of humorous resignation. 'As far as was possible, I simply ignored the whole affair. Patricia wasn't really upset. She's far from being a hysterical type, and when she came to tell us about it, she was much more astonished than frightened. There wasn't any kind of clue . . .'

'Nothing besides the diary was taken?'

'No . . . Oh, but there was one odd thing. Patricia's typewriter had been opened, and I imagine used. Of course, poor old Richard was in a state of complete panic. He's utterly devoted to that girl.'

'And yet,' said Fen, 'they weren't together during the game of hide-and-seek.'

MacAdam smiled; he looked tired. 'That was due to a ridiculous quarrel earlier in the evening. Nothing important, of course—Richard, who is *sérieux*, raised some portentous objection to playing children's games, Patricia said he was pompous, and so it went on. Naturally, Richard became vastly repentant almost immediately afterwards, but Patricia snubbed him, in her own placid way, and he's been running about all evening looking like a whipped dog.' MacAdam chuckled.

'Just one more thing. Had Louise Munro been behaving in any way oddly since she arrived?'

'Oh, yes.' MacAdam was looking at them from narrowed eyes. 'I think—in fact, I'm certain—that she was frightened of something. Or someone.'

7

As he went out, MacAdam almost collided with P.C. Scott in the doorway. He left with instructions that all except Janice and Noel, himself, and the remainder of the suspects, might now go to bed or otherwise disperse in whatever manner they pleased.

'*Get ivy and hull, woman*,' Fen sang as the door closed behind him, '*deck up thine house, and take this same brawn for to seethe and to souse*. I like the peremptory, patriarchal air of that carol,' he commented.

'Well, Scott, what results?' Wyndham asked.

'A blank, sir,' said the constable, swelling visibly with the consciousness of duty well performed. 'A complete blank. None of the guests knew or had heard of any of these persons'—he tapped the paper with the nail of his forefinger—'prior to August, 1939.'

'Which is unhelpful,' Fen remarked. 'Well, never mind.'

'What exactly was the point of the question, sir?' Wyndham demanded.

'It concerns the Forrest case. Hadow will be able to tell you more about it than I can, but I suggest that we leave him until last.'

The clock on the mantelpiece struck one.

'Well, sir,' said Wyndham, eyeing it sleepily, 'who do you think we should see now?'

'It hardly matters, really. What about this priest—Nathan?'

'Very good, sir. Scott, ask Mr Nathan to step in here for a minute. By the way,' Wyndham added when the constable was gone, 'isn't it odd that none of these guests should have *heard* of Hadow—he being a writer—before 1939?'

'He didn't start publishing until the war,' Fen explained absently; he seemed to be thinking of something else. 'Have you made any attempt to trace these gloves?'

'Not yet, sir. There hasn't been time.'

'Well, I suggest you show them to each of these people we interview. As they were left by the body, they're not likely to lead us anywhere. But we can try.'

In fact, the gloves proved to be Nathan's. He identified them without hesitation. He had left them, he said, in the pocket of his coat, and presumably anyone could have removed them. Obviously (he added rather uncertainly), if he had committed this appalling crime, he would not have used his own gloves; though on the other hand (here he grew noticeably depressed), he might have done, on the assumption that the police would suspect him the less for leaving so obvious a clue. It depended on the degree of sophistication one postulated in the criminal.

He had a light, quick, tenor voice, with a tendency to gabble; and Noel's description of him—'High church, arty, blue in the jowl'—had certainly covered his most salient characteristics. In addition, he was noticeably thin—though broad-shouldered—and possessed remarkably penetrating brown eyes. His general appearance was untidy, and his coat was speckled with dandruff on the shoulders, collar and lapels.

'*Jesus natus hodie*,' Fen chanted. '*Nowell, nowell—*'

'Just a minute, please, sir,' Wyndham interrupted. This persistent carolling was evidently fraying his nerves. 'Now, Mr Nathan, you were alone, I understand, during the game of hide-and-seek?'

Nathan was sitting forward in his chair, his bony hands clasped together on his knee.

'Yes, precisely,' he said. 'In point of fact I went to my own room. I'm sorry to say that on the whole I'm rather deficient in the party spirit. I was relieved when the gong was sounded five minutes earlier than had been anticipated.'

'Were you one of the earliest to return to the drawing-room?'

'I dont think so. Nor, for that matter, one of the latest. Several people were crossing the hall as I came down the stairs.'

'I see. Did you know Mrs Munro well?'

'Hardly at all. I met her for the first time when I arrived the day before yesterday. To me she was just one of a number of hardly differentiated "other guests".'

'And after you returned to the drawing-room?'

'I remained there until the crime was discovered. I think that quite a number of people can testify to my presence.'

In the hall outside, there was a low murmur of conversation as people went up to bed, and once they heard the front door open and shut, to allow the departure of an elderly couple who felt unable to stay in the house after what had happened. They apologised at length to MacAdam, who responded with suitable comprehension and penitence.

'And can you throw any light at all, sir,' said Wyndham, 'on either the attack on Miss Davenant or the murder of Mrs Munro?'

'As regards the former, no. I was unpacking in my room when it occurred. As regards the latter—' Nathan hesitated.

'Well, sir?'

Nathan gave the Inspector a quick and rather chilly smile. 'A small point, and probably it means nothing. As I returned to the drawing-room after the game, I saw someone emerge from the vestibule which leads into the long gallery.'

'Oh?' said Wyndham quickly. 'And who was that, sir?'

'His name is Simon Moore.'

8

Moore replaced Nathan, who returned to the others. He was scrupulously dressed, but offered a faint, unanalysable impression of shabbiness. There was a sort of generalised weariness about him, too: the weariness of a man who has spent his life striving for something which in his inmost heart he knows is not worth while—and has even then failed to obtain it.

He might have been forty years of age, with a tendency to plumpness and the dispiriting, automatic smile of the professional *bon homme* perpetually lingering on his lips. His black hair was remarkably thick and fine, and he wore rimless octagonal spectacles, which gave him a slightly transatlantic appearance. His manner throughout the interview, though superficially straightforward and agreeable, struck both Fen and Wyndham as being taut and strained. And there might be some justification for this, since his position had, obviously, its dangers.

He made no attempt to deny Nathan's assertion.

'Yes, I was in the vestibule,' he agreed in a soft, low-pitched voice. 'It's quite a comfortable little room, and I knew as well as anyone else did that the game wasn't going to be taken very seriously.

'Did you enter the long gallery at all, sir?'

'No. Not at any time.'

'Did you see anyone else do so?'

'Yes,' said Moore unexpectedly. 'That's to say I didn't see them—it was pitch dark. But, I heard them.'

'Them?'

'Him, then,' said Moore with a touch of impatience. 'Or her—I don't know which. It was only one person, anyway. I'd just finished groping about for a chair when this person came in from the hall. For some reason or other I sat quite still and said nothing—I think I imagined that after all Duncan *was* going about looking for people. At all events, I don't think that whoever it was can have known that I was there. I noticed'—he paused for a moment—'I noticed that he or she was breathing rather quickly and loudly, as though excited. But in the circumstances, that didn't surprise me much.'

'And you heard no one else go through into the long gallery?'

'No.'

'You're sure you can't say whether it was a man or a woman, sir? You see what I'm getting at, I've no doubt. Both Mrs Munro *and* someone else were in that gallery during the game of hide-and-seek.'

'Yes, I understand, but I can't help you. It was perfectly possible for anyone to enter the long gallery *before* I went into the vestibule. After the lights had gone out, I stayed put in the hall until most of the people had cleared off.'

'I see. Now, sir, did you hear any sounds from the long gallery while you were in the vestibule?'

'I heard sounds from all over the house,' Moore answered drily. 'Bumps and shrieks and giggles and whispers. You can't let a gang of people loose in the darkness, in a house which most of them don't properly know, without that happening. Mostly it was in the early stages, though, before everyone got settled. Where it all came from, I honestly can't say. One's sense of direction seems to go to pot in the darkness.'

'You mentioned whispers. If you heard whispering, it must surely have come from near by?'

Moore took off his glasses to polish them. His weak sight made him look oddly defenceless.

'I suppose so,' he said, 'but it might equally well have come from the hall as from the long gallery. Of course, I couldn't distinguish any words.'

'And when the gong was sounded—'

'I went out almost immediately. In fact, I was one of the first to get to the drawing-room. After that, I stayed there until—until I heard the news.'

'I'm afraid this is a personal question, but it must be asked. Were you in love with Mrs Munro?'

'No.' Moore flushed. 'But no doubt you've heard that I wanted to marry her.'

'Ah.' Wyndham evaded the slightly aggressive invitation to probe Moore's motives in the matter. 'You had asked her to marry you?'

'Yes. I asked her yesterday—that is, on the 24th. She refused.'

'I'm sorry,' said Wyndham with a bizarre and palpably insincere sympathy. 'Were you upset by her refusal?'

'Hardly. I intended to ask her again as soon as the opportunity offered.'

'Can you tell us *why* she refused you, sir?'

'She suggested that I only wanted to marry her for her money,' Moore replied coolly. 'That was her ostensible reason. Actually, of course, she was a minx. She got a great deal of fun out of having men tagging after her.'

'Was she particularly attached to anyone other than yourself?'

'She wasn't particularly attached to *me*, I can assure you . . . Anyway, the answer is no. She was prepared to allow almost any man to make love to her—up to a point—but apart from myself she had no regular devotees.' Moore paused, and as Wyndham said nothing, went on: 'I'm sorry to say that I didn't think her a very agreeable woman. She was what I should call a chaste wanton—suggestive of positively Turkish carnalities, but in practice as forbidding as a block of ice.'

Wyndham appeared to be considering the possible characteristics of Turkish carnality.

'As far as I knew,' Moore concluded, 'there was only one person to whom she was wholeheartedly and unselfishly devoted—her brother. And it seems that he's in prison.'

'Ah,' said Fen significantly. For some time he had been maintaining a gruesome and unnatural silence. 'You interest me enormously.' When Moore had gone, and P.C. Scott had been dispatched to fetch Ronald Neame, he drank some whisky and added: 'I suppose the point of your last questions was to discover if Louise Munro was likely to have made an assignation with anyone in the long gallery. Evidently it wasn't only likely, but virtually certain. Everyone seems to agree that she was as promiscuous as a rabbit.'

'As a rabbit,' Wyndham repeated, nodding mournfully. 'Though as to Turkish carnalities, I should have said rabbits were rather addicted to *them*.'

Richard Neame appeared promptly. He was a stolid man of thirty to thirty-five with a defensive air which Fen concluded was due less to present circumstances than to his avocation. Most schoolmasters acquire it, in one form or another; it is almost a necessity in dealing with the ghastly perspicuity of the young. With it went an authoritativeness which was vaguely offensive. It was evident, moreover, that he was far more concerned with the potential fate of Patricia Davenant than with the actual immolation of Louise Munro—regarding which, indeed, he displayed considerable indifference.

He announced, rather surprisingly, that during the game of hide-and-seek he had locked himself in a lavatory. He had wished, he explained stiffly, to be with Miss Davenant, but a slight disagreement earlier in the evening had made that undesirable. He had found the game trying, and thought it on the whole unnecessary. When it was over, he had returned immediately to the drawing-room.

'And what impelled you, sir, to join in the search for Mrs Munro?'

Neame appeared taken aback. He stammered a little. 'I simply—I simply felt that it was my duty to assist.'

'Quite so. And will you tell us what Mrs Munro said before she died?'

'All I heard was that Patricia was in danger.' Neame had lost some of his stiffness and spoke more vigorously. 'That was enough for me. If you'd seen the ghastly state that wretched woman was in . . .' His self-consciousness abruptly returned. 'Naturally, I left, and made straight for Patricia's—Miss Davenant's—room. Simon Moore went with me. She'd just finished changing when we arrived and, thank God, she was all right. We looked about the room a bit, and at last it occurred to me to make sure that her medicines and so forth were all right. I put a little of the tonic in my mouth, and asked her what it normally tasted like . . .' He gestured angrily. 'The rest you know.'

'Exactly sir,' Wyndham's tones were soothing. 'And you can throw no light on the previous attack on Miss Davenant?'

'I wish I could. I should like to get my hands on whoever was responsible.'

Fen regarded him thoughtfully. He had heard sufficient of Neame's infatuation with Patricia Davenant to make him suspicious of its sincerity. But that the man *was* infatuated he had now not the smallest doubt.

'Had you known Mrs Munro long?' he asked.

'Didn't meet her till I came here,' said Neame shortly. The subject of Louise Munro seemed almost to irritate him. And apparently he had some suspicion that heartlessness might be imputed to him, for he mumbled conventionally: 'Very tragic affair.'

He departed uttering various admonitions about the future safety of Patricia Davenant, the responsibility for which, he stated, rested entirely on the police.

'*He* didn't try to kill her, anyway,' said Fen after the door had closed behind him. '*Although at Yule it bloweth cool*,' he burst out suddenly, '*and frost doth grip the fingers . . .*'

He was cut short by the arrival of Sergeant Stokes, in a state of high excitement.

'I've been through Mrs Munro's room,' the Sergeant announced, 'and made two discoveries that I think'll prove to be important.' He beamed expectantly at his superior.

'Well, don't stand there,' said Wyndham, justifiably annoyed, 'with that oafish smirk on your face. What have you found?'

'First of all,' said the Sergeant dramatically, 'a letter which shows that Mrs Munro was blackmailing someone.' He handed Wyndham a plain white envelope with the flap tucked in. 'And second, what I'm pretty certain is Miss Davenant's diary.'

9

A stasis occurred while the provenance of the diary was checked and Patricia Davenant's fingerprints were taken. In the end it proved that the only prints on the diary were those of Patricia herself and of Louise Munro.

'So Mrs Munro took it,' said Wyndham blankly. 'And I suppose it was she who attacked Miss Davenant. But in God's name, why . . . ?'

He flicked over the pages of the little green-bound book. 'Surely there's nothing in this she could possibly want to see. It's little more than a list of engagements, and as far as I can see, there's no one in this party, barring Neame and MacAdam, who's as much as mentioned in it. And there's not a single damaging secret that I can make out. What do you think about it, sir?'

'I think,' said Fen from the depths of his armchair, 'that Louise Munro was as disappointed as you are; that she was expecting damaging secrets, too, and likewise failed to find them.'

'Is it possible that she was responsible for the strychnine?'

'And had a fit of death-bed repentance? It's possible,' Fen admitted grudgingly, 'but on the whole I don't think so. That would leave Louise Munro's murder out of account, and I'm certain these things are all bound up together. Believe me, there's only *one* murderer running around loose—and just as well, too,' he ended somewhat peevishly, 'or we should all be in our graves in a winking.'

'Well, now, sir—this letter.' Wyndham unfolded it to read it again. It was typewritten on a plain sheet of white paper, and ran: '*I am tired of blackmail. You may expect a visit from me soon.*' Wyndham flicked the edge of the paper with his forefinger. 'It would seem as though Louise Munro's blackmail victim had got sick of whatever extortions were going on and decided to put a stop to them once and for all. That sort of thing's been done often enough before.'

'It seems so,' Fen agreed, 'though I think there's an alternative explanation . . . The letter was found in that plain envelope?'

'Yes. *Apparently* it wasn't posted.'

'Ah,' Fen murmured absently. 'I rather think it must have been put in Louise Munro's room the evening everyone arrived—probably a short time before the diary was stolen . . . Yes . . .'

He fell silent. Wyndham saw that he was concentrating on some problem or other, and respected his absorption. But when Fen spoke again, it was only to say:

'What orders have you given Scott about this gang of suspects in the drawing-room?'

'Orders?'

'I mean, are you allowing them to move about the house at their own sweet will?'

'Lord, no. They've been in the drawing-room ever since we arrived, and there they stay until we've finished with them.'

'Of course, the evidence may have vanished before you got here,' Fen murmured obscurely. 'In that case, I'm not sure that an arrest would be justified . . . MacAdam's the man to ask . . .' He shook himself irritably out of his daydream. 'Anyway, Inspector, that precaution may save our bacon . . . Shall we see Patricia Davenant now?'

10

The clock struck a quarter to two as Patricia Davenant came in, but despite the lateness of the hour she looked fresh and untired. She was wearing a plain brown coat and skirt which set off the magnificent lines of her figure, and Fen observed that her make-up was so well applied as to suggest a professional interest in the matter. Unquestionably she was beautiful; but the chief impression one received was of an unthinking tranquillity, combined with a sort of naïvety such as one often sees in actresses, ballet dancers and other women whose job it is to display themselves publicly. She sat down, crossed her legs, and looked expectantly and unselfconsciously at the two men.

'What is your occupation, Miss Davenant?' Wyndham asked.

'I'm a model,' she replied directly. 'You know—magazine covers, advertisements, and so on.'

'Your age?'

'Twenty-five.'

'And you're engaged to be married to Mr Neame?'

She glanced at the diamond ring on the fourth finger of her left hand. 'Yes. I've only known him a few months, but I'm very, very fond of him.'

'You had a quarrel earlier this evening?'

'We've made it up now. It was nothing.'

'Still, it was enough to make you refuse to go with him during the game of hide-and-seek.'

Patricia regarded the Inspector wonderingly. 'I thought if I was stand-offish it would do him good,' she said; and added ingenuously: 'Some men who've made love to me say I'm not enough of a *coquette*.'

'Where did you go, during the game?'

'I? I hid in the cloak-room. You know—by the front door. I thought as it was near the starting-place Duncan wouldn't be likely to look there.'

'Didn't you understand that—well, that the game was more or less an excuse to enable'—Wyndham reddened, and becoming annoyed at this, reddened still more—'to enable people to get away together?' he concluded obliquely.

'Was it? I didn't realise.'

(And as a matter of fact, Fen reflected, it wouldn't occur to this girl that any excuse was needed for leaving a party it order to make love.)

Wyndham returned to the attack. 'I gather some accident happened to your dress?' he said.

'Oh, such a damned nuisance,' Patricia answered petulantly. 'In the darkness I got caught up on a hook or something, and my shoulder-strap broke. It wasn't a man or anything,' she added rather vaguely.

'So when the game was over, you went upstairs to change?'

'Yes. That's why I'm wearing these things. I didn't bring another evening frock.'

'And then?'

'Well, the first I knew of anything being wrong was when Richard and Simon came panting in to say I was in danger. Even then it took me ages to get anything coherent out of Richard.'

'What happened after that?'

'Happened?' Patricia felt in her handbag, brought out a tiny cambric handkerchief, and pinched the end of her nose with it in that delicate parody of blowing which women affect. 'Nothing really happened. Richard flapped about for a minute or two until Duncan came up to tell us about Louise dying, and trying to give the name of the murderer and so on, and then Richard flapped about again, and by the time he'd discovered the stuff in the medicine the police had arrived and we were all marched down to the drawing-room.'

'Do you know if you have any enemies, Miss Davenant?'

'I'm sure I haven't,' said Patricia. 'I think most people like me . . . Oh, well, I suppose *someone* doesn't, if my tonic really *was* poisoned, but I can't think who it could be.' She hesitated. 'Who was it stole my diary?'

'We think it was Mrs Munro.'

'Louise?' Patricia was almost indignant. 'But how *silly*: Why should anyone want to steal it at all?'

We were hoping you could help us over that.'

'Well, there's absolutely nothing in it. It's really only an engagement book.'

'Nothing that could—ah—compromise you?'

'Of course not.' Obviously Patricia did not in the least resent this question, but her blue eyes were wide with astonishment.

'Had you known Mrs Munro for long?'

'No, I only met her two days ago. I remember she arrived almost at the same moment as Richard and me, and Duncan introduced us in the hall.'

'You came here with Mr Neame?'

'Yes, we stayed together in a hotel in Thame last night. In separate rooms, of course,' Patricia explained gravely. 'Richard's very particular about that sort of thing.'

Wyndham, mindful of the traditions of the Force, suppressed a grin.

'But I still can't see why Louise should steal my diary,' said

Patricia, sincerely puzzled. 'I liked her, though of course she was terribly nervy.'

Fen asked a question. 'I believe your typewriter was used at the same time the diary was stolen?'

'Yes. Anyway, I found it open on the desk in my room.' Patricia frowned earnestly. 'Of course that *might* have been done *before* the diary was taken. I was one of the first to arrive, you see, and didn't bother to unpack much, and changed very quickly downstairs. And then later I found I'd forgotten a handkerchief, and went back, and it all happened. But anyway, it isn't my typewriter.'

Fen displayed interest. 'Whose is it, then?'

'I borrowed it about a month ago,' said Patricia. 'Someone told me I ought to write a book about my experiences, but I found I couldn't manage it. So I brought the typewriter here to give back. It belongs to Peter Hadow.'

11

'Well, Hadow is the last,' said Wyndham with a sigh of relief, when Patricia had been sent back to the drawing-room.

'And in some ways the most important, I suspect,' Fen rejoined thoughtfully. 'If I'm not much mistaken, he'll supply us with the motive—which at present is the most obscure feature of the whole affair.'

The novelist arrived yawning prodigiously. He had driven up that day from Torquay, he explained, and although some form of revelry might have kept him awake until this late hour, the effort of sitting about in the drawing-room had been almost too much for him. Wyndham apologised for this in his own dulcet way, and introduced Hadow to Fen. They settled down to the consumption of MacAdam's whisky, an oddly contrasted trio: Wyndham's bulky form fitting immovable into his chair, Fen tall, lanky and restless, and Hadow sprawled back, his dark hair tousled, his pince-nez clutched in his right hand, his mouth opening and shutting regularly, and his small, weak blue eyes drowsy and inattentive.

'Let me answer your questions before you ask them,' he said mildly. 'My name is Peter Hadow, my age thirty-four, my occupation the writing of detective novels. I arrived at this house about 10.37 this evening to find it as black and ghastly as the tomb, and was met at the front door by Duncan MacAdam, bearing a naked and tremulous light. While I was trying to discover the reason for all this, he ordered an aged man, whom I at first took to be the butler, to beat upon a gong, and when this unaccountable rite was over, went and switched on some lights. I was divested of my hat and coat, and taken into the drawing-room for a drink. People began to appear in numbers. I saw one whom I knew—namely Patricia Davenant—and was introduced to her betrothed, Richard Neame, with whom I've just been carrying on a turgid dialogue regarding the Sociological Significance of the Detective Novel. Of course detective novels have no more sociological significance than any other kind of novel, but he's not the sort of person who could ever be made to realise that. Poor dear, he has some fancy about the detective novel being connected with the rise of Nazism.'

Hadow paused to grin at Wyndham, who was eyeing him warily. It was apparent that Hadow was by no means entirely sober.

'Forgive the pseudo-literary chatter,' he went on. 'For some reason whisky always has this effect on me. *Le style, c'est l'alcoöl* . . . Where was I? Ah, yes.

'In addition to Richard Neame, I was introduced to an exceedingly pretty and forward wench named Janice, and to her predestined victim, a canny but none the less fated young man who tells me he's interested in Assyriology, though I hardly know whether to believe that. At about 10.45 or 10.50 Duncan took me up to my room and left me there, so that I'm not accounted for until I went downstairs ten minutes or so later. As a matter of fact I washed my hands and felt the bed and made a feeble attempt to unpack and peered into the wardrobe and did all the other things one does on arriving in a strange house . . . Anyway, I eventually returned downstairs—as I said. And the next thing was that just as I'd thought up an admirable word for a charade, we were all in the thick of it, with the girl I came here to meet desperately dead.'

Wyndham, who had been surveying the point of his pencil during this monologue, looked up. 'You came here to meet Mrs Munro?'

'I think of her as Louise Benest,' said Hadow a trifle inconsequently. 'Yes. I wanted to talk to her.' He glanced at Fen. 'You remember the Forrest case, just before the war?'

'The outlines,' Fen replied slowly. 'It was put rather out of one's head by the invasion of Poland. Would you mind running over it for our benefit? I gather you're more or less an expert on the subject.'

Hadow by now was observably less somnolent. 'It did take my fancy,' he admitted, 'to the extent that I decided to write a novel round it. Of course it wasn't for the sake of the novel that I went into the details of the affair. Crime as actually practised has little or nothing to do with the detective novel, which is a conventional-unreal *genre*, as purely imaginative as an interplanetary tale or a mediaeval cosmology. Naturally it has to be concerned with what's *possible*, but what's *probable* is practically outside its sphere . . .' Hadow stopped abruptly. 'What was I talking about?' he demanded.

'The Forrest case,' Wyndham reminded him severely.

'Oh, yes. Well, the thing got to interest me for its own sake, and I went on delving into it long after my book was finished.' Hadow paused to light a cigarette. 'It had one or two curious features, you see: the—third man, and the missing dagger . . .'

'You know it all occurred in Shrewsbury. I went there during the second year of the war, put up at the "Lion", and had a good look round. It's a pleasant town, not too large, with the Severn running round it in a kind of horse-shoe; at the centre of the horseshoe is the toll-bridge leading over to Kingsland and the Schools.

'The actual scene of the crime was the office of a solicitor in Pride Hill, which is, I suppose, the main shopping street. The office is a flat, really, about half-way down on the English Bridge side. You get to it by a flight of uncarpeted stairs leading up from an alley-way. The window of the main office overlooks a courtyard at the back, also reached from the alley-way. There's your setting. It hasn't any importance in itself; what happened there might just as well have happened at a dozen other places in the town.

'The protagonists are a night-watchman called Webb; P.C. Knight, of the Shropshire Constabulary; Edward Forrest; Louise Benest; her brother Charles; and a man who may or may not have been Andrew, Edward Forrest's brother.'

Hadow relit his cigarette, which had gone out. 'I don't know if all this is too detailed for you?' he enquired.

'No,' said Fen briefly. His manner was intent. 'Go on.'

'Louise and Charles Benest were living together at that time, in a house up on Kingsland. They had enough money of their own to avoid doing anything, and Charles had not, for medical reasons, been called up. He was about twenty-five, straightforward, ordinary, moderately intelligent; and he was devoted to his sister, as she was to him. Louise—Louise Munro to you—seems to have been a more unstable character than her brother, prone to fits of depression, and with another definite psychological kink which I'll tell you about in a moment. Of course at that time she wasn't very much more than a schoolgirl. Both the parents, by the way, were dead.

'In the last week of August, 1939, Edward Forrest arrived to stay with them for a week or two. Charles had met him at Oxford, and had apparently been fascinated by him to the extent of wholly overlooking the fact that Forrest had a basically childish mind—though superficially he was worldly, witty in a sixth-formish kind of way, and charming. Probably his motive in accepting the invitation had to do with Louise, but one doesn't know about that—nor does it matter much, now that he's occupying a plot of earth in a prison cemetery.

'He had only one relation, a brother who had been living for some years abroad. Note that word "abroad". Nothing more definite ever emerged on the subject. Moreover—and this is the important point—it's tolerably certain that the brother had changed his name and become a national of some other country. Ten years previously he had become involved in some trivial swindle, and had somehow contrived to leave England—after which no trace of him was ever found. That may sound fantastic, but there are two points to be borne in mind: (a) that he had not had a photograph taken since he was a child: and (b) that although in that Utopia to which we're all so eagerly looking forward everyone's movements will doubtless be recorded from font to coffin, there were plenty of loop-holes in those days.'

Hadow was absorbed in his narrative; all signs of tiredness had vanished.

'You see what I'm getting at,' he continued. 'The extraordinary *shadowiness* of this figure. Even his age remains uncertain. Unless he's changed very much, there are presumably still people in this country—landladies and so on—who could identify him, but after the lapse of years it would be a shaky business. One imagines that he himself was of that opinion otherwise he'd scarcely have returned.

'Edward Forrest referred to his brother, when he spoke of him to Charles and Louise Benest, as "Andrew", and that seems to have been his right name. The parents—poor folk—died quite early, and Andrew was left to look after his younger brother Edward. He worked, and scraped, and saved (obviously he was devoted to Edward), and he can't have been entirely without ability, because he managed to get together enough money to send Edward to Oxford, whereafter Edward got himself a job and became tolerably affluent. But in the meantime, Andrew had tried to hasten the process by the swindle aforesaid, and so vanished from the scene—until, perhaps, that evening of August, 1939.

'I'm sorry to take so long in getting to the actual crime, but after the trial of Edward Forrest, the presence of Andrew in England began to make itself felt; and for that reason it's important to understand how he came to be so exceedingly elusive. One thing is certain, I think—namely that Andrew didn't return to England with a passport. If you have some kind of boat, it's not at all difficult to get unobserved into any maritime country in the world. Two days after the affair in Shrewsbury, a small motor-launch was found abandoned in a cove near Brixham. Perhaps that was what he used—who knows?

'Naturally, all these facts about Andrew weren't known to Louise and Charles Benest—or at least not until the time of the trial, and then only partially. Andrew Forrest was a somewhat remote and improbable figure, and counsel didn't have much to say about him. Edward merely told the Benests that his brother was arriving by the late train on August 17th, 1939. Evidently they had kept in touch.'

Hadow paused. 'Well, it's pretty certain that he did arrive. A taxi-man remembers driving someone to the house on Kingsland. But it seems that the nearest he got to his brother was to hear the shot with which Edward Forrest murdered Webb the night-watchman in the office on Pride Hill.'

12

'That evening—August 17th, 1939—Charles Benest, Louise Benest and Edward Forrest got drunk together. Or perhaps it would be more correct to say that only Edward Forrest got seriously drunk. They did a round of the pubs and then returned to the house and went on drinking there. And they argued about crime.

'The discussion followed one of its familiar courses. It ended with Forrest's maintaining that to commit a successful crime, and get away with it, was the easiest thing in the world; and he offered to prove it, there and then, by committing a robbery.

'It's obvious that the others tried to dissuade him, but people when drunk are not easily dissuaded, and probably they felt obliged to go with him (since he persisted), in the hope of stopping him when it came to the point. As you'll hear, they didn't succeed.

'The victim Edward Forrest selected was a solicitor with whom Charles and Louise had had dealings in some matter of property-dealings which were unsatisfactory to them. They had mentioned his name to Edward Forrest earlier on the same day, and now nothing would satisfy him but that this unfortunate man's office should be the scene of the experiment; the drunk often develop an exaggerated sense of retribution.

'The walk from Kingsland to Pride Hill takes about a quarter of an hour, and it must have sobered Forrest to some extent—though not enough, unfortunately, to divert him from his purpose. He had left a hastily scribbled note for Andrew, indicating where they had gone, and why; and presumably Andrew's taxi passed them soon after they had set out.

'Well, they got to the office. It was one o'clock in the morning of the 18th. The streets were deserted and the street lamps out, but there was a half-moon which gave them sufficient light to be able to see what they were doing. One needn't expand this part of the story unduly. It's quite easy to imagine the efforts which the Benests made to stop Forrest's idiot scheme. The door in the alley-way, which gave on the stairs leading up to the flat, had a Yale lock; but it also had a glass panel at the top, and by breaking this Forrest was able to get in. The other two followed him up to the outer office; there they made a last attempt to prevent the whole silly business. But Forrest would have none of it; it wasn't a crime, he said; whatever he took, he'd return next morning by post; he merely intended to show that the thing could be done.

'So they left him there.

'Even so, they didn't go right away; it would have been better for them if they had. They lingered down below, and Louise went round to the courtyard at the back. There she saw the light go on in the main office, and Forrest drunkenly rummaging through the drawers of the desk. The fates had chosen to leave a loaded revolver in one of them. Louise deposed at the trial that he examined it carefully, opening and closing the chambers several times.

'The first outsider to arrive at the scene was Webb. It was his job to keep an eye on a whole block of houses up that side of Pride Hill, and he had heard the noise of breaking glass. One doesn't know whether he saw either of the Benests. Anyway, he went straight up the stairs to the office, and there Forrest was foolish enough to try and hold him up with his revolver.

'Louise saw the whole thing happen, and it was over very quickly. Webb realised at once that he had a drunk to deal with, and moved forward a step or two to reason with him; at which Forrest deliberately shot the man in the stomach. He died very quickly from internal haemorrhage.

'We come now to P.C. Knight, patrolling Pride Hill from the Kingsland direction, and with a belated wayfarer hurrying up behind him. It's one hypothesis, of course, that this wayfarer was brother Andrew. Knight caught only a glimpse of him, and that totally insufficient for identification purposes. The weak moonlight was to blame, and the sudden report of the pistol, which distracted Knight's attention. For a moment both men stopped dead. Then the constable ran forward to the alley-way. What became of brother Andrew—if it was brother Andrew—no one knows; he wasn't seen again, and presumably he cleared off as quickly as possible. In his position he could hardly wish to get mixed up with anything involving the police—whatever his affection for Edward.

'Knight, as I've said, ran for the alley-way, and entered the door at the bottom of the staircase leading to the office. But before he could get further someone overtook him and struck at him from behind with a knife. The wounds in themselves were not serious, but Knight overbalanced and struck his head on the hand-rail. He was unconscious for two minutes or so. Edward Forrest, panic-stricken, performed the insane action of flinging down the revolver (with his finger-prints all over it), and then fled; and Charles and Louise went back to Kingsland. But there had been sufficient noise to raise an alarm; the police were interviewing Charles and Louise half an hour later; and Edward Forrest was arrested next morning in Bristol.'

Hadow paused, lit a fresh cigarette, and swallowed his whisky at a gulp.

'Charles and Louise,' he resumed, 'being tolerably sensible people, made a clean breast of the whole affair, and Charles admitted to the attack on Knight; he had done it, he said, on a momentary impulse which he now recognised to have been insane, in the hope of keeping Louise out of the affair; and to anyone acquainted with the mutual affection of brother and sister, this seemed a perfectly plausible explanation. The weapon, it appeared, was a sharpish dagger of Indian design which was used in the outer office as a paper-knife. Charles said that he had picked it up with some vague idea of intimidating Edward Forrest, and had kept it in his hand when he left the flat; he added, moreover, that he had flung it down immediately after using it. But when the police looked for it, it had gone, and no trace of it has ever been found from that day to this.

'In parenthesis, I had a notion at one time that it might have been *Andrew* who attacked Knight, in the hope of getting his brother Edward out of the mess. But it soon became obvious that that theory wasn't tenable. For one thing, there was no earthly reason why Charles Benest should protect Andrew to get access to the dagger in time—and it certainly looks as though that was the weapon used, since it disappeared so completely. I only mention the fallacies in this notion of mine in case the same idea has occurred to you.

'Forrest came up for trial at the Shrewsbury Assizes in the autumn of 1939. In those days, if you remember, we were all in hourly expectation of annihilating German air-raids, so the case wasn't much noticed in the press. But I was already interested in some features of the case, and I managed to attend the trial.

'It lasted only a couple of days, and from the first the issue was in considerable doubt. There was no question, of course, as to whether Edward Forrest had actually shot Webb or not—the fingerprints on the gun disposed finally and effectively of that problem; but the defence maintained that the thing had been wholly an accident, and in addition that Forrest's drunkenness was evidence that no guilty state of mind existed. So the crux of the trial was Louise's assertion, which the defence wasn't able to shake, that Forrest had carefully examined the revolver on first discovering it. He, of course, denied this, and the trial really boiled down to his word against hers—in fact, to a matter of personalities, and the impression they made on the jury. Louise won hands down. The war had got people into a state of moral fervour, and the sheer inexcusable wantonness of Forrest's actions that night told heavily against him. He was brought in guilty and condemned to death.

'There were appeals for mitigation of sentence. They failed. Edward Forrest was hanged in January, 1940, and to all intents and purposes it was Louise Benest who hanged him.

'In some ways, Charles Benest was almost as unlucky as Forrest. His case came up later in the same Assizes, and of course under the same judge. There had been some question of indicting both him and Louise as principals in the second degree in the murder of Webb, but that was dropped, and Charles was charged with causing grievous bodily harm to prevent an arrest. In view of the fact that he pleaded guilty, there was considerable astonishment when he got the maximum sentence of fourteen years. That means that up to now he's done about half of it. Louise, of course, escaped altogether.'

Hadow smiled, a little grimly. 'We're coming now to the crux of the matter, in so far as it concerns what's been happening here. You'll guess that it has to do with brother Andrew. Evidently he regarded Louise as solely responsible for Edward's hanging, and in a sense he was quite right. On the day the execution was carried out, Louise was attacked in her own drawing-room, and an attempt made to strangle her. She didn't see the attacker, and the arrival of a servant drove him away before he could finish the job. There was no doubt that it was brother Andrew—she had had typewritten letters accusing her not only of his death, but also of instigating the crime for which he was condemned. Brother Andrew's affection for Edward had driven him a little crazy, you see; he wanted vengeance. Perhaps slashing a woman's bare back with a sharp knife would have satisfied him . . .

'Louise took the letters to the police, and asked for protection—which she got. No more letters arrived, and there was no further untoward incident. She married Munro, a rich man, and shortly afterwards he was killed in a flying accident. Apparently brother Andrew had vanished into limbo—until, that is to say'—with an expressive gesture—'tonight.'

Hadow stopped to refill his glass, and looked at them quizzically.

'Well, it's been a long story,' he said. 'But it seems to me that if you're looking for a motive, there it is, ready-made. Your problem now is to find out who, or what, is Andrew Forrest; and to that there just isn't any clue. He might be MacAdam, or Neame, or Nathan, or Moore—'

'Or, of course, yourself,' said Fen in an oddly colourless voice.

Wyndham stirred himself. 'There's one more thing, sir. You mentioned that Louise Benest—or Louise Munro, as I prefer to call her—had some kind of psychological kink. What was that?'

'Oh, yes, I forgot.' Hadow smiled. 'She suffered from genuine, *bona fide*, certifiable claustrophobia . . . What do you make of that?'

13

Hadow was conducted back to the drawing-room by P.C. Scott.

'*Heap on more wood, the wind is chill*,' Fen carolled gently. '*But let it whistle as it will, we'll keep our Christmas merry still* . . . Well, Inspector?'

'Well, sir: is that our motive?'

Fen nodded. 'I think so. Oh yes, I think so.'

'I've got to agree. But I scarcely see how the attempt to kill Miss Davenant comes into it—unless in some way she knows who the murderer is.'

'Very unlikely,' said Fen, and added provokingly: 'It's all perfectly natural, Inspector. It all fits.'

'It doesn't fit to me,' said Wyndham staunchly. 'I suppose now we shall have to go delving into the past history of all these five men . . . By the way, would Hadow have given us such a generous *resumé* of the case if he'd been Andrew Forrest?'

'We were bound to find out pretty soon about Louise Munro's connection with the Forrest case—in fact, as soon as I heard her maiden name I remembered the gist of the business. Besides, it was known that Hadow had come here specifically to talk to Louise Munro about it. That being so, he couldn't very well pretend ignorance.'

'Was his account correct?'

'Oh, yes, I think so.'

'But anyway'—Wyndham reverted to the previous subject—'I

don't see how I can hold *all* of those five on suspicion while we rummage into their pasts.' He stared blankly before him for a moment, and then said: 'Lord, sir, I'm stuck. Advise me what to do.'

'Just detain the one who's guilty. You've got plenty of evidence for that. Once you have him in your hands, you've got plenty of time to get him identified, trace his movements, and so forth.'

Wyndham sighed. 'If one only knew which . . .'

'Oh, I know,' said Gervase Fen blandly. 'I was tolerably certain after that first interview with Noel and Janice, and everything since then has gone to confirm my suspicions.'

Wyndham stared at him. 'You're joking, sir.'

'No, I'm not,' said Fen testily. 'I'm incapable of jokes at three o'clock in the morning.'

'Who do you mean, then?'

Fen told him.

'Well, I'm damned,' Wyndham commented unemotionally. 'I shouldn't have imagined . . . But why do you think so?'

Fen made certain explanations. 'Of course,' he concluded, 'it's *slightly* psychological. But still . . .'

'Psychological my foot!' Wyndham exclaimed vehemently. 'It's plain, simple and obvious, and I can't think how I was so stupid as not to see it. Oh, we'll have that gentleman locked up in less than no time.'

'I think we might try Patricia Davenant's typewriter first,' Fen suggested. "Also, there's a question I want to ask MacAdam . . . Let's get it all over and done with, and then we can go home. Have you got the letter? Good.'

They left the study and crossed the hall to the drawing-room. A dispirited little group was sitting round the fire.

'Hello,' said Fen. 'You all look very wan . . . MacAdam, do you let people know, when you invite them to your parties, what other guests are going to be there?'

MacAdam stood up to answer. His plump face was drawn

and tired, and his hair more dishevelled than ever. 'Yes, always,' he said shortly. 'Any objections?'

'None,' said Fen mildly.

MacAdam was very near anger. 'Inspector,' he snapped, 'is it really necessary for us to sit here all night?'

'In just five minutes, sir,' said Wyndham mildly, 'you'll all be able to go to bed. I shall be back shortly . . . By the way, where are Mr Carter and Miss Mond?'

P.C. Scott came up, red in the face. 'I'm afraid I'm responsible, sir. I allowed them to go into the library. They were very persistent, and I thought . . .' He stammered himself into silence.

Wyndham glanced at Fen, who said: 'They may as well make love while they can enjoy it. Not that it's all that enjoyable, anyway,' he added gloomily. 'Let's go upstairs.'

Patricia Davenant's room was all white—curtains, carpets, and rugs. The bed, the wardrobe and the dressing-table were of highly polished Indian rosewood, and the light came from frosted globes sunk in the ceiling. Patricia's clothes and belongings were scattered untidily about. A door on the right, which Fen investigated, led into a private bathroom. Fen pointed this out to Wyndham, who nodded.

'That would provide the opportunity,' he said. 'But to make sure we can ask about it.'

They found the typewriter, which was a portable one, and Fen screwed a piece of blank paper into it.

'How does it go?' he asked. 'Ah, yes . . . "*I am tired of blackmail. You may expect a visit from me soon*".'

He tapped away inexpertly for some moments. 'Damn,' he said. 'I've hurt my finger on the shift-lock.'

Wyndham compared the two sheets of paper. 'Yes,' he announced, 'I think the letter was obviously typed on this machine. You can see, for one thing, that the *m*'s out of alignment. But I'll get an expert to deal with it, for the purposes of the trial.'

Fen straightened himself, stretched, and yawned. 'So that's

that,' he remarked. 'Oh, my dear paws, how sleepy I feel . . . You'll search his belongings for the dagger, of course. And I should *think* there may be some prints taken from it, all duly and correctly attested— though of course a surface like that will keep prints for years, if it's not mucked about.'

'I'm very grateful to you, sir,' said Wyndham hesitatingly. 'If you hadn't pointed out that one simple thing to me, he might have been able to get clear of the country.'

'That's all right,' said Fen. 'Besides, I'm grateful to you, too. This business got me away from a children's party which descends on my house like a black cloud every Christmas Eve. And if there's one thing more horrible than violent death, it's the sight and sound of a large number of the young simultaneously enjoying themselves . . . Well, I suppose you'd better collect your man.'

'It'll be a pleasure,' Wyndham murmured. 'From almost every point of view, it'll be a pleasure.'

14

Actually it was Janice who had persuaded P.C. Scott to let them go into the library. Noel was too tired to be anxious for anything but bed. There was a faint glow in the middle of the heap of white ashes in the fireplace, and Noel put a log on top of it; it burned feebly for about a minute, and then went out. They huddled over it seated together on a small sofa.

'There,' said Janice. 'This is better, isn't it?'

'You seem to have no sense of cold whatever,' Noel answered ungraciously. 'You're full of disgusting animal vitality.'

'Are you really interested in Assyriology? How funny. Tell me how the Assyrians made love.'

'They made love in exactly the same way that everybody else makes love. And the only thing I'm interested in at present is my health.'

'Shall I sit on your knee?'

'Oh the whole, no. I wonder when we're going to be able to get to bed.'

'Not until the parson has blessed us with bell and book, Noel.'

'I have a bad cold.'

'Don't be so fussy, darling. Have you ever been in love?'

'Never.'

'Not with Patricia?'

'Not with anyone.'

'You may kiss me if you wish.'

'I don't wish.'

'On the whole that's just as well,' said Janice judicially. 'Because you're not very competent at making love.'

'Oh really?' said Noel, nettled.

'For example, if you'd never met me until this moment, how would you begin making love to me?'

'No, Janice, I refuse to be caught that way.'

'I'm not trying to *catch* you, idiot. Tell me what you'd do, and I'll tell you whether it's good technique or not.'

'Well, I suppose I should say something like: "You're really very beautiful . . ."'

'Yes, that's just the point, you see.'

'What's just the point, in God's name?'

'It's purely imbecile to trot out all that mildewed stuff.'

'One must *say* something first. A sort of warning. Like the red flag they put out before guns are going to go off.'

'No. It's quite superfluous.'

'I can't help that. It's a habit.'

'Very well. Go on.'

'Then I should say something on the lines of: "Your eyes are an enchanting blue."'

'They're brown.'

'I wasn't talking about *your* eyes. I was talking about the eyes of some hypothetical woman I've never met before.'

'My mother's eyes are brown, too. It runs in the family. Something to do with heredity.'

'Heredity. There's that limerick about . . .'

'I know it. Will you put your arm round me?'

'If you insist. But it's very uncomfortable for the man.'

'It's very uncomfortable for the woman, too.'

'Why do you allow it, then?'

'*I* always thought men liked doing it. One must throw them an occasional crumb. I think I'll sit on your knee after all,' said Janice, doing so. 'There. Isn't that nice?'

'It helps to keep me warm,' Noel admitted grudgingly.

'Darling, *why* don't you like me?'

'Janice, you're an intolerable little flirt. You should be spanked.'

'You may spank me if you like, but not too hard.'

'Don't you realise that no man has any use for a woman who runs after him?'

'Oh, no?' said Janice softly.

Noel took her up in his arms and deposited her firmly and not particularly gently in a chair.

'Understand this,' he said, 'once and for all: *I have not the slightest intention of marrying you or anyone else*. Now, is that perfectly clear?'

'Yes, Noel,' said Janice meekly.

15

After a week's honeymoon in Scotland, Noel and Janice returned south to act as witnesses at the trial for murder of Andrew Forrest. They stopped for a night in Oxford, putting up at the 'Mace and Sceptre', and after dinner went to see Fen at his rooms in St Christopher's. They found him biting a pencil and trying to write a detective novel; he was obviously relieved at having an excuse for neglecting it.

'Well, well,' he greeted them. 'All congratulations. I'm sorry I wasn't able to get to the wedding. Have you had a good honeymoon?'

'It's been very satisfactory, thank you,' said Janice demurely. Fen bustled about finding them drinks.

'You must tell us what's been happening,' said Noel, when they were at last settled. 'We've lost touch with everything.'

'His identity's been proved,' Fen answered. 'Which is most of the battle. And Crispin is proposing to write the case up. I suppose I shall have to get in touch with him about it—poor old chap, he gets terribly muddled . . .'

'I still don't understand how you *knew*,' said Janice.

'Ah,' said Fen complacently. 'Well, I shall now explain; and don't try to stop me, because it's a great and ancient tradition which must not be broken.

'Of course, the lynch-pin of the whole case lay in the words which Louise Munro spoke just before she died. I've no doubt you remember them—"*Patricia . . . in danger . . . help her*". And a little later: "*Mustn't be destroyed . . . I'll tell you . . . who . . .*"

'From the first, those words puzzled me, and I was careful to ask if you thought Louise was sane when she spoke them.

'MacAdam asked her the name of her attacker. Why on earth, then, didn't she immediately give it? Why, instead, did she trot out this stuff about Patricia being in danger? Because if Patricia was in danger, surely she could best be helped by Louise's revealing the identity of the criminal.

'Well, there seemed to me to be three possible solutions to this problem:

'(i) The person endangering Patricia was not the same person who had attacked Louise. I thought, on the whole, that that wasn't very likely, but it couldn't be ruled out, and I kept it in mind.

'(ii) It was Louise herself who endangered Patricia, and now she was repenting it. That again postulated two criminals in the party.

'(iii) The remark was addressed to Richard Neame, who, as we know, was infatuated with Patricia, and would be certain, on hearing she was in danger, to go to her assistance. Even if he were disinclined for some reason to do so, *someone*, in view of Louise's urgency, would have to go, and public opinion would unanimously expect that someone to be Richard Neame.

'It was this last hypothesis which gave me most to think about. At the time, naturally, I'd no idea whether it was true or not, but I went on considering it, while still keeping an eye open for anything which might confirm either of the other two explanations.

'The interesting thing about it, to me, was that I couldn't for the moment see why Louise should want to send Richard Neame away at all. If it was he who had attacked her, there was no clear reason why she shouldn't denounce him instantly, and in his presence; after all, there were three other men there who might be considered competent to handle him. I seemed to be up against a blank wall.

'And then two things happened: I heard that Louise's maiden name was Benest; and a blackmail letter was discovered in her room.

'Immediately I remembered the main outlines of the Forrest case—the curious episode of the missing dagger. In the first place that gave me the motive, which so far had been missing: brother Andrew was taking his revenge for the execution of Edward Forrest—the knife slashes in themselves were evidence of definite hatred, and not of a crime committed, say, for the sake of money. And in the second place, Hadow, when he was narrating the Forrest case for the benefit of Wyndham and myself, let out one staggering, all-important fact.

'Louise Munro suffered from claustrophobia; she could not endure to be shut up.

'Now, cast your minds back to the Forrest case. Brother Andrew, and the missing dagger, weren't the only oddities in it. There was in addition one psychological inconsistency which couldn't be ignored. Charles Benest was a steady, unimaginative, reliable young man. Is it conceivable that such a person, even to protect his sister, would rush up behind a policeman and stab at him with what was practically a toy dagger? Of course not.

'When he admitted to doing that, Charles certainly wasn't shielding Edward or Andrew Forrest; obviously he was shielding Louise, who suffered from an affliction of such a nature that imprisonment would have driven her mad. Charles loved his sister so well that he was prepared to take the blame for what she had done, and so went to prison for fourteen years; and she, though she was devoted to him, *dared* not admit her guilt.

'One could guess fairly accurately what actually happened (and incidentally, Charles Benest has confirmed it since). It was Louise who picked up the dagger in the outer office. Then, you remember, Louise and Charles left the building, though they remained down below, hiding when the night-watchman went in. Then Louise went round to the courtyard—alone, it seems, while Charles waited in the alley—and witnessed the finding of the revolver and the murder itself. Charles heard the shot. What, in the circumstances, would he do? Run away? Hardly; he wasn't that kind of man. He would—and he did—go up to the office. And Louise, running round from the courtyard to tell him what had happened, saw him go—and was in time, too, to see the policeman who shortly afterwards followed him. Plainly she was terrified in case her beloved Charles should seem to be involved in the murder. So she attacked the policeman. As you know, she was a much more hysterical character than her brother.

'No doubt she immediately threw aside the dagger, as Charles asserted that he did; and no doubt they were both very astonished when it wasn't found. It wasn't found, of course, because the "belated wayfarer" whom the constable saw had witnessed the entire business, and made off with it. And who could that belated wayfarer have been but brother Andrew?

'It's not easy at first sight to see *why* he took the dagger. But one's got to remember, I think, that he was—and will be, until he's hanged—a professional criminal. He saw the incident; he knew that the constable would not be able to identify the girl who attacked him; and consequently it was probable that the only evidence against her would be the dagger, with her prints on it, which she had so carelessly thrown away, and which would constitute, in his possession, a most agreeable weapon of blackmail. So he took it. He must have been considerably surprised when Charles confessed to the attack, but fortunately the value of the dagger was not thereby depreciated; he could still use it to blackmail Louise.

Then Edward Forrest was tried, and Louise's evidence was instrumental in hanging him. For the moment Andrew Forrest forgot about blackmail; he wanted revenge. He wrote Louise threatening letters, and on the day of Edward Forrest's execution he tried to kill her. She applied for police protection, and since he was cautious, and could afford to wait, he did nothing more for the moment. Time passed; Louise married a rich man; and it occurred to Andrew that before she was killed—and he still intended, with all his heart and soul, to kill her—she might as well be made, by his threatening to produce the dagger, to contribute to his private exchequer.'

Fen emptied his glass and re-filled it. 'Most of that I was able to work out as soon as I heard of Louise Munro's connection with the Forrest case. I remember that even at the time of the trial I was assailed by vague doubts as to whether Charles Benest actually *had* attacked the policeman. And as soon as the blackmail note turned up in Louise's room, I was damned well certain that he hadn't.

'Wyndham, in the first instance, got the meaning of the note the wrong way round; he thought that it was from someone who was being blackmailed *by Louise.* But as it happened, the wording was quite ambiguous, and I'd no doubt what the proper interpretation was. "*I am tired of blackmail. You may expect a visit from me soon.*"

'Andrew Forrest had got all the money he wanted out of Louise; now he proposed to have his long-deferred revenge. You see why MacAdam said that Louise was frightened.

'So far, so good. And how did all this new evidence react on my three hypotheses regarding Louise's last words? Obviously it explained just why she wanted to get Richard Neame out of the way. She was devoted to Charles, remember; only a pathological condition of mind—claustrophobia—induced her to let him go to prison in her place; and now she realised that she was dying, and her last thought was that the dagger must be preserved, her own guilt proved, and Charles released—his sentence, you know, had still seven more years to run. If she denounced Neame there and then, *he* would certainly not mention the dagger, and it might never come to light; if she spoke of it to the others in front of him, he might find a means of hiding or destroying it; it was possible, indeed, that he had provided against the contingency of arrest by arranging for some accomplice to do just exactly that—since he must have hated Charles Benest almost as much as he hated Louise. So she invented the tale about Patricia to get him away, relying on being able to tell the others about the existence of the dagger when he had gone. But she'd overestimated her strength. '*It mustn't be destroyed . . . I'll tell you who . . .*' And then she died.'

'But look here,' Noel interrupted, 'would he have *believed* such a tale?'

'There are three things to remember,' said Fen. 'First, that the previous attack on Patricia gave some plausibility to Louise's assertion; second, that Neame must have been absolutely staggered at finding his victim still alive, and have been incapable, for the moment, of lucid thought; and third, that in any case, he was glad of an excuse to get away. He must have expected to be denounced in the next few moments, and there might be a chance for him to make a dash for it in one of the cars. Of course,' Fen added parenthetically, 'Patricia was never in any danger at all.'

'The strychnine, though,' Janice interposed.

'Oh, Janice, don't you *see*?' Noel expostulated with some impatience.

'Be quiet, both of you,' said Fen waspishly. 'If you're not going to attend, we'd better abandon the subject altogether.'

'Oh, no, *please*,' Janice pleaded.

'Very well,' said Fen with obvious relief, 'I'll go on. I think we only need a brief account of what happened before, during and after the murder—now that the processes of detection have been exposed,' he added grandly.

'Andrew Forrest took the name of Ronald Neame and got a job as a schoolmaster. While he was blackmailing Louise, he investigated, and insinuated himself into, her circle of acquaintances and friends. And the time came when MacAdam invited them both to the same house-party at Rydalls. Neame knew that Louise would be there, since MacAdam was in the habit of informing people of their prospective fellow-guests, and he came well-provided—among other things, with strychnine—for any emergency. On the previous evening, he had stayed at the same hotel as Patricia, and had typed his last note to Louise—the one we found—on the machine Patricia had borrowed from Peter Hadow.

'Louise arrived at Rydalls at practically the same moment as Neame and Patricia, and she must have seen the typewriter among Patricia's luggage. Shortly afterwards, Neame left his note in Louise's room—or perhaps pushed it under the door. Louise must have been very frightened when she found it; but she remembered Patricia's typewriter, and when Patricia had gone downstairs, Louise went to try it out. She found—as we found later—that the note had, in fact, been typed on that machine. What conclusions she drew, one doesn't know, but evidently she was anxious to find out more about Patricia. She took the diary as being the most likely source of information, and Patricia surprised her just as she was leaving. There was a scuffle, and Louise got away.

'Neame's opportunity came when the game of hide-and-seek was proposed. The house would be in darkness, and he would be able (so he thought) to time things very comfortably. He arranged to meet Louise in the long gallery, possessed himself of Nathan's gloves and a knife from the kitchen, and when the lights went out was ready for what he had to do. He can't of course, have been aware of the presence of Simon Moore in the vestibule when he went through to the long gallery. He throttled Louise, and when, as he imagined, she was dead, mutilated her back with the knife. It must have been just after he had done this, and was preparing to leave—to be found, at the end of the game, in some other quarter of the house—that the first disaster (from his point of view) occurred.

Hadow arrived; the gong was sounded prematurely; the lamp at the other end of the long gallery went on; and he heard you coming up on to the terrace.

'So he picked up the body of the woman he thought was dead, and kissed her. And when you two had gone, he flung aside the knife and gloves, and went to join the other guests in the drawing-room. Since you stayed outside canoodling,' said Fen severely, 'he was able to get there well before you.

'Well, the search was organised, and he got his second shock: Louise was still alive. She spun her tale about Patricia, and he, no doubt, accepted it as an excuse for clearing out. But unfortunately, Simon Moore elected to go with him, and in the circumstances he couldn't give any excuse for leaving the house which wouldn't have made Moore instantly suspicious. He must have had a nasty few minutes before MacAdam came up to say that Louise hadn't, after all, named her assailant. In the meantime, of course, he'd seen through the purpose of Louise's Patricia-fabrication. Louise's connection with the Forrest trial would come out soon enough, and perhaps the business about the dagger. He was prepared for that in any event, and if Louise hadn't had the chance to speak, there'd have been no more case against him than against anyone else without an alibi for the time of the murder. But she *had* spoken, and he thought he might divert suspicion from the real purpose of her words by giving the Patricia-fabrication some basis in fact. He went into the bathroom and fetched out Patricia's bottle of tonic. He thought it had been poisoned, he said. And indeed, it had. He'd just that moment poisoned it himself . . .'

There was a long silence. Then: 'Poor Patricia,' said Janice quietly.

'She'll get over it.' Noel spoke very definitely. 'There never was such an extrovert as that girl. The moment she finds anyone or anything else to interest her, Richard Neame will be completely forgotten—probably is already. What s happening about Charles Benest?'

'The dagger was found, of course,' said Fen. 'And he'll be released, after a lot of formalities. He'll get no compensation for the seven years he was in prison, because he pleaded guilty. But after all, they were only seven years of war—not so much loss.'

'I still can't understand it being Richard,' said Janice. 'He seemed so dull and ordinary.'

'I think he was a schizophrenic,' Fen answered,' which means he didn't have to act the dullness and ordinariness. One half of him was the earnest educationist, the man who toiled and saved to send his brother to the University, the devoted lover of Patricia Davenant; the other half was a blackmailer, a swindler, and a murderer. It's a good thing that kind of person isn't born very often . . .'

He poked inexpertly at the fire with the toe of his shoe. Depression was very perceptible on his normally cheerful features. 'It was an ugly crime,' he said. 'I think he'll hang—and from every point of view he deserves to . . . Ah, well'—he reached for the whisky decanter—'*ad laetiora vertamus*.'

EDMUND CRISPIN

Bruce Montgomery, who wrote detective fiction as 'Edmund Crispin', was born at Chesham Bois in Buckinghamshire in 1921. His mother was Scottish and his father, an Ulster Protestant, worked in the India Office and expected that his son would also become a civil servant. As a child, Montgomery excelled in music, painting and writing, but he was a nervous, shy child and his parents would often recount how, on leaving a children's party at the age of seven, he had thanked the hostess for inviting him and explained that, although he had not enjoyed himself, it was not her fault. A degree of reticence stayed with him all his life and this may be partly explained by the fact that Montgomery had been born with two club feet, as a result of which he disliked all forms of sport intensely, although—perhaps surprisingly—he enjoyed swimming.

At Merchant Taylors' School, Montgomery won many prizes but was not popular. However, when he went up to Oxford, he blossomed. Red-haired and flamboyant, he was appointed organist and choirmaster at St John's College and, as well as playing music and attending choral evensong, he spent many hours in pubs in conversation with friends or solving the *Times* crossword, a life-long passion. He also read books and in his final year John Maxwell, then artistic director at the Oxford Playhouse, lent his friend a copy of John Dickson Carr's *The Crooked Hinge*. Montgomery stayed up all night to finish the book and so began a life-long passion for detective stories. As well as Carr, his favourite writers were Agatha Christie, Gladys Mitchell, Pamela Branch and H. C. Bailey. He also admired the early novels of Michael Innes, including *Hamlet, Revenge!* (1937), which features a character called Gervase Crispin. Montgomery liked the surname and, as he had red hair, was going to adopt 'Rufus Crispin' as his pen name until he learned of the existence of the crime writer Rufus King which prompted him to switch the forename to that of the illegitimate son of the Earl of Gloucester in Shakespeare's *King Lear*.

Montgomery's first detective novel, *The Case of the Gilded Fly* (1944), was written in only two weeks while he was still an undergraduate. His detective, Gervase Fen, is Professor of English Language and Literature at Oxford, a breezy don with a love of hairy tweeds and fast cars. He is named of course for John Dickson Carr's best-known detective Gideon Fell, and while Fen's penchant for puns and arcana certainly owe something to Fell, Fen is vain where Fell is merely immodest and the two detectives have *very* different builds. Perhaps taking a cue from Carr's mysteries written as 'Carter Dickson', Montgomery's Fen novels—particularly the earlier titles—combine detection and madcap humour; and he also took from Carr the quirk of breaking the fourth wall from time to time to address the reader directly.

In September 1943, after coming down with a second class degree in modern languages, Montgomery took up a position teaching English and Music at Shrewsbury School in Shropshire where his favourite lesson was to read aloud the ghost stories of M. R. James, another influence on his detective fiction. While at Shrewsbury, which would appear, thinly disguised, as Castrevenford School in *Love Lies Bleeding* (1948), he met regularly with another admirer of the work of John Dickson Carr, the poet Philip Larkin, whom Montgomery had met at Oxford. Together with Geoffrey Bush and others, Montgomery also formed The Carr Club, an informal society dedicated to the analysis of impossible crimes.

In 1945, Montgomery went to Devon, initially living with his mother at her home in Brixham and then in a bungalow near Dartington, which Philip Larkin claimed had had a bomb-proof cellar. Montgomery's intention was to write one novel a year 'for a living' and, inspired by the conductor John Hollingsworth, to compose an average of three small works and one large scale work 'for amusement'. In 1947, he became a member of the Detection Club and gave talks on crime fiction both locally and, in August 1949, on the radio, where he championed the virtues of detective stories on the BBC's Third Programme. At home, Montgomery played bridge; he also chaired meetings of the South Devon Literary and Debating Society and made appearances for charity as a *Brains' Trust* panellist. A first class pianist, he taught at the Torbay School of Music in Paignton and conducted the choral section of the Paignton Amateur Operatic and Dramatic Society as well as the Paignton Fairbairn Choir. Montgomery loved Devon, once saying that he wouldn't live in London for a thousand pounds and he was fond of comparing himself to Rex Stout's home-loving Nero Wolfe. A significant exception was the annual Detection Club dinner and for these Montgomery often travelled up to London with his near neighbour Agatha Christie who, unlike most people, always called him Edmund.

Montgomery had continued to write detective novels throughout the 1940s, working in a study that was lined with alphabetically ordered, jacketless books and which looked out towards Brixham Harbour and Torbay. But by 1950, it was clear that music was a good deal more profitable than literature and what would for over twenty years appear to be the last of his 'Crispin' novels, *The Long Divorce*, was published in 1951.

As a musician and composer, Montgomery was largely self-taught. In 1937, at the age of fifteen, he had played the organ at his sister's wedding and in 1938, '39 and '40, he played his own compositions as live accompaniment for pantomimes and revues performed by the Amersham Repertory Company. After moving to Devon, he performed regularly in local concerts and, in 1948, he and Geoffrey Bush conducted at London's Wigmore Hall. In a long career, Montgomery produced a major chorale, *The Oxford Chorale*, several songs and Shakespearean settings, as well as music for over 40 films, each of which would take him between four to six weeks to score. He composed the music for the first four of the *Doctor* comedies, based on the novels by Richard Gordon, and also for the first five *Carry On* films until he was sacked for missing a deadline. His favourite piece was another chorale, *Venus Praised*, but although his work was popular with audiences it was considered overly romantic by critics.

While composing music was his main occupation from the early 1950s, Montgomery did not abandon literature altogether. He reviewed books for the *Sunday Times* and edited anthologies. In 1957, he adapted a 1949 short story 'Beware of the Trains' for a series of radio plays by the Detection Club and, together with Anthony Berkeley and John Dickson Carr—by now a friend—he took part in *Connoisseurs in Crime*, a radio series in which a group of crime writers selected their favourite fictional and real-life cases for dramatization; Montgomery's choices were the baffling Pimlico poisoning mystery and Carr's 'Carter Dickson' novel *The Judas Window* (1938). He also continued to write short stories but these too petered out and the career of 'Edmund Crispin' appeared to be over.

Montgomery's musical career, however, continued to flourish with fees from his music making up two-thirds of his income. But he had always been a heavy drinker and by the mid 1960s his health was in decline and he fell into the hands of the medical profession, an experience that encouraged him to write six chapters of a novel for Macmillan called *What Seems to be the Trouble?* However, alcohol was not his only problem. His right hand was gradually being crippled by Dupuytren's Contracture, which causes the fingers to turn inwards, eventually making him unable to play the piano and compose.

In 1976, Montgomery married his secretary Ann Clements who had worked for him since 1957. And then in 1977, Gollancz published *The Glimpses of the Moon* (1977), the final 'Edmund Crispin' novel. The same year, Bruce Montgomery attended his final Detection Club dinner, desperately ill, and he died in 1978.

'The Hours of Darkness' is published for the first time in this volume though a version of the story, not featuring Fen, was broadcast on the BBC Home Service on 31 December 1949.

CHANCE IS A GREAT THING

E. C. R. Lorac

'I do hope you don't mind me popping in, Mrs Banks, but the fact is I'm so worried about my auntie.'

Mrs Banks, stout and fifty, sitting opposite her husband by the cosy kitchen fire, replied heartily. 'Come in, Miss Tiler, and welcome. Always pleased to see our neighbours, but what's this about your auntie?'

'Now you sit down here, Miss Tiler,' said Banks, nobly offering his own comfortable chair. (Banks was a plumber, and his feet often troubled him.)

Peggy Tiler, a smart, if somewhat flashy young woman in her twenties, looked a little out of place in the homely kitchen, but she took Banks's chair saying, 'Thanks ever so,' and began to pour out her troubles.

'She's so poorly, Mrs Banks. I took her to see the doctor and he said her heart was valvular or something, and there were murmurs and that she ought to be careful.

'Well, ever since then I've tried to make her go slow, but she won't, you know. She does too much, always scrubbing and that, as though the house mattered compared with her health.'

'Ar-rr' put in Banks. 'That's a woman all over. 'Ouse proud. Your auntie's always been the same. What I says is—'

'Now you be quiet, Banks,' said his wife firmly. 'You tell me what you're worrying about, dearie,' she added to Peggy, and Peggy went on:

'She comes all over queer, Mrs Banks. Goes all dizzy, and the other day she nearly fell down in the Tube, and she's that short-sighted, too. I don't think she ought to live in that house all alone. As you know, I've been staying with her nearly a month and I meant to go home next week, but I don't see how I can, with her being so shaky.'

'But I thought you was going to get married, dearie,' said Mrs Banks, and Peggy sobbed. 'So I was, and my Bob's ever so keen, but I'm the only relation auntie's got, and I don't see how I can leave her.'

'Well, that wants thinking about,' said Banks weightily. 'A chance is a chance and a girl oughtn't to turn her back on a good husband if so be one offers. Your auntie now—'

'Be quiet, Banks,' retorted his wife. 'Miss Tiler's quite right to think of her auntie—not that we wouldn't keep an eye on her, us having been neighbours nearly 12 years. I'd always pop in and welcome, and I'd sleep in any time she's feeling poorly.

'Now say if we settle it like this, dearie. You stay on another week, and if she don't seem no worse, you go back home and get busy with your trousseau and that, and if so be it's necessary, Banks'll drop you a line and tell you how auntie is. You just trust us to keep an eye on her, see?'

'Thanks ever so! That'd be a great weight off my mind,' said Peggy Tiler. 'Auntie'd be that cross if she knew I'd worried you, her being too independent to tell anyone she's poorly, but I just couldn't go away without saying something—and she goes that blue in the face sometimes, I'm real frightened.'

'I'm very glad you've told us, miss,' said the irrepressible Banks. 'As Mother says, we'll keep an eye on Miss Walton. Been friends and neighbours all these years. Couldn't do less.'

'And she's fond of you,' declared Peggy.

'And us of her,' said Mrs Banks. 'Now you rely on us, dearie, and though Banks didn't put it very well, chance is a great thing, so don't you go and miss yours. Never keep a young man waiting when 'e's ready with the wedding ring.'

'She's a smart piece, and I've no doubt she's snappy at demonstrating those electric gadgets,' said Banks later when Peggy had gone. 'But I wish 'er joy o' that Bob Hewson of hers. And that reminds me: Didn't Miss Walton promise to leave you her silver tea service and that gold watch of her dad's?'

'What a thing to say,' protested Mrs Banks. 'I'm ashamed of you—not but what she did promise, us having been neighbours so long, and her not too partial to that Peggy.'

'I wonder if the old lady put it down on paper,' ruminated Banks. 'When you nursed her over that bronchitis, she did mention a legacy. Be a pity if 'er wishes wasn't carried out.'

'There is that,' agreed Mrs Banks, 'but we can't do nothing about it, so it's no use worrying.'

'I'm not so sure of that,' said Mr Banks thoughtfully. 'I might put in a word, tactful like. I know what. I'll tell her I'm making a will meself, and ask her if she'd oblige by being a witness to same. That'll sort of break the ice. And you can say as 'ow it's everybody's bounden duty to make a proper will. So's to save all the nasty backbiting and unpleasantness you get after the funeral.'

'Now you stop it, Banks,' said his wife severely. 'If you so much as mentions the word funeral to Miss Walton, you'll put your foot in it proper. Why, with a heart like that she might pop off any minute if you upsets her, and what about a legacy then? I can see that Peggy Tiler showing respect to the dead by carrying out her auntie's sacred wishes, I don't think. If ever there was a Miss Grab-all, it's that Peggy!'

'A-rr-r, didn't I always tell you there was more in it than met the eye when Miss T. came over all attentive to auntie?' said Banks. 'And there must be a nice little bit in the bank, too, for

Miss Walton's lived very lady-like and comfortable all these years. Tell you what, Maggie, you make an 'abit of goin' in there last thing of an evening, just to see Miss Walton's comfortable and that, and I'll offer to fix that sink of 'ers she's 'ad trouble with, and maybe do that bit o' wiring so's she can 'ave the electric over 'er sink same's she been wanting. A little bit of neighbourly attention to lead up to me just mentioning about 'er will, see?'

'Maybe I do,' said Mrs Banks, 'but just you be careful. The trouble with you is that you thinks you're clever, and I 'appen to know you ain't, so don't go trying your tact stuff on with the old lady, or maybe you'll upset the blooming apple-cart.'

'Sorry to bother you, ma'am, but is there a party named Hewson here? Bob Hewson's the name.'

Miss Walton was turning out her kitchen, busy with pail and scrubbing brush; overhead the new electric light (fixed by Mr Banks) shone brightly, and Miss Walton turned quite proudly to the back door where the strange gentleman had just knocked and put his head in at the half-open door.

He had spoken politely, and Miss Walton replied cheerfully: 'I'm afraid you've got the wrong house. I'm the only person here. My niece has been staying with me, but she's just this moment leaving.'

'Sorry to have bothered you, ma'am, and thank you,' replied the other. He was a well set-up young fellow, and Miss Walton added, 'Try next door. Mr Banks knows everybody about here.'

He went away, murmuring thanks, and a moment later Peggy Tiler's shrill voice called: 'Auntie. Auntie. Be an angel and wait at the front door to watch for my taxi. I've brought my suitcase down, and the taxi's ordered, and now I've got a run in my stocking. I must mend it, or it'll run right down. If the taxi comes, tell him to put my case inside. I won't be a brace of shakes.'

Obligingly, Miss Walton went to the front door, thinking how nice it would be to have the house to herself again. Peggy meant well, but was always fussing over something.

Glancing down the little alley-way which separated her house from the Banks's, Miss Walton saw that her gentlemanly visitor was chatting to Mr Banks at the yard gate. A moment later Peggy came flying to the front door.

'Thanks a lot, Auntie, I've fixed it. You just go and carry on with your old scrubbing, but don't work too hard. I'll come and say goodbye when the taxi's come.'

'All right, dear. I'll just finish scrubbing that dresser,' said Miss Walton.

Mr Banks and his visitor saw the taxi arrive and heard Peggy yell loudly, 'Auntie, darling, I'm going now.'

She dashed into the house, leaving the front door open, and they heard her call: 'Auntie, I'm just off,' and a moment later her voice broke into a shrill scream of terror.

'Cripes! What on earth?' yelled Mr Banks, as his visitor leapt over the little fence and landed in Miss Walton's yard. Peggy still wailed loudly, 'Auntie! Auntie!' and Mr Banks was in the next door kitchen in 'two shakes of a duck's tail,' as he said afterwards.

Poor Miss Walton lay on the floor, her pail overturned beside her, floods of soapy water running around the flagstones. The visitor was bending over Miss Walton, and Peggy was wailing: 'She's fainted. It's her heart. Oo, I knew all that scrubbing was too much for her.'

'Better have a light on,' said Mr Banks. 'Heck, the bulb's gone phut, just when it's wanted, too.'

The visitor jumped to his feet and astonished Mr Banks by blowing a police whistle. 'Yelling won't help, Miss,' he said sharply to Peggy. 'You go and sit in the parlour and keep quiet.'

Another tall man appeared at the kitchen door. 'Surgeon—and make it snappy,' ordered the first man, and then a uniformed constable arrived. 'Take this lady into the parlour and stay there with her,' snapped the original visitor.

Well, I never did!' exclaimed Mr Banks. 'Is she very bad?'

'She's dead,' replied the other.

'I was afraid of this,' said Mr Banks, 'her heart was weak.'

'It was, was it?' rejoined the other. 'I'm a CID man. You can just stay where you are until I'm ready to talk to you.'

He looked round the kitchen at the overturned pail and the rubber kneeling mat just beside it, and scratched his head thoughtfully. Then he glanced at the new electric fitment overhead.

'Who fixed that up?' he demanded.

'I did,' said Mr Banks, 'and a good workman-like job it is too. Wires properly insulated, bakelite fittings all in order, so don't you go looking down your nose at me. Nothing wrong with it, except the bulb's gone.

'And why's it gone?' demanded the CID man. 'It was all right when I was here five minutes ago. Where's the main fuse box?'

Banks indicated the fuse box with a gesture of his thumb, and the CID man opened it.

'Main fuse gone,' he said. 'Now you just stay where you are and don't make trouble. There's some reason why that fuse went.'

'I'm not making any trouble. If you think my wiring's at fault I'll trouble you to call in the borough electricians,' said Mr Banks with dignity.

The CID man lifted the bucket thoughtfully and set it on the rubber kneeling mat. It was very thick rubber.

'A-rr-r . . . see what you're getting at,' said Banks. 'That's insulated, that is. Try the dustbin, mister. You've got something there. And kindly remember I was talking to you next door when this 'ere occurred.'

The CID man went and rummaged in the ashes in the dustbin and returned shortly with a length of flex, fitted at one end with an adapter for plugging into the bulb socket.

The other end of the flex was untwisted into its two separate wires, one wire being stripped of its insulated covering for several inches. Both wires were still dripping with soapy water.

'The wickedness of it!' exclaimed Mr Banks. 'You see what she did?'

'You be quiet,' said the CID man. 'It's fingerprints that will settle this job. There wasn't time to wipe them off.'

Both the electric bulb and the adapter on the flex showed Peggy Tiler's fingerprints.

Without assistance from Mr Banks, the CID man re-assembled the contraption with which Peggy had killed her aunt. She had connected her flex by means of its adapter to the bulb socket.

The bared half of the flex wire was run into the bucket of water, the other half was balanced over the edge of the bucket, hanging clear, but in such a manner that it would have slipped into the water when the short-sighted Miss Walton plunged her hand into the bucket. The result was to make a complete circuit and thus bring about a lethal electric shock.

Although the bucket had stood upon the rubber mat to insulate it, Miss Walton, standing upon the damp flagstones of the kitchen floor, had earthed the apparatus when she touched the bucket.

When he was allowed to go home, Mr Banks gave a graphic account of the affair to his wife.

'The CID man was after Bob Hewson. Peggy's chap. He's a con man, and due for a stretch. The detective noticed at once the light 'ad failed, and 'e looked a bit old-fashioned at me . . . Poor old lady, if she 'adn't been so short-sighted she might've spotted them wires.'

'And think of Peggy getting 'er auntie out of the kitchen so's she could fix that up! I never did!' said Mrs Banks. 'Did Miss Walton ever make that will, Banks?'

'No she didn't. I suppose it'll all go to the Crown now,' said Banks sadly. 'No other relatives. That's another chance lost.'

'Chance lost, indeed!' said Mrs Banks. 'I reckon you 'ad a lucky chance yourself, that CID man being with you the identical moment it 'appened.'

'Maybe you're right,' said Mr Banks. 'I always said chance is a great thing.'

E. C. R. LORAC

Edith Caroline Rivett was born in Hendon, North London, in 1894. As well as two novels under her own name, she wrote over 70 book-length detective mysteries under two pen names: 'E. C. R. Lorac', who was assumed by many contemporary critics to be a man, and the less ambiguous 'Carol Carnac'.

Carol Rivett was largely brought up in St John's Wood, also in North London, and she attended the prestigious South Hampstead High School, one of Britain's leading girls' schools. After leaving, she became an art student at the Central School of Arts and Crafts, specialising in design, embroidery and calligraphy. She quickly gained employment as a school arts mistress, which she remained for many years, and she also supplemented her income by selling her own work and accepting private commissions. Rivett's work as a letterer was widely admired, and for eleven years she also worked on an illuminated book recording the benefactions made to the Abbey since the time of Edward the Confessor. However, Rivett's most significant artistic work, at least as far as readers of this volume are concerned, will be the logo she designed for the Detection Club, the dining club for mystery writers established in the late 1920s.

In the 1930s and 40s, Carol Rivett lived in South Devon where she was the arts mistress at a girls' boarding school, Blatchington Court, and she was very active in community affairs, raising funds for charities such as the Red Cross and the Royal Devon and Exeter

Hospital by, for example, sitting on a local Brains Trust alongside the Dowager Countess of Devon and other local luminaries. After the war Rivett moved to Aughton, a small village in Lunesdale, Lancashire, where she lived for many years with her sister Gladys. She continued to play a role in public life, for example opening exhibitions of the work of local artists, presenting prizes at local schools, and giving talks on the detective novel, as she did in 1953 as part of an exhibition mounted by the National Book League to mark Queen Elizabeth's coronation.

While Carol Rivett wrote some short stories in the 1920s, it was not until the comparatively late age of 36 that she attempted a novel, a detective story published in 1931 under the title *Murder on the Burrows* and credited to 'E. C. R. Lorac', the initials being of course her own and the surname an inversion of the name Carol. More than 40 more titles would follow and in 1936, in a similar approach to that taken by her contemporary Cecil Street, Rivett began a second series of novels, this time writing as Carol Carnac, the surname drawing on a remote but illustrious branch of her father's family. Rivett's two strands of books are pretty much indistinguishable in style, and while it is sometimes suggested that the Carnac books are all set in the North of England and the Loracs in the South, that is not the case. Generally, her plots are not particularly complex or challenging but they hold interest for their originality, and though some of her characters can be rather bland, others—particularly victims and murderers—are more memorable. Almost all of her books have an extremely strong sense of place, especially those with a rural setting. This was doubtless because Rivett set them in places she knew well—several early titles take place in London, especially St John's Wood and Regent's Park, including the political mystery *The Organ Speaks*, while others such as *Fire in the Thatch* are located in Devon, where Rivett lived in the 1930s. Several of her later books are set in Lancashire's Lune Valley and the surrounding areas, where Rivett lived after the Second World War; these include *Rigging the Evidence* (1955), which features a manhunt in Swaledale, and the highly regarded late novel *The Double Turn* (1956), which deals with the investigation of the death of the eccentric housekeeper of an aged and unfashionable artist.

As 'E. C. R. Lorac', Rivett's main character was Chief Inspector Robert Macdonald, a sound—if stolid—police officer who enjoys nothing better than a walk in the countryside. Like Rivett, 'Mac' prefers the single life and in around 30 novels he investigates with the help of Detective Inspector Reeves. As well as the novels and short stories in which Mac appears—the finest of which, arguably, are the serial murders story *Policemen in the Precinct* (1949) and the political mystery *Crime Counter Crime* (1936)—there is a single radio play, *Bubble, Bubble, Toil and Trouble*, in which Mac investigates death on a farm, *apparently* the result of natural causes. Most of the Carnac books also centre on two policemen, Inspector Julian Rivers and his sidekick Inspector Lancing, who are similarly methodical in their investigations.

Under her own name, Rivett wrote two 'straight' novels which have well-drawn characters and an undertow of humour. In the first, *Outer Circle* (1939), a seventeen year old girl—alone in the world—has an illegitimate child after a passionate love affair with a self-centred pianist whom she met in the Outer Circle, a road encircling Regents Park near Rivett's childhood home; in the second, *Time Remembered* (1940), a widow and her impetuous young niece have various adventures and eventually find happiness.

Carol Rivett remained active until her death in 1958. Although she is not seriously considered to be one of the true greats of the Golden Age, her work remains very popular. Her books have been difficult to obtain for many years but happily they are gradually becoming available again with reprints by the British Library and others.

'Chance is a Great Thing' was published in London's *Evening Standard* on 8 August 1950.

THE MENTAL BROADCAST

Clayton Rawson

I leaned across the magic shop counter and watched The Great Merlini put a drop of machine oil in the hinge of a Talking Skull.

'Jim Thompson,' I said, 'is gathering contributions for a book of tricks. He wants one from you.'

The skull in Merlini's hands wagged its jaw experimentally and Merlini threw his voice. The skull said, 'We just put the finishing touches on a new illusion—Sawing an Elephant in Two. Would he like that?'

'I doubt it,' I said sceptically. 'His readers might have difficulty getting such a big saw. Besides, he wants something impromptu and spectacular.'

'Particular, isn't he?' Merlini handed me a deck of cards. 'Here, look at this deck and make sure the cards are all different.'

I did. They were. I said, 'Okay.'

'Good. Take the deck into the next room, select and remember one card and bury it in the deck. Like this.' He demonstrated. 'Hold the deck face down, pull a group of cards at random from the middle of the deck, look at the card on the face of the group, drop them all on the deck and square it up. Then come back.'

This method of selection sounded familiar except that instead of trying to glimpse the top card as I always did, Merlini made it quite obvious that he had not seen any card. I scowled, went into the next room and did as directed.

When I returned he took the deck and said, 'You know the approximate location of your card in the deck, don't you?'

I nodded. He cut the deck a couple of times. 'I also want to be quite sure that you haven't any idea of its location.' He shuffled the deck and then handed it to me. 'Just to make sure, you shuffle it too.'

As I did so, he took a handkerchief from his pocket and blindfolded himself. 'You chose a card while in the next room,' he said. 'You know its name, but not its location. I know neither. I shall try to discover both—the card's name by mindreading, the location of the card by clairvoyance.' He took the deck from me and dropped it into his side coat pocket.

'Finally, by means of a highly developed sense of touch, I shall try to cut the cards at that exact spot and produce the card whose name is locked within your mind. And I shall do all that while blindfolded!

'First let me see how your mental transmission is this evening. I'll name a card at random—the Jack of Clubs. Please answer mentally whether or not that is your card. Just think either "Yes" or "No". Hmmm! Somebody must be operating a faulty electric appliance somewhere in the neighborhood. There's quite a bit of static. But your thought waves do come through faintly. You are thinking: *No*. Is that correct?'

It was, so I said, 'Yes.'

'Good. And since the Jack of Clubs is not your card we might as well get rid of it.' He reached into the pocket that held the deck, brought out one card, showed it to be the Jack of Clubs and tossed it aside.

Then he brought out another card—the Nine of Hearts—and displayed it. 'Is this your card?' he asked. 'Answer mentally, yes or no.' He concentrated a moment and then very positively and quite correctly said, 'You are thinking: *No*. Is it the same suit as your card? Answer mentally. Hmmm! Still *No*. Is the card I hold a red card? Oh, it is. Is it a Diamond? *No*. Then it must be a

Heart and—concentrate, please. You are thinking that it is a spot rather than a court card, that it has quite a number of spots. You are, in fact, thinking that it is the Nine of Hearts! Thank you very much. Now that your mental broadcasting set is warmed up we'll get down to business.'

His hand went into his pocket and brought out two cards. He held one in each hand. 'Look at this card closely,' he said. 'Good. And now this one. That's fine. Your thought is that they are both red cards. I'll discard one.' He tossed it aside, and brought another from his pocket. 'Red or black?' he asked. 'Answer mentally. Black. Good. Now which card is the same colour as the one you chose when you were out of the room—this one or this one?' He hesitated, then threw the red one aside. 'You are thinking: Black. Is that correct? It is. Thank you. Do I hold a Club or Spade? You are thinking: Spade. You chose a Spade but not the *Three* of Spades I have here. Is that correct?'

It was, so I admitted it.

Merlini continued, 'Your thoughts are coming in quite clearly now, so clearly, in fact, that I believe I have divined the name of the chosen card.' His hand went into his pocket. 'I shall try now to discover its location in the shuffled deck clairvoyantly. I have a feeling that it is the twenty-fourth card from the top.' His fingers riffled the cards. He brought one card from his pocket. 'The twenty-fourth card. And, if you have been concentrating correctly—your card. When I show it to you, please tell me aloud whether or not I am correct, but do not name the card. Is it yours?'

He turned the card around. It was the card I had chosen. I said so.

'Good,' he said, 'and your thought waves also tell me that this card which you chose, while in the next room, is the *Eight of Spades*!'

He whipped off his blindfold, tossed the Eight of Spades aside and took his bow. 'Do you think Jim will like that one?' he asked.

I nodded. 'I think he might—provided he's got space for all that patter.'

'Patter!' Merlini snorted. 'That's not patter. That's build-up. It's a way of getting a maximum of effect out of a few not very new but subtle angles. You don't appreciate . . .'

He scowled at me, muttered, 'Patter!' in an exasperated tone and then turned, walked into his inner sanctum and slammed the door behind him.

'Hey!' I objected. 'You didn't tell me how . . .'

His door opened again and he put his head out. 'Patter!' he said disgustedly. 'You can figure it out for yourself.' The door slammed again.

I sat down and waited. 'He's got to go out to eat sometime.' Then I had an idea. If Merlini had memorised four cards and placed them in his pocket before starting the trick, that would explain how, in spite of all the shuffling, he knew what the names of those first cards were.

As for locating the card I chose when out of the room—well, if he scratched the edge of the top card of the deck as he picked it up to begin the trick, that might help too. All he'd need to do then would be cut the cards and hold a break above the scratched card. When he demonstrated how I was to select a card, he pulled a group of cards from the deck just below the break, showed me the card on the bottom of the group, and dropped it on top of the deck. This would put the scratched card back on top of the deck when he handed it to me. And when I went out of the room and selected a card in the same manner, the card I looked at and remembered would be replaced directly on the scratched locator card.

When I returned, he took the deck and cut it a couple of times. On the last cut he broke the deck just above the scratched card and cut it to the top. The chosen card would then be on the bottom. He shuffled, palmed the chosen card off, and handed the deck to me to shuffle. His right hand went into his pocket at the same time, left the palmed card there and brought out the handkerchief with which he blindfolded himself.

Merlini later calmed down enough to admit that I had doped it correctly. 'And sometimes I plop a spot of wax on the back of the locator card so that the victim, after selecting a card, can give the deck an overhand shuffle before he comes back into the room.

'I like the trick because the out-of-the-room choice looks so completely impossible and because, the moment the chosen card is palmed off and in the pocket—from there on it's all presentation. If you lay an egg it's your own fault and if you wow 'em you can take the credit for that too. Anybody with money can buy tricks and anybody with a little imagination can invent 'em, but selling them to an audience is something else again. A pinch of showmanship and a few teaspoonsful of build-up are worth a trunk full of gimmicks. Presentation is . . .'

I had heard him give that lecture before so I said, 'Excuse me, but your pull is showing.' Then I jumped for the door.

I just barely managed to duck the heavy brass lota bowl he threw at my head.

CLAYTON RAWSON

The son of a railway clerk, Clayton Rawson was born in Elyria, Ohio, in 1906. He became a magician before he was eight years old and magic—and mystery—remained the driving force for the rest of his life. In an interview many years later, he explained that he spent most of his spare time making things appear and disappear, or in turning up at parties 'carrying a cross-cut saw and asking to borrow a lady'.

Rawson attended Ohio State University and in 1927 he was appointed as editor of *The Sun Dial*, the University's humour magazine. He graduated in 1929 and, later that year, married Catherine Stone. The couple moved to Chicago where Rawson found work as an illustrator. He also began writing in earnest, with a series of humorous stories for *College Life* magazine and pieces for various professional magic journals. In the mid-1930s he began his first novel for which he created a detective, the Great Merlini, a retired magician who runs a shop selling magic supplies. *Death from a Top Hat* (1938) was an immediate success and was filmed in 1939 as *Miracles for Sale*. To help establish the mechanics of the novel's plot Rawson built and furnished a series of 'murder rooms', which he then photographed for the first edition. In later years he would claim that the novel had taken longer than expected to write because he had been constantly distracted by the need to chase the family cat away from the models.

While other writers of detective stories would incorporate magic and magic tricks into their plots, this was the essence of Rawson's work and *Death from a Top Hat* features mind readers, magicians, spiritualists and escape artists.

For his third novel, *The Headless Lady* (1940), Rawson spent a week performing as a sideshow magic attraction with Russell Brothers' Circus as they played in western Pennsylvania in 1939. Merlini would appear in one more novel and over a dozen short stories, several of which were used by *Ellery Queen's Mystery Magazine* as the basis for reader competitions; another was printed on a jigsaw which, on completion, revealed the final clue to the mystery presented in the story. And Merlini was also the name under which Rawson himself would perform magic, and he used it for short pieces like *The Mental Broadcast*.

Using a house name, Rawson also wrote pulpish novellas featuring the Great Diavolo, another magician who investigates even more outré mysteries, featuring murderers who might be an invisible man or a genuine vampire; Rawson's Diavolo stories were collected in *Death out of Thin Air* (1941) and *Death from Nowhere* (1943).

In 1942, Rawson's final novel, *No Coffin for the Corpse* was published, and it was filmed the same year as *The Man Who Wouldn't Die*; as in *Miracles for Sale*, the Great Merlini did not appear, his role being given to a private eye created by Rawson's friend Brett Halliday.

In 1945, Rawson and Halliday—together with Anthony Boucher and Lawrence Treat—founded the Mystery Writers of America, which presents the annual Edgar Awards, and it was Rawson who proposed the MWA's annual banquet at which the Edgar for Best First Novel is presented. Rawson himself would receive awards from the MWA including in 1962, on the 113th anniversary of Edgar Allan Poe's death, the 'Cask of Amontillado' mystery award for his work in keeping alive 'the intrigue of mystery'. Rawson also served as the first editor for the MWA's newsletter, *The Third Degree*, whose title he had proposed, and he also coined the magazine's famous slogan 'Crime Doesn't Pay—Enough'. In 1948, Rawson became editor of *Clue*, 'a guide to mystery' for which one of his Edgars was awarded, and he would remain very active in the MWA for the rest of his life.

In 1952 the MWA's president Lawrence G. Blochman, vice-president Will Oursler and Rawson were part of a team engaged by Twentieth Century Fox to promote a film, *5 Fingers*, which concerned the activities and eventual exposure of one of the most infamous spies of the Second World War. In response, the MWA writers enlisted a couple of former soldiers, two actresses and a beauty queen to carry out a series of stunts involving the acquisition of blueprints for sensitive buildings and, incredibly, the planting of fake bombs on the New York subway, the Holland Tunnel, the George Washington Bridge and even inside the New York Police Department.

In 1963, Rawson took over as managing editor of *Ellery Queen's Mystery Magazine*, where he remained until his death in 1971 in Port Chester.

'The Mental Broadcast' was first published in *My Best: The Best Tricks from the Best Brains in Magic* (1945), edited by James G. Thompson Jr. I am grateful to Stephen Leadbeatter for drawing it to my attention.

WHITE CAP

Ethel Lina White

When Tess Leigh washed her hair, one June evening, she involved the issue of life or death . . . On the surface it seemed merely a matter of a trivial change of habit. Instead of going bare-headed to work, she had to wear a cap.

The reason was that her thick wavy hair became unruly if she exposed it to the open air too soon after a shampoo.

The turban was made from a white Angora scarf and was ornamented with a lucky brooch of green-and-white enamel in the shape of a sprig of white heather. Inside the band was stitched a laundry-tape marked with her name in red thread.

It was a glorious morning when—disdaining the trams—she set out to walk to the Peninsular Dye-Stuffs Corporation, where she was employed as a stenographer. The industrial town was built upon rolling moorland whose natural beauty had been destroyed; but the Council had acquired a range of hills—the Steepes—as its lungs and playground. About 1,000 feet in height, they were dominated by the mountain-peak—the Spike—which rose another 3,000 feet into the air.

Tess walked with the rapid ease of youth, swinging the suitcase which held her holiday-kit. From time to time she looked up at the Spike—sharply outlined against a cloudless blue sky. It helped her forget the smoking chimneys of the factories and also to calm her spirit—for all was not well either with her work or her love.

She had only herself to blame for her heart-trouble. No one at the Peninsular could understand why she had been taken in by the cheap glamour of Clement Dodd. She was attractive, athletic and possessed of a sweet yet strong character. Fearlessly outspoken, she had deep sympathy with the underdog and always rushed in to champion any victim of injustice.

As she approached the majestic pillared entrance to the factory, she felt a reluctance to enter which was becoming a familiar sensation.

She knew that she was not the only employee to feel that suddenly sinking heart and lagging foot, in spite of the fact that old John Aspinall—who founded the Peninsular Works—had striven to make it a model factory. He had arranged for the health, comfort and recreation of his workers. There were extensive grounds, a swimming pool, an excellent canteen and various athletic clubs.

These good things remained after his death when his son—Young John—went to the USA to study American methods, leaving his brother to direct the corporation. Brother Eustace was a lazy inefficient man who was content to sink to the status of a puppet government after Miss Ratcliffe had bought a controlling interest in the Peninsular.

She was a wealthy, keen-witted woman with a lust for power. Soured by lack of social sovereignty through her failure to marry a titled husband, she strove to become a Power in commerce. Part of her policy was to use the brains and experience of the men employed by the Peninsular. While she was professing interest in them, her keen brain was mincing up their suggestions and theories until they emerged as facts—for which she took all the credit.

Unfortunately the process was accompanied by corresponding human wastage, when gradually the atmosphere became poisoned because employees feared for their jobs. Most of the small-fry were too insignificant to be vulnerable, but Tess stood out from the bulk of the stenographer-staff, because of an unlucky incident.

The Peninsular ran a rifle club in connection with the municipal shooting-range. One day, Miss Ratcliffe visited them and gave what practically amounted to a demonstration in marksmanship. Tess, who was also expert, welcomed her only as a worthy opponent and challenged her to a match which she won by a narrow margin.

'Bad show,' commented her friends. 'After this, she will have her knife in you.'

In addition to anxiety for her job, Tess was beginning to fear that Miss Ratcliffe was developing her specialized interest in Clement Dodd. As chief accountant of the Finance Department, he frequently visited her office although he denied any personal element to Tess.

Tess's frown deepened as she passed through the gates and entered the grounds—gay with lilac and laburnum. Although it was the half-holiday, the model factory repelled her like a prison. As she gazed wistfully up at the soaring Spike, she suddenly saw a bird circling over its rocky summit.

'Don,' she called to a tall stooping man with grey hair and a classical profile, 'Don, do you see what I see?'

He shaded his eyes with a shaking white hand.

'It must be an unusually large bird to be visible at this distance,' he remarked. 'Can it be an eagle?'

'Of course it's an eagle,' cried Tess exultantly. 'Oh, isn't he a real king of birds? So free and splendid. I've a passion for eagles. The sight of one in captivity makes me see red.'

The old man did not respond to her interest for he was gazing eagerly at an impressive black saloon-car which had just driven up to the main entrance. As a majestic blonde ascended the steps, he glanced at the clock tower.

'Miss Ratcliffe sets us an example in punctuality,' he

remarked. 'In confidence, I have an appointment with her. My poor wife has resented the overtime I have given to the corporation. The fact is I was staying late to work out a system of reorganisation for several of the departments, to submit to Miss Ratcliffe . . . Now I believe I am going to reap my reward. My letter states that the subject of the interview is "important clerical changes".'

As she looked at his flushed triumphant face, Tess had a sudden pang of misgiving. Originally a schoolmaster, Don was a man of superior education. For the sake of a delicate wife and daughter, he had commercialised his scientific knowledge in the Peninsular Laboratory. He was intensely proud of his intellectual family and his cultured surroundings, where every book and picture was the result of selective taste.

'Don't count on it,' she warned him. 'Everyone knows that Ratcliffe is a rat.'

A short girl with a dark fringe and an important air looked at her sharply as she hurried past. She had chosen an unfortunate moment for her remark, since the energetic damsel was Miss Ratcliffe's secretary. Donovan, too, was visibly distressed by her imprudence.

But Tess smiled at him and entered the great hall to clock in.

A young man came forward to meet Tess as though he had been watching for her arrival. Ted Lockwood made no secret of his feeling for her. It was one of Nature's mysteries why she had rejected him for Clement, since he was so suited to be her opposite number. She had a mechanical mind so could appreciate the fact that he was a clever engineer. Like her, he was a fine athlete while he seasoned his sound qualities with a sense of humour.

'Will madame lunch with me?'

'Sorry, Ted,' replied Tess. 'I'm eating with Clem. Have you seen him around?'

'In the sick-bay. He's got a hangover and Matron's fussing over him. If a woman wants to be maternal, it beats me why she doesn't marry and set up her own outfit.'

'Meaning me?' asked Tess with customary bluntness.

'Yes, Tess.' Lockwood's face was grim with resolution. 'Why won't you face the facts? The most successful marriages are founded on mutual interest—and you and I have the same tastes. How will you make out with an artistic bloke like Dodd?'

'Oh, not again, Ted,' pleaded Tess wearily.

She had no further chance to brood for she always worked at high pressure. As the subject of the dictation was technical matter which exacted her entire attention, she welcomed a break, in order to freshen herself with a wash. The men's and women's cloakrooms were built off a central domed hall with a white marble drinking-fountain, which was a popular meeting place.

When she entered it, a group of employees were talking in excited undertones as they gathered around Clement Dodd. He was a tall slim-waisted youth who would have made a pretty girl, but for thin mobile lips. He spoke with a stressed Oxford accent while his manner to women of all ages was that of a courtier.

'Heard the latest casualty?' he asked Tess. 'Poor old Don's got the K.O.'

As Tess stared at him in dismay, he lit a cigarette.

'Afraid he asked for it,' he said casually. 'Too big for his boots. That line does not appeal to our lady-boss.'

'It's a real tragedy,' exclaimed a woman who dyed her grey hairs. 'He was nearly due to retire. Now he'll lose his pension. What will become of him?'

'Hush,' whispered a typist. 'He's coming in.'

His head held high, the old scientist approached the group. He cleared his throat before he made an announcement after the fashion of a Headmaster addressing his school.

'I have just resigned my position. I have never been happy in a non-scholastic atmosphere. Now I shall hope to resume my academic career. I wish to take this opportunity to thank you for your loyal support and cooperation.'

Although his lips quivered. he managed to make a grand exit.

As she watched him, Tess grew suddenly hot and giddy.

'It's cruel—hateful—abominable—' she stormed. 'That horrible woman has thrown him out just to save his pension.'

'Cool off, you young volcano.'

Tess felt herself pushed down on a chair. Although she recognised Lockwood's voice, she barely saw him through a shifting mist. She gulped down the glass of water which he drew for her and then gave him a grateful grin.

'O.K.?' he asked. 'What was the matter? You went first red and then white.'

'Temper,' she replied frankly. 'Only it's a bit more than that. Just before I left Canada, I was in an air crash. Since then, if I get too steamed up, I have a blackout. The doctor told me I'd grow out of it very soon, but he warned me not to get excited.'

'What's it like?'

'Foul—and frightening. Everything turns black and I drop into a sort of sleep. The doctor explained that sleep was my salvation, but it scares me because when I wake up, I can remember nothing. I go right out.'

The rest of the morning dragged itself out. Worried about Don, she forgot to concentrate on her work with the result that she had the greatest difficulty in reading back her outlines. As she was typing her notes, she noticed that Miss James—Ratcliffe's secretary—had entered the room and was whispering to the supervisor.

Although she vaguely expected it, her heart knocked at the summons.

'Miss Leigh. Please report at once to Miss Ratcliffe.' . . .

Seated at her desk, Miss Ratcliffe looked a model of impersonal

Administration—correct to form and polished in every detail. Her dark suit was perfectly built and her silver-blonde wave faultless.

'Miss Leigh?' Her voice was languid. 'Ah yes. I am sorry that your services will not be required after today. You will receive a week's wages in lieu of notice. This is no reflection on your work—but we have to reduce the staff.'

'But Miss Ratcliffe,' gasped Tess, 'there must be some mistake. My speeds are the highest in the office and—'

'This is not a personal matter.'

'But it is personal.' With characteristic courage, Tess dared to interrupt the tyrant. 'If it were not, I should be expected to work out my notice. I have a right to know the reason.'

'The reason is this,' she said. 'You have been disloyal.'

With a guilty recollection of unguarded remarks, Tess could not deny the charge. Instead she sank her pride to make an appeal.

'I don't want to inflict a sob-story on you, but I really need this work. I came over here from Canada when my parents died and I have no friends in England. Jobs are so scarce at present. Will you give me a second chance? I promise you I'll do better in future.'

Miss Ratcliffe looked at her with cold impersonal eyes as she touched her bell.

'My decision is final,' she said.

As Miss James bustled into the office and opened the door pointedly, Tess had a sudden vision of the eagle beating his great wings over the mountain top. The memory flooded over her, filling her with a wave of power.

She realized that she too was free and able to meet Ratcliffe on equal ground.

'You are a cruel, petty woman,' she said. 'The most junior typist has more right in the Peninsular than you have. You've bought your power—not earned it. And instead of using it, you abuse it. When worthwhile people are dying every day, it is a crime for you to be alive.'

She was conscious of passers-by in the corridor who paused to look into the office before Miss James pushed her outside and shut the door.

On her way to the cashier's office, she met Don in the corridor—stooping like a defeated man.

'The Gestapo's got me too, Don. I'm sacked.'

'I'm deeply grieved,' he told her. 'But your conscience is clear, while I have something to regret . . . When I first had news of my—my resignation, I was so stunned that—in trying to save myself—I threw someone to the lions. That hurts most.' He added regretfully with a lapse of his grand manner, 'Besides, it did me no good.'

As the admission sank in, fitting the circumstances of her own dismissal, Tess felt that she had been struck by the hand of a friend.

'You,' she muttered as she turned away.

The second shock made her feel numbed to reality. After she was paid off, she went to the cloakroom and mechanically changed into white slacks and a rose-red pullover. Her hair was beginning to get bushy, as she drew her white cap over it, in an instinctive desire to look her best when she met Clement.

She waited for Clement for a long time in the canteen, but he did not appear. Presently she accepted the disappointment with dreary fatalism. Too overwrought to eat, she went out of the Peninsular grounds. All she wanted was to escape to the Steepes and climb the rough ascent to the Spike—to stand on the mountain-top and meet the healing friction of the wind.

Owing to its precipitous quarried sides, the Steepes were accessible from the town by a small funicular which carried patrons up the face of the cliff. The girl at the turnstile who collected the tickets was a local character. Abnormally sharp, although she looked a child, her mop of red hair had gained her the obvious title of 'Ginger'.

'Does it bring you luck?' she asked as her quick eyes noticed the white heather brooch on Tess's cap.

'You may have the lot at bargain-price,' Tess told her bitterly.

On the summit of the Steepes stretched a wide level expanse of threadbare turf where a cafeteria as well as chairs and tables were provided for the community. The bulk of the holiday-makers used to congregate there, eating, drinking, reading and playing games; but it was deserted that afternoon owing to a circus performance in the town.

Tess struck off along a narrow path which wound, like a pale green ribbon, amid clumps of whinberry and stems of uncurled bracken. Farther off, on the left, the ground sloped down to the Rifle-Range.

She threw herself down on the heather. She wanted the consolation of contact with primeval things. With a springy cushion of twigs supporting her head, she gazed up into the clear blue sky, when she noticed the flicker of wings.

Again the eagle was circling around the summit of the Spike, reminding her of her impulse to climb to the mountain-top. It was a long rough walk, for the steep track zigzagged continually across natural obstacles of bog and rock. Even the optimistic guide-book stated that two-and-one-half hours were required for the ascent.

Swinging to her feet, she had a clear view of the path leading to the Rifle-Range. Two figures—pressed closely together—stood upon the slope. Even at that distance, it was impossible to mistake the sunlit shimmer of the woman's silvery-blonde hair or the slack grace of her companion.

As she watched them, Dodd threw his arm around Miss Ratcliffe and bent his head, as though seeking her lips . . . At the sight, the blood rushed to Tess's head. Again she felt the blast of furnace heat while a wheel seemed to spin remorselessly inside her brain.

Recognizing the terrifying symptoms which heralded a

temporary extinction, she fought with all her strength to resist them, but while she was struggling, a rush of darkness swept over her like a black rocket. As she fell—face downward—on the heather in her last moment of consciousness, she noticed the watch on her outstretched wrist.

It was 3 o'clock.

It was 4 o'clock. Tess stared at her watch with frightened eyes. Only an instant before it was 3 o'clock. A whole hour had been rubbed out of her life . . .

She pressed her fingers to her eyes as the memory of Clem's treachery overwhelmed her. The knowledge made her feel not only miserable, but cheap and ashamed, so that her dominant instinct was to hide. Soon the holiday-makers would be spreading fanwise over the lower slopes of the Steepes.

Shrinking from the ordeal of meeting someone from the Peninsular Factory, she rose stiffly and looked around for her cap. To her annoyance, she could not see it and, after pulling apart the nearest clumps of heather, she had to give up the search. Stampeded by the sound of distant voices, she ran over the rough until she reached a slippery bank of turf which dropped sheer to a narrow ledge above a worked-out quarry.

A perilous climb along the rocky rim brought her to a shallow depression in the hillside which offered her sanctuary. When she leaned back in the hollow, she seemed perched upon a lip of some bottomless abyss. For a long time she lay there—watching the pageant of clouds which rolled past like a stormy sea.

When she forced herself to look at her watch, she grimaced.

'Gosh, it's late. Well—I've got to face people again.'

In spite of this resolution, she made a circle to avoid passing the crowd around the cafeteria. She could not understand the force of the instinct which warned her to remain hidden.

As she clicked through the 'OUT' turnstile, she noticed that

Ginger was staring at her. The scrutiny alarmed her vaguely for it revived her dormant dread of her lost hour.

'Where did I go?' she questioned. 'What have I done? Do I show the marks of it in my face? Why does that girl stare at me? Oh, dear heart, I wish Ted was with me.'

Now that her infatuation for Clement had been shrivelled by the knowledge of his treachery, her heart turned instinctively towards Lockwood. On the homeward journey, while she sat upon the hard wooden seats of the tram and watched long lines of mean houses slide past, the lines of Kipling's poem swam into her mind.

'The Thousandth Man will stand by your side
To the gallows-foot—and after!'

She lodged in a comfortable house which belonged to a florist. It welcomed her like a haven, that evening. The flowers had never looked so beautiful in the sunset glow when she walked through the garden. The shabby dark green sitting room was cool and a meal was spread on the table, so that she had only to make her tea from the electric-kettle.

She was feeling refreshed and stimulated when her landlady entered the room to remove her tray.

'What news?' she clicked. 'Is it really true she's been murdered?'

'Who?' asked Tess, with a pang of foreboding.

'Your Miss Ratcliffe, of course. It's all over the town that she's been shot dead.'

As Tess stared blindly at her landlady, the scrape of the gate made the woman glance through the window.

'It's Mr Lockwood,' the announced. 'I'll go let him in.'

'I knew he'd come. I knew he'd come,' Tess told herself.

As he entered, she turned away and stood with clenched fists and locked jaws, fighting for self-control. She heard his step beside her but he did not speak until they were alone.

'Tess . . . Darling.'

The new tenderness of his tone broke down her defences. Clinging to him, she pressed her face against his shoulder.

'We mustn't waste time,' he said. 'A copper will soon be here to question you. First of all, remember I'm with you, whatever you've done . . . Did you kill her?'

Her face grew suddenly white as she repeated his question with stiff lips.

'Did I kill her? I don't know . . . Tell me, has my cap been found?'

'Why?'

'Because it's gone. I had a blackout. I can't remember anything . . . But my cap might tell me where I went.'

Lockwood's face grew grim as he heard her incoherent story.

'I know you are innocent,' he told her. 'But this is not exactly a water-tight yarn. Keep off it as much as you can. Don't lie, but let the police fish for themselves.'

'But why are they coming to me?'

In her turn, Tess listened to his account of the tragedy. A member of the Rifle-Club had found Ratcliffe's body lying in the rough beyond the targets, about 4.30. She had been shot through the heart at close range. The doctor estimated the time of death as between 3 and 4—but probably about 3.30. As Tess's rifle was found lying near, the police had made inquiries about her at the Peninsular Works, when they had learned about her dismissal and her subsequent threats.

He had just finished his story when the garden gate scraped again.

'It's the detective-bloke,' Lockwood warned Tess. 'Don't forget I'm standing by.'

Inspector Pont reminded Tess of an uncle who grew prize dahlias. He was big and dark, with sleepy brown eyes which revealed nothing of his mental process.

Tess met him with the desperate courage of one mounting the scaffold.

'I am Tess Leigh. I am prepared to sign a statement.'

'Not so fast,' said the inspector. 'You'll be warned when I'm ready for that. I want to know if you remember making any of these remarks about the deceased?'

As Tess read the typewritten paper he handed her, her face flamed.

'Only one person could have told you these things,' she said. 'That's Clement Dodd . . . Yes, I did say them. All of them—and more. They are true. She was a cowardly tyrant for she hit people who could not hit back. Cruelty or injustice always make me see red.'

'The turnstile girl at the Steepes has told me you were up there from between 2 and 6,' Pont said. 'What were you doing during that time?'

'Walking,' replied Tess.

'Where?'

'I don't know . . . It's no good asking me. I've been in an air crash which has affected my memory. I was terribly upset . . . But I walked.'

'Did you lose your cap during your walk? The turnstile girl tells me you were wearing one when you clicked-in, but that you were bareheaded when you returned.'

'That's right. But I don't know where I lost it. I tell you—I don't know.'

'I'd like a description of it.'

After the inspector had entered the particulars in his notebook he turned towards the door. Lockwood noticed the glint in his eyes when he spoke to Tess.

'That cap's got to be found. I'll have bills out tomorrow. Meantime, a notice goes up on the Station-board. I don't expect any results tonight, but hold yourself ready to come and identify it.'

Directly the door closed, Lockwood held Tess tightly in his arms.

'I'm standing by you,' he said. 'We'll wait together.'

She was not comforted because she knew that he too was feeling the same strain of suspense. She felt his start when the telephone bell began to ring in the hall.

'I'll take it,' he said quickly.

When he returned, his smile was unnaturally broad.

'We're going for a joy-ride,' he told her. 'My bus is parked outside.'

The journey to the Police Station had a nightmare quality. The lines of smoke-grimed houses seemed to flash by so that Tess—who was dreading the end of the ride—caught her lip when the car stopped under the blue lamp. Still in an evil dream, she stumbled into a tiled hall, when an open door gave her a clear view into a room.

Standing under the glare of an unshaded electric bulb, Clement Dodd was smoking a cigarette. He appeared entirely at his ease until he saw Tess. His face grew red and he turned his back to avoid meeting her eyes.

'This way,' said a constable.

Supported by the pressure of Lockwood's arm, Tess followed the man into another office where Inspector Pont was seated before a table littered with official papers.

'Yours?' he asked, holding out a white Angora cap for her inspection. She glanced mechanically at her name printed inside the band and nodded assent, before she realised that he was smiling at her.

'My congratulations,' he said. 'This cap was brought in by two hikers—strangers to the district—who chanced to see the notice on the board. They say they picked it up among the rocks on the top of the Spike, soon after 4 this afternoon. As the official time for the ascent is two-and-one-half hours and the deceased was alive at 3, according to medical evidence, it stands to reason that you could not have committed the murder and afterwards climbed the mountain, all within an hour.'

As she listened, Tess's head reeled, for she realized that the story was full of holes. Before she could protest, Lockwood grabbed her arm.

'Miss Leigh's our champion athlete,' he told the Inspector. 'Thanks very much. I'll run her home now.'

'I may ring you later,' remarked the Inspector. 'I am going to chat with another party. If you're interested, you could take your time going out.'

Tess understood the reason for his wink when they reached the hall, for after the detective entered the room where Clement Dodd was waiting, he left the door slightly ajar.

'There's just one point I want cleared up, Dodd,' he said in a loud, cheerful voice. 'It's common knowledge that two articles were found on the scene of the crime. One—a rifle—has been identified as the property of a stenographer—Tess Leigh. The other article has still to be identified.'

'But her name's inside the band.' Clement spoke quickly and confidently. 'Besides, everyone knows her white-heather brooch.'

'I was referring to a pencil stamped with "PENINSULAR",' remarked the Inspector. 'The cap you describe was picked up at the top of the Spike at 4 o'clock this afternoon.'

'That's a damned lie. I saw it—'

'You saw it?' prompted the Inspector as Dodd broke off abruptly. 'Go on. Now that Miss Leigh has a perfect alibi, I must go further into your own movements.'

He shut the door and Lockwood dragged Tess outside to the car.

As they reached the front door of Tess's lodging, they heard the telephone bell ringing in the hall, when, once again, he rushed to receive the call.

When he rang off, his face was beaming.

'Dodd's confessed to the crime,' he said. 'The Inspector said he was in such a state of nerves after he made that slip that he cracked directly they got to work on him. It appears that old Donovan—when he was ratting for Ratcliffe—found out that Dodd had been embezzling money from the accounts. He told Ratcliffe and she taxed Dodd.

'As usual, she pretended that she alone had been so clever as to discover the fraud, so he reasoned that if he bumped her off, no one would know. I am assuming old Don blew the gaff from something he said to me. Dodd admitted that he got Ratcliffe to come with him to the Range, to talk it over, so it was a cold-blooded crime.'

As she listened. Tess felt almost light-headed with relief.

'Oh, it's wonderful to know I never killed her. And I'm glad Don didn't give me away. It was Clem he "threw to the lions" . . . I was feeling that I could trust no one. And then—you walked with me to the gallows-foot. And after—'

Lockwood began to laugh as he interrupted her.

'I've some good news for you. It didn't matter before. Nothing mattered then but you . . . But Eustace has asked Daddy to carry on until young John returns from America. Looks as if the good times are coming back to the Peninsular . . . But what's the girl frowning about now?'

'My cap,' replied Tess. 'If it had been found near the body, I should be convinced that I had killed her. I should have confessed to it—and Clem would not have been brought into it. I should have cleared him . . . But how did that cap get on the top of the Spike? I passed out between 3 and 4. Besides, no one on earth could have made the climb in that time.'

'No one on earth,' said Lockwood. 'But what about someone in the air! There's a simple and natural explanation. My hunch is that Dodd saw you asleep after he shot Ratcliffe—in that white rig you'd be conspicuous on the heather—so he stole your cap and placed it beside the rifle, to frame you. That's why he crashed so badly. Nothing rattles a liar so much as to be disbelieved when he is telling the truth—and he knew it was inside the range. There was no wind, but probably it stirred a bit in the breeze.

'Enter Mr Eagle. He sees something white and fleecy moving on the heather. He swoops down on it, soars up again, realises he's been fooled and drops it again in disgust . . . By the luck of the air currents, it fell on the top of the mountain instead of the lower slopes. You owe your perfect alibi to your friend—the eagle.'

ETHEL LINA WHITE

One of twelve children, Ethel Lina White (1876–1944) was born in Abergavenny, Gwent, on the border between England and Wales. Her father was a builder and the inventor of an award-winning composite material called 'Hygeian rock cement', which found use in paving and for the construction of prisons. White and several of her siblings worked for their father's business in various capacities, continuing to do so after he died in 1901 when her mother Eliza took over the business. Eliza White died in 1917 and, for reasons that are unclear, the family lost all their money during the First World War. White and her two younger sisters then moved to London where the three all found employment: White as a clerk with the Ministry of Pensions; her sister Dora as a secretary and Marjorie as an illustrator.

By this time, White had just turned 40 and had had several short stories—generally concerning romantic entanglements—published in magazines such as *The Strand*, *The Idler* and *The London*. While working for the Ministry she continued to write short fiction and she also completed *The Port of Yesterday*, a play about a man who finds himself haunted by the memory of his first wife. After leaving the Ministry and supported by her sister Dora, who kept house, White also wrote her first novel, *The Wish-Bone* (1927), in which a young woman evades marriage by running away with a man whom she subsequently discovers to have a lunatic wife. In her second novel, *'Twill Soon Be Dark* (1929), a young man strives for fame and fortune and, after achieving it, returns to his home town only to find his childhood sweetheart on trial for murder. If the themes of her first two books were familiar enough, her third was extraordinary by any standards for *The Eternal Journey* (1930) recounts the life—or, rather, the lives—of a young woman who may be a witch as she kills her cousin in 1794, sacrifices her own life for a friend in 1931 and then marries for love . . . in 2331.

Although none of these early books was especially successful, their reception was sufficiently positive to convince White that she should continue to write for the rest of her life. This was the Golden Age of crime and, as she had incorporated murder and elements of suspense in two of her first three books, it was not surprising that she should try her hand at a full-length novel. The result, *Put Out the Light* (1931), is a cleverly constructed story in which, contrary to the generally accepted convention, the murder comes late on. With its focus on the victim's paranoia and her dread of ageing, the novel demonstrates what is most distinctive about White's work: her interest in the psychology of her characters and how it shapes their response to the situations in which they find themselves.

During the 1930s and early '40s, White wrote many short stories, some of which were syndicated in the United States, and she also wrote several other superb novels of mystery, including *Wax* (1935) and *Step in the Dark* (1938). But it was Alfred Hitchcock's film of her sixth crime novel *The Wheel Spins* (1936) that brought White lasting fame. The film, *The Lady Vanishes*, was released in 1938 and when it finally had its premiere in Abergavenny in February 1939, White was there as the mayor's guest of honour. She would go on to write eight more books including *The Man Who Loved Lions* (1943), in which an eccentric millionaire uses a private zoo in the grounds of his Surrey home to wipe out his enemies, and her final novel, *They See in Darkness* (1944), which features a chain of murders, an asylum and a sinister cult of nuns, the Sisters of Healing Darkness.

White died in Chiswick in 1944 while another of her late books, *Midnight House* (1942), was being filmed. Raymond Chandler was among those with a hand in the adaptation, which also incorporated elements of White's short story 'The Cellar', and the resulting picture, *The Unseen*, was released in 1945. After her death, other short stories were adapted for television while the novel *Some Must Watch* (1935) was filmed and released in 1946 as *The Spiral Staircase*. As a novelist, White may be all but forgotten but she will be long remembered as the mind behind those two truly great films of suspense, *The Lady Vanishes* and *The Spiral Staircase*.

The short story 'White Cap' was first published in the *Akron Beacon Journal* on 31 January 1942.

SIXPENNYWORTH

John Rhode

The scene is the lounge of the Spotted Dog. At the back of the stage is a bar counter. About the room are scattered a number of small tables (three will be enough) each with a shaded electric table lamp, and chairs arranged around it. The walls of the room are hung with antique weapons, presumably collected at various times by the proprietor. A pair of duelling pistols, Malay krises, Gurkha kukries, Zulu assegais, Moorish scimitars, anything in fact that can be got together. Among them, but not conspicuously so, is something really sharp, preferably an Italian stiletto. There is a single door for entrances and exits. The time is after blackout, and all the lamps are switched on except on one of the tables, which should be the one nearest the door.

The *dramatis personae* are:

FREDDY, the barman. He has only been at the Spotted Dog that day, having replaced his predecessor, who has been called up. He is keen enough on his job, but obviously quite new to it. He seems unable to remain in his proper place behind the bar, but is continually fussing around the room, fiddling with the chairs, picking things up and putting them down again. In a word he is restless, and clumsy with it at that.

MR HAROLD PALMER. He is stout, bald-headed and very hail-fellow-well-met. You might take him for a successful commercial traveller. He is staying at the Spotted Dog, having arrived there that morning.

THE STRANGER. Tall, somewhere in the late thirties, with a keen intelligent air about him.

DIANA, The Stranger's Companion. Early thirties, good-looking and vivacious. This is the first visit of the Stranger and his companion to the Spotted Dog, and indeed to the neighbourhood. They arrive in a car.

MRS JANE FREAN, and her friend, MRS VERA TERRY. They are grass widows, their husbands being called up for service, Frean in the Army, Terry in the Air Force. They live together in the town, and are frequent visitors to the Spotted Dog. Both young and inclined to be skittish.

MISS JULIA WESTGATE. Jane Frean's aunt, elderly and garrulous.

(The curtain rises, disclosing Jane and Vera sitting at one of the tables, not the one with the unlighted lamp. Each has an empty cocktail glass in front of her, and they are chatting vigorously. Freddy is pottering about with a tray, picking up empty glasses. His balance of the tray is most precarious, and the glasses tinkle about alarmingly. He is perpetually tripping over everything that comes his way. He is, as he is intended to be, distracting.)

JANE: (*leaning forward confidentially*) . . . and, do you know my dear I couldn't buy a single yard of it. I went into every shop in the town but it was no use. They hadn't got any left, and they weren't expecting any more for ages.

VERA: Yes, I know, it's the same with everything. I don't know what I shall do when Hugh comes home on leave. He adores onions, and there simply aren't any to be had.

JANE: He'll have to do without, like the rest of us. You needn't worry about our husbands, dear. Men always know how to give themselves a good time.

VERA: (*slyly*) And, some of us girls too. What about last week when young Tom Harley was here?

JANE: (*in obvious alarm*) Hush! Don't speak so loud. If Cecil ever heard about that I don't know what would happen. Shall we have just another? No darling, really! It's my turn this time. Freddy!

(*At this sudden call, Freddy almost drops the tray he is carrying, which, at that moment, is fortunately empty. He retrieves it by a supreme effort, and bustles up to the table*)

FREDDY: Yes, mum.

JANE: (*speaking to Vera*) What shall we have this time?

VERA: (*consideringly*) I don't know, darling. I think I'd like a Maiden's Kiss.

JANE: That's quite a good idea. Two Maiden's Kisses, please, Freddy.

FREDDY: (*eyeing her in complete bewilderment*) I beg your pardon, mum.

JANE: (*impatiently*) Two Maiden's Kisses, I said. And see that you mix them properly.

FREDDY: Yes, mum. Certainly, mum.

(*He picks up the two empty glasses and puts them on the tray in such a way that they rattle together as he goes off. During the following dialogue he goes behind the bar and scratches his head. The order has evidently defeated him. At last, in desperation, he seizes a cocktail shaker, into which he pours a little from each of a dozen bottles chosen at random. Finally he adds a lump of sugar and a dash of Worcestershire Sauce, and shakes the mixture violently*)

JANE: (*aside*) I can't think why on earth they ever took that man on. He doesn't seem to know what he's doing half the time. I believe he's daft.

VERA: He's only here on trial for a week. The man who was

here before has been called up, and they had to take whoever they could get.

JANE: Well, if he lasts a week he'll be lucky. Oh, did I tell you that I heard from Cecil this morning?

VERA: No, how thrilling. Had he any news?

JANE: Oh lots. His regiment is going to move next week. I've forgotten the place he's going to, but it's all very hush-hush. I'll show you the letter. I've got it here in my bag.

(*She fumbles in her bag, taking out a variety of feminine adornments, but failing to find the letter. Meanwhile she continues*) No, it isn't here. I must have left it on the mantelpiece in my bedroom. I do hope the housemaid won't read it. Cecil would be furious if he knew. Or perhaps I dropped it in the bus when I opened my bag to buy a ticket.

VERA: (*consolingly*) I don't suppose anyone will trouble to read it, dear. Husbands' letters aren't interesting enough. Hugh's aren't, at all events. He writes about nothing but what he's doing at that silly old aerodrome of his.

JANE: Yes, I know. They never seem to think of us. Here are we, struggling to make both ends meet on what they choose to allow us, while they're having a jolly good time.

(*By now Freddy has completed his devil's brew. He looks at the cocktail shaker, then at the row of glasses on the shelf, uncertain which to choose. In the end he selects two enormous brandy glasses, and puts them with the shaker on the inevitable tray. Bearing this, he shuffles proudly to the table. He puts the glasses on the table and half fills each of them with a mixture which looks, and probably tastes, like red ink. Jane, who has been powdering her nose meanwhile, becomes aware of these astonishing drinks*)

JANE: What in the world have you got there, Freddy?

FREDDIE: Two Maiden's Kisses, mum. You'll find they've got plenty of bite in them. And that'll be five shillings, if you please, mum.

JANE: Five shillings. I never heard of such a thing. Think again, Freddy.

FREDDY: (*firmly*) That's right, mum. Cocktails are half a crown each in this lounge. We might manage to make a slight reduction if you could step into the public bar, mum.

JANE: (*impatiently, as she takes a note from her bag and puts it on the tray*) Oh go away—(*Freddy does so, and Jane turns to Vera*) I said the man was daft. And I've never seen a Maiden's Kiss like this in my life. (*She picks up her glass, sniffs at it, and at last takes a cautious sip.*) Oh. I'm awfully sorry, my dear, but I'm afraid—

(*She is interrupted by the tumultuous entry of Miss Westgate, very much muffled up and carrying bag, umbrella, and quantities of parcels. She trips across the room to the occupied table and warmly embraces Jane and Vera, scattering her belongings on the floor as she does so. Freddy rushes forward to assist, and a scramble ensues. Finally order is restored and Miss Westgate flops into a chair*)

JANE: (*hopefully*) Was it mustard by any chance, Aunt Julia?

(*Miss Westgate shakes her head. Vera tackles the question in an equally helpful spirit*)

VERA: Matches, perhaps. They're getting very scarce nowadays.

(*Freddy has been hovering about Miss Westgate's chair, anticipating an order. Now he thinks it time to take a part in the game*)

FREDDY: (*brightly*) Marmalade, mum.

MISS WESTGATE: Yes, of course, that was it. (*She turns round and surveys Freddy approvingly*) You seem to be a very intelligent young man.

FREDDY: (*bowing gracefully*) Thank you, mum. And is there anything that I can get you?

MISS WESTGATE: I think I should like a little something. What have you got there, my dears?

JANE: (*Hastily*) I don't think you would care for it, Auntie, it's hardly in your line. Won't you have something else?

MISS WESTGATE: Well, perhaps I should enjoy a glass of port. I always think port's so refreshing.

FREDDY: Very good, mum. (*He hurries off behind the counter and searches wildly for a bottle of port. Finding it, he shakes it vigorously, and looks around for a suitable receptacle. A liqueur glass catches his fancy. He fills this and carries it on the biggest tray he can find to Miss Westgate. Meanwhile—*)

MISS WESTGATE: (*in a tone of extreme confidence*) Do you know, my dears, I met Mr Huntly while I was out this afternoon. He is in the special police, and he hears everything. Such a nice man, too. I'm sure he'd be so gentle with anyone he caught doing anything wrong . And of course I promised that I wouldn't say a word about it.

JANE: About what, Auntie?

MISS WESTGATE: Oh, didn't I tell you? About that bomb that fell just outside the town the other day. He went to measure the crater. Wasn't it brave of him? Don't you think so, Vera, dear?

VERA: (*doubtfully*) Well, I don't know. The beastly thing had gone off, hadn't it?

MISS WESTGATE: (*shaking her head*) Oh, yes, it had gone off. But, as Mr Huntly said, you never know. Anyhow, he went to measure the hole it made, and he told me how big it was. Of course, I promised not to repeat it, but I'm sure he wouldn't mind my telling you.

JANE: (*rather intrigued*) And how big was it, Auntie?

MISS WESTGATE: (*in a tense whisper*) Two hundred yards across, and a hundred feet deep. I'm sure that's what Mr Huntly said it was. But you won't say a word to anybody about it, will you? Hush. Here comes the waiter.

(*Freddy arrives with tray and glass. He puts the latter in front of Miss Westgate, spilling a goodly proportion of its contents in the process*)

FREDDY: There's a nice glass of port, mum. Very strengthening it is, they say. And that'll be a shilling, if you please, mum.

MISS WESTGATE: (*horrified*) What? A shilling for a glass that size!

FREDDY: (*leaning over and speaking confidentially in her ear*) It's a very fine old vintage port, mum. There aren't half a dozen bottles left in the whole country, and it's worth a guinea a drop. It's only sheer good nature that lets the guv'nor sell it at all.

MISS WESTGATE: Well, it seems a lot of money to me. (*She begins to fumble in her bag, and in all sorts of unlikely places about her person*) Now, wherever did I put my purse? I know I had it when I went out shopping, for I always pay cash for everything. I don't believe in running up bills, they always come in at the most inconvenient time. (*The purse at last rolls out of one of the parcels and falls on the floor. Freddy retrieves it and hands it gracefully to Miss Westgate, who opens it*) Thank you, waiter, I knew it must be somewhere. (*The purse is bulging with nothing but coppers, which Miss W. counts out one by one*) One, two, three, four, five, six, seven, eight, nine, ten, eleven, twelve. And there's an extra half-penny for you, my man.

FREDDY: (*in a tone of overwhelmed gratitude*) Thank you so very much indeed, mum. I've a wife and ten children at home, and this'll help to keep the nippers in shoe leather.

MISS WESTGATE: Ten children. A man of your age?

FREDDY: Well, mum, there were ten when I last counted them, and they keep coming. Excuse me.

(*Mr Palmer has just entered. He stops just inside the door and looks around furtively. Freddy, from behind the counter, watches him with interest. By way of occupying himself he picks up a siphon and begins polishing it vigorously with a very wet and dirty cloth. Mr Palmer walks to the bar*)

MR PALMER: (*brusquely*) Double whiskey and soda.

FREDDY: (*urbanely*) I think we can manage the whiskey, sir. (*He picks up a bottle of one brand of whiskey and pours a generous measure of this into a pint mug. Then he picks up a bottle of another brand and adds some from this*) That's a pretty safe double, sir. White Cat and Black Chief. You can't beat 'em. But I'm not sure about the soda. Excuse me.

(*He dodges from behind the counter and bolts from the room like a shot rabbit. Meanwhile Mr Palmer looks intently at the three women who are chatting away in animated fashion. Scraps of their conversation are audible*)

JANE: —embarking at Bridport. Two whole Army Corps, Cecil told me. I don't know how many men that means but I expect it will be quite a big boat-load.

VERA: But how thrilling. Where are they going to?

JANE: (*darkly*) Ah. That's a terrible secret. But I know, for Cecil told me and said I wasn't to breathe a word. They're going to the Galapagos Islands, and they're going to invade Italy by way of Cape Horn.

(*Mr Palmer has left the bar and is drifting quietly across the room towards the three women. All at once he recognises Vera and comes up to her with an ingratiating smile*)

MR PALMER: Well, I never. If it isn't my old friend Mrs Terry. I'm so delighted to meet you again, for I had quite lost sight of you. But don't let me interrupt you ladies' conversation.

(*But Vera is at least effectually interrupted. She leaps up and shrinks back*)

VERA: You!

MR PALMER: (*pleasantly*) Yes, me. You recognise your old friend, surely, Mrs Terry? And by and by, when you've a moment to spare, we'll have a little chat about old times together, won't we?

(*Freddy has reappeared, carrying a packet of something. He regains the counter*)

FREDDY: (*imperiously*) Excuse me, sir.

MR PALMER: *Au revoir*, Mrs Terry, we shall meet again, I'm sure. (*He strolls back to the counter*) Well, what is it?

(*Freddy puts the packet on the counter, it is now seen to be labelled 'Finest washing soda'. He puts his fingers into the packet, produces a lump of the stuff and poises it gracefully over the tumbler*)

FREDDIE: (*deferentially*) Your soda, sir. How much would you like? Say when.

MR PALMER: (*hastily*) Here, take that stuff away, you damn fool. It's soda water I want. Look! (*He seizes the siphon and squirts some of it into the tumbler. Meanwhile Vera, very much shaken, has sat down again. She picks up the Maiden's Kiss, and takes a good gulp at it. This results in coughing and spluttering*)

JANE: Vera, darling, whatever is the matter?

VERA: (*weakly*) It's the cocktail, it tastes terribly strong.

JANE: (*impatiently*) No, no, I don't mean that. The gentleman who spoke to you just now. Do you know him?

VERA: (*slowly*) Oh, yes, I know him. (*with sudden fervour*) Jane, let's get away quickly, now.

MISS WESTGATE: (*sensibly*) Nonsense, my dear, he won't let you. In my young days I never ran away from a man.

JANE: (*maliciously*) Did they run away from you, Auntie?

MISS WESTGATE: I always knew how to keep men in their place. They never ventured to try any of their nonsense with me.

(*Vera, whose hands are trembling, tries to cover her confusion by a lavish application of cosmetics. Miss Westgate, ignoring the slightly awkward incident, goes on talking volubly*) It's most interesting, what you were telling me just now, Jane, I knew a man once who went to the Galapagos Islands. He said that his only companions were turtles, and that he had to kill his favourite one to make soup of, just like a City Alderman.

(*During this conversation, Freddy has again emerged from*

behind the counter, and is prowling restlessly about the room. The extinguished lamp attracts his attention. He goes up to it and tries the switch. Nothing happens. He holds it upside down and shakes it; still nothing happens. At last he has a bright idea. He takes out the bulb and holds it to his ear, as though he expected it to purr at him. Then he lays the bulb down, and takes various articles out of his pocket—pencil, bundle of keys, handful of change—and tries in turn to make them fit the holder. At last, disgruntled by his failure to produce any improvement he puts back the bulb and wanders away. As he does so, enter the Stranger and his companion. The three women are still chatting. Mr Palmer is standing at the counter, obviously listening to their conversation. The Stranger glances significantly at him and then significantly at his companion. Freddy dashes forward and almost forces them into the chairs round the extinguished table)

FREDDY: (*engagingly*) And what would you and the lady like to drink, sir?

THE STRANGER: (*to his companion*) What are you feeling like this evening? (*aside to Freddy*) Who is that standing by the counter? I'm pretty sure I've seen him somewhere before.

FREDDY: (*confidentially*) Him, sir? That's Mr Horace Palmer. He's staying at the hotel, sir. Very nice gentleman. Would you like me to introduce you?

THE STRANGER: (*hastily*) No, don't trouble to do that. (*to his companion*) Well, what about it, Diana? Made up your mind yet?

DIANA: My dear man, you know very well that it never takes me long to make up my mind. I'll have a gin and bitters.

THE STRANGER: That's not at all a bad idea. I shall follow your example. (*He beckons to Freddy, who has drifted away again*) Waiter! Two gin and bitters.

FREDDY: (*nods with complete comprehension*) Yessir. Two gin and bitters, sir. (*He retires behind the bar to execute this order*)

THE STRANGER: (*animatedly to his companion*) That's the chap, surely? What do you think? They said we might possibly find him here.

DIANA: He's just like the description they gave us. But the name wasn't Palmer. It was—

THE STRANGER: Hush! Some people have long ears. He's listening to what those women are saying at the other table, now. And as for his name, I expect he changes that as often as it is convenient. Keep your eye on him.

DIANA: What are you going to do?

THE STRANGER: Wait for a bit and see what he does. We've got plenty of time. He can't get away from us now, and if he attempts to leave the room I'll follow him.

(*Meanwhile Freddy has been busy behind the counter. He takes two tankards from the shelf and measures into each a noggin of gin from the bottle. Then he holds them in turn under the tap of the barrel resting on the counter. He produces a flaming top, and proudly carries them to the Stranger's table*)

THE STRANGER: (*his attention distracted from Mr Palmer to the tankards being planted down in front of him*) Hullo! What the dickens have you got here, waiter?

FREDDY: (*pained*) Gin and bitter, sir. That's what you ordered. A spot of gin and the rest bitter beer. Very fine drink if you've got a cold coming on. Just you try it, sir.

DIANA: (*amused but slightly suspicious*) How long have you been serving here, waiter?

FREDDY: This is my first evening, mum. I'm here on trial.

THE STRANGER: (*eyeing the contents of his tankard*) You'll be on another sort of trial if you get poisoning any of your customers. Now just you take these away and bring us what we ordered. A single gin in a glass with a dash of Angostura. And bring some water with it, understand?

FREDDY: (*quite unperturbed*) Yessir. (*He replaces the tankards on the tray, then wanders off round the room picking up empty glasses. Everybody is concerned with their own affairs, and taking no notice of him. The three women engrossed in conversation, Mr Palmer has left the counter and edged towards them. The Stranger and Diana are watching him furtively*)

DIANA: (*to the Stranger*) I don't see why we shouldn't have a light on our table. Switch it on, there's a dear.

(*The Stranger puts out his hand to the switch and presses it. All the lights go out immediately, plunging the room into complete darkness. Pandemonium ensues. Things happen in the following order: Freddy drops his tray, which falls with a terrific crash. Feminine exclamations*)

VERA: Oh! That clumsy waiter. He's spilt his tray all over my frock. Do get a light, somebody. I'm so frightened!

MISS WESTGATE: (*soothingly*) It's all right, dear, it's only a fuse that's gone. I remember when that happened once when I was in a room alone with a man, and—

(*But her virginal reminiscences are interrupted. There is a gurgling cry followed by a heavy thud on the floor. Vera screams hysterically. A sharp scraping of a chair, and the sound of rapid footsteps. Then a crunch as of broken glass stepped upon*)

THE STRANGER: (*commandingly*) Keep still everybody. Waiter! Where are you?

(*There is a perceptible pause before Freddy replies*)

VERA: Oh! What is it? What's happened? Hasn't anyone got a match?

FREDDY: I'm here sir, behind the counter, looking for a candle. I know there are some here if only I could lay my hands on them.

THE STRANGER: Well, hurry up and find them. And don't let anybody else move.

(*Silence for a few seconds, broken only by Vera's whimpering. At last a light appears, Freddy has found a candle and lighted it. He sticks it in the neck of the first bottle that comes to hand. For the next minute he continues very deliberately to light candles and stick-them in bottles until he has quite a row of them along the counter.*

In the dim light of the first candle, the room is revealed. The Stranger is standing with his back to the door, a revolver in his hand. Diana is sitting very still, intently watchful. Jane and Miss Westgate are still in their chairs, but Vera has started up, and is standing appalled, the broken cocktail glass at her feet. Her frock is stained red and is wet.

But Mr Palmer is the centre of attraction. He is lying face down on the floor, half way between the counter and Vera, and sticking from his shoulder is the handle of a stiletto. As this sight is revealed, Vera screams and shrinks back from the body against the wall. Jane and Miss Westgate seem too paralysed with horror to move)

THE STRANGER: (*sternly*) Keep quite still, please. (*He pockets his revolver and walks across to the body. He kneels down beside it and then stands up again*)

THE STRANGER: (*quickly but impressively*) This man is dead. A stiletto has been driven into his heart. And someone in this room must have killed him.

(*Gasps of horror from the three women at the table. Diana, still watching them intently, takes a cigarette from her case and lights it. Freddy, quite unconcerned, finishes lighting the candles. Then he jumps lightly on to the counter and sits there, drumming his heels and surveying the scene. Miss Westgate is the first to find her tongue.*)

MISS WESTGATE: (*decisively*) If the poor man has been killed, the police ought to be sent for. I've always understood that when you find a body the first thing to do is to send for the police. I'm sure Mr Huntly—

THE STRANGER: (*interrupting her*) I don't think we need trouble Mr Huntly. I am Inspector Waghorn of the Criminal Investigation Department, Scotland Yard.

JANE: (*who is gradually recovering from the shock*) How terribly thrilling. Vera, dear, do sit down and let me mop up your frock. You look so uncomfortable standing against the wall like that.

(*Vera starts, and looks at the red stain on her frock. Until now she has not realised its presence. She touches it with her fingers, then holds out her hand before her. Her fingers are seen to be wet and red*)

VERA: Oh, what is it? Where did it come from?

(*Jimmy takes no notice of her, but walks to the table at which Diana is sitting*)

JIMMY (i.e. THE STRANGER): I want to see all your identity cards, please. And I'll start with you, Diana.

(*Diana smiles, opens her bag and produces her card. Jimmy reads it*)

JIMMY: Diana Waghorn. Yes, I know the address, thank you. (*He gives her back the card and walks to the table at which Miss W. and Jane are sitting. Jane has her card ready and gives it to him*)

JIMMY: Jane Frean, local address. Thank you. (*He turns enquiringly to Miss W., who is fumbling feverishly in her bag*)

MISS WESTGATE: It must be here somewhere. I've always kept it in my bag since I heard the Prime Minister tell us on the wireless that we must always carry our cards with us. At least I think it was the Prime Minister, but it may have been somebody else. I always get so confused with all these different people telling me what to do. I—

JANE: (*interrupting this flow*) I expect it's in one of your other bags, Auntie. (*She turns to Jimmy*) This is my aunt, Miss Julia Westgate. She lives at Number 14 Church Street, in this town.

JIMMY: Thank you, Mrs Frean. (*He steps up to Vera*) And you, madam.

(*Vera makes an obvious effort to pull herself together*)

VERA: (*faintly*) My card. In my bag. There on the floor, by my chair. (*It is evident that but for the support of the wall she would fall—*)

JIMMY: I think that you had better sit down. (*He takes her by the arm and leads her to the chair. He picks up the bag, then beckons to Diana. She crosses the room, takes the bag from him, opens it and finds the card*)

DIANA: Vera Terry, with a local address.

JIMMY: Thanks. (*to Vera*) Now Mrs Terry, did you know that man there? (*Vera shakes her head, then becomes aware of Jane's eyes fixed upon her*)

VERA: I—I knew him once, very long ago. He was never a friend of mine.

JIMMY: No, I imagine not. Perhaps you can tell me his name?

VERA: I—I've forgotten.

JIMMY: Try to remember, Mrs Terry.

VERA: (*desperately*) Well, if you must know, it was Hogwash. Mr Julius Hogwash.

FREDDY: (*suddenly and loudly from the counter where he is still sitting*) That's not the name he gave when he signed the visitor's book here.

JIMMY: (*turning to him*) What name did he give?

FREDDY: He called himself Mr Harold Palmer, and I heard him telling the Guvnor that he's travelling in rocking horses. And he never paid for that double whiskey he ordered.

JIMMY: (*brusquely*) I'll hear what you've got to say later. (*He turns back to Vera, and points to the stain on her frock*) How did that happen, Mrs Terry?

VERA: (*wildly*) I don't know! Something must have got spilled on it, something red and sticky.

JIMMY: Yes, I noticed that. You told me that this Mr Hogwash or Palmer was not a friend of yours. Was he an enemy?

VERA: Oh! I hated him! He knew something about me and threatened to tell my husband. I thought I had escaped from him by coming here. And then—

JIMMY: And then he met you and, well, died. (*He walks to the wall against which Vera was seen standing. There is a conspicuous gap and an empty hook amid the array of weapons hanging there. He looks at it then walks to the body and withdraws the stiletto, wiping it as he does so. He hangs the stiletto on the empty hook*) That seems to complete the decorative scheme, don't you think so, Diana?

DIANA: Yes, that's where it was hanging when we came in. I noticed it particularly, for it's just like one that used to hang in a house where I once worked. But, if you don't mind my saying so, I fancy that you're barking up the wrong tree.

JIMMY: (*amused*) Very likely. But what exactly do you mean? (*Diana makes no immediate reply but picks up Jane's glass*)

DIANA: Excuse me, Mrs Frean. (*She takes a sip from the glass then puts it down hastily with a wry face*) My word. That's a new one on me! (*She rubs her finger delicately on Vera's frock, then sucks it reflectively*) No one could possibly mistake it. That's not blood, Jimmy.

FREDDY: Quite right, that's not blood. That's a Maiden's Kiss. A speciality of the house.

JIMMY: Shut up! (*he turns to Miss Westgate*) Did you know Mr Hogwash, Miss Westgate?

MISS WESTGATE: (*Indignantly*) Certainly not. I could never be on speaking terms with a man with a name like that. I call it perfectly disgraceful.

JIMMY: (*to Jane*) And you, Mrs Frean?

JANE: I never saw or heard of him before this evening.

JIMMY: And I know he didn't happen to be on your visiting list, Diana. (*He leaves the table and walks up to the counter, where he surveys Freddy with marked disapproval*) Now we'll deal with you. Let's have a look at your identity card, to begin with.

FREDDY: (*shaking his head*) Sorry, sir, it's in my other coat, the one I wear when I'm walking out. I'll slip upstairs and fetch it, if you like.

JIMMY: (*sternly*). You'll stay just where you are and answer my questions. What's your name?

FREDDY: (*glibly*) Frederick Theophilus Henry. At least that's the name my godfathers and godmothers gave me at my baptism. But those who love me call me Henry.

JIMMY: And your surname?

FREDDY: (*with suspicious promptitude*) Cholmondely-Marjoribanks.

JIMMY: You'd better be careful. How long have you known Mr Hogwash?

FREDDY: (*evasively*) Oh! Not very long. Only since this morning when I took on this job.

JIMMY: I see. And what did you do when the lights went out?

FREDDY: Oh, I was that startled, I dropped my tray and then I remembered that I'd seen a packet of candles behind the counter, so I went to look for them.

JIMMY: H'm. It was fully a second or two after the lights went out that this man was murdered. What were you doing during those few seconds?

FREDDY: Why, groping my way back behind the counter, I tell you. I had to go carefully, for I didn't want to run into any of the tables and upset them.

JIMMY: You heard the sound of Mr Hogwash's body falling?

FREDDY: Oh, yes, I heard that right enough. I wondered whatever it could be.

JIMMY: Did you? And where were you when you heard the sound?

FREDDY: I'd just got behind the counter and I was trying to lay my hand on that packet of candles.

DIANA: (*who has been listening intently to all this*) Is there any broken glass behind the counter?

(*Jimmy leans over and looks*)

JIMMY: None that I can see. Why?

DIANA: Because there's plenty lying in front of the counter, where Freddy dropped the tray. And I distinctly heard a crunch as someone stepped on a piece of broken glass, at least a second or two after the body had fallen.

JIMMY: Yes, I heard that too. And it wasn't I who trod on the glass when I went to the door. (*To Freddy*) Where exactly were you standing when the lights went out?

FREDDY: (*pointing*) There, just beside where those three ladies are sitting.

JIMMY: Yes. That's where he must have been, for when he dropped the tray he spilt some beer or something over my arm.

JIMMY: (*to Freddy with sudden inspiration*) What made you drop the tray?

FREDDY: Haven't I told you? I was so startled when the light went out that I let go of it.

JIMMY: You seem pretty easily startled. Wartime nerves, perhaps?

FREDDY: (*defensively*) Well, it would have given anyone a turn. How was I to know the light was going out suddenly like that? I'm in charge here when the guv'nor's out, and anyone might have slipped behind the counter and pinched the money out of the till. And then where should I have been?

JIMMY: Where were you? That's the point. Not behind the counter, I'm pretty sure of that . . . And there's another thing. What made the lights go out?

FREDDY: The fuse must have busted. They do sometimes, and then you've got to put a new one in.

JIMMY: (*impatiently*) Yes. I know all about that. But fuses don't bust, as you call it, without some cause. Diana, just look round the house and see if there are any lights on, will you?

(*Exit Diana. She is absent only a second or two*)

DIANA: There are lights on all over the house, as far as I can see. It's only in this room that they're out. And they went out, if you remember, when you tried to switch on the light at our table.

JIMMY: Yes, I remember that. (*To Freddy*) How was it that there was no light on the table you showed us to?

FREDDY: (*volubly*) That's just what I can't make out. The other tables were all right. And just before you and the lady came I tried to make that one work, but I couldn't. These ladies saw me.

MISS WESTGATE: Yes, that's right, Inspector. I saw him trying to make the light work, and I thought that he didn't seem very clever at it. I was expecting him to get a shock any minute.

FREDDY: (*feelingly*) I got the shock all right when I saw Mr Palmer lying on the floor like that!

MISS WESTGATE: (*severely*) An electric shock, I mean. I always think it's very dangerous to touch those things. If anything goes wrong at home I send for a proper electrician at once. I remember that one day—

JIMMY: (*with a silencing gesture*) Please, Miss Westgate. (*To Freddy*) Why did you show us to a table where you knew the light would not work, when there was another one vacant?

FREDDY: (*easily*) Oh, it's a very nice table. I think it's the best in the room. Real Chippendale from the Tottenham Court Road. Besides, look what a cosy position it's in. I thought you and the lady would be nice and snug there.

JIMMY: In spite of the fact that the light wouldn't work. I wonder if I could find out why it wouldn't.

(*He walks over to the table and picks up the lamp standing on it. Miss Westgate and Jane, scenting a discovery in the air, get up and follow him, leaving Vera, who seems too overcome to move. Diana crosses the room watchfully in their wake, taking care to keep between them and the door. Jimmy takes the bulb from the lamp and looks into the holder*)

JIMMY: (*quietly*) Bring me one of those candles off the counter, Freddy.

(*Freddy obeys with obvious reluctance. He slides off the counter, extracts one of the candles from a bottle, and carrying it like an acolyte, offers it to Jimmy*)

JIMMY: (*impatiently*) What's the good of that? I want something to put it in, don't I?

FREDDY: (*pained*) You didn't say you wanted the bottle too. You only asked for a candle.

(*He returns to the counter, sticks the candle in the bottle and returns with the two complete. He hands these to Jimmy and then slides off towards the door*)

JIMMY: (*commandingly*) Here, you, come back. We don't want any more of your tricks. Get back behind the counter. That's your proper place.

(*Freddy obeys. Jimmy watches him until he is safely behind the counter, then turns his attention once more to the lamp. He turns it upside down. A sixpence falls out of the holder, and drops on to the table*)

JIMMY: (*as he picks up the coin*) Now, that's what I call really ingenious. A complete short circuit. As soon as the switch was put on, the fuse would blow, and all the lights on the circuit would go out. And that's just what happened.

(*He strides to the counter and confronts Freddy*)

JIMMY: Now listen to me. You know well enough that if you showed anyone to that table, they were pretty certain to try to switch the light on, didn't you?

FREDDY: (*brazenly*) Well I thought they might, and perhaps make a better job of it than I had.

JIMMY: I made a good enough job of it from your point of view. Of course you slipped the sixpence into the holder when you were pretending to try to put things right.

FREDDY: I? If I'd been up to anything like that I'd have used a farthing, not a sixpence. Sixpences don't come my way often enough for me to chuck them about like that.

JIMMY: I'm not so sure about that. But the sudden darkness

was a wonderful opportunity for a murderer. The weapon was ready to hand hanging over there on the wall. It was only the work of an instant to take it down and to stab the victim with it. But you shouldn't have trodden on that bit of broken glass on your way back to the counter. And there's still one thing that I don't understand.

FREDDY: A clever chap like you. What is it?

JIMMY: (*impressively*) I'll tell you. This man Julius Hogwash was a notorious blackmailer. I rather think that explains Mrs Terry's knowledge of him. (*He turns to Vera, who has looked up, startled at the mention of her name*) She had fallen into his clutches. Is that not so, Mrs Terry?

VERA: (*in a strangled voice*) Yes, yes, but—

JIMMY: It is no affair of mine how that happened. The man is dead and whatever he knew died with him. (*He turns back to Freddy*) I was on his track, and that is why I came in here just now. I should have taken the first opportunity of arresting him, quietly. (*He pauses for an instant*) Why did you kill him?

FREDDY: (*in a quiet but impressive voice*) Look in his pockets. (*Jimmy moves swiftly to the body, drops on one knee and runs his hands rapidly through the dead man's pockets. He rises, holding a sheaf of papers, which he carries to the candle on the table*)

JIMMY: Hullo! What have we got here? Secret documents.

FREDDY: (*easily*) Yes, that's right. Your Mr Hogwash was the ablest spy in the country. I knew he had those papers, and I didn't intend that he should get away with them. That's what I followed him for.

JIMMY: You? And who may you be, I'd like to know?

FREDDY: (*with a graceful gesture in Miss Westgate's direction*) That lady might be able to tell you.

MISS WESTGATE: I? Why, I've never set eyes on you before this evening.

FREDDY: Possibly not, dear lady. But your intuition told you the truth. Not so very long ago, you told me that I was a very intelligent young man.

MISS WESTGATE: (*puzzled*) Well, yes, I believe I did. But I don't see what that's got to do with it.

FREDDY: It's got everything to do with it. Intelligent is the very word. You see, I'm not a barman at all, really. I'm an Intelligence Officer. And now will someone tell me whose job it is to dispose of that body?

JOHN RHODE

'John Rhode' was a pseudonym of Cecil John Charles Street (1884–1964), one of the most prolific writers of the Golden Age of crime fiction. In a career spanning over 40 years Street published 144 novels, a handful of short stories and various non-fiction articles and books, including two full-length biographies and a study of the notorious Road House murder. He also wrote a few radio plays for the BBC, including *The Strange Affair at the Old Dutch Mill* (1938) and *Death Travels First* (1940), and a short series entitled *The Thoughts of a Detective Story Writer* (1935), in which he considered why people like detective stories and how they are constructed. During the Second World War, harking back to his work as a propagandist for the British Government in the so-called Great War and afterwards in the build-up to the 1921 Anglo-Irish Treaty, Street also wrote a programme for the BBC on *The Auxiliary Fire Service* (1940) to raise awareness of its vital role in protecting citizens from the consequences of the Luftwaffe's bombing.

Early in his writing career Street wrote thrillers, but the bulk of his work comprises detective stories of the classic mould: there is a crime, there are clues and there are suspects; there is an amateur detective, working—more or less comfortably—alongside the official police; and there is a solution, often involving an ingenious device, many of which Street would create and test himself. In the

1930s and '40s, he was very well regarded, and not only in Britain: his work sold well in America and, as noted in Street's obituary in *The Times*, 'the Japanese editions delighted the author particularly'.

Street also played a central role in the early years of the Detection Club, the dining club for mystery writers that still exists today. He wired up 'Eric the Skull', which is still used in the Club's membership ritual, and he edited *Detection Medley* (1939), the Club's first short story anthology. But despite such evidence of what one might term clubbability, Street was not regarded as an easy man to know. He was reticent when not in familiar company and he had only a few friends, the closest in the Detection Club being John Dickson Carr, the American writer who served at one time as the Club's secretary. With Carr doing the bulk of the writing, the two even collaborated on a novel, *Drop to his Death* (1939), which may well have been inspired by an incident in 1925 in which Street fell down a lift shaft.

As well as 'John Rhode', Street also wrote crime fiction as 'Miles Burton' and as 'Cecil Waye', and used other pseudonyms for non-crime books, including I.O., which stood for Intelligence Officer. As his work in the First World War had earned him a Military Cross and the Order of the British Empire, he did not regard his crime fiction as particularly significant. Nonetheless, although the majority of his books are not currently available, he remains extremely popular and first editions—where they can be found—are highly collectable.

Sixpennyworth is published here for the first time. It may well have been written by Street for performance by a local amateur dramatics group, and I am grateful to the late Michael Lane for drawing it to my attention.

THE ADVENTURE OF THE DORSET SQUIRE

C. A. Alington

I had been showing Ivor over Durham Castle, and in the room with the four-post bed had told him the inevitable story, how Mr Justice Hawkins was found in his nightshirt in front of the dressing-table holding in his arms a fainting chambermaid wearing his Judge's wig.

'What I like about the story,' I said, 'is the inexorable way in which one thing leads to another. If Hawkins hadn't stayed in bed, the maid would never have tried on his wig before the glass; if he hadn't crept out and looked over her shoulder and said *Boo!* she'd never have fainted. You might even say that it could never have happened, if the bed hadn't been a four-poster.'

Ivor was silent for a moment, and I saw in his eye a look which I have come to know only too well. If Ivor has a fault, it is his habit of capping one's best stories, and I had a feeling that he was going to do so now.

'That's quite true,' he said. 'Inevitability's the test, and the greater results you can get from one cause the better. It reminds me of what happened once when I was staying with old Tom Wetherby down in Dorset. It was a precious dull party, and I never expected anything to happen, but we had five or ten minutes of the most hectic experiences I've ever known.'

'Why, what happened?'

'And all from one cause too. You often hear people say that the old days were the ones for adventure, and how romance vanished with the coming of the internal combustion engine, but this couldn't have happened except in a mechanical age. I don't suppose electricity's really made by internal combustion; but still, the principle's the same!'

'What *did* happen, anyway?'

'And perhaps it wasn't exactly romantic either,' went on Ivor dreamily, taking no notice of my question, 'unless you call hysterics romantic. Anyhow, old Wetherby's never been the same man since.'

As I didn't know what sort of man he'd been before, I was not interested and said so; but Ivor was not to be ruffled.

'You let me tell the story in my own way,' he said. 'It isn't easy to tell it at all, for so many things happened at once. And it's all flat contrary to the law of unity they used to jaw about at Oxford. However, I'll do my best.

'As I've said, it was rather a sticky party. Wetherby has no idea of choosing his guests to match one another, and we had precious little in common. It used to be rather a jolly place while his wife was alive, and he'd only asked me because she'd been rather fond of me in old days.

'Besides me, there was his son Bill, whom I hardly knew, and a friend of his called Simpson—rather a little rabbit, I thought—the sort of health fiend who has a remedy for every sort of disease, and travels about with most of them.

'Then there was an American journalist, very competent and rather boring; and a Major Endicott and his wife. He was a red-faced, blustering fellow with a bad temper, always suspecting everyone of designs on his wife, though why anyone should have looked at her oftener than they could help I couldn't see. She was an elderly lady made up to look like thirty, but if she deceived the Major she deceived no one else.

'That's all the house-party. The Vicar'd come in to dine, to make us an even number, and a pretty dull evening we had. It was a foul night, raining and as dark as pitch.

'Well, after dinner, four of us settled down to Bridge. I was playing with the Vicar against Wetherby and Endicott. The others sat about for a bit and then drifted off to bed. Bill Wetherby and Simpson were motoring to Scotland next day and had to make an early start, and the two ladies said they were tired.

'Our game wasn't a success; the Major's cards were bad and his play was worse, and his temper worst of all. I forgot to say he'd brought an ill-tempered brute of a collie with him; I hate visiting dogs. He made a scene with the house-dog, whose temper wasn't any too good either.

'At last, about half-past eleven, the Major had a really good hand; he called a grand slam, and really looked like making it for once, when every light in the house went out! They went on again in ten minutes, but a good deal had happened by then.

'As it happened, none of us had any matches, and there weren't any on the table. The Major got up to look for some, and trod hard on the local Cairn, which bit him smartly in the right calf. He let out a yell and the collie sprang to his aid; in a moment the two dogs were at each other's throats, and the cards scattered on the floor.

'I don't know if you've ever seen a dog-fight in a dark room full of furniture, but I expect this one went pretty well along the usual lines. Both dogs got a firm grip, and both owners stood by shouting and cursing.

'The Vicar and I weren't in the centre of the stage, of course, but we each did our bit. I stumbled on the fender and swept off half the ornaments on the mantelpiece; he made a nervous leap on to the seat of a springy arm-chair and took a header over the back of it. I heard him groaning a bit and crawling away, so I guessed that his neck wasn't broken.

'Well, after two or three minutes of this, in the course of which the card table had gone over, and all the other small tables where matches were likely to be, we heard the door open and saw a gleam of light; it was Parkins, the butler, with a torch and a bundle of candles in his hand.

'We hailed him like a party of shipwrecked mariners. Unfortunately, the dogs heard him too: I suppose they'd had about enough of each other's hair, or perhaps the light startled them; anyhow, they released their grips, gave a pair of blood-curdling barks, and went for Parkins as hard as they could, the collie leading by a short head.

'I don't blame the man. He turned and bolted back through the door, slamming it behind him as he went, and we heard him making very good time up the stairs.

'So there we were, left in the darkness once more—darkness and silence, for the dogs seemed to have made it up, and there was no sound except the low moans of the Vicar and the curses of Major Endicott, whose bite was beginning to hurt. Suddenly we heard the sound of a pistol shot from upstairs. Curtain: end of Act I.'

'How many acts are there going to be?' I inquired.

'Two, I think, and an Epilogue,' answered Ivor, 'but I've never worked it out properly before. But before I go on, I must explain the geography of the house. There was a flight of stairs up from the hall, and two bathrooms on your right, when you got up. The passage went away to the left, and my bedroom was at the far end; the rest of the guest rooms were on either side—old Tom had his rooms up another staircase.

'Well, the scene now changes to the upstairs passage, and the time goes back about five minutes. The two ladies had gone to bed, and Bill and Simpson were in the bathrooms. Bill had thought he'd save time in view of his early start by shaving overnight, and Simpson had decided to have a bath on general grounds. They were both in their bathrooms when the lights went out.

'Bill's hand slipped and he cut himself badly; he's one of the old-fashioned brigade and sticks to a cut-throat—not that he couldn't have done himself some damage with a safety. I saw a detective story the other day which was based on the theory that one can't, but that's all rot—anyhow, Bill was well and truly cut and he could feel the blood pouring down. Naturally he hadn't any matches in his dressing-gown, so he did his best with a towel and then decided to get back to his own room and get a light.

'Of course he knew the house very well, but you know how it is in the dark: one always thinks one's been twice as far as one really has, and so, when he reached what he thought was his own door, it was really one short, and he blundered into the room of Miss Annie K. Schwab.

'That wouldn't really have mattered, if it hadn't been for the conversation at dinner. There'd been some burglaries nearby, and she'd taken the talk about them rather seriously; so when Bill came stumbling in, she thought she was for it, and having a gun by her bedside (she'd boasted at dinner about her shooting) she picked it up and loosed off at once. Luckily for Bill, he'd taken a toss over a chair in front of the door, or his number might well have been up; he didn't wait for any more but slipped out on all fours a good deal faster than he'd come in.

'When he got back to the passage, he straightened up and paused for breath, and that was where the second bit of bad luck came in. It was just at that moment that Parkins rushed up the stairs. He happens to be one of those blokes who faint at the sight of blood, and Bill had blood enough about him for any reasonable purpose. He was still clutching the gory towel and all the coat of his pyjamas was dripping; it was a really good cut. Parkins got one glimpse by the light of his electric torch, and one was enough: he dropped in a dead faint, and the torch went out as he fell. Bill hurried forward to help, stepped on one of the candles and went head first down the stairs.

'Meanwhile, Miss Schwab was not idle. She had no idea of

merely scaring off the burglar, but meant to catch him, so, grasping her little torch in one hand and the smoking revolver in the other, she came out into the passage. But when she saw Parkins lying obviously dead, the woman in her came to the surface; with a piercing scream she flung herself on the body of the murdered man and went into a fit of hysterics. As she fell, her torch went out also. Curtain: end of Act II.'

Ivor paused for a moment.

'But where was Simpson all this time?' I asked. 'We left him in the other bathroom.'

'I've no doubt he wished you had,' said Ivor cryptically. 'Simpson only comes into the Epilogue, but he had a pretty rotten part to play. You'll hear all about him later on.

'Well, to go back to the Library. There we were in the dark, trying as well as we could to give first aid to the Major. The pistol-shot startled us a bit, but old Tom said it must be a car back-firing. We started looking for matches again; but the room was in such a fearful mess that we couldn't find anything. I suppose we spent two or three minutes like that, and then there came a ring at the bell, and a hammering at the front door.

'That seemed to promise something, so we made our way as best we could into the hall, and old Wetherby opened the front door. There was a policeman with a bull's-eye.

'"Beg pardon, Sir Thomas," he said, "but 'earing a shot . . ."

'"Oh, you heard it too, did you?"

'The constable referred to his note-book and read with ill-concealed pride: "11.37, 'eard a shot, proceeding from Wetherby Manor."

'"'Earing a shot," he went on, "and knowing as there was burglars about, which is why I was 'ere at all, as you might say . . . But, begging your pardon, Sir Thomas, it looks to me as if the rain was a-coming in."

'He flashed his bull's-eye on the floor, and, sure enough, there was a steady stream of water flowing down the stairs.

'The Vicar had perked up wonderfully when he saw the water; he was an old Cambridge Rowing Blue—'

'Oh come, Ivor!' I expostulated.

'Well, have it your own way! All I can tell you is, the hall was getting to look jolly like the Cam at low tide. He said it had been raining uncommonly hard when he came in.

'"Nonsense!" said old Wetherby testily. "It's a pipe burst. No, by Jove!" he went on, feeling the water with his finger. "I'll tell you what it is—some silly ass has left the bath running. Let's go and see who it is. Bring your lantern along, Willis; all our lights have fused."

'Guided by Willis, we slowly splashed our way up the stairs. When we rounded the first flight we came on Bill, weltering, as they say, in his gore; his fall had knocked him out and he looked a pretty ghastly sight.

'"Good Lord!" cried Sir Thomas, "what on earth's happened?"

'At that moment, a shriek rang out from the floor above—"I've killed him! I've killed him!"

'The constable had lifted Bill's head. "Well, killed 'im she 'asn't," he said: "not but what she's 'ad a middling good try at it."

'Bill opened his eyes; the water which was coming down steadily must have helped to revive him.

'"Poor old Parkins!" he murmured.

'"What's happened to Parkins?" asked his father.

'"It might be 'im as 'as been killed, as you might say," suggested the constable.

'I was just going to suggest that we'd better find Simpson and get hold of one of his remedies when Miss Schwab's voice came down the stairs, fraught with all the intolerable pathos of the Middle West. "I'm a m-m-murderess!"

'Sir Thomas rose to the occasion.

'"Here, Major," he said. "You and the Vicar look after Bill; we must go and see what's up—and stop this infernal water too."

'We splashed up the rest of the stairs: there was Parkins, lying on his back and Miss Schwab rocking herself to and fro and keening, as I believe it's called in the best circles. The body was beginning to show signs of animation.

'"I've k-k-killed the b-b-burglar!" she sobbed hysterically.

'"Nonsense, woman!" said Sir Thomas angrily—his feet were very wet by now—"That's Parkins, and he's no more dead than you are. Turn off those taps!" he roared to me, and I forced my way upstairs into the near bathroom. Luckily, Simpson had left both taps running, or Bill might have been scalded to death.

'Well, we sorted things out by degrees, and were just beginning to see daylight, with the help of the two torches we'd recovered, when we became conscious of a dull howling proceeding from somewhere along the passage. We made our way in the direction of the sound, which proved to come from the lift. Thomas, the footman, had been on his way up in it, when the power failed: he'd been stuck half-way ever since.

'We gave him what spiritual consolation we could, and he seemed to be responding to treatment, when suddenly the lights came on, and Thomas flashed past us at what seemed incredible speed on his way to the roof.'

'But what about Simpson?' I asked. 'I suppose it was Simpson who'd left the taps on; but where was he all the time?'

'Ah, where was Simpson?' repeated Ivor. 'That's just what we all wanted to know. The search for him began as soon as we'd parted from the footman, and I can tell you, Sir Thomas was thirsting for his blood. No one likes to have his house a foot deep in warm water.'

'But what happened to him?'

'The Simpson story is really very simple; he was in the bathroom when the light went out, and like Bill, he thought he'd go to his room for matches. He'd got half-way down the passage when the shot went off, and, not being one of Nature's lions, his only thought was to get to cover. He found a door-handle beside his hand, turned it and slipped in; it wasn't his fault that it was

Mrs Endicott's room he got into. The shot had wakened her up, and finding her light wouldn't work, she struck a match. I don't know what it showed her, but it showed Simpson that she wore a wig—wore it by day, I mean. He didn't strike me as a very bright young man, but he had sense enough to realise he wouldn't be popular if he were spotted. He dived for a sofa which he'd seen in the matchlight, and that was where he was when the lights went up.'

'Why hadn't he come out before?'

'Well, somehow there never seemed quite the right moment; there was a lady howling in the passage for one thing, and he was only very lightly clad. Of course, that cut both ways when the Major found him, and there looked like being a very ugly scene, but luckily he'd got some patent cure for dog-bites, and that eased matters. But he wasn't at all happy about it, and when we came down to breakfast next morning he'd vanished. Of course Bill wasn't fit to travel, and I gather Simpson had started for Scotland on foot, No, I was sorry for Simpson, but I know he had a patent stuff for curing sore feet, so I dare say he was all right in the end!'

C. A. ALINGTON

The Very Reverend Cyril Argentine Alington was born in 1872 in Suffolk, England. The intelligent and hard-working son of a vicar, he attended Marlborough School and later Trinity College, Oxford, attaining a double first and fellowship of All Souls. An academic to his bones, he returned to his old school in 1896, this time as a master, before taking up a similar position at Eton in 1899. In 1901, in parallel with his teaching career, Alington was ordained an Anglican priest and, in 1904, he married the Hon. Hester Lyttleton. In 1908, he was appointed as head teacher of Shrewsbury School, and in 1917 he succeeded his brother-in-law to become the head of Eton College, an achievement considered remarkable for a man in his forties. As a head, Alington was popular with his peers and not afraid to express an opinion. Somewhat ahead of his times, he supported the teaching of ecology, championed the provision of scholarships for children from a disadvantaged background, and railed against overloading of the curriculum and the forced conversion of left-handed pupils to right-handedness. He was also respected by the parents at his schools for his clear, Christian leadership: on one occasion he gated the entire school after Eton's senior cricket team ran amok in Windsor, and on another he expelled two boys for their 'liaison' with the actress Tallulah Bankhead.

In 1933, Alington retired from his beloved Eton and, at the age of 61, was appointed the Anglican Dean of Durham, a position he would hold for many years. He continued to speak up for what he believed to be right, criticising some verses of the Bible as un-Christian, protesting against the pre- and post-war militarisation of the Northumberland coast and lobbying successfully against construction of a power station near Durham. Most remarkably perhaps, in 1946, despite the death of his son—a Captain in the Guards—during the Second World War, Alington welcomed 1,100 German prisoners of war to a Thanksgiving service in Durham Cathedral, offering his 'German brothers' the 'warmest of thanks' for helping to bring in the harvest.

Throughout his life Alington was also a popular speaker, addressing organisations like the Parents' Association, although his views were sometimes contentious; for example he criticised the focus of some churchmen on the concept of original sin. At other times he could seem absurd, and not only to modern eyes: when awarding prizes at a girls' school in 1931, he asserted that a woman's place was in the home and that the reason there were few great women artists was that women, while far more courageous and practical than men, were simply incapable of being artistic.

But it is for his schoolmanship and writing that Cyril Alington is best remembered. In the 1910s, he wrote two delightful studies of life at Shrewsbury and in 1922 his first novel, *Mr Evans*, a detective story set against the background of a test match between England and Australia. Alington would go on to write other detective stories including a series featuring the Venerable James Castleton, Archdeacon of Garminster. While *Archdeacons Afloat* (1946), *Archdeacons Ashore* (1947) and most of Alington's other crime fiction was well regarded at the time, some critics considered his books to be 'anaemic' given the relative absence of violence. As well as writing detective stories Alington also reviewed them, and he agreed to be the public face of the so-called selection panel for Collins' Crime Club, apparently (but not actually) recommending which titles the imprint should publish.

In parallel with his career as a detective story writer, Alington also maintained a steady flow of non-fiction books throughout his life. The majority have religious themes and others relate to the history and day to day life of Eton. There is also a history of Durham cathedral, a 'semi-religious' autobiography and an insightful post-war 'political and personal survey' of Europe. As well as books, Alington wrote hymns and poetry—including the famous 'To the School at War', a poem written in 1916 and taken up by schools around the country. He also wrote two comic operas, very much in the vein of Gilbert and Sullivan and, as 'S. C. Westerham', he wrote a Wodehousian novel, *Mixed Bags* (1929), for which he was praised, if ambiguously, as being the first head of Eton 'who has ever accomplished light fiction'.

Cyril Alington died in 1955 and he was buried at Durham Cathedral. 'The Adventure of the Dorset Squire', one of a series of stories, was first published in March 1937 in *Pearson's* Magazine, and I am indebted to Stephen Leadbeatter for drawing my attention to its existence.

THE LOCKED ROOM

Dorothy L. Sayers

'All my family are eaten up with superstition,' said Betty Carlyle.

'Are they really?' Lord Peter Wimsey looked back through the open french window to the drawing-room they had just left. He did not know his host and hostess well; he had met Arthur Deerhurst at the Club several times, and had come down to Pidley Manor to give an opinion on the value of the library, being, among other things, an authority in a dilettante way on ancient editions.

He knew Deerhurst vaguely by repute as a hard-living man, of more family than intellect, who had a habit of dropping more money on the turf than his inherited estate could well afford in these days of heavily-taxed unearned increment. He saw his host now, a big, dark, finely-groomed animal, making amiable conversation to Mrs Poulton, the vicar's wife. The Rev. Thomas Poulton, in a reciprocal spirit, was telling Mrs Deerhurst about the forthcoming Church Bazaar, over a small cup of coffee into which Wimsey had seen him drop three large lumps of sugar.

Mrs Deerhurst was plaintive and pretty in a fragile way. She was one of those porcelain women who arouse, according to temperament, all the brutality or all the sentimental chivalry of their attendant males. In her clinging Worth draperies she looked a little out of her element; their bold outlining of the limbs seemed an outrage on anything so essentially and delicately withdrawn. Amelia Sedley, thought Wimsey, in the robes of Cleopatra.

A little apart from the group stood Deerhurst's step-brother, Anthony Severin—a fair, nondescript-looking man, whose only surprising feature was his pallid appearance. His build and expression suggested athletics and country sports. Lord Peter had tackled him before dinner, and discovered that he had no conversation of any sort. As a matter of fact, his contradictory exterior was easily explained. Wimsey—a detective by instinct as well as by training—had interrogated his own man-servant, Bunter, and Bunter, though he had only been a couple of hours in the house, had, as usual, all the facts at his finger-tips. Mr Severin had been a great outdoor gentleman—a very hard rider to hounds and a champion polo and tennis player. The explosion of a shell at Vimy Ridge, however, which had nearly blown him in two and had buried him under half a ton of earth, had ended all his activities and very nearly ended his life. Confined to the house, and at times to his bed, he had taken to hand-work of various kinds as an employment, and turned out marqueterie boxes, repoussé work, and art-jewellery with the same pathetic and unimaginative industry as those other stricken soldiers whom Peter had seen in the hospitals, embroidering their regimental emblems on black satin cushion-covers.

'They say he bears it beautifully, my Lord,' said Bunter, 'and never complains.'

Lord Peter looked interrogatively at the narrow, piquant face beside him.

'Oh!' said Betty, 'I don't mean that they believe in crystal-gazing or Mrs Baker-Eddy, or in old Cuthbert Deerhurst who is supposed to clank about the passages in the Chapel wing. I mean they believe in all the funny superstitions you find embalmed in Victorian novels. Like the one about first kisses, for instance.'

'What is the superstition about first kisses?' inquired Lord Peter.

'Oh, don't you know? Don't say you've got it too. About a girl's first kiss makes her feel all different and as if Heaven had opened in a fiery glow and swept all the stars away. That kind of thing.'

'And doesn't it?'

'Never—at least, hardly ever. One can't prove a universal negative, can one? And of course most women lie hopelessly about that sort of thing—especially to men. But I know I simply *hated* my first—if I hadn't been absolutely abjectly devoted to the person, I couldn't have stood it for a second—and it seemed to last a hundred years.'

'Oh!' said Wimsey.

'Had you there,' said Miss Carlyle, triumphantly. 'You were just opening your mouth to say "Perhaps it was wasn't the right man." Confess: weren't you?'

'Perspicuous woman! I won't say no.'

'Well it *was* the right man—and I'd been simply longing for it, and working up for it ever so long—or perhaps you think I couldn't have been?'

'Well, no,' said Lord Peter. 'I'm gettin' along, you know—first grey hair 'n' all that sort of thing. I've outgrown one or two superstitions with my Erin suits.'

Betty looked at him.

'I'm not sure,' she said, 'that you may not turn out to be one of those refreshing, untrammelled spirits. But perhaps it's only London. It's lovely to meet a London person again—we're all so earnest down here. When I get back to town shall we go and dine somewhere?'

'We will go to Verrey's,' said Lord Peter, promptly, 'where the food is good, and there's no music worrying you an' makin' you belt the bones of your soul.'

'You are not superstitious,' said Betty, 'or you'd have said the

Carlton. But I was going to widen your outlook about something. What was it?'

'Kisses,' said Peter. 'Their origins and habits.'

'Oh, yes—my first kiss. Do you know, when it happened, the only thought in my mind was slugs.'

'Oh, Lord!' said Wimsey, really disconcerted.

'Yes, slugs. Something awfully smooth and damp and alarmingly muscular. Are you feeling hurt in your vanity?'

'Why should I?' said Wimsey. 'Nothin' personal about it. It wasn't me, you know. I'm sure I'd know if I'd ever met you before—even in the dark.'

'Most men I've tried that remark on take it as an insult to their sex.'

'Not at all,' said Wimsey, 'not at all. I was just deducin' the outward aspect of the—perpetrator, what? Was he biggish, clean-shaven, full-lipped, rather vain and not without experience?'

'He was. I begin to believe that you really are rather priceless as an amateur detective.'

'That was an easy one.'

'How was it done? At least, I understand the clean-shaven, full-lipped and not-without-experience part. But big? And why vain?'

'Vain—first because he was so well-shaved. Most people who have confided their experiences to me complained of bristles.'

Betty chuckled.

'And secondly, because, when you told him about it, later on, when you were cross and you were both gettin' fed up with the experiment, you unloaded your impressions on him, and he sulked.'

'Wizard! And why big?'

'You like big men.'

'How did you know it?'

'When we were introduced you sized me up, and decided I was not tall enough.'

'You're terrible.'

'Now you're flatterin' my vanity. But my mind is growin' fast. And what are the family superstitions?'

'Oh, they've all got them. So have Mr and Mrs Poulton, though they're dears. They never read anything later than Victorian novels, and they're full of them.'

'I know—like the one about dogs and little children having an unerring discernment of virtuous and villainous people.'

'Yes—Mrs Poulton has that badly. And the one about always having a baby if you miss the last train home.'

'And the one about husbands always bein' thunderstruck if they hear there's a youngster on the way.'

'Yes—so improper of them really. And the one about consumption being a beautiful, poetic disease where you just fade away without any symptoms but a genteel cough. Whereas everybody who has anything to do with it knows it's perfectly beastly. Father died of it.'

'Beastly rough on you,' said Wimsey. He put his hand over the small fingers invitingly stretched out on the verandah railing, and added, 'What is Mr Deerhurst's superstition?'

'Oh, Uncle Arthur? He and Anthony Severin both have the same one, only it takes them different ways. They think all women are alike.'

'I get you,' said Wimsey, 'they say "That's just like a woman". Or they ask "Do women notice whether a man's well-dressed?"'

'Exactly. It's no good my telling them that women are just as different as men. Uncle Arthur says, "What you want is a fellow who'll carry you off your feet. Women like to be bullied." And Anthony thinks women like a dog-like devotion—he says, "Find some good man who'll care for you and make a home for you, Betty, and you'll give up wanting to be independent."'

'Which *do* you like?' inquired Wimsey.

'Well—I'm engaged, as a matter of fact,' said Betty, 'but he isn't quite either one or the other. And he hasn't any money, so I haven't told them anything. He's a writer.'

'Not a payin' job as a rule,' said Peter, 'but if you get on with him that's the chief point. No wonder you're bored with bein' stuck down here,' he added, elliptically.

'Oh, it isn't that,' said Betty—'He's in Austria, anyhow—cheaper, you know, till his book's finished.'

'Yes, but this place doesn't provide a heap of distractions. When do you get back to Piccadilly Circus?'

'Next month. Will you really take me out?'

'Rather. We'll run round like anything.'

'I *do* miss people.'

'Of course you do.' Peter tightened his grip a trifle.

'Lord Peter?'

'Yes.'

'Do you think—it's unfair—and horrid—wanting to "go round like anything" when he's in Vienna?'

'Not a bit. Don't give way to the family superstition. Let's walk to the end of the verandah.'

'I thought somehow you were going to be an untrammelled spirit,' said Betty, demurely, following him out of the lamplight into the rose-scented gloom.

'I keep my intellect surprisingly, in spite of my advancing years,' said his lordship, 'though I don't mind saying that your mention of slugs rather tends to cramp the style.'

'Not noticeably,' said Betty.

'No?—I think the next will be a better effort—how's that?

'Thank you,' said Betty. 'You're not without experience either, are you?'

'What a thing to suggest!—Here, don't go!'

'Oh, I feel much better now. Quite cured. I'm going in.'

'That's not fair. I was just getting nicely set. Besides, you haven't told me about Mrs Deerhurst's superstitions yet.'

'Oh, I'll leave you to deduce them. They're too many to count. One is, that I oughtn't to stick out here all night!'

'You're a vampire,' said Peter. 'All right—just a minute. You're quite sure that nothing in the shape of—er, slugs or fish or anythin' came floating into your mind just now? I have my share of vanity, you know.'

'Nothing at all of that sort,' said Betty.

'That's all right. Because I had a kind of fleetin' impression myself—'

'Of what?' cried Betty. 'Oh, you brute!—something horrid? You didn't! What was it?'

'I won't tell you,' said Peter.

'You are a perfect horror,' said Betty, 'and you've restored all my self-respect.'

She ran rather hurriedly into the drawing-room. Peter pulled out his cigarette-case.

'Unsettlin',' he said to the moon, 'uncommonly unsettlin'. So many nice things are.'

He followed her more slowly.

It was on the third day of Wimsey's visit that the telegram arrived. In the interval his lordship would have been intolerably bored, had it not been for Betty Carlyle. She assisted him in viewing the household from a detached and cynical standpoint, and she was pretty enough and sufficiently in love with her writer in Austria to make her cynicism attractive, even to a man. Lord Peter found her far more conversable than Mrs Deerhurst, who worried him by an aggressive womanliness. She laid exquisite fingers on his arm in the moonlight, and explained that she hated the material aspects of life. Men, she said, were apt to be brutal—there were certain things—certain reticence—which they could not understand—did he remember Jeanne in *Une Vie*? '*Elle en voulait en sa coeur a Julien de ne pas comprendre—de n'avoir point ces fines padeurs, ces delicatesses d'instinct, et elle sentait entre elle et lui comme un voile, un obstacle*'—de Maupassant! Ah, there was a man who understood women, but he, of course, was a writer of genius, and to be a great writer Mrs Deerhurst always felt a man must have a great deal of the woman in him. Didn't Lord Peter think so?

Lord Peter replied that he felt sure de Maupassant would have understood Mrs Deerhurst perfectly.

Deerhurst, it appeared, had other traits in common with the objectionable Julien. He was always grumbling at his wife's extravagance. 'Though he spends *much* too much on those wretched horses. Of course, he never *tells* me what our income is—I always think that such a bad habit in English husbands, don't you?—but I'm sure my poor little frocks don't cost a twentieth of what he has spent on that horse of his—*Listening-In*—it's to run in the Derby, and he's backed it to win I don't know how many thousands of pounds.'

From Deerhurst himself, Wimsey heard about *Listening-In*, in greater detail. It appeared that that promising young creature—by *Marconi* out of *Electric Spark*—was indeed carrying the whole fortune of the house of Deerhurst on his chestnut back. 'All this place,' said the owner, gloomily waving his stick towards the acres of park and meadowland, 'is mortgaged up to the hilt. It's a damned rotten country under this fool Coalition Government—nothin' but grindin' the faces off estate-owners. And now these dirty Labour fellows comin' along, shoutin' for a Capital Levy—capital, indeed! Why, there are fellows on my own land that would have the cheek to vote Labour, when they've simply been livin' on me for years. Suck the blood out of one, that's a fact—as bad as the women. Take my wife, now. Frocks, frocks, frocks, and wantin' to go everywhere, when she knows I ain't got a penny to spare. And whining to Anthony Severin all day about not bein' understood.'

Lord Peter indicated that being misunderstood was surely

only a feminine accomplishment, like powdering the nose, designed to lend additional charm without deceiving anybody.

Deerhurst passed over this epigram without appearing to hear it.

'To hear my wife talk,' said Deerhurst, 'you'd think she was too delicate-minded to live. Fact is, she enjoys working a man up till he can't sit in his chair, and then she sniffs and says he's misunderstood her, and what a pity it is people can't be friends and leave all this love-business out of it. Look at poor old Anthony, with a blue ribbon round his neck, eatin' out the palm of her hand. She's my wife, and it suits me all right as it is, but I tell you frankly, Wimsey, in Anthony's place I'd wring her neck. There's only one way with women, and I may say I understand 'em—'

Lord Peter, delicately escaping from this discussion of his hostess, told himself that Deerhurst might say so, but that that didn't make it true. He presently sought out Betty and asked whether it was only another superstition to say that the man who boasted of understanding women invariably turned out to know nothing whatever about them. Betty considered with her head on one side.

'I think sometimes,' she said, 'he may understand *one* woman quite well—but then he generalises from her to the others and is quite wrong.'

When Peter could not find Betty to talk to, he would run away into the workshop where Anthony sat patiently hour after hour, fashioning hideous trifles from metal and glass. Severin talked little, and Wimsey would chatter or smoke silently as his mood took him, turning the hammers and pliers and other tools over in his long, nervous hands, dipping into books on New-Art Decoration and Metallurgy, or poking a thin, overbred nose into the scraps and filings on the floor. 'Every serious-minded detective,' he would say, 'should devote himself to the study of rubbish.'

One day they discussed literature. Severin had learnt to read books since his illness, and spoke with simple pride, as of an achievement.

'I used to be awfully ignorant,' he said, 'I knew nothing about poetry and feeling and all that sort of thing. Just huntin' and games, and girls now and then, of course, but I never thought much about it. What a lot of books these women write nowadays, what? S'pose they have to spit it out somehow. I never realised what brutes we were, you know—I suppose you know all about that sort of thing?'

Wimsey was a little baffled by this wistful question.

'It's my belief', he said, 'nobody knows anythin' about it at all. Least of all the fellows who think they do. Only thing I'm sure of is that it don't do to get pokin' into other people's affairs. Between the tree and the bark, eh? Sure to get one's fingers pinched.'

'Rotten thing seeing a woman hurt, though,' muttered Severin. His eyes wandered to the table on which his pipe lay between the pages of a fashionable feminist novel. Peter reflected that Anthony's reading was obviously edited with care.

The telegram was brought up from the village post-office, in company with a cardboard dress-box, by one of the under-footmen after dinner. Mrs Deerhurst, with a delighted little cry, had pounced upon the box and called upon Betty to come up with her *at once* to try on her new frock for the Reed-Swayntons' dance. 'Telegram?—Oh! I think Mr Deerhurst's in the garden somewhere, Thomas, you might take it out to him. Lord Peter, you *will* excuse us just a minute, won't you? I'm so *terribly* thrilled. If you're very good—and if it's really a success—I'll come down and show it to you. Come along, Betty darling!'

They ran off, twittering. After a few minutes Peter, by a happy accident for which he was subsequently deeply thankful, discovered that his cigarette-case was absent, and started off in quest of it, leaving Anthony Severin knitting his patient brows horribly over a work by Dorothy Richardson. A search in his bedroom failed to discover the cigarette-case, and he rang for Bunter, who arrived, in a Maskelyne & Devant kind of way, with the missing object in his hand, having found it, where its master had left it, in the Italian summerhouse. Thus armed, Wimsey proceeded leisurely downstairs and across the hall—then paused with his hand on the knob of the drawing-room door. After standing a moment or two, ears cocked, he withdrew, backwards, with delicate steps, like a cat retreating from a lighted cigarette-end, till he regained the staircase. Then, with a swift and silent motion he fled upstairs, and caught Bunter just disappearing from the back landing.

'Bunter!'

'My lord?'

'Family row goin' on. No business of mine. Never interfere in delicate situations. But if there's anythin' I ought to know, you know you can tell me. Give me my cigars, and I'll have a hot bath at 10 o'clock.'

'Very good, my lord.'

Mr Bunter made his way down the back staircase, and his master retired unobtrusively to the Dutch Garden and smoked there in peace, beyond those voices.

At 10 o'clock Peter came in. The house was ominously quiet. On the stairs he met Betty, white-faced and tearful.

'Oh, Lord Peter—' she said helplessly, and stopped.

'Can I do anything?' asked Wimsey.

'I don't know. There's been such a scene. Uncle Arthur's lost a lot of money—the horse has gone wrong. It was so unfortunate Aunt Celia coming down in her new frock just that minute. He knocked her down—but I really don't think he meant to do it. Anthony got her away—Oh! Lord Peter, I'm frightened. Uncle Arthur—I've never seen him so violent. He said he'd—said he was sick of everything—What happens when people go bankrupt? He's got a revolver in his desk—'

She broke off. Peter put his arm round her.

'You're a comfort', said Betty, 'but I must go to Aunt Celia—she's making *such* a fuss. But I feel as if Uncle Arthur was more important really. She doesn't understand how dreadful it is for him to have lost all that money. She doesn't think he *means* anything. The fact is, she *enjoys* a row!'

'Here, steady on,' said Peter, 'do I understand that Deerhurst's been threatening to blow his brains out?'

'Yes. He said he was done for—'

'Well,' said Peter, equably, 'I don't for a moment suppose he will. Hardly ever happens that way, y'know. Usually fellow partakes of a hearty dinner and seems particularly cheerful before he goes and does it. Very seldom he goes blowin' about it beforehand. Statistics of suicide—gloomy readin' in a general way, but comfortin' in the present case. Cheer up, old thing. I'll go and seem him if you like.'

'Will you?—Oh, do!'

'Nothin' for him to blow his brains out about. Told him this afternoon the library would fetch twenty thousand easy. Sell it for him tomorrow. No sense doin' one's self in in the circs. Deerhurst ain't the fellow to mind pawnin' the family Bible. I'll remind him about it.'

'Bless you!'

'You embarrass me, Betty. I say, I suppose when that writin' bloke of yours comes back he won't let me kiss you any more. Hope he stays away. Don't sit comfortin' your aunt all night, but go to bed. So long.'

'You're a darling,' said Betty, and ran upstairs.

Lord Peter tried the library door. It was locked and an infuriated voice shouted thickly, 'Go to hell!'

'It's only me,' said Wimsey, mildly, 'I've left a book I wanted.'

'I tell you to go to hell!' said the voice.

'But see here, old bean—' expostulated Peter.

'I'll see you damned if you don't clear off,' said his host.

Peter bent his ear to the door, and heard the sizzle of the siphon.

Something in the familiar sound comforted Peter, and put to flight the vague uneasiness which had been creeping into his mind. He released the door-handle, and a half-formulated decision was abandoned at the same moment. Presently he found himself halfway upstairs, muttering to himself, 'Either have done it straight off or opened the door.' He frowned, considered a moment, and then, apparently satisfied, entered his own room. Bunter received him respectfully.

'I understand, my lord, from the under-footman who brought the telegram and is walking out with the young woman at the post-office, that the horse *Listening-In* has unfortunately fractured a limb. Mr Deerhurst had backed it to win to the tune of £10,000, your lordship, at 3 to 1—a very regrettable affair. A slip in the stable, I understand, my lord.'

'I see.'

'Mrs Deerhurst's maid informs me that Mr Deerhurst carried on in the most shocking manner, my lord, when he saw Mrs Deerhurst's new gown, calling her names in the heat of the moment which it would not be my place to repeat to your lordship, and saying that she was set upon ruining him. Mrs Deerhurst was hurt by the suggestion, I understand, my lord, and her replies were what, if it became me to express an opinion, I should characterise as tactless. Deerhurst then caught her by the arms and threw her down, and it took all the efforts of Miss Carlyle and Mr Severin to get him away. I am very sorry to say, my lord, that the small Dresden vase upon the revolving bookcase, which your lordship admires so much, was unfortunately capsized and broken in the struggle. The maid—her name is Gwendolen—ran away at this point, having remained long enough to overhear what was not her business, without lending the slightest assistance, but it was not within my duty to pass any comment upon her conduct. The head footman tells me that he saw Mrs Deerhurst run upstairs crying, with her head bleeding, and Mr Deerhurst banged into the library and slammed the door. Then Mrs Deerhurst rang for Gwendolen, and she's up there now.'

'And Mr Severin?'

'Mr Severin went upstairs after Mrs Deerhurst, my lord, but when Miss Carlyle came up he went to his workshop.'

Peter paused, in the act of transferring his cigarette case and handkerchief from the pocket of his dinner jacket to the dressing-table.

Bunter—unwitting instrument of doom—spoke:

'Your bath water is ready, my lord.

Peter put the handkerchief and cigarette-case down on the polished slab.

'After all,' he said, 'perhaps—'

Lord Peter opened his eyes reluctantly as Mr Bunter drew the curtains aside.

'Mornin',' Bunter. Hullo! Has my watch stopped?'

'I took the liberty to call your lordship somewhat earlier,' announced Mr Bunter, 'under the unusual circumstances. It is a very fine, warm morning, my lord, and I fancied your lordship would wish to rise. Mr Deerhurst has unhappily destroyed himself.'

'What!' cried Lord Peter, starting up in bed, his sleek, yellow hair tumbling into his startled eyes. 'God forbid!'

'Not at all, my lord. Mr Deerhurst has shot himself in the library with his army pistol, which is clenched in his right hand. The under-footman found the library door locked on the inside this morning and gave the alarm. The window being shut and the inside shutters bolted, with the bars up, and Mr Deerhurst's valet coming to say that his master's bed had not been slept in, they broke a door-panel in, and found Mr Deerhurst dead in his desk chair, shot through the head. Which suit will your lordship wear today?'

'The dark grey,' said Wimsey at the wash-stand. 'Wait half a tick—I want to soap my ears. Right you are. Drive on.'

'The under-footman,' pursued Mr Bunter, 'having made a study of criminological works, besought the other servants, with an eloquence which I might call impassioned, not to move the body, and I am happy to say that I was able to be on the spot in time to support his very proper suggestion. Mrs Deerhurst flung herself on the body, my lord, in a highly emotional manner, but Miss Carlyle was able to persuade her not to destroy the evidence. A very capable young lady, my lord, if I may make so bold. The chauffeur has gone for the medical man and the police, and as soon as I could be sure nobody was going to take any rash step, I came to rouse your lordship. The family is in the library. If I might express an opinion, my lord, I think a dark purple tie would be more appropriate to the melancholy occasion than reseda.'

'I daresay you're right,' said his lordship. 'When did this happen?'

'The medical evidence has not arrived, my lord', replied Mr Bunter with due caution, 'but the body is very nearly cold, and rigor is perceptible in the jaw and neck.'

'That may mean anything from about 6 to 8 hours.'

'The cook says she thinks she heard something like a door slamming about midnight, but she paid no particular attention.'

'That sounds quite likely. I say, Bunter—I didn't expect it.'

'No, my lord.'

'Ought I to have? I don't know. The door was locked?'

'And the key on the inside, my lord.'

'And the shutters bolted. Must have meant to do it after all. He left no letter?'

'We saw none, my lord.'

'Well, let's have another look. Where's Mr Severin?'

'He came down at the alarm, my lord, but it is one of his days of severe pain. They had to carry him back to bed, my lord.'

'Poor devil. Come on. Let's get there before the police. Oh! And I say, Bunter, wire to town and put off my engagements for today and tomorrow. We shall be hung up here over the inquest'.

The bullet had shattered the right temple, and the body of Arthur Deerhurst lay sprawling in the desk chair, pitched forward across the large blotting-pad, which was steeped in a sinister red stain. The right arm hung to the ground, a heavy army revolver clenched in the stiff fingers. Lord Peter verified the clutch as a true cadaveric spasm, noted the contraction of the facial muscles and the position of the body, propped between the table and the extreme verge of the revolving chair. He then examined the papers upon the desk, which consisted chiefly of a number of amateur efforts to figure out Deerhurst's financial position—with many miscalculations and much writing of carrying figures in the margin. Deerhurst seemed to have been engaged in this dismal work of accountancy when he fired the fatal shot. The last sheet lay with the pen upon it under Deerhurst's arm. Peter, cautiously peering at it without disturbing anything, was attracted by the letters 'Libra—' ending suddenly in a little leap of the pen. With a changed expression, he stood up and looked curiously about. On a small occasional table near the desk stood a bottle of whisky, a siphon, and a half-filled glass. This Wimsey scrutinised with great attention, sniffing it, as though making a mental record of its strength. He walked over to the door, took out the key, looked at it through a lens, replaced it, and then, returning to the window, made a careful examination of the shutters and the heavy bar which secured them.

At this point the doctor and the local police arrived together, and were brought into the library by Betty Carlyle. The girl came over to Peter who, after some aimless wandering about, had taken up a position on the far side of the table, leaning against the bookcase.

'It's happened,' she said. 'What did he say last night?'

'He wouldn't let me in,' said Peter.

'You don't think it would have made any difference—' said the girl.

'I don't think so,' replied Wimsey, a little absently. He did not move from his position, but his eyes watched the doctor and the police-sergeant.

'Afraid there ain't much doubt about this, ladies and gentlemen,' said the latter, rising ponderously from an examination of the revolver. ''Ere's the weapon wot the deed was done with akshally in the pore gentleman's 'and, and the windows as you might say 'ermitically fastened, and the door locked and the key inside. It stands to reason—jest for the sake of argument, now—any other party 'ad come in, 'e wouldn't a' locked the door again be'ind himself, not leavin' the key in—and I think Dr Robbins will bear me out w'en I say as the position of the 'and about this 'ere weapon is completely true to nature. Haccident you might call it, if you was so minded, but these 'ere papers and the wire as come last night, together with the locked door, looks more like tempery insanity. Now, doctor, if you've finished, I think we can move the gentleman.'

'Mr Deerhurst appears to have been killed sometime about midnight,' said the doctor. 'The shot was fired from very close quarters, and death must have been practically instantaneous. There will, of course, have to be a formal post-mortem, when, *ex abundantia cantelae*, we shall extract the bullet and compare it with the weapon. But everything appears very straightforward. A very sad and shocking occurrence, Miss Carlyle. How is Mrs Deerhurst?'

'I think you should see her, doctor. She is dreadfully upset.'

'Poor soul, yes!' said Dr Robbins, manifesting a highly efficient degree of sympathy. He blew his nose. 'I am quite ready, Miss Carlyle.'

The body of Arthur Deerhurst was removed by the under-footman and the younger of the two constables. The sergeant remained, packing papers, revolver and other scraps of evidence into a bag. He stooped under the table with a grunt, and brought to light the shell of the exploded cartridge. Lord Peter stood where he was, thoughtfully fitting his toe into a design on the Turkey carpet.

'Finished here now, I think, sir,' said the policeman, when he had briefly duplicated Wimsey's inspection of the door and window. 'Not much doubt, I'm afraid. This 'ere cartridge come out o' that weapon. Now, as to these 'ere 'igh words I've 'eard mentioned as passing last night, was you a witness to that, sir?'

'No,' said Peter. 'I was in the garden at the time.' He took out his pouch and began to fill a pipe.

'Very good, sir. Well, I'll 'ave to ask you not to leave the 'ouse till after the inquest, but I don't suppose we'll be botherin' you much.'

'That's good,' said Peter, with a vague giggle, 'embarrassin' thing givin' evidence, what? Apt to contradict yourself and all that sort of thing.'

He dropped his pouch. 'Damn the thing.' The officer marched out to interrogate his witnesses. Peter turned, took a book from the shelf behind him, and wandered into the conservatory, apparently absorbed in a rare commentary on S. Thomas Aquinas.

The inquest on Arthur Deerhurst, with the usual verdict and the usual comments, had been over nine months. In the clubs, men had said it was a dashed bad business, and had forgotten. There was a rumour that the widow—exquisitely inconsolable for half a year—was spending much of her time at Bordighera in the company of Sir John Merrion. In the fogs of London the world discussed the latest murder—a husband shot by his wife's young lover, and the part the woman had taken in egging the boy on to crime. Queues sat through the night outside the gates of the Old Bailey, and it was eagerly debated whether the grim verdict brought in by the jury was according to law or only according to justice. Lord Peter, who had secured a seat in court throughout the trial, came home on the last day to his flat at 110 Piccadilly, and sat thoughtfully beside the fire, with a volume of S. Thomas Aquinas on his knee. He did not read it, but his long, nervous fingers moved monotonously, stroking the back of the binding.

The bell rang. Bunter was heard, respectfully inquisitive, in the hall. The door opened.

'Miss Carlyle.'

Betty came forward to the fire, loosening her furs. Her impertinent face was graver than Peter was accustomed to recall it. He greeted her enthusiastically.

'This is simply toppin',' said he.

'You're sure I'm not disturbing you?'

'Far from it, I was gettin' beastly humpy all by myself. Feelin' ten years younger in the last ten seconds. Tea, Bunter, with crumpets. Come and get warm. Uncommon nasty sort of weather, what?'

'You really *are* a dear, as I've mentioned before,' said Betty. She sat down in an enormous arm-chair and stretched out damp little feet to the blaze.

Tea went merrily. It was not till the last crumpet was disposed of and the table cleared by the discreet Bunter that Lord Peter relaxed his air of nonchalance.

'What's the trouble, Elizabeth?'

'You've realised I had an ulterior motive? I'm worried.'

'Not your friend in Austria, I hope.'

'Oh, no!—He's in London now, and we're going to be married next month. No. But Sir John Merrion is a cousin of mine, and they say that he—that Aunt Celia—Peter! I *must* know—who killed Uncle Arthur?'

Wimsey started.

'My dear child—why seek to go behind the finding of a coroner's jury?'

'Don't play about with me, Peter, I'm deadly serious. I must know.'

'It concerns nobody now.'

'It concerns John Merrion—and me. But I'll leave it alone if you'll tell me in so many words that you believe Uncle Arthur killed himself . . . Will you?'

Peter opened his mouth, caught Betty's eye fixed on him, hesitated, shut his mouth again, took out a cigarette, tapped it, put it back in the case, and said:

'No.'

'I thought you would say that.'

'Why?'

'From the way you gave evidence at the inquest.'

'Good lord! Women are terrors. And they've got 'em on juries now. Who then shall be saved? I say, d'you mind if I smoke a pipe?'

'Peter, tell me the truth.'

'Look here,' said Peter quietly, 'you realise that if it was not suicide, it was—'

'Murder,' said Betty.

'Yes. Well—do you want to bring the murderer to justice, or to compound a felony?'

'Isn't that what you're doing—compounding it?'

'I may take a risk which I would refuse to pass on to you.'

The door opened. Bunter entered with the evening paper.

'I thought your lordship might wish to see this,' he said.

It was a short paragraph, headed: ENGLISHMAN DIES AT CANNES, and ran:

> 'Mr Anthony Severin, well-known before the War in sporting circles, was found dead in his hotel bedroom this morning at Cannes. Death was apparently due to an overdose of veronal, a bottle of which was found half-empty

by his bedside. Mr Severin suffered severely from injuries sustained at Vimy Ridge, and was obliged to use this drug to obtain sleep when the pain was excessive. Doubtless last night he accidentally took more than his usual quantity. Previously he had complained of pain, but appeared otherwise in his usual health and spirits. His death will be deeply regretted by the many friends who honoured and esteemed him.'

Peter handed the paper to Betty.

'There is no felony now to compound,' he said, 'Severin died last night.'

Betty read the paragraph. 'Poor Anthony', she said. 'Oh, Peter—it was Anthony?'

'Yes.'

'Thank God. I thought—I had a perfectly *horrible* feeling—'

'In justice, perhaps,' said Peter, without pretending to misunderstand her, 'but not in law.'

There was a long interval.

'Tell me,' said Betty, 'how did you know? And how did it happen? I was sure—by instinct at least, I was sure *you* were sure—but even then, I couldn't think how you *could* be sure, with all that evidence. There was the revolver in Uncle Arthur's hand—I thought one couldn't imitate what-you-may-call-it spasm like that? And then the door bolted on the inside and the shutters bolted—did he get in by the window? He *couldn't* have bolted that on the inside after him. Was there a secret panel or something?'

'No,' said Peter. 'And I was horribly afraid that even those dolts of policemen would find out the truth. But I counted on the universal superstition—one or two more to add to your collection, Betty.'

'What superstitions?'

'First, that if you find a bloke shot, with a discharged pistol firmly clasped in his hand, he must have shot himself. And secondly, that if you find a dead cartridge which fits a discharged revolver, that is the revolver it fitted, and thirdly that if you find the key inside a locked door, it's proof positive that it was locked from the inside.'

'How—?'

'I'll tell you how I know. To begin with, there was Severin's superstition about women. That they were tender, delicate beings who couldn't bear passion or brutality in a man. Your aunt, Betty, lives by rousin' passion, and she just enjoys brutality.'

'Uncle Arthur understood her very well, really. Just as you said. Only he thought women were all the same.'

'But Severin didn't. She told him pathetic stories, and gave him books, and worked him up—'

'Anthony was rather a lamb really, but so stupid, poor dear.'

'Betty, do you know, I nearly as anything went up to talk to Severin the night of the row. I wish to God I had: it's been makin' me feel every kind of a slack beast ever since. But I'm so damn fond of stickin' my nose into other fellows' business—and just that once I said, "Hang it all, I won't."'

'Oh, Peter—did you guess?'

'Well—not really—I only thought he'd be upset. Honestly I never dreamed he would—'

'Don't worry now. Poor Uncle Arthur and Anthony! It can't be helped any more now. Tell me what you found.'

'Well,' said Wimsey, 'when I came into the study I thought Deerhurst really had made away with himself. It looked uncommonly like it. First thing that surprised me was the whiskey in the glass. Now why should a fellow suddenly shoot himself in the middle of a very mild whiskey and soda? If he'd tossed off a stiff peg almost neat and shot himself then, I could understand it, but the glass looked and smelt so jolly friendly and peaceable.'

Betty looked dubious. 'He might have forgotten to finish if he was worried.'

'Yes—but that was not the only thing. The next was the accounts he was trying to make out. One sheet, headed "Assets", had the word "Libra–" on it.'

'Was he going to write "Library"?'

'I think so. Well, I'd told him that very day that the Library would fetch thousands if he sold it—quite enough to haul him out of *this* tight corner. Now, why should a man suddenly leap up and shoot himself in the very act of writing down a handsome asset? If he'd been working on his debts, now—Besides, the pen had leapt at the "a" of Libra– just as though something had startled him. That was the moment when the locked door opened, and he saw Severin standing behind the desk with an Army pattern revolver.'

'Oh.'

'Yes. The bullet that shot Deerhurst was fired by Severin. All those Service revolvers take the same make of cartridge—naturally. I think that Severin came down to call Deerhurst to judgment, so to speak. Possibly he only meant to threaten him in the first instance. In fact, it's quite probable that Deerhurst fired the first shot. Anyhow, he snatched his own revolver out of the desk drawer where it lay handy. Perhaps they exchanged some pretty pointed back-chat. In any case, they both fired pretty simultaneously, I fancy—that would be the sound like a slamming door the housekeeper heard. Severin's shot took effect. I daresay he was a bit appalled at first, but it wouldn't be the first dead man he'd seen by a long chalk. He probably saw pretty quickly how easily the thing would be taken for suicide. He just tip-toed out, re-locked the door, padded up to bed—and collapsed, as we know he did.'

'But where did Uncle Arthur's shot go to?'

'It went here.'

Wimsey took up the big volume of S. Thomas Aquinas. In the middle of the back was a bullet hole. Opening the book, he displayed the bullet, buried deep in a discursive on the Holy Trinity.

'When I tumbled to what might have happened, I looked along the bookshelves, and just bagged the book. I didn't see quite why—well, I mean—damn it all—men in love do rotten silly things, and the poor blighter had been damnably worked up. But I nearly made a ghastly floater even then. I'd clean forgotten about the cartridge till I saw it on the floor, just where those bally policemen were rooting about. Lord! I thought we were all done in then, an' me with this bally old doctor of the Church in my hand giving the whole blame show away.'

'Oh, Peter—how did you manage?'

'Shoved my foot down and said my prayers.' Peter opened a drawer in his desk and brought out a pill-box containing the missing cartridge. 'Then picked the bally thing up under their eyes. Lord! It was a squeak, though. There, m'lud, the evidence is complete.'

'Except the door.'

'Oh yes. I forgot.' He rummaged once again in the drawer, bringing out a small pair of long, flat-nosed pliers, such as are used by jewellers. 'I sneaked this later out of Severin's workshop. If you'd examined the keypad of the study door, you'd have seen that the barrel projected nearly through the keyhole—as this one does.'

He walked across to the door, which had the key on the outside, and inserting the pliers into the lock, nipped the barrel from the inside. A turn of the wrist shot the bolt across.

'Those blamed policemen,' he said sadly, 'never even saw the little bright scratch each side of the key where the pliers had gripped it. I'm glad they didn't.'

'You're some detective', said Betty.

'I happened to get the right line on the thing from the start,' said Peter. 'But the real criminal is out of reach of the law. *She* knew, of course. What happened, by the way, between her and Anthony?'

'They had a fearful row and he went abroad. I never knew which—'

'No. Of course not.'

'I say, Peter—poor old John is going to have a thick time. He has all Anthony's superstitions.'

'You can do nothing then. He must dree his weird, Betty.'

'I wish I'd never guessed,' said Betty, and burst into tears.

'It don't pay, really,' said Peter, 'to be so darn clear-sighted. Have a cocktail.'

DOROTHY L. SAYERS

Other than Anthony Berkeley, Dorothy L. Sayers is the single most important figure in the history of British classic crime in the 1920s and '30s.

As well as creating one of the greatest of the 'great detectives' of the Golden Age, she edited three important anthologies that demonstrate the genre's heritage and breadth. Through her insightful reviews in the *Sunday Times*, which were recently collected in *Taking Detective Stories Seriously* (2017), Sayers highlighted the best and worst of the genre and, with her colleagues in the Detection Club, she worked to raise standards and build public appreciation of good detective fiction. She was also in the vanguard of the pseudo-scholarship surrounding Sherlock Holmes, and she showed through her own studies that the experience and intelligence of detective story writers made them uniquely well placed to analyse notorious real-life crimes.

Dorothy Leigh Sayers was born on 13 June 1893 in Christ Church Cathedral School, Oxford, where her father was chaplain. A phenomenally gifted child, Sayers was educated at the Godolphin School and won a scholarship to Somerville College, Oxford where she read modern languages and medieval literature, achieving first class honours in 1915 and completing her Master's degree in 1920. Sayers' first appearance in print was with a poem, 'Lay', in the 1915 edition of the annual *Oxford*

Poetry anthology. This was followed swiftly by two collections of her poetry, *Op. I* (1916) and *Catholic Tales and Christian Songs* (1918), and poems also appeared in the *Oxford Magazine* as well as in other anthologies such as *The New Decameron* (1919).

After graduating, Sayers worked as a teacher before, in 1922, becoming a copywriter with S. H. Benson Ltd, a London advertising agency where she remained until 1931, working on contracts with the Guinness Brewery among others and coining arguably the best known phrase about the value of publicity: 'It pays to advertise!' Her first detective novel, *Whose Body?* (1923), introduced Lord Peter Wimsey, a wealthy collector of rare books with a nose for murder, owing as much to Wodehouse's Wooster as to Conan Doyle's Holmes, and Wimsey's foil and friend, Detective Inspector Charles Parker, who eventually marries Wimsey's sister. *Whose Body?* was followed by eleven other crime books including her only non-series mystery, an epistolary novel, *The Documents in the Case*, co-written with Robert Eustace, as well as *Murder Must Advertise* (1933), inspired by her time with Benson's, and *Busman's Honeymoon* (1937), adapted from the script of a play co-written by Sayers and Muriel St Clare Byrne, who had been an English tutor at Somerville.

Such is Wimsey's enduring popularity that he was revived in 1998 by Jill Paton Walsh, who completed *Thrones, Dominations*, a novel that Sayers had left unfinished, and has since written three original Wimsey mysteries. 'Lord Peter' also appeared in short stories—21 of them—as did the preternaturally cheerful wine salesman and rhymester, Montague Egg. There are also several superb non-series short stories and an excellent late radio mystery, *Where Do We Go from Here?*

A proto-feminist in some (but not all) ways, Sayers also created Harriet Vane, a detective novelist who was perhaps an idealised version of herself. Vane first appears in *Strong Poison* (1930) where she is on trial for murder, and while their romance is not without its complications she and Wimsey eventually marry.

In many of her novels, Sayers went beyond the conventions of detective fiction at that time by using the form to explore contemporary issues, such as the ethics of advertising or the mental illness that would now be termed post-traumatic stress disorder in *The Unpleasantness at the Bellona Club* (1928).

Outside the field of crime fiction, Sayers is also recognised for her scholarship and for her theological and religious works, in particular her translation of Dante's *Divine Comedy*, which was completed by her god-daughter and biographer Barbara Reynolds. It is perhaps the most accessible version of the work, and is noted for the ingenious way she preserved the rhyme of the original as well as its sense. She also wrote a number of religious studies including the popular radio serial *The Man Born to Be King* (1941), which re-told the life of Christ, and *The Zeal of Thy House*, about the rebuilding of Canterbury Cathedral, where it received its premiere.

Dorothy L. Sayers died in 1957 at her home in Witham, Essex, where in 1994 the flourishing Dorothy L. Sayers Society erected a statue to commemorate the centenary of the author's birth.

'The Locked Room' by Dorothy L. Sayers is a previously unpublished short story held in the collection of the Marion E. Wade Center, Wheaton College, IL, USA. The manuscript remains in the collection of an anonymous donor; hence, the Wade Center's copy is the only publicly available version of this work. A Lord Peter Wimsey detective story, the original manuscript is 38 pages, typed, signed with revisions by Sayers; the Wade Center manuscript number is DLS/MS-104.

ACKNOWLEDGEMENTS

'NO FACE' by Christianna Brand copyright © Christianna Brand 2019. Printed by permission of A M Heath & Co. Ltd Authors' Agents.

'Before and After' by Peter Antony © the estates of Anthony and Peter Shaffer.

'Exit Before Midnight' by Q Patrick copyright © the estate of Hugh Wheeler.

'Room to Let' by Margery Allingham printed by permission of Rights Limited.

'A Joke's a Joke' by Jonathan Latimer copyright © the estate of Jonathan Latimer 1938.

'The Man Who Knew' by Agatha Christie copyright © Christie Archive Trust 2011. All rights reserved. Agatha Christie® is a registered trade mark of Agatha Christie Limited in the UK and elsewhere.

'The Hours of Darkness' by Edmund Crispin printed by permission of Rights Limited.

'Chance is a Great Thing' by E. C. R. Lorac copyright © the estate of E. C. R. Lorac 1950.